THE
FOREVER
ENGINE

D0377308

BAEN BOOKS BY FRANK CHADWICK

How Dark the World Becomes
The Forever Engine

THE
FOREVER
ENGINE
FRANK
CHADWICK

BAEN

THE FOREVER ENGINE

This is a work of fiction. All the characters and events portrayed in this book are fictional, and any resemblance to real people or incidents is purely coincidental.

A Baen Books Original

Baen Publishing Enterprises
P.O. Box 1403
Riverdale, NY 10471
www.baen.com

ISBN: 978-1-4516-3940-7

Cover art by Adam Burn

First Baen printing, January 2014

Distributed by Simon & Schuster
1230 Avenue of the Americas
New York, NY 10020

Library of Congress Cataloging-in-Publication Data

Chadwick, Frank.
The Forever Engine / by Frank Chadwick.
pages cm
ISBN 978-1-4516-3940-7 (pbk.)
1. Steampunk fiction. 2. Science fiction. I. Title.
PS3553.H2184F67 2014
813'.54--dc23

2013037566

Printed in the United States of America

10 9 8 7 6 5 4 3 2 1

CONTENTS

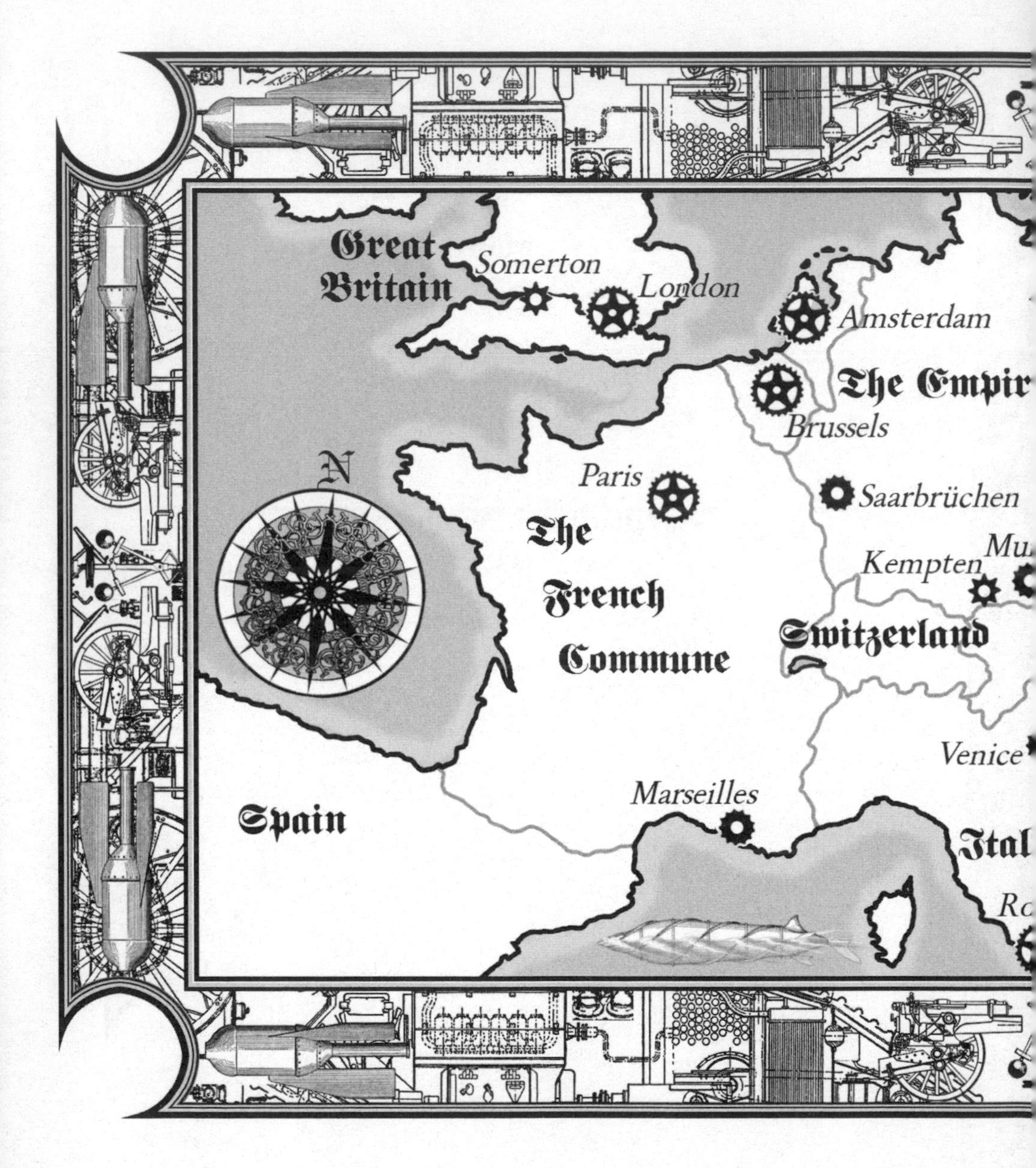
Great Britain
Somerton
London
Amsterdam
The Empir
Brussels
N
Paris
Saarbrüchen
The French Commune
Kempten
Switzerland
Venice
Spain
Marseilles
Ital

The Empire Of Russia
Warsaw
Germany
The Austro-Hungarian Empire
Vienna
Buda-Pest
Transylvania
Újvidék
Croatia
Bosnia
Belgrade
Wallachia
Bucharest
Višegrád
Kokin Brod
Sofia
Serbia
Bulgaria

THE FOREVER ENGINE

"Now I am become death, the destroyer of worlds."
—Robert Oppenheimer, July 16, 1945,
(quoting the Hindu scripture, *Bahagavad Gita*,
upon seeing the Trinity atomic-bomb test)

ONE

August 2, 2018, Wessex, England

Reggie Llewellyn was the most casual killer I ever met, but I didn't hold that against him. If I'd known he was behind the trip to England, you couldn't have gotten me on the plane at gunpoint—not because of who he was, but what he represented. But I didn't know. Not until it was too late.

My internal alarm started sounding from the moment I walked in the front entrance of WHECOL—the Wessex High Energy Collider facility. I expected an overweight, white-shirted rent-a-cop guarding a civilian research complex out in the sleepy English countryside. Instead I faced four hard-eyed soldiers dressed in camo fatigues and packing assault rifles. Their stares followed me in unison as I crossed the polished marble floor, but I looked straight back at them. If they wanted to intimidate someone, they'd have to wait for the next guy through the door.

Well, maybe I was a *little* intimidated, but the trick is never to show it.

I'd barely cleared security when a greeting echoed through the foyer.

"*Jack Fargo!* There you are!"

Although I hadn't heard it for a decade, I recognized Reggie's voice at once. And I knew nothing here was what it seemed.

We shook hands, and Reggie beamed at me. Reggie always beamed—sort of crazy that way. My anxiety at seeing him was mixed up with some pleasure as well, and that surprised me. Lots of surprises that day, and more to come.

Unlike the guards, he wore a pressed service uniform. He wasn't much different from the young subaltern I'd known in Afghanistan—deeper laugh lines around the eyes, hair clipped shorter, mustache showing some gray in the jet black, and different rank insignia on his shoulder straps. Well, he looked a little jumpy, too, which I'd never seen in him before.

"They made you a major, Reggie? The British Empire is doomed."

"The Empire's been finished for some time," he said. "If your education system were better over there, you might have noticed. How have you been? I was quite sorry to hear about your wife and . . . well . . ."

The sudden tightness in my throat surprised me. "I'm okay. Tough time. My daughter Sarah and I got through it together."

Reggie nodded in sympathy. "I'm glad to hear that. Well, then . . ." He gestured down the broad marble corridor into the facility, and we walked side by side. I didn't know what was really going on here yet but decided my best bet was to play along with the original premise of my trip and see where that led me.

"So, let me get this right," I said. "You started digging the foundations for a new wing and stumbled on some possible Roman artifacts? Not that I'm complaining, but why fly a historian all the way from Illinois to evaluate a cultural resource site? Isn't Cambridge around here somewhere?"

"Oxford is closer, actually, but it's a fair question. Some discretion in this matter is required. When I realized we might have need of someone conversant with ancient history, I recalled that you are a very discreet fellow. More than that, I know you will tell me the truth, with neither fear nor favor. You are honest—to a fault, as I recall."

"So I've been told. Thank God for academic tenure, huh?"

"Yes. We don't have that in the army. Fortunately, excessive honesty is not a failing from which I suffer."

He grinned that toothy grin, the one that looked like a tiger about to make a kill. Reggie and I had worked well together a long time ago, but there were good reasons I'd chosen academia instead of a more active career. These days my most vicious fights were over who was going to be the next departmental chair. Reggie knew a surprising amount about my post-military career. That made me nervous.

We stopped in an open, well-lit, but deserted office area.

"The technical staff is preparing for another test," Reggie explained. "We do these mostly at night, when the clerical staff is gone."

He studied me for a moment, as if deciding how to open the conversation. He took a clear plastic coin case from his trouser pocket and handed it to me.

"Give me your professional opinion of this."

Since the Brits had brought me a long way at some expense, I took my time studying the coin, but I pegged it in about two seconds.

"Roman silver *denarius*, first century CE, reign of Emperor Galba. Supposedly."

"Supposedly?"

"Well, it's counterfeit—a really good one. Too good, actually. It looks as if it were struck last year, not over nineteen hundred years ago."

"But other than that you'd say it was authentic?" he asked.

"No. The inscription places it from the third year of the reign of Galba. The thing is, Galba's reign only lasted about seven months before he was killed and replaced by Otho."

I handed the coin back.

"Weren't coins ever struck . . . in anticipation of an event?" he asked.

"Not a couple years in anticipation, and especially by Galba. About the only thing memorable about him was his stinginess."

"You're certain, Jack? I brought you in on this because people tell me you're one of the top men on Roman coins these days. I need to know. Are you absolutely certain?"

"Yup, one hundred percent."

Lost in thought, Reggie frowned at the coin in his hand and said nothing.

"What gives?" I said. "You didn't fly me all the way here from Chicago to tell you what any Roman numismatist could."

"It is not counterfeit."

I started to insist otherwise, but stopped. What was an American historian *really* doing in a British high-energy physics lab guarded by armed soldiers, looking at a phony silver coin that wasn't phony? Had to be, but wasn't. Reggie wasn't worried about disturbing a cultural-resource site, and suddenly I had absolutely no curiosity about what he really wanted.

"Well . . . sorry I couldn't be more help. Give me a ring next time you're in the States, Reggie, and I'll buy you a drink. I can find my own way out."

He laughed. "You know it's not that simple."

"Sure it is, because I don't know anything yet, and I intend to keep it that way. You asked for my professional opinion, I gave it to you. *Adios muchacho.*"

"It is *not* counterfeit."

"Oh, fuck you, Reggie! My daughter starts her freshman year of college in three weeks. I don't know what sort of cloak-and-dagger Indiana Jones bullshit you've got going on here, but whatever it is, it's not my department. I used to be an army translator. That's it. Now I'm a historian and a single parent, and I have things that need doing. You aren't on my list."

"Of course I understand how you must feel, Jack. But before you say anything else, why not have a seat and read these papers? Please."

He held out a folder with the seal of the U.S. Department of the Army.

Son of a bitch! I'd been set up.

I snatched it, sat at an empty desk, and found nothing surprising in the folder: my change of status from unassigned reserve to active duty with a pay grade of W-4, recertification of my top-secret security clearance, and orders assigning me to temporary duty with Wimbish Detachment, Military Provost Guard Service, Major Reginald Llewellyn commanding.

Provost Guard Service, my ass. Reggie was SAS—the British elite special operations force—and I figured the four goons at the front door were as well.

The last document was the British Official Secrets Act form. I scribbled my signature, the date, and handed the folder back.

"I'm out of the world-fixing business, Reggie. If I'm not back in time to take Sarah to college, I will have your ass, SAS or not."

He beamed and took the folder.

"Imagine how *terrified* that makes me!" Then the smile left his face. "The question of who would actually have whose ass may be academic, however. What did you just call it? The world-fixing business? Believe me Jack, you do not appreciate how apropos a term that is. If we are not successful here, there is a distinct possibility our world as we know it will not survive."

I studied him for a moment, but he didn't look like he was trying to snow me. He looked a little frightened. I'd never seen him look frightened before. "Okay, you've got my attention. Here's the deal: I'll help you out on this, but I will not, under any circumstances, do anything I will be ashamed to tell my daughter. Is that understood?"

"Assuming we live through this, I wouldn't recommend telling her anything, old man. The Official Secrets Act—"

"Fuck the Official Secrets Act."

His eyebrows rose a bit at that, but then he smiled ruefully.

"Very well, conditions understood and accepted. And you'll be happy to know that we won't be jetting anywhere to do our work, or have any annoying people shooting at us. That is not the sort of danger we face. No one knows what we are doing here."

"Yeah, including me. So what *are* you doing?"

He sat in the chair beside the desk and looked at me for a moment.

"It's . . . something of a time machine, I suppose," he said.

"A *time* machine? Bullshit."

"I hardly believe it myself. It wasn't meant to be. It was intended as a weapon, very hush-hush. I don't completely understand how it was supposed to work, something about quantum-tunneling projectiles going straight through the Earth without actually touching it, that sort of thing. I suppose that's all academic now, in any case, because that's not what happened. When they test-fired the device, it sent the projectile out as planned, but instead of it appearing at the target point, a *different* object appeared back here, at the launch site."

"And what happened to the projectile?" I said.

"No idea. So far as we can tell, it simply vanished. They've done quite a number of test fires. The projectile always disappears. The accelerator brings back a small solid object—sometimes rock, sometimes a molten slug of metal, but sometimes an intact artifact. Artifacts from the past, Jack. Artifacts from *our* past, we thought, until this."

Reggie tapped the coin with his finger. I looked at it again, looked at the coin from the third year of a reign which, in our world, had lasted only six months! For a moment blood pounded in my ears; the room spun. I leaned back in the chair and held its arms to steady myself, breathing slowly and evenly.

"This . . . this can't be right. A *time* machine? A different past? How do you know all that? Maybe it's just a movie prop you snagged by accident from the Fox back lot."

"I understand how you feel. Honestly, I doubt you can say anything I didn't say myself when I first heard about all this. If you want the technical explanation of radioactive decay dating and something I think they called electron-cloud shift, one of the boffins can trot it all out for you later. I don't really understand any of it myself, but I know when people are lying and when they absolutely believe they are telling the truth. You do as well, don't you? Well these scientists are telling the truth. And they are frightened."

I stared at the coin. *Emperor Galba, huh?*

"Okay. If it's not from our past, then what gives?"

"Of course there are as many theories as there are boffins—circular time, infinite universe—but the most dangerous, the one we must act on, is that someone else has accessed the past, perhaps someone from our future—or perhaps even us—and either deliberately or inadvertently altered it."

I shook my head. "No way. We still *remember* our past, we still have museums full of artifacts from it. How can the past change and the present stay the same?"

"Well, of course it cannot. But the theory involves a temporal event wave. If you drop a rock in a pond on one side, its effects are not felt immediately on the opposite shore, but eventually they reach there. The notion is a change in the past takes time—whatever that means in this context—to manifest its effects in the present, that it moves forward through time destroying the presents it passes through and replacing them with the alternate. The wave simply has not yet reached us, but when it does . . ." His voice trailed off.

"Everything changes," I said. "But we won't know it changes. As far as we know, it will always have been like that, right?"

"It's more than that, I'm afraid. My mother was married before she married my father. Her first husband, who as far as I know she loved very much, fell down the steps of the church as they emerged on their wedding day, broke his neck, and died. Several years later she met my father, married, and I am the result. But had her first husband not found his death in remarkably unlikely circumstances, I would never have existed. Someone else would have, in all likelihood, but not me.

"I don't believe in predestination, Jack. Although we've never spoken of anything so esoteric, I don't think you believe in it, either, or you would not behave the way I have seen you do.

"Men like us believe we make our own destiny, to the extent we are able, and for everything beyond that the gods roll the dice. Leaving aside whether someone else would have saved your life in Khost that one time had I not been in the world, what is the likelihood *you* would exist at all? How many times in your ancestry, stretching back thousands of years, do you suppose a future hinged on whether a man looked to his right and saw the love of his life or to his left and saw the woman he settled for instead? The gods rolled the dice, Jack, and as a result of all those rolls, here we are. But change something and, aside from its direct effects, the table is cleared, the game begins anew, and all those dice are rolled again. What are the chances they will all come up exactly the same? And what if even one of them is different?

"No, when this temporal-event wave passes, it may leave a world full of people, but they will be entirely *different* people. I cannot conceive that you or I or anyone we know and love will actually be among them, no matter how much some of them may coincidentally resemble us. We will all be dead. Well, we will never have existed, but I'll let the philosophers argue that distinction in whatever time they have left. To me it amounts to the same thing."

It was a terrifying prospect, or at least would have been if I believed any of it. Wave effects taking time to move through time, theories spun on top of other theories, none of it was real. But across the desk Reggie absentmindedly tapped the plastic coin case.

That damned coin was real. I felt sweat on my forehead. *What if . . . ?*

The lights dimmed for a moment and came back up. I heard a soft chime from somewhere deeper in the facility.

"Ah," Reggie said. "Firing up the accelerator for tonight's test shot. They're sending something really large back this time, so we'll see what we get in return. The white lab coats think there's some sort of conservation of matter and energy thingie at work—we send something back and automatically displace an equivalent mass here to keep things in balance."

"How long have we got if this wave-effect theory is real?" I asked.

"We don't know, but they're playing with different settings, power and that sort of thing, trying to find as many artifacts from different times as possible and see if they match our expectations, or if . . . well, they are somehow *different*."

"And you want me to look at whatever shows up here."

"Precisely. We need you to look for historical discrepancies like this coin. We have a few other historians I'll introduce you to shortly, but to my mind you're the key, Jack. You see, you always had an eye for detail, for little things not quite right, and a preternatural ability to see relationships no one else could. That's why we really need you here: first to find out how much time we have, and then to help formulate a plan. If someone has altered our past, we need to change it back, and I suspect we will have only one opportunity to do so."

I sat back and thought about that, and I didn't much like it. *This* was their plan? Poke around, see what turned up, and hope *I* could pull a quantum rabbit out of the hat? *Jesus Christ!*

He drew a polished metal flask from his pocket, took a drink, and handed it to me. I noticed his hand trembled as he did so. I'd never seen Reggie's hand shake. I took a long pull. Irish—Reggie always preferred Irish to Scotch.

"If I'm going to do this," I said, "I need to talk to someone from the physics side, someone who can explain things in English instead of foot-long equations on a blackboard. I'll need to see the existing artifacts as well. Presumably you have a database started?"

"Yes."

"Okay. I need to know the plan, the logic of their search for artifacts, and see if we can tweak that to get better results. Well, that's a start."

"Right. I'll go find the others, introduce you to the team—*your* team. I knew you were the right man for this." He rose and turned to leave.

"One more thing, Reggie. I want to call Sarah. My phone's not going to screw anything up, is it?"

"No, certainly not, but you may have trouble getting a signal once the accelerator starts, so I'd call now." He left through a door opposite the side we'd entered, and I took out my phone.

"Call Sarah." I heard the line ring at the other end three times, and then she answered, voice foggy with sleep.

"Mmm . . . hello?"

"Hey, kiddo, it's just me. Sorry I woke you."

"Mmm . . . Dad?"

"Yeah. Go back to sleep. I just called to let you know I'm safe and sound and . . . to tell you I love you."

The sleepiness vanished from her voice. "Dad, what's wrong?"

"Nothing. Everything's fine. I'm—"

The lights dimmed again, more this time, and flickered. The phone crackled, the connection starting to breaking up. ". . . *ad . . . oo . . . and . . .*"

"I can't hear you, honey. The connection—"

My phone sounded the three quick beeps of a dropped call. The lights came back up, brighter than before, and an alarm chimed from deep within the facility. I started to redial, but the phone just displayed the *searching for service* message. Reggie burst back through the door looking confused and alarmed.

"Something's gone wrong," he said. "I'm not sure what, but you'd better go back to the front entrance for now."

I slipped the phone in my pocket and started to stand.

The world turned white, unbearably hot. The thundering roar of dying atoms and molecules tore through every nerve in my body and drowned out my scream of agony, and all I could think was, *the event wave!*

TWO

Somewhere in England

I lay in a bed, my eyes bandaged. Those bandages on my eyes frightened me more than anything else, more than the waves of pain that washed over me and made me cry out and try to sit up. Someone spoke, someone pricked my arm, the pain left, and for a while I floated in a narcotic fever dream.

In the dream Sarah needed a bigger bed. I got one of those kits from Ikea, and Tommy Nash, my platoon sergeant, came over to help. We had the parts spread all over the floor, trying to figure out which peg G went into which socket M, while Sarah stood in the doorway watching. She was small, though, only about six years old, with short brown hair like mouse fur. How could she go to college when she was so tiny?

After ten minutes, she asked, "How many hillbillies does it take to put together a bed?"

I laughed and grabbed for her, but she ran away giggling.

I turned back to Tommy, but he was dead, his legs blown off by an RPG round. He lay on the riverbank and his blood stained the water of the Darya-ye Helmond pink, but only for about ten meters downstream. Then it turned back to the same muddy brown as always, and you'd never even know he'd been there.

Then I was back in the bed of pain. People spoke to me. I answered, but don't remember what I said or if it made any sense. Probably not.

Eventually my senses sharpened and I asked whoever was there not to give me any more of the pain medication. Hard to do. I liked the meds, had started looking forward to my shots.

The more my thinking cleared, the less everything around me made sense. Where was I? What had happened to me? I couldn't see because of the bandages, but what did my other senses tell me?

I was still in England. The nurses' rural accents were barely intelligible and the food was terrible. The fare that morning, stewed kidney paste on toast, smelled like urine. Who but the Brits would eat that stuff?

The scent of alcohol, soap, and another strong chemical I couldn't place hung in the air, but I didn't hear any of the normal background noises—PA systems, monitor beeps. The breeze brushing my face and the smell of flowers meant an open window instead of central air. That was odd. And just as odd, they actually injected the pain medication with hypodermics. Why not just add it to my IV drip?

No IV drip.

Maybe I was in better shape than I thought.

A doctor—older fellow from his voice—talked with me about my burns. My back and upper arms would scar, but not my face. My hair was already growing back. They expected my eyesight to recover, though they wouldn't know for certain until the bandages came off. I asked about Reggie and the others. He declined to discuss any other cases, but only after enough of a hesitation to make me fear the worst.

Had my daughter been notified? The doctor didn't know but promised he'd look into it.

A police inspector interviewed me. Beyond the large explosion, he had no idea what had happened. I couldn't fill him in, not without going to prison for violation of the Official Secrets Act, but I told him I'd talk to someone from military intelligence out of London. I repeated my request twice before he got it. Apparently the British police did not reserve their most intellectually promising officers for service in rural Wessex.

The doctor removed the bandages from my eyes the next day. Even through blurry eyes, my surroundings looked wrong. No monitors. The bed wasn't adjustable, just a brass poster with no railings to restrain restless patients. The nurses wore long sleeves, long dresses, and long hair tucked up under little round white caps. *Maybe a private Mennonite hospital?*

Yeah, maybe. But that damned coin suggested an alternative. I tried to avoid dwelling on the implications but couldn't. Had there really been an event-wave passage? Was I in an altered world, and if so, *how* altered? But if the world had really changed, why did I remember the way it had been? Why weren't *my* memories changed? No, none of that made sense.

The military intelligence guy showed up the following day: a slender, dark-haired captain in his late twenties named Gordon, in his own words "sent out from Horse Guards."

My vision had improved to about eighty percent or so. He wore a red uniform tunic and dark blue trousers, like the foot guards in front of Buckingham Palace. Why send someone from the Guards? Why wear the ceremonial uniform? And besides, the Horse Guards wore blue, not red.

I had learned enough British history to remember the Horse Guards barracks once housed the headquarters of the British Army. "Horse Guards" had been shorthand for Army Headquarters—but not for the last hundred years. So maybe that had changed—or not changed, I guess.

Gordon started. "You understand, Mr. Fargo, that this whole affair is quite a serious matter. The village of Somerton was all but destroyed, between the blast and fires. Over a hundred people died, and Copley Wood is still burning. Now what's all this nonsense about some secret law?"

He took out a pocket humidor, stuck a cheroot in his mouth, and lit the cigar from a big, sulfurous match. In a hospital!

A nurse came in with a pitcher of water, and when she didn't bat an eye at the cigar, my pulse increased and sweat broke out on my forehead. I remembered Reggie's words: *it's something of a time machine.* My breathing became labored, as if my ribs had fused and would not expand to inflate my lungs. *A hundred years? No, too crazy. But that damned coin . . .*

"Are you unwell, Mr. Fargo?" Gordon's tone told me the question was *pro forma*; he didn't really give a damn.

"What year is it?"

"You don't remember?"

"What year is it, goddammit?"

"No need to be a bore." Disdain saturated his voice. "It is 14 September, the year of our Lord 1888."

Sarah! Somehow I had to get back to my daughter. Crazy. She wouldn't be born for another century, or might not be born ever, but I couldn't believe that. As hopeless as it might sound, one thought came to me and stuck: wherever I was, *whenever* I was, *if there was a way here, there had to be a way back.*

Gordon was talking again, and I knew I had to pay attention. I needed an ally, and Gordon was my best candidate.

"I'm sorry, Captain, what were you saying?"

"I wonder if you could identify this item."

Careful to keep the object out of my reach, he held up a flat sliver of aluminum and plastic. He needn't have bothered—there wasn't anyone in this century to call, even if the plastic buttons and screen weren't melted and fused into the frame. A bandage covered a still-healing burn on my right hip about where the phone had rested in my pocket.

"It's my . . . oh boy. It's called an allphone. It's a communication device and . . . um, a web-access tool."

"I see." Gordon made no attempt to hide his disbelief. "And this ring found beside you. Can you identify it?" He handed Reggie's ring to me. Soot still blackened the crevices. My throat tightened,

"It's a class ring of a friend. You say it was beside me. My friend . . . ?"

"Deceased. All we found was the one arm and part of a skull, both badly charred. What does the inscription signify?"

Reggie dead? Reggie was . . . indestructible.

I looked up from the ring. What an odd question from a British officer.

"RMA Sandhurst? It means the Royal Military Academy at Sandhurst."

He frowned. "Interesting. And the number 2006?"

"His year of graduation." I watched his face for reaction. Mounting anger replaced his disbelief.

"Two thousand and six you say? *AD?* What do you take me for?"

What did I have to lose? Nothing. So I told him everything—who I was, when I'd been born, why Reggie had called me in, what the Wessex project was attempting, and the little I knew about what went wrong. I left out the part about trying to change the past back to what it had been, not knowing whether this time was part of the reality I wanted to save or the one I would have to extinguish to do so.

All that took a while. By the time I was done he was on his second cheroot and his anger had given way to contempt. He sat and smoked his cigar for a while, saying nothing. It's a good interrogation technique—people like to fill the silence with sound. I filled it with my own silence. After a few minutes he gave in.

"You expect me to believe all this rubbish?"

"Not really."

"Then why waste my time with it?"

"It's all I've got, Captain Gordon. The truth. Who could make something like that up?"

"Some arrogant American scoundrel could. You think foreigners will believe any silly twaddle you invent. An attack on an English village gone wrong, an attempt to shift the blame to the British military—you could at least have done some research. The Royal Military Academy is at Woolwich, not Sandhurst."

Anti-American bias on top of everything else. So much for my potential ally. Time to change direction.

"Maybe you better put me in touch with the American embassy."

"That will be difficult, as I am sure you already know. Your ambassador was sent packing a month past. I shall be greatly surprised if we are not at war with the United States within the fortnight."

My startled expression pleased him.

"You are under arrest for espionage, Fargo, if that really is your name. I don't know what happened at Somerton village or why all those people had to die. We'll get to the bottom of it, though, I assure you. And I will see you swing for it."

THREE

September 20, 1888, Wessex, England

A constable appeared outside my door after Gordon left. I needed some time alone anyway. Either I really was one hundred and thirty years back in time or I was in the hands of intelligence operatives who had gone to a lot of trouble to fool me. As unlikely as that second option seemed, it was at least physically possible. But time travel? Absolutely unbelievable . . . except for the coin.

The coin. Reggie's ring had made it through with me, and my allphone sort of had. What about the coin? Gordon hadn't mentioned it, or anything else that might have come through.

I picked at my dinner, which was a small meat pie—some sort of bird, I assumed, since the top of the pie was garnished with its little amputated feet. Nice touch. It was okay, but there were too many things on my mind for me to have much appetite. Was it time travel, or was I enmeshed in the gears of the most complicated and improbable intelligence scheme I'd ever heard of? Never in my life had I so wished to be in the clutches of ruthless and diabolical villains; the alternative *really* sucked.

If I was in the past, *which* past was I in, mine or that coin's? There was the business with the Royal Military Academy being at Woolwich instead of Sandhurst, but the more I thought about it, the less sure I was that proved anything. I didn't know where it had been a hundred and thirty years ago—why not Woolwich?

I'd been thinking about the war talk as well. We'd never gone to war with Britain since the War of 1812, but we'd had some diplomatic bumps. I just wasn't sure if any of them were this serious—or if this one was as serious as Gordon had portrayed it. He hadn't said there was a war, only that he expected one. Maybe that was just his wishful thinking. This might still be the unaltered past.

But if the event wave hadn't hit my present, how had I gotten here? Possibly the malfunction at WHECOL was simply that, a massive accident which I'd managed to survive. If so, this was my unaltered past and I was, as Reggie's SAS troopers in Afghanistan used to say, *proper* fucked. No one in my unaltered past would have the means of building a high-energy particle accelerator, even if I had any idea how to go about doing it. My only hope was the event wave had already passed and altered this past enough to give me something—*anything*—to work with.

But if it had, why did I still have my memories? Why did I even exist? Was the event wave still someplace between 1888 and 2018? If so, how long did I have before it caught up to my childhood, my life? When it did, would it wipe me out? Or would those early memories fade first, one at a time, until it got to the Wessex event itself and then erased whatever was left of me.

When the nurse took away my dinner dishes, I asked for paper and pencil. I thought that if I could write down the critical information, then I could read it and keep acting, even if my memory of those events started to go. Or if it was going to snuff me out, I should write about that world I'd lived in, leave some concrete record of it having existed. The paper and the graphite in the pencil were from this time; the event wave wouldn't erase them. It wasn't a living, intelligent being, just a force of nature, like an avalanche.

For a long time I stared at the blank paper. Where should I even start? What was there to say about the entire history of a world that stood in danger of extinction? What was it about that world which made it so important I had to preserve it? Finally I picked up the pencil and began to write.

Dear Sarah,

I can't imagine you will ever read this, but just writing it makes me feel closer to you, across the unimaginable gulf which separates us. There are things about me I need to tell you, should have told you before I left for England, but I put them off out of fear and shame. But as I sit here and think of you, of the young woman you have become, I know you are strong enough to hear them. . . .

Two days later Gordon returned with a suit of civilian clothes. I was already up and in my robe, but he tossed the clothes on the bed.

"Put those on. We're taking the express to London."

I'd grown impatient, was anxious to start on whatever journey lay before me, but despite that my heart sank a bit. There had still been the faint possibility I was in my own world and had simply been fooled into thinking otherwise. Now that possibility was gone. Someone could have dummied up a hospital room to look like a century ago and hired a dozen actors to play their parts—London was a different proposition. So I was in the past. Now the question was, *which* past?

"Hurry up, damn you," Gordon snapped. "We haven't got all day."

"A little touchy today are we, Captain?" I asked as I started to dress. "Have the boys upstairs overruled your plans for a hanging?"

"Never fear, you'll have your trial and then we'll hang you. It will be closed door, of course; we have some experience dealing with spics. But first there are some gentlemen who would like to ask you a few more questions."

"I'll be happy to talk to your people in London," I told Gordon, "but I've already told you everything I know. I don't have much more to give."

He didn't answer me; he just smiled. Actually it was a nasty little smirk, which wasn't a good sign. I'd read enough *Flashman* novels to know what that meant. Those old-time Brits had a code of honor and standards of behavior, unless they didn't think *you* were a gentleman. In that case they didn't feel much need to act like gentlemen themselves, so this could get pretty ugly. Making a run for it started sounding good.

My only real hope was things had actually changed here, and done so in a way that left me some sort of return route. I knew next to nothing about physics, and when you know that little, anything is possible, right? So my first priority was figuring out if this really was my own past or that coin's. I specialized in ancient Rome and the Near East, not nineteenth century Europe, but I knew more than the average Joe on the street. Reggie had picked me in part because I had an instinct for little things not quite right. I'd need to focus that, look for subtle differences, something the average person might miss.

Gordon included a long overcoat with the clothes, but it seemed like a nice day and so I carried it over my arm. Gordon and I, with two big constables in tow, walked out the front door of the hospital. I felt a breeze, heard the drone of machinery; a shadow fell across the broad stone steps ahead of us. I looked up.

Three hundred meters above us was . . . an ironclad? It was big, really big. It had too many surface features to be a balloon, things that looked like gun mounts and observation platforms, with shining brass railings and evenly spaced rows of massive rivets, the kind that hold steel girder bridges together. The drone grew louder as it passed overhead. Black smoke escaped from a stack in the rear, dispersed into a dirty gray wake by three large propellers that apparently drove the ship forward. I had no idea what held the damned thing up. An intense downdraft enfolded us, and piles of dried leaves on the lawn exploded into a swirling red-brown blizzard.

"Okay," I said to no one in particular, "so much for subtle differences."

I don't remember much about the carriage ride. I suppose I was still dazed, but I started paying attention again once we got to the train station—a little place out in the countryside called Creech St. Michael Halt. The locomotive hissed and throbbed nervously, reeked of hot rusty iron and sulfurous coal, and looked longer and more powerful than I remembered Victorian steam engines looking in Sherlock Holmes films.

Sherlock Holmes films? Flashman novels? And I called myself an historian? This was getting pathetic. Why couldn't this event-wave thingamajig have dropped me in fourth-century BCE Achaemenid Persia? At least I knew my way around there.

Gordon led the way with the Bobbies to either side of me. The one on my right slipped his hand around my elbow—not making a show of manhandling me, just letting me know he was there. Gordon looked through the open doors until he found an empty compartment and motioned us to follow him in.

The compartment was pretty much what I expected: dark wood paneling and brass fittings, a gaslight overhead, and a well-thumbed copy of *The Times* left on the overstuffed seat. Gordon sat facing me while the constables sat opposite each other by the windows.

"Where in London are we going?" I asked.

"You will see in good time," Gordon answered.

"Who are these gentlemen I'll be talking to?"

"All in good time."

"Look, if you could just—"

"Do be quiet, Fargo. There's a good spy."

Be quiet. Sure. I was on a train about to take me to an interview with people Gordon had broadly hinted were going to torture me—if necessary—to find out what I knew. Since I didn't know anything they were interested in, it was hard to see how this was going to end happily for anyone, but especially for me.

I picked up *The Times* and looked it over. Doing a quick scan was hard—these guys still had a lot to learn about newspaper layout, things like headlines and organizing from most to least important.

A penny had been removed from the pendulum counterbalance of Big Ben, which would slow the clock by four-tenths of a second per day. Seems it had been running slightly fast. No one knew why, but a panel of study was being formed. Swell. There was a report on the Royal Horticultural Society's flower show, another grisly murder in Whitechapel—when was Jack the Ripper running around?—and a letter from an unnamed correspondent about a Fenian Army massing in the U.S. Pacific Northwest. It also alleged several acts of sabotage against the Canadian Pacific Railroad near Vancouver.

Fenians—Irish separatists. I remembered there had been a border incident after the Civil War when a bunch of Irish veterans got together and tried to invade Canada, hold it hostage for an independent Ireland. Not much came of it, although it had been a big deal at the time. It seemed to me it had been earlier than the 1880s, though; weren't Civil War veterans getting long in the tooth by now?

Then another article caught my eye. The Foreign Office announced its acceptance of the credentials of General William Ransom Johnson Pegram as the new ambassador to the Court of St. James from the Confederate States of America. General Pegram had expressed his government's sympathy with Great Britain's current difficulties *vis-a-vis* the United States of America.

"Son of a bitch! Those assholes actually *won?*"

Gordon and the Bobbies eyed me with disapproval, and I tossed the paper aside.

The train started up, gathering speed quickly.

I couldn't believe it. *The South won?* I wasn't just in an altered history, I was in some stupid "Lost Cause" wet dream. If this place had taken a pass on emancipation, what other horrors had it decided it just couldn't part with?

This place? As if there were somewhere else? No, this was all there was now. This was it. I had already spent too much time in a hospital bed. Whatever trick I was going to perform to fix all this, I had better get going on, and right away.

Son of a bitch.

FOUR

September 23, 1888, London, England

Like a ghostly demon, London enveloped me in sulfurous tendrils of mist and smoke that smelled of hot metal, burning coal, and rotting garbage. The open air train platform stood at least twenty feet above street level, held up by iron girders. It reminded me of the Chicago Loop's "El,"—the elevated train—or what it might have looked like a century ago. My gaze swept across the faint powdering of dirt and coal dust blowing across the platform's walkway, the rust-streaked metal uprights and railings with their damp, grimy look, and then the city.

Brick and stone buildings rose into the sky, taller than seemed right for the period. Many larger ones sported an iron girder tower on top, with dirigibles docked to several of those. Two large flying machines droned slowly through the smoke and haze, but I couldn't tell if they were also dirigibles or more of those flying ironclads.

The people on the platform around me wore ankle-length coats in dark colors—browns and grays and dusty blacks. They conversed with muffled voices, hair hidden under hats, faces behind goggles and dark fabric masks. Many women wore elaborate dark veils tucked into the collars of their coats. They reminded me of Afghan women in burkas, at least in their impersonal anonymity. But instead of hiding their shape, their coats exaggerated the female figure, accenting ample bosoms, flaring from narrow waists out over bustled skirts. The women glided across the platform with a deliberate grace I found seductive and creepy at the same time.

This wasn't the London I had expected, but I had already abandoned my attachment to expectations.

"This way, Fargo," Gordon grunted from under a rubberized mask that included both goggles and air filter. Two different Bobbies now accompanied us, having taken over from the rural constabulary at Paddington Station, our port of entry to Greater London. The Wessex men had, in retrospect, been easy-going compared to these two. Like Gordon they both wore goggles and masks. Their uniforms seemed darker and were augmented by thick gauntlets and taller helmets. They had a lean, tough look compared to their more portly country cousins, and black varnished wooden truncheons dangled from wrist thongs. One of them poked me in the back for encouragement. I'd put on the long coat they gave me, but no face protection was offered. My eyes burned already.

Ten minutes on a metro train brought us to a smaller station deeper in the city—St. John's Square, the sign told me. Two flights of wrought-iron steps took us down to ground level, where horse-drawn cabs clip-clopped along crowded, litter-strewn streets, side by side with worn-looking freight wagons and one smoking steam-powered autocarriage. Most of the people here didn't have elaborate masks and goggles. Instead, men in threadbare coats with collars turned up wore handkerchiefs tied over nose and mouth, and watched the Bobbies warily through red-rimmed eyes. They knew more about this world than I did, and they were afraid of the uniforms. Point taken.

We walked briskly for two blocks, then up the stone steps of a brownstone house, a knock, a few exchanged words between Gordon and a doorman, and we moved from the gloom of the streets into the gaslit twilight of the interior.

Heavy furniture, that was my first impression: big wardrobes, massive dark wood tables with legs carved to look like lion paws, overstuffed chairs, leather couches, and heavy brocade curtains hanging from near the high ceiling, puddling on the floor. Thick oriental carpets, bunches of them, carpets on top of carpets. Big oil paintings in heavy gilt frames covering whatever wall space was left—landscapes, seascapes, pictures of the moors or heaths or whatever, and one portrait of an angry old man whose eyes seemed to follow me as we marched through the front room.

"Who's your decorator?" I asked. "Count Dracula?"

But it was just bravado, just whistling past the graveyard. The place had me spooked.

Up a broad flight of polished wood stairs, down a hall, and finally to a pair of sliding doors. Gordon knocked, the doors slid open a crack for a moment, he exchanged a few hushed words with whoever was inside, and then the doors slid open to let us in.

"You two wait out here," he ordered the Bobbies. "And you mind yourself in here, Fargo. I have a revolver."

He patted his right coat pocket to let me know he meant business.

We entered what I guess they called a sitting room. Four men conversed in the center of the room, and they turned to look me over without warmth. All wore dark suits except for one in an army uniform—same red tunic and dark blue trousers as Gordon but heavier with gold braid. Gordon joined them after gesturing for me to wait by the door.

One of the older men smiled and shook Gordon's hand, and Gordon returned the smile. First time I'd seen him show any warmth at all.

This was supposed to be my interrogation, and I was here, but nothing was happening, so I figured we were waiting for someone else to show up. I glanced around the room. There were a couple love seats and wingback chairs set away from the walls but leaving a large open area in the center of the room covered by a single oriental rug. By the standards of the rest of the place, or what I'd seen of it, this room was sparsely furnished.

The double-paneled door we came through was behind me, and drapes on the opposite wall covered two windows, so that must be an exterior wall. As I faced the exterior wall, I had a fireplace to my left and then another double-paneled door on the wall to my right, so two ways in and out if you didn't count the windows. Good to know if I had to make a break for it. I wasn't sure where I'd run to, but I had a very bad feeling about this place.

Under the odor of cigar smoke, the room was filled with that same unfamiliar chemical scent I'd noticed at the hospital, and it seemed to be coming from the windows. Was that a room deodorizer of some kind? Maybe. It reminded me a little of Listerine.

"What's that smell?" I asked, and the gang of five turned to me with startled expressions, as if a statue or caged animal had suddenly spoken.

"I beg your pardon?" one of them asked after a moment.

"That chemical odor. I smelled it at the hospital and now here, but I don't recognize it. I think it's coming from the drapes."

They exchanged looks—confused, unbelieving, impatient.

"Carbolic acid," the tall officer snapped, and the five went back to their conversation, but the three men in suits stole glances back at me.

Carbolic acid was an early disinfectant. I'd probably have recognized its odor from high school chemistry class, except I took biology and physics instead.

The paneled doors to my right slid open and another man strode purposely toward us, his eyes taking in the conversational group and then locking on me. He wore his big shock of reddish-brown hair, graying at the temples, like a well-groomed lion's mane. His dark suit looked expensive, carefully tailored.

"Colonel Rossbank, gentlemen. So this is the fellow. What do we know of him?"

His voice filled the room without straining—a voice accustomed to filling rooms.

"Good day, Sir Edward," the tall officer, presumably Colonel Rossbank, answered. "Aside from his preposterous story, I'm afraid we know nothing. The Americans profess ignorance, of course."

"Of course," Sir Edward answered. He stopped a couple feet away facing me, hands clasped behind his back under the tails of his coat, and he leaned forward and squinted at me as if I were some sort of museum display.

"*Quo usque tandem abutere, Catalina, patientia nostra?*" I asked him.

The five others shifted with surprise and muttered to each other, but Sir Edward barked a short laugh.

"Damn me if I wasn't about to ask you almost the same thing. 'How long, Cataline, will you abuse our patience?'" he translated. "Cicero's ringing denunciation of Cataline's base treason—very apropos, although I rather think of *you* in the role of Cataline. Now, what is a spy doing quoting Cicero? Oh, that's right! You're pretending to be an ancient historian, aren't you?"

"Marduk belu rabu uihdiema, ana ia'ati." I answered. This time he didn't laugh. His face clouded over with uncertainty.

"I'm afraid I am unfamiliar with that passage, or even the language."

"'Marduk the great lord rejoiced in my pious deeds, and gratefully blessed me,'" I translated in turn. "It's ancient Persian, a passage from the Babylonian Cylinder of Cyrus the Great, which, as I recall, currently resides in the British Museum."

He studied me seriously for several seconds, arms folded across his chest and eyes narrow, before giving a slight nod.

"Very well, I accept your academic credentials, Professor Fargo. I am Sir Edward Bonseller, personal secretary to the prime minister. You will understand, given the circumstances, if I do not offer my hand. Have you met the others?

"Well, you know Captain Gordon, of course. Colonel Rossbank is director of the military intelligence department at Horse Guards. Professor Tyndall is retired from the Royal Institution, but circumstances have conspired to interrupt his well-deserved rest. I hope you are well, sir."

The older man who earlier had greeted Gordon with affection was frail and birdlike, with a high forehead and a fringe of white hair around his chin and skull like the ruff of an owl. He now patted his side coat pocket, much the same way Gordon had.

"I am armed, Sir Edward, which is more to the point." His accent had a trace of Irish, and his voice, reedy with age, nearly cracked as he spoke. "They killed poor Huxley last evening. Had you heard?"

"Yes. You have my sympathy, Tyndall. Damned shame. That makes six, doesn't it?"

"Aye, six with Huxley. Of the entire membership of the X Club there remains only Hooker, Frankland, and myself, and this scoundrel came within an ace of getting me." He pointed at me. "Louisa and I were visiting relatives in Somerton when this fellow blew half of it to pieces."

That could put you on edge, I supposed. I was probably going to have a hard time convincing him it was all just a coincidence, scientists being generally skeptical of the notion that something "just happened."

"Tyndall is one of our most respected physicists, and Professor Thomson is another," Bonseller continued, gesturing to a man of similar age but stout and full-bearded, bearlike in physique. "Thomson's come down from Glasgow University, where he holds the chair in physics, to help us sort your story out. He's helped the government on a number of thorny matters. Good to see you again, Billy."

"A wonder I can see at all, dragged down from my clean Sco'ish air into this sewage dump," he answered in a soft brogue. "What's keeping you from doing something about the blasted air, Eddie? Waiting till Tyndall here makes his second million off patented respirators?"

"Damn your eyes," Tyndall hissed back, and the heavy-set Scotsman turned toward him, the malice between the two men suddenly as obvious as a bloodstain.

Bonseller held his hand up to cut off the argument

"Oh, and Meredith is the cabinet's science advisor," he added, finishing the introductions.

The last one was younger, probably in his late thirties or early forties, pear-shaped and balding, with only a sparse moustache for facial hair. His eyes darted from Bonseller to me, to the window, the door, the floor. He bobbed his head nervously in acknowledgment.

"Now, let's get to it, shall we?"

They grilled me for over an hour. Bonseller asked most of the questions, with Tyndall chiming in on technical matters at first, but then becoming more involved as the questions turned from my "story" to a detailed description of the future from which I came. All of them reacted with surprise when I told them the outline of our space program, having put men on the moon and an unmanned rover on Mars. That interrupted the session while they had a huddled and heated consultation in the far corner of the room. When they started again, they asked more about powered flight, and when I told them the broad outline of some of the newest aircraft, they were impressed but confused. I could see why.

Colonel Rossbank had a few questions about the armed forces of my time, but the capabilities I described were so unbelievable he quickly lost interest and lit a cigar. Gordon followed his lead with a cheroot of his own. Meredith sat at a writing desk and took notes, and Thomson, the heavy-set Scottish physicist, remained quiet and paced the room, chewing on the stem of an unlit pipe, his face always in silent motion, alternating between concentration, surprise, disbelief, and then understanding.

The birdlike Tyndall finally shook his head in exasperation.

"The story is remarkable for its detail and consistency. Genuinely remarkable. But it is simply beyond belief."

"Nonsense," Thomson said, his first spoken word since my interrogation began. "There is not a thing in the world he describes which is not explainable by direct extrapolation from our own existing scientific principles."

Right then I decided the big Scot was my guy. I could have kissed him.

"Oh, rubbish!" Tyndall snapped back. "This inter-web thing is extrapolation? Of what?"

"His high capacity computing machines are simply an improvement on our analytic engines, but with mechanical calculation and memory replaced with electric functions. That accounts for both the miniaturization and the higher calculation speed. Electric storage of data is clearly possible, something like that American laddie Smith argued for, recording sounds with permanent magnetic impressions on wire."

"Smith? Smith who? What are you talking about?" Tyndall demanded.

"Oberon Smith, I think he's called. It was in *Electrical World* last year, Tyndall. You really should keep up on your professional reading. As to electrical as opposed to mechanical functioning, it's nothing more than development of a Crookes tube into something more than a curiosity. The American mathematician Charles Pierce has already proposed a means by which logic operations can be carried out by electric switching circuits."

Tyndall sniffed and turned away, looking all the more like an offended owl.

"I'd call that a mighty leap," he said

"Aye," Thomson agreed. "But thus do we advance, by mighty leaps."

"And the ability to access these machines from anywhere, without wires?" Bonseller asked, but Tyndall instead of Thomson answered.

"Obviously some sort of electromagnetic communicator propagated through the aether. I suppose it could utilize Hertz's waves." He turned to Thomson. "As was reported in *Annalen der Physik*, last year."

Thomson smiled and bowed slightly to him.

"That's right," I put in, because it was time to insinuate myself into the group. "Hertz was one of the early pioneers in wireless research."

Things were going better than I'd expected, a lot better. They obviously had some sort of advanced science to work with. I figured if they could manage to make great big ironclads fly like balloons, they knew something we didn't. Now if I could get Tyndall and Thomson to kiss and make nice, I had three potential allies: the Irish owl, the Scottish bear, and, most importantly, the English lion Bonseller. I'd known men like him before—men who could open doors. Men who thought the world could be fixed and they were just the guys to do it. Dangerous men, but useful ones, too, up to a point.

I heard a thud out in the hallway, where the Bobbies were waiting, and then what sounded like a scuffle.

"What the devil's going on out there, Gordon?" Colonel Rossbank demanded.

"I'll find out, sir."

Rossbank shook his head and dropped his cigar in a brass spittoon.

"I'll sort it out. I need some air."

He walked to the doors and slid one back.

"What's all this, then?" he demanded, but he suddenly choked in pain, staggered backward a step or two, and fell, blood spraying across the floor.

We stood frozen as two dark shapes filled the doorway, paused for an instant to scan the room, then an arm snapped and a blade flew through the air. Tyndall staggered back, eyes bulging, blood bubbling from his throat and mouth. He turned as he fell, for a moment the light of a gaslight sparkled from the diamond stickpin in his cravat, and then he collapsed twitching to the floor.

"NO!" Gordon shouted, his voice rising almost to a scream.

Blood pounded in my ears, and my perception became jerky, strobelike: shouts, curses, scrambling bodies, overturned furniture, and one of the dark shapes raising his hand and pointing at me.

"'Ere 'e is. Git 'im!"

The other's hand, holding a steel blade rose, and snapped toward me.

FIVE

September 23, 1888, London, England

The dagger wasn't meant for me. I heard Bonseller cry out in pain and fear, and that shocked me into action. I staggered away from the door, my feet clumsy, balance screwed up. Nothing around me made sense, because my heart rate had gone through the roof and a lot of frontal brain functions were shutting down, but I remembered enough to start tactical breathing. Inhale for a five count, hold it for a five count, exhale for a five count, wait for a five count, start again.

Someone grabbed me by the right arm, one of the men from the door. He wore some sort of black coverall and a black cap. His mouth twisted open in a grimace showing me yellow and black jack-o'-lantern teeth, and his breath came as a physical shock almost as potent as the thrown knife. A blade flashed toward my face, and I tried to twist away, but his grip was strong. The knife stopped millimeters from my throat.

"Come wi' us or you're a dead 'un," he growled.

I nodded mutely.

Exhale for five, hold for five . . .

Three serving-platter-sized metallic spiders scrabbled past my feet, making whirring, clicking noises.

What the hell?

The other man in black yanked down the big drapes from the window, pulling the curtain rod and mounts away from the ceiling in a small shower of plaster dust. Light exploded in through the large window, and I saw a smoky rectangle of the London skyline. He kicked at the window, and glass shattered.

"Where's the bleedin' coin?" the man holding me shouted as he pulled me toward the window.

"I . . . I don't—" I stammered.

"Here!" someone yelled. I recognized Meredith's voice. His plump hand appeared from behind the overturned writing desk, holding a melted slug of clear plastic.

Inhale for five, hold for five. Vision came into sharper focus, legs grew steadier. Around the periphery of my vision the old blackness crept, the blackness I thought gone forever.

Where was Gordon and his revolver? Tyndall's pistol was in his coat pocket on the floor. No time to get it. The man at the window had his back to me as he used his fist to knock out the remaining broken shards of glass. The thug holding me shoved me toward the window and let go to reach out to grab the coin.

Action without thought. Two long steps to launch myself into the air, catch the man at the window with both of my feet squarely in his back. Kick hard to transfer momentum to him, come down in a crouch as he plunged screaming out the window. Anticipation, experience, memory—indistinguishable.

With neither thought nor emotion I rose and turned to the other thug and I knew my face was as empty as the abyss. Did I know it then or know it later? There was no then or later. He hesitated, his knife held wrong for a throw.

"Halt in the name of the crown! Hands up!"

Gordon!

Face white, pistol raised and shaking, Gordon stood at the double paneled door through which Bonseller had entered. The thug didn't even glance back at him. Instead, his eyes flickered to the open window behind me. He licked his lips, calculated, then lunged toward me.

I sidestepped, Gordon's pistol fired, the sound exploding like thunder in the confined space of the room. The man staggered forward and fell against the window sill, then straightened, put his foot on the sill, and jumped.

Through the window, I saw the thug swinging from a rope ladder a dozen feet from the building, and as I watched, he rose up and away, and the blackness behind my eyes fled with him.

I stuck my head out farther and looked up—some sort of elongated powered balloon. The chugging engine rose in volume as the balloon gained speed and disappeared up and into the mists. Thoughts returned.

What the hell was going on?

The pistol barked again, and a slug slammed into the windowsill above my head, throwing splinters of wood and glass into my scalp. I flinched to the side and then dove for cover behind a heavy leather sofa. Thomson was already there, kicking one of the metal spiders away.

"Nicely done, laddie," he said.

"Tell that to Gordon."

The pistol fired again, and a slug blew through the back of the couch, showering us with horse-hair furniture entrails.

"Captain Gordon!" Thomson shouted. "Cease fire, ya great bloody idiot! I'm back here, and Fargo is on our side, not theirs."

"Yes, for God's sake stop shooting." That was Bonseller's voice. He sounded weak, but he wasn't dead. I helped Thomson to his feet and then hurried over to Bonseller's prone form. Gordon stood in the doorway uncertainly, pistol drooping. A mechanical spider scrambled toward him, he fired his revolver, knocked wood from the floor six inches to the side, fired again, and then again, finally hitting it.

"Damn," he muttered. Several men in suits pushed past him from behind.

I knelt beside Bonseller. He was trying to sit up but having a hard time. Blood soaked his left sleeve around the hilt of a throwing knife that was buried in his arm above the elbow. I grabbed his upper bicep in my left hand, my thumb on the pressure point to cut off the blood flow.

"Take it easy, Bonseller. You're bleeding a lot. The knife must have nicked an artery. I'm going to put a pressure bandage on it."

I started to pull open his coat, when a mechanical spider scrabbling across the floor bumped Bonseller's leg. It stopped and locked steel mandibles on his calf, then made a loud whirring sound, started vibrating, and Bonseller cried out in pain. I felt an electric shock through my thumb and jumped back.

"Son of a bitch!"

I kicked the spider away from Bonseller and grabbed his arm again. He trembled from the shock and groaned but didn't seem much worse otherwise. He still needed a compression bandage, so I unbuckled his belt and pulled it out as gently as I could.

"Stand away from Sir Edward, Fargo," Gordon ordered. I hadn't even noticed him walk up. He raised the shaking revolver, pointed it at my forehead, and cocked the hammer back.

"You're dry, Gordon," I told him, "unless that's a seven-shooter."

Gordon looked at his revolver in confusion.

"Oh, put the bloody gun down, man," Thomson ordered. "And where did you get off to, anyway?"

"I went for help," he explained.

"This may hurt a bit, but I need to get this knife out of the way," I said. I took the handle in my fist, made sure I was lined up squarely, and slid it up and out of the wound, trying not to make things any worse. Bonseller gasped but made no other signs of pain. More blood oozed out of the slit in the coat, but not much. I wrapped the belt three times around Bonseller's upper arm over the wound and pulled it tight. He drew in air sharply as I did, but he took it pretty well, all things considered.

"That should hold you until a surgeon can stitch you up. Just make sure you keep the pressure on the wound."

I looked up as the room filled with excited servants, men who looked like clerks, and two who looked more like police detectives or bodyguards from their grim composure. Meredith, supported by two men, rose weakly from behind the overturned desk. Most of the others clustered around us, but a few checked Tyndall and Colonel Rossbank for signs of life. Gordon drifted over to stand by the silent form of his older friend, his empty revolver dangling limply in his hand.

"A couple of you find something to use for a stretcher," I ordered, "and get rid of these damned spiders. Somebody else get a carriage, or whatever you use to get people to the hospital. And grab the bad guy I pushed out the window; it's only two stories down, so he's probably still alive, and maybe mobile. *Hurry!*"

The closest ones looked uncertainly from Thomson to Bonseller.

"Yes, yes," Bonseller said. "Get to it."

Two of them dashed for the door, and a couple others started looking for lightweight furniture—good luck with that.

"You got a favorite hospital, Sir Eddy?" I asked.

"St. George's on Grosvenor Place, and damn you for a cheeky bastard. 'Sir Eddy' indeed. What of the others? How is Tyndall?"

I was sure Tyndall was dead; the thrown knife had severed his carotid artery. I glanced over to the doorway where Rossbank lay. One of the detective-looking men stood and spread an overcoat over his motionless form. Past them, through the open panel doors, I saw the still form of one of the Bobbies.

"Tyndall and the colonel are both dead, probably both constables as well. Everyone else seems okay." I sniffed and looked around.

"Someone shit their britches. Was that you, Gordon?"

Publicly humiliating him might cause problems later, but I didn't care. Survivor's high does that. Gordon's already-red face turned a brighter shade, and he shot me a look of hatred and shame all mixed up together.

The truth was all of us who'd been in the room—Bonseller, Thomson, Gordon, and probably me as well—had bright red faces by then. It's the normal response of the circulatory system to danger; first it chokes off blood to the extremities to concentrate it in the core organs, so the face goes white. Then, when the all-clear sounds, the blood comes pounding back into the skin—instant tomato face. Bonseller's complexion was the first to start to lose its color again.

"I'm feeling a bit lightheaded."

"Yeah. You're probably going to faint," I told him.

"I dare say. Billy, you are in charge here until I'm back from the hospital. Try to sort all this out, will you? And don't let Gordon shoot anyone."

People with purpose bustled in and out of the room, giving reports to Thomson and getting orders. I sat on the leather sofa that had a bullet hole through its back, looked at the small pile of broken mechanical spiders, one of their legs still twitching and clawing the air, and I collected my thoughts.

Thomson came over and sat down heavily on the sofa next to me. He exhaled shakily.

"I'm still a bit overwhelmed by all this," he said. "But you're a very cold-blooded fellow, aren't you?"

In response I held out my hand. It trembled uncontrollably.

"I think I might throw up," I added.

"If so, do it now, while Gordon is off changing his trousers. You wouldn't want to give him that satisfaction, would you?"

"For an old, fat Scotsman you're pretty observant."

He chuckled.

"You have a knack for making insults palatable, Fargo, damn me if I understand how.

"We've asked you a great many questions today. I'd say you've earned some answers of your own. I imagine you have more questions than I can address all at once, so for now, which one is most important to you?"

One question?

Why did the bad guys want Tyndall dead? Why did Tyndall think I was part of that? Why did the bad guys want the coin? Why did they want me? What were those spiders? Why does London have elevated trains instead of a subway? What's wrong with the air? How did the South win? What the hell holds those flying ironclads up?

"How do I get back to my daughter?" I said.

He leaned back on the sofa and examined me. I could tell he had no answer, but the question interested him.

One of the clerks walked through the door and hurried over to us.

"Professor Thomson, the villain who fell from the window is conscious and his injuries do not seem life-threatening. We have him in a room off the front parlor for now. To where should we have him taken?"

"I think we'll talk to him there. Find Captain Gordon and have him join us, would you?"

He turned to me as the clerk left.

"Come along, Fargo. I will tell you honestly that I cannot imagine how it is possible to return you to your time, but I know of one man who might help us. First, however, we must attend to this business."

When we got downstairs, Gordon was already questioning the thug, had already finished in a sense.

"This blackguard won't tell us anything," he announced in disgust as soon as we arrived. I glanced over at the fellow—thin in the face, wiry-looking, but a thick torso under his coveralls. His face was skinned up, nose broken, with blood caked around his mouth and chin. He sat on a sofa with his left leg propped up on it.

I walked over and had a look at his leg, touched it below the knee, and he winced in pain. The trouser leg was bloodstained, and the irregular bulge suggested a bone sticking out of the skin.

"Nasty compound fracture you got there. If a doctor doesn't take care of it, you could end up with gangrene, lose the leg."

He licked his lips, and sweat trickled down the side of his face.

"So what? Dead's as dead, either way."

At least that's what I thought he said. He dropped almost all the consonants, leaving a series of vowel-like grunts, so it was hard to tell for sure, but I was starting to get the hang of some of the accents and the meter of the speech. I could read and speak Latin, ancient and modern Greek, Aramaic, German, Spanish, French, and a half-dozen Middle-Eastern and Central-Asian languages and dialects. You'd think I could decipher Cockney English.

"He won't tell us anything," Gordon repeated.

I ignored him and leaned forward, rapped the fellow lightly on his chest. Under the fabric it was hard, rigid, and made a muffled *thunk*.

"Thought so. That first shot of yours didn't miss the other one, Gordon. These guys are wearing some sort of body armor."

"Body armor?" He came over and leaned forward to rap it himself. "Well, damn me if he ain't."

"You tell him you were going to see him swing for this, no matter what?" I asked.

"Of course I did."

"Yeah, and now he won't talk. What a shocker."

"If you think you can do any better, be my guest."

I couldn't imagine doing much worse. I pulled over an armchair to face the sofa and noticed Thomson take a chair near the door. Gordon remained standing, pacing back and forth, scowling ferociously. Good. I didn't know if these guys had come up with *Good Cop, Bad Cop* yet, but if not, it was about time.

I looked the guy over. Scars on his face and knuckles told the story of a violent life. Hard eyes told it better. Red-rimmed, bloodshot eyes, broken veins on his nose to match—a life of alcohol as well as violence. But he looked strong now, in a lean, ratlike way, and clearheaded. There was life in his eyes—not exactly hope, but defiance and self-respect. This wasn't a hired tough; this was a man with beliefs.

His pupils were dilated. All mixed up in the smells of sweat and soot, the smells of the man and his world, there was something else, something herbal and smoky. Marijuana? Maybe so.

"What's your name?" I asked. He hesitated. "What do you want me to call you?"

"Grover'll do."

"Would you like a smoke, Grover?" I asked. The question caught him by surprise, but then he shrugged.

"Could do."

"Captain Gordon, give him one of your cheroots."

"I'm damned if I will! These bastards killed Tyndall."

"Just do it, man," Thomson ordered softly.

Gordon threw the small cigar onto the couch. The prisoner snatched it, put it in his mouth, and grinned.

I took a match from Gordon, struck it, and the prisoner puffed the cheroot to life. The room filled with its aromatic smoke, and he leaned back in relaxed pleasure, his pain and fear momentarily forgotten.

"Captain Gordon has told you that, no matter what, you'll hang. Well, that's not much of a surprise, is it? Two constables, a colonel, and one of the most respected scientists in England all dead—hard to imagine they'll let you off with a warning. My guess is, the time you spend here, smoking that cigar, is probably going to be the best time you have left in your life, so savor it. From here on out it will either be just so-so, or truly horrendous. You understand that, right?"

His smile faded a bit, and his eyes grew thoughtful. After a moment he nodded.

"Okay, good. You probably aren't going to betray anything important to us, so instead let's see if you can satisfy our curiosity about some smaller things. Professor Thomson figures he knows who you work for. Who's that again, Prof?"

"The Old Man," Thomson said.

I watched the thug's face. If Thomson was wrong, I'd have seen disdain or triumph. Instead I saw nothing, a wall.

The Old Man. *The Old Man of the Mountain?* That would explain the smell of cannabis. The timing was about eight hundred years off, though.

"Well, whoever. Here's what I'm curious about. I get that he's killing some group of guys, and Tyndall was next on the list. But why did he want me? And why the coin?"

The prisoner took the cheroot from his mouth and studied the ash for a moment, considering his answer.

"Well, 'e's a collector, see? Go' to collect all the li'l shiny bits what come frew the 'ole."

"The hole?"

"The 'ole in time. 'E's already got lots o' shiny bits. Don't think you're the first, do ya?"

The hole in time! I sat up straight and leaned forward.

"I need to find him."

Grover's expression clouded over as if he realized he'd said too much. "'E'll find you, soon enough."

"Yeah, well, he's got his schedule and I've got mine. Where is he?"

I figured I knew the answer—Syria. That's where The Old Man of the Mountain—*Shaykh al-Jabal* in Arabic—had been based along with his cult of *hashshashins*—fearless killers, from whom the word assassin derived. The story was they took hashish before a mission to fortify their courage and dull the pain of any wound or injury they might suffer. That had always sounded pretty far-fetched to me, and London was a long way from the cult's recruiting area, but it wouldn't be the screwiest thing about this place. Not even close.

Grover's face tightened, and his eyes narrowed to slits. Everything up until then was bragging—this approached betrayal, and I had the feeling he would never voluntarily betray The Old Man.

"Look," I said, "if he's as good as you think he is, you'll be doing him a favor. I'll go charging in there, he'll grab me, and then he'll have what he wants. Besides, he'll know we're coming, right? If he knew about me and the coin, he knows everything going on here."

We stared at each other, me daring him to talk, him calculating the angles. As I watched, I realized I was seeing the workings of an intelligent and sophisticated, if unschooled, mind. Now he was trying to figure out which play made the most sense, but not for him, for his boss.

"Stuff it," he finally said.

Here was someone with brains, guts, and loyalty, even honor in his way, and this society had just discarded him. Then along came someone who recognized gemstones, even damaged ones lying in the gutter, and had swept him up. This wasn't my world, and I was glad it wasn't, because it was in bad trouble.

I gathered the plan had been to throw me in prison after the interview. Things having turned out as they had, they decided against prison, but that left my domestic arrangements up in the air. It turns out there were bedrooms on the third floor of the house for unexpected guests like me. I also found out the house had a name—Dorset House.

A maid—she couldn't have been more than ten or twelve—showed me to my room and brought some cold cheese sandwiches and a pot of lukewarm tea. She also pointed out, with much blushing, the commode down the hall, where I was pleasantly surprised to find a functioning flush toilet.

I turned in early but had trouble getting to sleep. I wasn't used to sleeping in odd places. A hospital, a bed-and-breakfast, that's different. Those are places with labels, so you know how you're supposed to feel about them. Dorset House—what kind of place was that? Also, I wasn't sure when I was going to get a clean change of clothes, so I slept in the raw. The bed was cold and the sheets stiff and scratchy. I could have used a change of bandages on my burned back as well, but that would have to wait.

My thoughts didn't help me doze off. Sitting in the interview room with Grover, the Cockney *hashshashin*, for just a moment I'd felt closer to an answer, closer to the way home. But since I'd come to this thoroughly screwed-up place, all I'd seen were hostile faces, violent death, and a London right out of a bad acid trip. I'd played this game of looking for allies, planning my next move—for what? Even if I found some "hole in time," what then? How much closer would I be to finding what had altered my past and then undoing it? Not one inch. Lying there alone in that cold bed, I felt impossibly far away from anyone and anything I had ever cared about. And in that cold darkness, I couldn't believe there was a way back to the warmth and light. I just couldn't.

SIX

September 24, 1888, London, England

The next morning an older maid woke me up with tea—hot for a change—some crisp toast held upright in a silver toast rack, and the news that I was wanted downstairs as soon as I could dress. I'm not sure why, but a hot cup of tea, and the thought of someone—even assholes—waiting for me, restored my confidence.

"Outrageous! Do you hear me? It is bloody outrageous, and I will not bloody have it. I *will not!!*"

I paused in the doorway, glanced around the office, and saw three red-faced junior officers at rigid attention—with Gordon the reddest of them all—in front of the ranting older officer. I recognized the two others with Gordon as the men I had taken for detectives the day before. Thomson sat in a chair in the corner, puffing on his pipe and lost in thought. He noticed me at the door and took the pipe from his mouth to wave me in.

The tall, stout officer turned his ferocious glare on me. His eyes narrowed and his gray moustache bristled like the whiskers on a walrus.

"So, the mysterious Mr. Fargo joins us. Because of you they said my 'talents' were needed here, in the Intelligence Department. They're bringing that doddering old fool Baker back from India to give him my seat on the Army Board. That was Wood's handiwork, I'll wager. Well damn Wood, damn the Board, damn Rossbank for getting himself killed, and damn all of these fools for not dying in place of him!"

"Don't forget to damn me," I said.

"*Damn you*, sir!"

"Fargo, allow me to introduce the new director of military intelligence," Thomson said from his chair. "Major General Sir Redvers Buller, VC. General, as you correctly deduced, this is Professor James Fargo of the University of Chicago."

VC after his name meant Buller had the Victoria Cross, Britain's highest award for heroism, the equivalent of our Medal of Honor.

"University of Chicago?" Buller said. "Never heard of it."

"Be patient," I answered. "It wasn't founded until 1890, but we managed to make a name for ourselves fairly quickly. *Redvers*. Do your friends call you 'Red'?"

"Damn you, sir, they do *not*. Americans must prize a particularly thick sort of professor. Just what did you intend by taking on two armed assailants?"

"I intended not to go with them."

"Damned foolish, if you ask me," he said.

"Well, you guys have been so nice to me, I couldn't bear to leave."

"'Better the enemy you know' was more likely your motive," Buller muttered.

There was more than a little truth to that.

"I think this 'Old Man' may be the only one who can get me back to my time," I said. "I want to have a nice long talk with him about that, but not as his prisoner. So I'm going to need some help."

Buller stood there for a moment and stared at me.

"Indeed," he said finally. "And you expect us to provide that help?"

"Yup. You want him, and I appear to be the key to getting him, or at least bringing him out into the open. His henchman said as much. So you need me for bait, and I need you for muscle. It's a match made in heaven."

Buller snorted and looked to Thomson, who simply raised his eyebrows in reply.

"And I suppose I'm to trust you because you turned on your captors," Buller said. "But you did not raise a finger until after Tyndall and Rossbank were dead. How do I know the entire episode wasn't staged just to put you in our good graces?"

"You're director of military intelligence. In my time I'd know what that means. Here, not so much. Is this just another assignment, or have you actually done this stuff before?"

"'Done this stuff before?' Listen to this fellow, Thomson. You actually believe he is a professor of *anything*? He talks like a guttersnipe."

"Well, he *is* American," Thomson answered.

"Hummph. I was chief of intelligence in the Ashanti campaign and again in the Sudan in '82, so, yes, I have 'done this stuff' before. What of it?"

"You'd give a lot to have a source inside the highest level of your enemy's counsels, right? Sure you would," I said. "But once you had it, would you risk it just to get a second one?"

"What are you insinuating, Fargo?" Gordon demanded.

Buller turned on him.

"Found your voice, have you, Captain? He is insinuating nothing; he is stating the obvious. We already have a viper in our midst. How else could they have found out about both Fargo and the artifact? As I'd say you were the principal suspect, your outburst is hardly surprising."

"Me?"

"Yes, you," Buller answered. "I must say, Gordon, for a serving officer that was a remarkably unconvincing display of marksmanship. You put pistol bullets all over the place, missed almost everything you aimed at, but your very first shot hit the henchman square in the back. Or should I say square in the body armor?"

The color drained from Gordon's face, and he shook his head.

"No, sir. It wasn't like that!"

"No, perhaps not," Buller continued. "Perhaps that shot was as wild as all the rest. Were you really aiming for Fargo, but couldn't hit him any better than anything else?"

"*No*, sir. I swear it, upon my honor!"

"If, as I suspect, you are a damned spy, you have no honor, sir, so your oath is hardly reassuring."

Enjoyable as it was to watch Gordon getting roasted over a fire—and it really was—I knew I had to step in before this careened out of control.

"No, it can't be Gordon," I said.

General Buller's eyebrows went up a little in surprise, and for the first time he looked at me with genuine interest. I learned something about him right then. Everything he'd done up until then had been a deliberate performance, and everything he'd seen and heard had been exactly what he expected, until I came to Gordon's defense.

"Go on," he ordered.

"You can fake voluntary reactions, but not involuntary ones. He soiled himself. It's a common but completely involuntary response to sudden danger. He was as surprised as the rest of us."

"*You* didn't soil yourself," Buller observed.

"I knew I was in for a long and stressful day, maybe even torture, so I took a tactical dump on the train right before we got to London."

"And what, pray tell, is a *tactical dump*?" he demanded.

I told him.

Thomson laughed, and one of the young officers snickered, which made Buller frown all the more fiercely.

"You never filled your trousers in combat, General?" I asked.

His scowl grew even darker and his face reddened.

"Different matter altogether," he snapped. "Water's always bad on campaign; a soldier learns to live with dysentery. Not the same thing at all."

"No, of course not," I said.

"Damn you, Fargo. How do you explain his convenient marksmanship? Hasn't it occurred to you he may have been trying to *kill* you?"

"Yeah, but I decided against it. Use your head, General. If he works for a guy who wants to 'collect' me, whatever the hell that means, why would he want to kill me? No, his shooting makes perfect sense. You've been in tough combat before or you wouldn't have a Victoria Cross, so think about it.

"His stress level was through the ceiling, so his hands shook, and he'd lost fine-detail resolution in his vision. He couldn't *see* the sight on the end of his pistol. His first shot was pure muscle memory; he raised his hand, and it automatically pointed where his eyes were looking. After that he started thinking about it, trying to aim, and so he put bullets all over the place."

Buller studied me carefully for a few seconds, and I could almost see the gears turning in his head as he thought it over. He'd probably never heard it explained that way before, but if he really had seen a lot of combat, it would make sense.

"Loss of fine-vision resolution, involuntary responses, *muscle memory*—how do you know all this?" he asked.

"I'll tell you some day. But right now you've got a more pressing problem, don't you?"

"Yes, the spy. Well, that's thin soup, Fargo, but it's the only soup we have, I'm afraid. Damned if I'm certain why, but I think you're right. Blast you, Gordon! My life would be a deal easier if you were guilty."

Buller waved the three rigid officers to ease and sat down behind the large wooden desk. I found a chair.

"I'm a fair suspect myself, I suppose," Thomson said. "I knew all the details concerning Fargo's story, and I was on bad terms with Tyndall and the other X Club members."

The same thing had already occurred to me. I liked Thomson, but that didn't change the facts.

Buller opened a folder on his desk and studied its contents, frowning in thought.

"Your argument with the X Club was public, Professor, but I hardly consider it a motive for these killings. Your position is rather sensible, if you ask me. All this Origins of Species nonsense the X Club members spouted—I knew my grandfather, by God, and *he* was no monkey."

Across the desk I saw Gordon's face tighten, but he said nothing. Buller turned to me.

"Professor Thomson disproved all that rubbish, you know, but the X Club johnnies still stuck with it. Rather thick of them, if you ask me. Not to speak ill of the dead, of course."

"Disproved it?" I asked.

Thomson shifted uncomfortably in his chair and cast a guilty look at Gordon.

"I . . . ah . . . calculated the age of the Earth based on its internal temperature and the rate of cooling of its component elements. It is not old enough for the processes Mr. Darwin outlines to have played out . . . at least not in the fashion he describes."

He looked down and away when he was finished. Maybe he felt uncomfortable bringing up a disagreement with the late lamented Tyndall.

"Right, but that's hardly a motive for you to go around killing them," Buller went on. "Rather the other way, I should think. Between Sir Edward's staff and this department, a dozen men knew or could have known of Fargo and his story. Thomson, did Sir Edward ask you to consult on the Vickers lightning-cannon project?"

"The *what?*" Thomson sputtered.

"No, I didn't think so," Buller said with a nod. " There were cases of sabotage, such as the Vickers workshop, which I think are also linked to this spy, whoever he is. You weren't positioned to assist in those. No, I had already ruled you out. *Damn* you, Gordon. Why couldn't you have been the bloody spy?"

"Sorry, sir," Gordon answered with a hint of sarcasm and Buller glanced up sharply at him.

Buller played the blustering, gobbling British general, but there was clearly more to him than met the eye. Rossbank's body was hardly cold, Buller had been head of Military Intelligence for probably twelve hours at the outside, and he was already up to speed on the leak and the most likely suspects. I wasn't crazy about the guy, but that was impressive.

"Carstairs, Burroughs, you are both dismissed," he said.

The two other officers barked "Sir!" in unison and stamped out of the office. Once the door closed behind them, Buller looked at us.

"Well, that's it, then. You three are the only ones in this whole business I can trust. Trust is perhaps too strong a word in your case, Fargo. Let's just say I am certain you are not a spy for the Old Man. The same is true for you, Captain Gordon."

Buller moved the folder to the side and opened the one under it.

"You are with the Northumberland Fusiliers, I see," he said after a moment.

"Sir."

"The First Battalion fought in Afghanistan eight years ago. You were a subaltern then, weren't you?"

"Yes, sir."

"Good opportunity for a young chap to show what he's made of. But you stayed in England, exchanged places with a subaltern from the Second Battalion, lad named Collingwood."

Gordon shifted his weight from one leg to the other and frowned. "Yes, sir."

"He was killed in action, I see. Where was that?"

I saw the color come to Gordon's face. His ears burned cherry red. When he didn't reply, Buller looked up at him. Gordon licked his lips before answering.

"Kandahar, sir."

"Yes, that's right. I missed that show. Down in Zululand, you know."

"Yes, sir."

"Then last year your second battalion rotated with the first, got overseas service at last. It's seeing some lively action out on the Northwest Frontier. You exchanged out again, I see, with a captain named Winthrop. Is *he* still alive?"

"Yes, sir."

"Lucky chap," Buller said.

Gordon dropped his hands to his side and came to attention.

"Will that be all, sir?"

"No, damn you, it will not. I know the army is full of worthless young gentlemen who think soldiering is nothing more than hunting foxes in Yorkshire and gambling away their father's money in London. They exchange out with poorer officers whenever their battalion ships overseas. The poor ones can't afford the mess dues back in England and so go on campaign, seduced by the prospect of prize money. They end up doing all the bleeding and damn the army for still allowing it. But you, Gordon! You had your chance to prove yourself yesterday, and you ran."

"I went for help!" Gordon protested.

"*Went for help?* You ran into the others outside the door and so had to turn around and come back. Otherwise like as not you'd have kept running all the way to Horse Guards."

"If you believe that—"

"*Shut up, damn you!*" Buller roared, his searing rage no longer a pretense. Sweat broke out on Gordon's forehead and he seemed to wilt in the furnace of the general's contempt.

"I won't say what I believe," Buller resumed after a moment. "If I did, I might have no choice but to give you a revolver and some privacy. I can't afford that. Much as I loathe the idea, you are the only officer in this entire department whom I can trust. Whatever else you are, Gordon, Fargo has convinced me you are not the spy."

Gordon glanced at me, but there was no gratitude in his eyes.

"You fancy yourself an intelligence officer," Buller continued. "I will tell you this much: an intelligence officer isn't worth a box full of backsides unless he's out in the field. So that is where you are going, all three of you.

"Professor Thomson, I cannot order you, but the Crown would be extremely grateful—"

"Of course I'll go," Thomson said. "I owe poor Tyndall that much. We should never have let a scientific disagreement divide us so bitterly all those years."

"Splendid. Lest there be any misunderstandings, *you* are in charge of the expedition."

"Where would you have us go, and to what purpose?" Thomson asked.

Buller looked at each of us in turn.

"Investigate the Somerton site. The police already have done so, and we have their report, but there's nothing in it. This talk about a 'hole in time' is worth looking into, though. The incident at Somerton was not a unique occurrence. We received a cable from our embassy in Berlin which reports another similar detonation in southern Germany—Bavaria, actually—at precisely the same time.

"After you've learned what you can from the Somerton site, go to Bavaria. I'll have a Royal Navy flier ready to take you—quickest way and no embarrassing questions from fellow passengers. Contact the Bavarian State Police. They have already agreed to cooperate. You will jointly investigate the reports of the explosion near Kempten, Bavaria, in the Allgäu Alps. Find out what happened and what role this Old Man had in the business. Follow wherever it leads, Thomson, and sort this business out."

Out in the hallway the three of us paused for a moment, but Gordon stared straight ahead, as if Thomson and I weren't there. He straightened his tunic and then walked away without a word.

"That lad's carrying too many rocks in his pockets," Thomson observed. "Tyndall was his uncle, you know. They were quite close."

"Well, he better get his shit together or he'll get us all killed."

"*His shit together?*" Thomson chuckled. "Aye, that's one way to put it. Now, where are you staying?"

"Here I guess."

"Nonsense. Come along to my club. We'll have a wee bit of lunch and then see about providing you with some proper clothing."

"That sounds okay. Some jeans, running shoes, and a couple sweat shirts and I'll be good to go," I said with a smile.

"I have no idea what you're talking about, but it doesn't sound like proper attire to me. My tailor will kit you out, though, no fear. You'll have to look your best when we meet Lord Chillingham."

We started down the broad stairs, and I saw the butler at the bottom holding our coats, calm and emotionless as a robot. I'd only been here a few days, but one of the things which already struck me was how people were so careful about not showing their humanity to anyone of a higher social station. I bet this butler loosened his collar and roared with laughter with his pals, tossing back a pint or two in the pub, but you would never know it to see him here, standing like a statue.

"Who's Chillingham?" I asked Thomson. "Is he the man you said might help me?"

"*Lord* Chillingham, and best not forget it, laddie. He won't find you as amusing as I do. He doesn't find anything amusing, so far as I can see. No, he's not the man I mentioned earlier. Lord Chillingham. All the soot and smoke in the air over London—and Manchester and Birmingham are worse—is mostly from Chillingham's foundries and mills. Ever since he bought up the patents to Henry Bessemer's process, he's had a stranglehold on heavy industry. He's also the Lord Minister Overseas, the real power behind the foreign ministry, colonial affairs, and particularly military intelligence. I imagine that's the reason the general's so upset. Buller was Quartermaster General until yesterday, safe and sound on the Army Board. Now he's at Chillingham's mercy. Well, we all are now, I suppose."

I knew at least something about British government, but I'd never heard of a Lord Minister Overseas.

"Aren't ministers from the House of Commons? What's with this Lord Minister thing?"

"The Common Cabinet comes from the lower house, but cabinets come and go as Parliament changes. The Lords are—more permanent. Their two ministers—Home and Overseas—well, they're the ones to worry about."

"In my time the House of Lords is pretty powerless," I said.

Thomson slipped into the coat the butler held open for him and looked at me a moment before answering.

"Now, that's a revolutionary idea," he said. "Were it mine, I'd keep it to myself."

"Okay. So who's the guy who may be able to help?" I asked.

"We're fortunate he's even in the country, it's only a temporary visit. He's speaking at the Royal Society tomorrow. I'll send my card and ask him to meet with us afterwards. A remarkable man, especially considering he's a foreigner of quite humble origins."

"Yeah, you have to be careful of those foreigners of humble origin," I said.

He glanced at me to make sure he understood what I meant and then squinted as he smiled. "Aye," he answered, "present company included. This fellow's eccentric, of course, perhaps even a bit mad, but only a madman would take your story seriously. His theories are certainly excuse enough for a suite at Bedlam. I suspect it will take some very unconventional thinking to sort out a way to duplicate the event which brought you here."

That, I thought, was probably an understatement. And simply reversing the event wasn't enough. I had to figure out a way to go farther back in time, find out what had changed the course of history, undo it without making any other changes, and then get back home. Of course, I couldn't tell anyone here that was my plan, because it involved undoing *this* history to restore my own, and they probably wouldn't like that idea.

So whoever this guy was, he had better be really smart.

"What's his name?" I asked.

"Nikola Tesla, although I doubt you've heard of him. He's certainly a very creative thinker, but he doesn't have the sort of organized, methodical approach likely to leave a lasting mark on the world."

SEVEN

September 25, 1888, London, England

When Thomson told me we'd meet Tesla at Burlington House off Piccadilly, I imagined an anonymous brownstone like Dorset House. Boy, was I wrong. At first it looked like a massive gray stone three-story building, with columns and balconies and stuff all over it but regularly enough placed that they had a sort of grace in their repetition. Our carriage took us through an arched gateway in the center, and it turned out Burlington "House" was actually *four* massive buildings enclosing a sprawling rectangular courtyard.

"This is somebody's house?" I asked.

"Not for over a century, and it wasn't always this grand. They added the east and west wings about fifteen years ago. I think they did a splendid job matching the original architecture, don't you? The Royal Society has the east wing."

"Yeah? So where are the Illuminati?"

He chuckled. "Nothing so sinister or romantic as that, I'm afraid. The other wings house the Royal Academy, the Chemical Society, the Linnean Society, and the Geological Society. There may be a few other small organizations housed here and there in odd corners."

A crowd of dark-suited men flowed slowly out of the main entrance to the east wing, breaking into animated conversational knots here and there.

"Tesla's talk must be finished," I said. "Looks like he gave them something to chew on."

"I'm not surprised. He's lecturing on his theory of a force-bearing aether."

"The luminiferous aether?" I asked. As I recalled, these Victorian scientists had been big on that until the theory got shot full of holes.

"No, not the light-bearing aether, but a force-bearing one, which he claims is entirely different. The luminiferous aether is a propagating medium for thermal, radiant, and electromagnetic energy, but he speculates about a deeper, rigid propagating medium for force—gravity primarily, but also more fundamental forces which bind matter itself together. I understand he believes this force-bearing aether is also the source of mass itself, that without it mass would have no meaning or means of exerting effect on other objects."

I wasn't a physicist, but I'd watched enough episodes of *Nova* to know that this force-bearing aether thing Thomson was talking about sounded a lot like the Higgs field, the omnipresent field which gave all particles in the universe mass—or at least those which actually *had* mass. Maybe these guys were smarter than I gave them credit for.

"Ah . . . General Buller has cautioned me not to mention anything we know about the Old Man of the Mountain," Thomson added as the carriage pulled up. "If you would accept a word of advice, I would not make any mention of your space exploration program, either. It may complicate things."

Probably good advice. Things were already plenty complicated as they stood.

We left the carriage and made our way up the steps to the door. With the lecture attendees still leaving, this was like swimming down the Columbia River when the salmon were coming up. A doorman took our overcoats and tried not to stare at my ill-fitting and unmatched clothing—my own new duds wouldn't be ready for a few days. As I handed my coat over, I saw my hand tremble and felt sweat break out on my forehead. Why?

I was scared, that's why. This meeting might very well determine my fate, even the fate of my world. Until I actually did the meeting, there was still the possibility, the hope, Tesla could whip up a miracle. But once it was over, and if no miracle emerged, I'd have exhausted one more of my very limited options.

"You say 2018?" Tesla asked in a fairly pronounced eastern-European accent. He leaned forward, his curiosity aroused. "So you are from *future*, not past. Most interesting."

The way he said *interesting* didn't make it sound like a good thing.

"You didn't seem to have a problem with me being from a different time, so why not the future?" I asked. Thomson and I had already told him as much background as I was willing to let go of, and he had reacted with interest rather than incredulity. The date of the Wessex accident was different, though. That brought him up short.

"Unsettling," he answered. "It is one thing to accept relics dredged up from past, animated museum exhibits. But a fully formed man from the future—that suggests a level of determinism in the affairs of men I find troubling. What if you were to tell me what I am known to have done in future and I do something different? Or better still, what if I were to find ancestor of yours and kill him before he produced necessary offspring? Would you disappear?"

"Beats me," I answered, not entirely truthfully. He studied me, his brow creased by a slight frown—partly from concentration and partly irritation. I looked him over again—tall and slender, black hair cut short and parted in the middle, neatly trimmed black moustache, high forehead, dark deep-set eyes, thin straight nose. He wasn't a bad-looking guy, but there was something remote, almost incomplete about him, as if he existed simultaneously in two worlds and all you saw was the part that happened to be in this one.

What did I know about Tesla from my own time? Not much. He was smart, and he was crazy—probably more smart than crazy. He'd come up with wireless communication and alternating current, both of which transformed the world. Some argued those two innovations *created* the modern world. He also had a lot of screwy ideas that never panned out.

"It is a pity you are professor of ancient history rather than physics," he said. "I am certain you could answer many questions both I and Dr. Thomson have."

"I know a little about physics. There were programs on TV—well, think of them as lecture series by prominent scientists. My daughter, Sarah, got interested in physics and we watched a lot together."

"Ah, your hobby?" Tesla asked.

"Well, it's one of my interests. I'd rank it below football but way above synchronized swimming." That clearly meant nothing to him, so I forged on ahead. "I don't understand the math, but I know a little of the basics from a layman's point of view. Take your idea of a force-bearing aether. It's very similar to what scientists in my time call the Higgs field."

I explained the Higgs field the same way I had to Thomson, then had to get into the Higgs boson, got tangled up in what a boson was, and started losing them. I'd been a teacher for the better part of ten years. I thought I was a pretty good one, but I was making a hash of this. I took a breath and paused a moment to gather my thoughts.

"Okay, all matter is made up of particles, and there are two types of fundamental particles: fermions and bosons. In a nutshell, fermions are particles with mass which combine to form atoms, which in turn form molecules and then all other matter. Have you heard of atoms and molecules?"

"We've heard of them, but let us say the atomic and molecular theory of matter is not generally accepted in the physics community," Thomson said.

"Most members of the so-called physics community are fools," Tesla replied. "Existence of atoms and molecules has long been recognized in chemistry. Please continue."

"Okay, fermions are particles with mass, the building blocks of the material universe. Bosons are force-carrying particles with no mass. So if a fermion, a particle with mass, bumps into another one, it imparts some of its momentum to that particle by giving up and transferring a momentum-carrying boson.

"A Higgs boson is the manifestation of interactions between fermions and the Higgs field, but it's more than that. It's what actually gives a fermion mass. The more powerfully a fermion interacts with the Higgs field, the more Higgs bosons it has, and so the more massive it is. Think of the Higgs field as a rain shower and a fermion as a person who walks through it. The more absorbent the person's clothing, the more water it absorbs from the rain and so the more wet it becomes. But once the clothing becomes saturated, the rest of the water just runs off. It can only get so wet."

Thomson said nothing but chewed on his pipe, frowning in thought, eyes distant and unfocused.

"Interesting theoretical explanation of the property of mass," Tesla said after a moment.

"Not a theory," I answered. "Scientists in my time had isolated and observed Higgs bosons in high-energy particle accelerators. It's the real thing."

"Tell me of this—what did you call it?—high-energy particle accelerator," Tesla said.

I did, and he listened thoughtfully, occasionally nodding in understanding. When I explained the Wessex particle accelerator as a weapon which had instead produced this time-shift effect, he smiled and almost laughed, but I couldn't tell exactly why. He was definitely an odd fellow.

Thomson came back into the conversation then. "The use of a rotating electromagnetic field to produce this effect naturally made me think of you, Mr. Tesla. I know of no one more knowledgeable about the subject, with the possible exception of Mr. Edison."

That must have been the wrong thing to say, as Tesla's face immediately clouded with anger.

"Edison knows nothing. He makes his discoveries without *a priori* hypotheses. He simply tries a thousand different mechanical combinations—or has his hired lackeys do so—until something works. He has no idea how or why it does so. He is not a scientist. He is a *tinker*, and a thief to boot!"

I remembered something about the disputes between Tesla and Edison from my own time. Edison had clung to direct current and Tesla had promoted alternating current, eventually winning what people called *The Current War*. Maybe I could use that to settle him down.

"If it's any consolation," I said, "before he died, Edison said his greatest regret in life was not listening to you on the controversy over alternating versus direct current."

Tesla looked at me, his eyebrows rising in surprise.

"That is interesting," he answered, "since he stole my plans and ideas for alternating-current generators and is manufacturing them even now. That is why I returned to Europe. There is nothing left for me in America."

Shit! No Current War here, apparently.

"Listened to you about compensation," I added quickly, making it up as I went. "If he had paid you fairly, and you had stayed and worked with him, who knows what you might have come up with together?"

Tesla studied me for several seconds, eyes calculating. Then he looked away.

"Edison is a man of appalling personal habits, a filthy man, and with no interests beyond accumulation of wealth. I could not have worked long with him."

"I have never met the man," Thomson said, "but I confess I have heard similar judgments from others. We are doubly fortunate you were available. Surely this must excite your scientific curiosity. Will you help us understand this phenomenon?"

Tesla looked at him and I could see something about the question amused him, some private joke.

"I do not know if I can shed light on this matter. It is too soon to say for certain." That wasn't what I was hoping to hear, especially after he'd seemed so engaged in the physics discussion. "There is much to absorb," he went on, "much to think about. But I have previous engagements on the continent which I must attend to."

"We are bound for the continent ourselves," Thomson said. "Would you consider joining our party and traveling with us?"

Tesla looked from Thomson to me and considered the possibility, but then shook his head.

"No, I am afraid that is not possible. I will think more on this matter, though, that I can promise you. If something comes to me, how can I find you?"

"You can contact us through the British consulate in Munich," Thomson said.

"You travel to Bavaria then."

"Well . . ." Thomson shifted in his chair, perhaps thinking he may have said too much. "Only in passing, but we will keep them informed. I would ask you not to share that information with anyone else."

"Of course," Tesla answered and then turned to me. "Your situation here must be very difficult, Dr, Fargo. I wish I could have been more help."

"So, did you buy all that?" I asked Thomson once we'd flagged down a horse-drawn cab.

"Buy? I'm not sure I . . ."

"Did you believe him?"

Thomson's confusion showed clearly in his face. Scientists are easy to fool because they are trained to accept the world at face value.

"He knows more than he's letting on," I said. "What's he doing here in England?"

"I told you, this talk. Well, now that you mention it, *he* contacted the society and offered to give the speech, as he was already in the country. Why? Do you think that's significant?"

Everything is significant.

EIGHT

October 1, 1888, Essex, England

Less than week later I felt like a proper Londoner. I had my own respirator and goggles, even if they were tucked away in a leather shoulder bag. I also had a hat.

I was forced to agree to the practicality of a hat in this environment—that or comb dust and cinders out of my hair every time I came in from outdoors. I never liked wearing hats and I had avoided them altogether after leaving the army, but now I had a closet-full of the damned things.

That was only a slight exaggeration; I had a hat for everyday "walking out" wear, one for formal occasions, a sporting hat, a shooting hat, a hunting hat, and a riding hat. I had a hard time telling the everyday, formal, and riding hats apart, since all three were black silk top hats, but the tailor assured me they were all necessary and Thomson agreed. Since the British government was paying the bill, who was I to argue? After all, the British government got me into this mess. Maybe not *this* British government, but what the hell—this one was handy.

I wore my formal hat and formal evening wear today, wore it for the first time since it was delivered yesterday afternoon. I always thought I'd look good in white tie and tails, and I was right. Nevertheless, I couldn't help remembering what Thoreau said on the subject: *Beware of all enterprises that require new clothes.*

"It looks tight across your midsection," Thomson said. "You should have let the tailor cut it more generously."

"I'm about to lose some weight," I answered. "It would have ended up looking baggy."

"If I had a shilling for every gentleman who's told his tailor that, I'd be a rich man."

"You *are* a rich man," Buller put in, his first words since climbing into the horse-drawn carriage at the train station. He was resplendent in his own dress uniform, which looked unlike any British Army uniform I could remember seeing—all black with shining black silk tapes across the front and looping around the sleeves, and topped by a fur cap with a tall, slender black and red plume. The coat was heavy with decorations across the chest, including a couple of big multipointed silver stars.

The carriage lurched in the rutted road and turned into a long, shaded drive. As we rounded a bend I saw what I took to be our destination—Larchmont Hall, stately and serene, perched on a low hill and surrounded by painfully disciplined formal gardens.

Buller, Thomson, and I had taken the train from London out to a place called South Woodham Ferrers-on-Crouch. Its name was almost longer than the village main drag. The large and ornate four-horse carriage waited for us at the station and carried us to the hall where Lord Chillingham would receive us.

"So, let me make sure I've got this right. We are going on a critical mission but we couldn't leave yet because first we had to meet this Lord Chillingham, and before we could do that I needed the right *clothes*. Is that about it?"

"Don't be an ass about this, Fargo," Buller growled. "Keep your mouth shut in there unless you're spoken to directly. If asked for your view, either agree with his Lordship or say you don't have an opinion."

"And for heaven's sake," Thomson added, "don't be sarcastic, much as I am sure that will pain you. This is no joking matter, laddie. Chillingham is an Iron Lord, makes a fortune from industry instead of agriculture, although God knows he has land enough for that as well. That makes him dangerous—he actually *does* things for his money, instead of just owning land and paying someone to collect the rents."

"Their Lordships don't usually take to money with the scent of sulfur on it," Buller said. "I suppose if you've got enough of it, they make an exception."

"That and the fact that Lord Chillingham is from one of the oldest noble families in the British Isles," Thomson added. "Thomas St. John

Curnoble, twenty-eighth earl of Chillingham and Adderstone. He was rich *before* he bought the Manchester Iron Works."

"They've been rich ever since King Harold stopped a Norman arrow with his eyeball at Hastings," Buller muttered.

It didn't sound as if I was going to like this Chillingham guy much. On the other hand, if he was some new breed of noble, a "get your hands dirty" take-charge guy, maybe I could find some common ground.

The carriage stopped at a side entrance where a butler waited for us.

"Follow me," he ordered and then turned and entered the house.

"Servants and tradesmen's entrance," Buller said quietly, almost to himself. "Been some time since I've had to go in one of those."

He heaved his bulk up from the seat, squared his shoulders, and walked through the door with the quiet resignation of a man marching to the gallows. Thomson fidgeted with his gloves as we followed, but in we went.

Quiet. That's what Larchmont Hall was like inside: quiet and bright. Light flooded in through windows and French doors while white lace sheers floated in the soft breeze that carried the scent of flowers in from the garden. I breathed in slowly. Rose. Gardenia. Jasmine. Hyacinth.

Quiet, bright, and clean-smelling: anyone fresh from the noise and gloom and stench of London would instantly recognize this as Heaven. There was both irony and symmetry in that: first render the cities hellish, then construct a refuge from your own handiwork.

The long halls and open rooms seemed to stretch on endlessly. Mirrors everywhere accentuated the effect. Here and there I caught sight of a servant moving silently and gracefully from room to room. The butler led us, his velvet-slippered feet silent on polished hardwood floors. Our own shoes clumped and banged incongruously, no matter how carefully we trod. The sound echoed in the halls of light, somehow seeming to defile this sacred oasis of calm.

Three grown men tried to tiptoe down the hall like schoolboys following a teacher to the principal's office, trying to keep up but not draw attention to themselves, to their guilt and awkward inadequacy. Buller, a brave soldier—even if he was an overbearing asshole—walked gingerly on the balls of his feet, almost stumbled from the effort in his tall riding boots, and looked foolish doing it. That brave old soldier looked foolish, and I think that's what finally got me.

I stopped walking lightly.

Clump, clump, clump.

After a half-dozen steps the butler turned and scowled at me.

"Bite me, pal," I told him

"*Fargo!*" Buller hissed. "Mind your tongue."

"Give it a rest, General. If Chillingham wanted it quiet, he'd either put in rugs or have us leave our boots at the door. This is just a head game."

"Aye, that may be," Thomson said softly at my side. "But in his castle, he chooses the game."

Maybe so, but I noticed both Buller and Thomson walked more easily after that.

The butler took us to a sitting room with large glass doors facing the garden. It caught the early afternoon sun perfectly, and I had the feeling there must be different rooms in different parts of the hall used at different times of the day just for the way they caught the light. And of course the light changed at different times of the year. I always wondered what the deal was with all those rooms in old manor houses. I guess if you wanted to have rooms that always got the light *just right*, you probably needed a house this big.

Chillingham looked younger than I expected, early forties probably. His brown wavy hair grayed at the temples so perfectly I wondered if he dyed it. He had the physique of an active man but not too active—someone who rode but did not shovel out the barn afterwards. I saw no glint of humor in his eyes at all; that's always a bad sign.

He sat in a large wingback chair with a small dog in his lap—a black Scottish terrier. The terrier was alert and interested in the three of us, but not inclined to bark. We did not alarm him, because he knew that nothing threatening ever entered this house. Lucky little dog.

"Lord Chillingham," Buller and Thomson said together and bowed from the waist. I took Buller's advice and kept my mouth shut. I nodded with enough energy I'm sure someone might have mistaken it for a bow. Chillingham didn't seem inclined to take offense.

Instead, he sighed.

"Yes, very well, General. Let's hear it."

Buller launched into a detailed outline of the mission. I wasn't sure our host was even listening. He was more interested in his little dog. But then the door opened, and the butler crossed to Chillingham's side. Buller stopped speaking, but Chillingham motioned him to continue. He did so, but with less assurance as the butler leaned forward and whispered in the lord's ear.

Chillingham frowned, and for the first time looked alert and mentally engaged. The butler straightened, and Chillingham's gaze wandered to the French doors, swept the garden, and then lost focus in the afternoon clouds as his mind grappled with the new problem. Buller stopped speaking again, and this time Chillingham did not notice. For several seconds the only sound was the caress of the sheer drapes against the doorframe in the light breeze.

Chillingham's mouth hardened, his attention returned to the room, and I knew he had made a decision.

"Very well then," he said to the butler. "We'll follow the fish course with a claret. It's too early in the meal, but there's nothing for it."

The butler nodded and glided from the room. Chillingham's eyes wandered back to us, he seemed to remember we were there, and the look of intent concentration flickered away, replaced by bored irritation. He waved for Buller to continue.

"We—ah—where was I?"

"Somewhere in Bavaria," I volunteered.

Chillingham glanced at me, and one eyebrow went up slightly before he looked back at Buller.

Buller resumed his narration of our plan, such as it was. From this point on it was all wishes and dreams as far as I was concerned. We had no clue what we were getting into and would be making things up as we went. Operations like this work when you know exactly what's going to happen at every step and rehearse it a couple times. This sort of "Go in there and see what you chaps can accomplish" approach almost always ends in disaster, but it was my only ticket to the Old Man.

While Buller droned on, I had time to think about Chillingham. He wasn't at all what I had expected. Any thoughts I'd had of winning him over were long gone; he wasn't interested enough in this mission, or me, to even listen to my pitch. His mind was more on tonight's dinner than this operation, and, despite the contempt that initially made me feel, the more I thought about it, the less certainty I had on the subject. I didn't know who was coming to this dinner or what would be decided there, but Chillingham did not strike me as a stupid man. For him the dinner was more important. Maybe he knew something I didn't.

And maybe he had about as much faith in this "mission" producing positive results as I did.

Buller finished, and Chillingham turned to look me over, noticed me studying him, but showed no reaction to that one way or another.

"And why are you helping us in this enterprise, Mr. Fargo?"

"To get back to my time," I lied.

"I see. I read enough of that long report of Captain Gordon's to make me wonder why you would want to. Considering the enthusiasm with which your society embraces its lowest, least-cultured elements, it's small wonder your world is in such a frightful state."

"As opposed to how peachy things are here," I said.

He looked at me through eyes incapable of registering either respect or contempt. He looked at me through the eyes of a farmer inspecting his livestock, but his eyes narrowed as he did, and I saw measurement and calculation and an inhuman coldness unlike any I'd ever experienced.

"Precisely," he said.

NINE

October 2, 1888, Aboard Her Majesty's Aerial Ship Intrepid, *Aloft Over the English Channel*

"Lift-*wood*?" I asked. "You mean to tell me this thing is held up by *wood*?"

"I assure you, laddie, I was as surprised your time does not have it as you are that ours does," Thomson answered.

We stood inside the massive lower hull of the flyer, looking down at row upon row of broad, thin wooden slats, arranged like louvers in a door.

"Go ahead and touch them," he told me. "They're real enough. Only touch the top surfaces, though, unless you want the skin stripped off your fingers."

I knelt on the catwalk, reached out, and ran my fingers lightly along an upper edge.

"Are they always so hot?"

"No. As we ascend, their temperature increases. We don't know why the temperature rises when they climb and drops as they descend, but my theory is it has to do with potential energy. A good trimsman keeps the climb shallow enough to avoid thermal distortion. The angle of the plane of the wood with respect to the center of mass of the world determines the amplitude of lift."

I sat on the catwalk, leaned my back against one of the steel ribs of the hull, and looked at the rows of louvers, their positions controlled by an elaborate array of brass and steel gears and thin control cables running up to and through the overhead. As I watched, the louvers adjusted slightly, two here, five over there, keeping the flyer in trim.

Thomson and the others had figured out I was from a different future right away, but they'd done a good job of keeping it to themselves. It had been obvious to them once I talked about our "amazing" space-exploration program, which had finally put an unmanned rover on Mars in the twenty-first century. That's why he hadn't wanted me to tell Tesla about our space program—it would have let him in on the secret as well. Men from this world had been visiting Mars since *1870!*

And they had liftwood. It grew on Mars.

"Back at the hospital I felt a downdraft when one of these things went over. I thought maybe it had big fans inside or something. Instead it's got these wood slats, but when we took off I noticed a lot of wind underneath. So how do these things work?"

"There is some controversy over that. The panels clearly do not block the effects of gravity. Since there are lifting panels between us and the ground, we would not feel the gravitational pull of the Earth below us, or would feel it with reduced effect. Nevertheless, we clearly do feel it.

"The accepted explanation is that the louvers exert a repulsive force on whatever they come in contact with, but only do so parallel to the axis of strongest proximate gravitational attraction. The mechanism of this repulsion, and the source of the energy which produces it, remains a mystery, but it is one to which I believe you may have provided the answer."

"Me?" I said. "What does time travel have to do with it?"

"Not time travel," he answered, "but rather your explanation of matter in terms of small particles, particularly those—what are they called? Bosons? Those bosons which carry force and are exchanged.

"The difficulty with the standard explanation of liftwood's function is that it seems to allow for violation of conservation of matter, energy, and momentum. If you float something heavy and then drop it, you generate a good deal of kinetic energy at the impact point, and appear to do so for free."

"Nothing's free," I said.

"Quite right, and there is some historical evidence from Mars's past that in fact the entire momentum of the system is preserved. I now believe that liftwood does not actually repel matter which comes in contact with it, but rather exchanges momentum with it."

"What momentum? The air isn't moving."

"Of course it is," he said. "It is spinning around the Earth's axis and hurtling through space as the Earth revolves around the sun. Each particle of air has enormous momentum. What remains a puzzle is why, or how, liftwood is able to selectively borrow the momentum parallel to the pull of gravity, but organic constructs are extraordinarily sophisticated. We cannot even begin to explain how a chameleon's skin can so quickly react to its surroundings and duplicate them as a form of visual camouflage. Your time has extraordinarily advanced computing machines. Do you have one as quick, sophisticated, and compact as the brain of a seagull?"

"I don't think so," I answered.

"No, and mind you a seagull is not a particularly intelligent bird."

I looked back at the rows of louvers. They vibrated softly, in tension between gravity and the restraints of the gears holding them in position.

No, not gravity—*momentum*?

"Let's get out of here," I said. "This place gives me the willies."

We made our way through the doorway, back out into the rhythmic clatter and bustle of the engine room, and I felt better right away. I was tired of complicated men and impossible science. I paused and took a good long look, breathed in the steamy smell of oil and hot metal. Here were men dirty and sweaty from work, real work—lubricating the big reciprocating engines, fine-tuning a dozen different-sized valves on the steam lines, shoveling coal into the hungry boilers, shouting to be heard over the pounding beat of the flyer's heart. They worked with confidence and economy of motion—a well-practiced team. I was nearly overcome by a desire to be part of that team, to take off my shirt and just start shoveling coal.

"Do you mind, lad? I'm starting to melt," Thomson said.

Her Majesty's Aerial Ship *Intrepid* was damned impressive. I'd been on the old cruiser *Olympia*, Dewey's flagship at the Battle of Manila Bay, and *Intrepid* reminded me of her. She had a broad, shallow hull. A narrow superstructure, topped by the wheelhouse, ran most of the way along the upper surface, all dark iron, steel, and polished brass, along with bleached white wooden decks and rich varnished interior woodwork. The flyer bristled with guns. One large steel turret dominated the main deck forward and another crowned the stern superstructure. More guns were mounted to fire broadside from the superstructure, and a sort of sideways turret on each side of the deck mounted another gun each. They called those *sponsons*. They could fire up and down as well as to the sides.

A small housing below the hull held the ship's compass. It had to be below the hull because the liftwood interfered with it. It didn't stop it from working, it just made it slow to change, like a gyroscope. Later, as we leaned on the brass railing and watched the distant clouds drift by, I asked Thomson how that squared with his new theory of how liftwood worked.

"I'm not certain," Thomson said, "and if I know anything, I should know that. I designed that compass, the one in use in every Royal Navy vessel. It is not simply a navigational aid, it is also a precision scientific instrument. The navy has ships all over the world and they've been mapping the magnetosphere since—well, the 1830s, as I recall. Still are. This cruiser's taking magnetic readings all along its course."

"Since the 1830s? And you're not done yet?"

"The magnetosphere is not absolutely stable, you know, laddie. The north and south magnetic poles drift over time, and there are other anomalies worth mapping. For the last year we've noticed a very slight weakening in the electromagnetic field. That's the main reason the Royal Navy adopted my compass; it's the most accurate and sensitive navigational instrument the service has ever had."

"If you do say so yourself," I said.

He smiled but I saw sadness there as well.

"Yes, you're right. It is a very good compass, but still—just a compass. As I grow older, most of my work seems little more than tinkering: the transatlantic cable, the adjustable compass—simply toys by your day, I imagine. I wonder if I've done anything which will be remembered once I'm gone. Tell the truth—you've never heard my name, have you?"

"Nineteenth century science isn't my field," I said.

"Yet you knew of Edison."

"He's American—hometown boy makes good."

"And Hertz?"

"They named radio waves after him. A car rental company, too."

But the truth was, I knew a half-dozen or more scientists from about this time: Edison, Hertz, Faraday, Marconi, Kelvin, Babbage, Darwin, Planck, Tesla, of course—but not Thomson.

"Now Tyndall—there's a scientist who's left his mark on the world," Thomson said.

I'd never heard of Tyndall, either, but I didn't think that would make Thomson feel any better about his life. Besides, I had problems of my own.

I'd found out how the South won its independence: Lincoln had died in 1862 from typhoid fever. It made my heart ache again just standing there thinking about it. Everyone thinks strategy is all about generals, but it's more about the men who stand behind them. Hamlin, his vice president, apparently just didn't have what it took to get the job done, so the war effort faltered. McClellan won the election in '64 and made peace. That's how the South won—not anything they'd done, just some microscopic organism.

Typhoid fever. *Son of a bitch.*

In the midst of the post-war malaise which gripped the North, a young inventor named Edison heard a lecture on the luminiferous aether and decided America needed a new challenge, a new frontier to re-spark its spirit of purpose and adventure. A year of obsessive-compulsive experimentation later and he had a working aether propeller. So far so good. The problem was, when he got to Mars, there was a breathable atmosphere and life.

"Yes, there's a troubling difference," Thomson had said when he told me all this other stuff. "Mars has very small polar caps, but they are slowly growing, have been for several centuries as near as we can tell. I actually believe that is at the root of the collapse of the great civilizations there, the gradual cooling and drying of the world. It's not just its seas which have disappeared. It's also losing its cloud cover. I suspect that kept the world warm, rather like a greenhouse."

That was about the first scientific thing I'd heard here which made much sense. I knew a little about our own Mars expedition plans. They included some long-term terraforming involving melting the polar caps, which were mostly CO2, to release the greenhouse gases, get the planet warming, and cook an atmosphere from Mars's own frozen gases and the moisture locked in the soil. I wondered what it would have taken to do that naturally a couple billion years earlier, long enough for life to have evolved. A really big meteor strike at the pole? Sure, that would probably do it.

The problem was, now I was not looking at "fixing" a change in history as recent as the Roman emperor Galba. Now I had to figure out how to rearrange the solar system. Well, somebody apparently did it, so somebody could undo it. Maybe I was that somebody.

Yeah, maybe.

The sky stretched before us seemingly to infinity, dusted with a handful of clouds ahead and above us, and a wispy, uneven floor below. Through breaks in the clouds I could still see the blue-gray water of the English Channel and the approaching green outline of the Belgian coast. By then the sun was low in the sky behind us, the deck dark in the shadow of the hull, the clouds below us turned from white to pale orange, with dark, well-defined shadows and pink highlights.

This was real. I could never dream this sunset, and I felt tears run down my face.

"What is it, lad?"

For a moment I couldn't even find my voice. Thomson put his hand on my shoulder.

"My daughter doesn't even *exist* here," I whispered. "How can it be this beautiful?"

TEN

October 3, 1888,
***Aboard Her Majesty's Aerial Ship* Intrepid,**
Aloft Over the Franco-Belgian Border

"We cruise at twenty knots," Captain Harding, *Intrepid's* skipper, told me the next morning. We stood together in the wheelhouse and shaded our eyes from the glare of the sun rising almost directly ahead of us. Twenty knots, at two thousand yards to the nautical mile, put our speed at about twenty-two or twenty-three miles an hour. It felt as if we were hardly moving at all.

"We can keep this speed up day in, day out, for a week," Harding went on. "There is very little vibration from her machinery. My first aerial command was *Uxbridge*, a *Macefield*-class gunboat based out of Alexandria. She'd do thirty-three knots, if you coaxed her and had the engineer sit on her safety valve, but she'd vibrate and shake to beat the devil. Bucked like a whore."

The petty officer helmsman beside us grinned at that.

"It's true," Harding insisted. "Ride her too hard and she'd start leaking steam everywhere. Not the whore, mind you."

"Smoke off the starboard quarter," one of the lookouts called from the masthead above us. "Twenty degrees high."

Harding raised his binoculars and scanned the sky.

"Mr. Conroy, what do you make of her?"

Ensign Conroy, the young officer of the watch, raised his own glasses.

"Converging course, sir, making . . . I'd say fifteen knots. Three stacks, turrets fore, aft, and ventral—I make her *Invincible*, sir."

He pronounced it as a French name, however, not English. *On-ven-SEEB-luh.*

"Close," Harding agreed, "But *Invincible*'s been shifted to the Pacific. That's her sister, *Gloire,* as sure as there's a hole in your backside. We'll pass close enough to exchange honors. I believe we'll go to action stations, Mr. Conroy."

"Action stations, sir," Conroy repeated. He pressed a red-painted lever near the engine telegraph and five bells sounded in rapid succession, followed by several seconds of silence, then five bells again.

Crew members boiled from hatches and scrambled to man the open gun mounts. The twenty red-coated marines formed in two ranks on the superstructure, and another officer climbed the steps to the wheelhouse. After a few minutes, Thomson joined us as well.

"Well, this is exciting!" he said, still puffing from the climb up the companionway to the bridge. "Another flyer, I see. We aren't expecting trouble, are we?"

"No trouble," Captain Harding answered. "Just a French cruiser, and we'll pass close enough to smell the garlic. Trimsman."

"Aye, sir?" a petty officer at the rear of the wheelhouse answered.

"Let's bring her up even with the Frog. Ten percent positive buoyancy."

"Ten percent positive buoyancy, aye, aye, Captain." The petty officer stood before a double bank of tall levers, about twenty of them in each row. He released the hand brakes on two of the levers and pulled them back slightly, then locked them, waited, and adjusted two more. I felt the deck tilt very slightly up toward the bow then level again and for a moment I felt slightly heavier.

"Holding at ten percent positive buoyancy, sir," he reported after a few seconds.

"What's the glass read, Mr. Conroy?" Harding asked.

"Four-twenty, Captain."

"Very well. We'll come up to five hundred fathoms and level there," Harding said.

"Aye, sir. Level at five hundred fathoms."

At six feet to the fathom, that would put us at three thousand feet, about a kilometer—not very high for a jumbo jet, but plenty high for a thousand-ton ironclad.

I could pick out more detail on the French flyer now, even without binoculars. It had a different look from *Intrepid*. Its turrets sat higher in front, and it didn't seem to have much deck forward. With an underslung gun turret aft, like a bomber's belly turret, its profile looked a little more like an aircraft than a flying ship, but only a little. I never saw an airplane with three smokestacks.

"Coming up on five hundred fathoms, Captain," Ensign Conroy reported.

"Very well. Trimsman, neutral buoyancy."

The petty officer made more adjustments to the forest of levers, studied his spirit levels and plum line, and then adjusted one more.

"Ship neutral, Captain."

We had drawn closer to the French ship, and it slowly changed course to parallel ours. As we were moving faster, we would overtake the other aerial cruiser and pass it in a few minutes. I could make out her flags; a large tricolor flew from the mainmast amidships, and a blood-red ensign fluttered from the stern.

"She'll follow us for a while, but we're coming up on Saarbrüchen in a quarter hour. She'll turn back for home rather than go deep into German air space," Harding declared.

"Is that red flag some sort of naval ensign?" I asked.

Harding snorted.

"Not by a long shot. She's flown by *La Garde Rouge,* the Commune's pet bully boys."

"The Commune?" I repeated.

"Mr. Fargo is not conversant with recent European political history," Thomson explained. "He's from . . . the west." He turned to me. "The Commune took control of the French government in 1871, during the war with Germany."

"You're a cowboy, Mr. Fargo?" Harding asked. "You must be a cowboy who lives in a bloody cave if you've never heard of the Commune."

Right, the Paris Commune. But in my world it had lasted—what?—a couple weeks?

La Garde Rouge—the Red Guard. I wondered how "red" those French really were. Wasn't Karl Marx still wandering around somewhere?

"No shooting today, though, right?" I asked.

Harding turned and looked at me for a moment before answering.

"No, Mr. Fargo, not since '85. The politicians will yammer a while longer before we start shooting at them again. Soon enough, though, I'll wager."

He turned back ahead, and in a couple minutes we passed abeam of the French cruiser, close enough that I could see the expressions on the French officers as they returned the salutes of our officers—proper but unsmiling. There was as much recognition over there as there was here that the next time they saw each other it might be through powder smoke and across a bloodstained deck.

That might explain why we were getting so much help from the Germans—nothing like a common enemy to make the children play well together.

I looked around the wheelhouse.

"Where's Gordon?"

Conroy exchanged a look with the other officers and Thomson cleared his throat before he spoke.

"I imagine Captain Gordon is still abed. He had quite an evening."

The three of us had eaten in the small officers' mess, but I'd left right after dinner and turned in early. In the week we'd spent in England getting ready to leave, I'd gotten back in the habit of rising before dawn and running. This morning I'd taken my run on *Intrepid*'s deck, round and round the superstructure. Two miles before breakfast had done wonders for my attitude. But by the time I'd left the officers' mess the night before Gordon had been tipsy, and was still going strong.

"Well he's got ten hours to sleep it off before we land in Munich and find out what the Bavarians know," Harding said. "Do you suppose the young gentleman can be persuaded to rise before sunset?"

Damn. Munich in ten hours? The stately progress of the flyer had lulled me into a false sense of complacency. There would be things I would have to do, things I never thought I'd do again, things I dreaded doing, but would have to do. I needed to get my head squared away about that, and time was running out.

I had a mental checklist I'd been making. Gordon wasn't on it. If Gordon couldn't make the world safe for Bonseller and Lord Chillingham's England, it was no skin off my ass. If I managed to do what needed doing, that England wasn't going to be around much longer anyway.

It wasn't my world. It would sure as hell take more than one pretty sunset to make it so.

Nine hours later we dropped down through the scattered clouds to find the Bavarian countryside below us, afternoon sunlight sparkling off the rivers and making the wooded hills and fields spreading out to either side seem to glow with life. The snow-peaked Alps rose to our right above nearly invisible clouds on the horizon and, like *Intrepid*, seemed to float impossibly in the air. The ground was higher and wilder looking to the south, and the rivers, a series of them perpendicular to our path like successive finish lines, flowed north to feed the Danube for its long journey east.

Thomson and I stood on the open flying bridge beside the wheelhouse. He pointed out three moving shapes far below us and handed me a pair of binoculars. The objects were some sort of powered land vehicles, with caterpillar tracks as near as I could tell, and enclosed. Big, too, about the size of locomotives, but they moved across open ground, not on railroad tracks. They each sported a few gun mounts.

"What the hell?"

"Imperial German land ships," Thomson answered, "moving south. Quite formidable. Odd to see them on Bavarian soil—although Bavaria is part of the empire, of course, especially since the old king was deposed."

"The Kaiser?"

"Good heavens, no! The Kaiser is secure, but Bavaria—its place in the German empire is ambiguous. It is a kingdom within the empire, more than a province but not exactly sovereign. Its foreign policy is directed from Prussia, but its heart, I think, is still with Austria. The old king, Ludwig, was mad and his brother Otto, the new one, is worse, but this Luitpold fellow, the prince regent, actually runs things now. He seems levelheaded enough. I don't envy him his job."

"So we're getting help from whom? Germans? Prussians? Bavarians?"

"Yes," Thomson answered and laughed. "General Buller's contacts were through the German General Staff in Berlin, but the Bavarian *Stadtpolizei* have jurisdiction over the incident site. They'll assist us, under instruction from Berlin."

"How happy are they going to be about that?"

"We'll see soon enough," he answered.

Maybe the maneuvering Prussian land ships were meant as a reminder to the locals of who was in charge. Maybe not. I gestured down toward them, now well astern.

"Reinforcements?" I asked. Thomson's eyebrows went up in surprise at that but then settled back as he thought it over. He was a scientist and viewed this as a fact-finding mission. I don't think it had occurred to him until then that we might have to fight for information, or that the Germans might have anticipated something like that and were getting ready to back us up. *Intrepid* might be useful to us for something other than its speed.

Ahead of us I saw the dark mass of a city—Munich. While smoke rose from countless chimneys, it was nothing like the oppressive industrial smog of London. Dozens of multicolored balloons, some spherical, some sausage-shaped, floated above and near the city. As the clouds drifted and the sun setting behind us touched the distant city, a thousand windows reflected the light and sparkled like diamonds.

"I hear it has come back to life since the old king was deposed," Thomson said from beside me. "Like a fairy city, isn't it?"

It was. In the distance I saw a light on the outskirts of the city flickering with particular brilliance and regularity. When it paused, I heard a loud clacking from above us, on the catwalk above the flyer's bridge. A crewman manned a large searchlight with louvered metal shutters, and as he worked the lever controls the shutters opened and closed, flashing light back to the city.

"Aldis lamp," Thomson explained. After several more exchanges, the signalman slid down the ladder and disappeared into the bridge. Ten minutes later Captain Harding joined us and handed Thomson a message form.

"It came in my personal code," Harding said.

Thomson read the note, and his eyebrows went up a bit.

"I didn't know he was in Bavaria," he said.

"He was supposed to be in Italy, last I heard," Harding replied.

"Who?" I asked.

Thomson folded the message and put it in his coat pocket before answering me.

"We will see the Bavarian police tomorrow, but tonight we are to meet with Baron Renfrew in Munich. Baron Renfrew is—"

"Yeah," I interrupted. "I know who Baron Renfrew is."

"You *do?*" Thomson said. "Extraordinary."

"I'm just full of surprises."

Baron Renfrew! Now, this was an interesting development, but not a very cheery one. I'd never even heard of Lord Chillingham, and my brief meeting with him had left a bad taste in my mouth. *Renfrew . . .*

ELEVEN

October 3, 1888, Munich, Bavaria

Baron Renfrew summoned us to a private home in Ludvigsvorstadt, a suburb between the landing ground—the *Fliegerplatz*, they called it—and the city center. We climbed aboard a carriage and set out to meet him.

Large balloons still floated aloft in the early evening, and a small cigar-shaped one passed overhead no more than fifty feet up. Instead of a basket, the gas bag supported a contraption like a tandem bicycle without the wheels, the chain drive turning a whirring propeller in back. A young couple pedaled vigorously, and the woman waved to us as they passed over. I waved back. That looked like fun.

At first our carriage made good progress down the broad, tree-lined Landsberger *Strasse*, with a sprawling rail marshalling yard to our left and a mix of small parks and suburban townhouses with steeply peaked gabled roofs and brightly painted wood shutters and flower boxes framing the windows. After ten minutes we came to a stretch filled with people, and the carriage slowed to a crawl.

The good news was the crowd was in a festive mood. I had grown used to the somber clothing of London and the surrounding countryside. Bright colors dominated the crowd here, with a lot of men in *lederhosen* and jaunty alpine hats and women in elaborately embroidered aprons over flaring skirts worn just short enough to show the layers of ruffled petticoats underneath. Wealthy women in expensive gowns wore their hair up in elaborate twisting towers, and even their austerely dressed consorts sported green sashes around their ample middles and green scarves wound about their tall silk top hats. What I found particularly interesting, though, was the extent to which the wealthy and common seemed all mixed up together, and thoroughly enjoying themselves.

The sun touched the horizon behind us and promised a beautiful, warm autumn evening. I heard distant music from ahead of us and to the right, a dozen oompah bands battling for supremacy and cheered on by well-lubricated vocal sections a thousand or more strong.

"Somebody's having a hell of a party," I observed unnecessarily. "*Was ist das?*" I asked the driver.

"*Der Wies'n*," he answered with a broad grin.

Wies'n? My German was rusty, and Bavarian was slangy, but that sounded like *The Meadow*.

"What's The Meadow? A festival?" I asked in German.

"*Ja.* The October festival."

Of course: *Oktoberfest*. That explained the music and crowds of amiable drunks dressed in colorful local costumes.

"People come from all over for the fest?"

"*Ja.* Most from the south and Austria, but some from farther. Not many Prussians," he said and laughed. "Carnivals, too, come from all over, but more from the east. Damned gypsies steal everything."

"What's he saying?" Gordon asked. I remembered he didn't speak German but Thomson did and provided him a translation. Gordon looked bored and annoyed while Thomson remained distracted, preoccupied with our impending meeting. I couldn't blame him for being nervous.

So far I liked Munich better than London. Folks at least had a sense of fun. Maybe Bavaria was an international backwater, but there might be some advantages to that. Now we'd see what Baron Renfrew could do to screw things up.

We met in the parlor of a small but tastefully decorated private home, nothing like Dorset House. The furniture was lighter in design and color, the walls papered with pastel stripes and adorned with a few inviting landscapes—apparently the Bavarian countryside we'd just overflown. Large windows would have let in sunlight during the day, but it was early evening by the time we arrived and the curtains were drawn for privacy. Renfrew waited for us seated on a loveseat beside a strikingly attractive woman.

Portraits of important people are idealized representations. Even though I'd seen dozens of portraits and photographs of Renfrew, I was prepared for something less impressive. Actually, the portraits didn't do him justice. He stood taller than I did, which put him over six feet, and he had a good fifty pounds on me, maybe more. Some of that was fat, but not all of it. I thought of Thomson as bearlike, but Renfrew physically dominated the room.

He rose to meet us, which is more than Lord Chillingham had done in our brief meeting. Renfrew wore his dark hair cut close to his head and his beard trimmed in the tight pointed style so familiar in all the paintings and photographs. The pictures failed to capture the animation in his face, or the intelligence and humor in his eyes. He looked deadly serious in all the pictures and sort of distracted, looking up and away as if his mind was somewhere else. Today his mind was right here.

Thomson made the introductions and "Baron Renfrew" shook our hands, shook mine particularly vigorously.

"I've heard a good deal about you, Professor Fargo. You have had an adventurous few weeks since appearing so explosively in our midst. I assume Dr. Thomson has told you who I am."

"It wasn't necessary, Your Highness," Thomson put in. "He already knew."

"Really? How is that?"

"I'm from Illinois, Your Highness. I have relatives from a little town southwest of Chicago called Dwight."

He face broke into a wider smile, and he nodded.

"Yes, I remember that village quite well. I hunted there—oh, it must have been twenty years ago now. Stayed with a local gentleman named Spencer. Quite good shooting. Lovely countryside. They don't still talk about my visit in your day, though, surely. It was just a hunting trip."

"No, Your Highness, they don't talk about it, but your stay made such an impression in the town, they named the local park after you."

"What? Albert Edward Park?"

"No, sir. Renfrew Park."

"*Renfrew* Park?" He laughed. "Oh, that's quite good! Yes, very gratifying. Thank you for telling me."

Baron Renfrew was the title Prince Albert Edward, son of Queen

Victoria, Prince of Wales and heir apparent to the British throne, and who at least in my timeline would later become King Edward VII, used when he wished to travel informally and without a lot of fuss. It was the most modest of his many titles, and its use told everyone involved he was not visiting officially or on state business; he was there purely for pleasure.

I again glanced at his female companion, still seated on the loveseat, and tried not to stare. She wore her shining blond hair swept up in what I thought of as Gibson Girl style, with a few soft curling strands framing a heart-shaped face, clear skin, and broad, inquisitive blue eyes. Her riding habit, jet black except for white ruffles at her throat and wrists, flattered her figure. I saw no rings on her fingers, no ear rings, brooches, or any other jewelry except for a small silver locket suspended from a chain around her neck. Smoke curled from the slender cheroot she held in her hand.

The Prince of Wales followed my glance.

"Allow me to introduce my friend, *Mademoiselle* Gabrielle Courbiere. Gabrielle, this is Dr. Thomson, Captain Gordon, and Professor Fargo."

I followed their example and bowed. Thomson murmured *enchanté,* but Gordon remained tight-lipped.

Prince Albert Edward—affectionately called "Bertie"—gained fame for his love of the good life, particularly his liaisons with some of the most beautiful women in Europe. The basis for his attraction to *Mademoiselle* Courbiere was obvious, but why the British crown prince was playing footsy with a French woman when Britain and France seemed ready to start shooting at each other any minute, and why he had brought her to this meeting, were, well—interesting questions.

"Have you been riding, *Mademoiselle*?" Thomson inquired politely.

"Non, I prefer the riding *habite*. It is how I wear the trousers without scandalizing the small minds." To illustrate her point, she flipped back the slit skirt to show the tightly fitted black trousers underneath, tucked into gleaming riding boots. She crossed her legs and drew on her cheroot, then blew a smoke ring. Thomson colored, and Gordon turned away with a disapproving scowl.

What was interesting, at least to me, was how devoid her gestures seemed of artifice. Her words and the uncovering of her legs could easily have been an act either of provocative challenge or playful flirtation, but instead they were surprisingly matter-of-fact. If she was a steamy seductress, she wasn't working it very hard—at least not for us.

The prince took a large cigar from his inner coat pocket and trimmed the tip off with a pocket knife, talking as he did so.

"Professor Thomson, I understand that you are in authority over this expedition."

"Yes, Your Highness, I am."

"Splendid. I wonder, then, if you would do me a little favor. A personal favor, you understand—entirely unofficial."

Thomson shifted uncomfortably.

"Well—of course, your Highness, if it is within my power and does not jeopardize our expedition."

"Be so good, then, to take *Mademoiselle* Courbiere along, would you?"

Gordon snorted in derision, and the prince's face immediately lost its easy charm and casual humor, as if a massive thundercloud had blotted out the sun, and I was again aware of how physically imposing he was. Gordon's face reddened, and Thomson seemed nearly beside himself, shifting from one foot to the other as if he had to go to the bathroom.

"But Your Highness, a lady . . . do you know where we're going?" he asked.

The prince struck a match and then carefully lit his cigar, the silence stretching out as he puffed, puffed again, turned the cigar, examined the coal, and then blew out the match.

"Do *you*?" he finally asked.

There was a moment of awkward silence.

"Well. . . in a general sense. That is, there are . . . some specifics still to work out. We were hoping the Bavarians—"

"The Bavarians know a little," the prince cut in. "*Mademoiselle* Courbiere, on the other hand, knows a great deal. So were I you, I would add her to your party. Now, if you will all excuse me, I have an appointment with a baccarat table."

He kissed Gabrielle's hand, and he was gone.

"Highly irregular," Gordon said once the prince's footsteps faded.

"Oh shut up," I said.

He turned and glared at me, opened his mouth as if to speak, but then scowled and turned away.

"He has a point, Fargo," Thomson said. "This is a highly sensitive mission, and the young lady is . . . well—"

"What?" I demanded. "A French *spy?* Is that what you think? Don't be ridiculous."

"Well . . ."

I turned to Gabrielle.

"*Mademoiselle* Courbiere, are you a spy for the French Commune? Are you an agent of the dreaded *Garde Rouge*?"

She shrugged.

"Oui."

I stared at her, and she returned my gaze without blinking. She was absolutely serious.

TWELVE

October 3, 1888, Munich, Bavaria

"Do you understand, lass, how awkward this is?" Thomson asked.

"Of course," she replied. "The times they are awkward for us all. But we carry on, *non*?"

"Give me one good reason why we shouldn't arrest you right now," Gordon said.

"I have broken no laws, and you have no authority in Bavaria."

That was actually two good reasons, but pointing that out would have seemed rude. Besides, she left out the best reason—she was a special friend of the Prince of Wales.

"Just tell us what we need to know and we'll take care of the rest of this business," Gordon snapped.

"*Non.* I must accompany you, for to be certain the interests of France they are served." She shrugged again, as if to say there was nothing more to discuss.

"Look, you guys may not like the idea," I said to Thomson and Gordon, "but this trip is likely to be long, stupid, and end up with us dead, facedown in the mud, unless we get some real intelligence, and quickly. Let's add up what we know: he's called the Old Man of the Mountain and he's a really bad guy. That's not a lot to go on, and according to . . . *Baron Renfrew*, the Bavarians can't help much. Where are we even going to start looking?"

Gordon answered. "If he is not somewhere near the site in southern Bavaria—"

"He is not," Gabrielle put in.

"*If* he is not," Gordon continued, "then obviously Syria. I would imagine either the Lebanon or Ante-Lebanon mountain ranges, where his original predecessor lurked."

"*Non,*" Gabrielle said. "He is not in the Syrian mountains."

"He's the Old Man of the *Mountain*," Gordon shouted back. "What do you mean he's not in the bloody mountains?"

"*Oui*, the mountains, but not *those* mountains."

Gordon sank down in a chair against the wall, and Thomson shook his head.

"He's in Serbia, isn't he?" I asked.

"Don't be an ass, Fargo," Gordon said, but Gabrielle looked at me, and her eyes widened slightly in surprise.

"How did you know this?"

"I didn't for sure, not until your reaction. It was just a hunch—a speculation."

Thomson laughed for the first time since we got the Aldis lamp message. He sat in an overstuffed armchair and pulled his pipe out of the pocket of his jacket.

I expected Gabrielle to react with irritation, but instead she nodded thoughtfully. "Upon what was this speculation based?"

"I didn't see it until we were in the chart room of the *Intrepid* and I looked at their large globe. Because of the projections used, large-scale flat maps distort straight-line distances, but on a globe you can see them more clearly. We know there was an energy source at one end of this effect—the Wessex collider in my time. What if there was one at the other end as well?"

"But the other incident was here in Bavaria," Thomson said.

"The other *reported* incident was in Bavaria, but what if the real effects were at two power sources with an echo effect in the center? The Allgäu Alps are on a straight line and exactly centered between Wessex and Serbia."

Gordon snorted in derision. "You expect us to believe you reasoned all that through based only on two explosions?"

"No, but it was enough to make a guess. My first pick was southern Bavaria and my second was Syria, like yours. But if Syria and the Alps were out, Serbia was worth a shot."

"That was very logical," Gabrielle said.

"Do you mind, my dear?" Thomson held his pipe up for Gabrielle to see. She shook her head and drew on her cheroot. Thomson began packing tobacco into his pipe, and behind me Gordon lit one of his own cheroots. I supposed this sharing of smoke was a step toward a sharing of information, and perhaps even international peace and harmony, which were all good things, but it *was* getting hard on my lungs.

So we were back to the question of whether Gabrielle Courbiere would accompany us. The problem, in the end, was one of trust. How could we trust Gabrielle's information to be sufficient to warrant her inclusion unless she shared it with us? But once she did, how could she trust *us* to take her along? It was the sort of problem best solved by repeated and generous infusions of distilled alcohol, but all we had was one bottle of dry sherry, and Gordon put about half of that down just to take the edge off his hangover. At least after that he stopped shouting so much, which made the negotiations go easier.

"Okay, here's what I suggest," I said. "*Mademoiselle* Courbiere, tell us what you know about the Old Man except how to find him. If the information's good enough to convince Dr. Thomson to bring you along, you're in. If you don't trust us to deliver on that promise, tell us what we need, as we need it, to find him. What do you say?"

"*Oui,*" she said without hesitation. "If this is acceptable with the doctor, for me it is good."

Thomson drew on his pipe and looked intently at her.

"Forgive me asking, *Mademoiselle*, but . . . are you really a spy?"

"*Oui,* Doctor. For three years now I have been the agent of *Le Direction Centrale des Renseignements Généraux,* the DCRG."

"But . . . how?"

"Oh, it is simple. I am quite intelligent, and men find me attractive. They will often tell me almost anything for the possibility to mate with me, even if later that possibility it is not realized."

Thomson and I must both have stared at her for a moment, he in shock and me in puzzled admiration.

"Lass," Thomson finally said, "for a spy you're disarmingly honest. The truth is, the more I think on this mission, the less prepared I feel to accomplish anything. We do need help. If what you tell us now is useful, I'll take you with us and accept any additional assistance you can provide."

She nodded firmly.

"*Bon.* We have a considerable *dossier* on this man who calls himself *le Vieil Homme de Montagne*. He takes this name to cause fear, *oui?* He has assassinated over thirty men that we know of. His agents use the hashish, like the *Hashassiene* in the Holy Lands during the Crusades, but he is an ethnic Serb born in Austrian Croatia."

"Born when?" I asked.

She pursed her lips and looked up. "On 10 July, 1856."

She had a pretty good memory for numbers.

"So he is what? In his early thirties? Younger than I would have thought," I said.

"Young, *oui*. Perhaps *le Jeune Homme de Montagne, n'est-cepas?*" She looked at us and smiled, then added, "I made the joke."

We smiled back at her, but it wasn't exactly a knee-slapper.

"We know little about his early life," she continued, "but he studied the electrical engineering at the *Polytechnique Autrichien* in Graz. We first began collecting information on him six years ago when he moved to France."

"He lived in *France*?" Gordon shouted from his chair by the window. "Why in God's name didn't you arrest him when you had the chance?"

"We did not know his identity as *le Vieil Homme de Montagne* until recently. He had broken no laws when he lived in France, *mon Capitaine*. We do not arrest people simply for being disagreeable. You, for example, would be quite safe there."

I chuckled at that, and Thomson suppressed a smile of his own.

"While in Paris he worked for *La Compagnie d'Edison*, then in 1884 he traveled to your country, Professor Fargo, but a year later there was a dispute with *Monsieur* Edison and he returned to Europe. It was not long after his return that the first attacks by *le Vieil Homme de Montagne* took place."

I shot Thomson a look and saw him bite through his pipe stem in surprise, then spit out the end.

"Good God, you can't mean Nikola Tesla!" he exclaimed.

"Ah, you have heard of him."

THIRTEEN

October 4, 1888, Aboard Her Majesty's Aerial Ship* Intrepid*, Aloft over Bavaria

When we reboarded *Intrepid* the next morning and Captain Harding learned our party now included a representative of the DCRG, he did not react well. After a number of loud and intemperate words, Gabrielle Courbiere, looking every bit as lovely as I remembered from the previous evening, but that day wearing a dark purple riding habit, found herself installed in the crew's mess hall with an armed Marine guard at the door for company. She was not a prisoner, certainly not, not by any means. She was simply under no circumstances to leave the mess hall. About an hour after we were airborne, Thomson and I looked in on her. Gordon sniffed at the idea but came along anyway.

We found her enjoying tea served in a white porcelain navy mug. When we sat at her table, she raised her hand and called the mess steward.

"Jerome, would it be a trouble to bring my friends some tea? Ah, *bien*. *Merci*, Jerome." She smiled at him as he brought our mugs, and he floated back to the galley, soaring on the thermals of that smile. Give her a week and she'd be running the ship.

"Lass, I appreciate your assistance in this," Thomson said once we'd sipped our tea and settled back. "But I have to wonder why. What is your official charge with respect to our mission?"

"None," she said. "Officially I am not here. There would be much discord in the Chamber of Deputies were it known the DCRG was cooperating with British military intelligence. The same with the

House of Commons, *n'est-cepas*? But my immediate superiors ask me to do this thing, and I say *oui*."

"Just out of the goodness of their hearts?" Gordon demanded. "I've followed the Old Man's campaign of assassinations and terror, and I've never heard of any of his attacks being directed at France."

"That is true," Gabrielle answered. "The majority of them have been in Great Britain, Germany, and Austria-Hungary. There have also been four assassinations in Turkey, two each in Italy and Bulgaria, and single assassinations in five other European countries. Those are Greece, Wallachia—"

"Yes, yes." Gordon cut her off. "I know all that. The point is, none in France. So what interest does your agency have in this matter?"

"Your country and Germany attempt to isolate us," she said. "Well, not the entire countries. We have many friends in both places, but Lord Salisbury's government in your country and Chancellor Bismarck's in Germany oppose us. Very well. So now we reach out to Austria-Hungary and Turkey as friends. The attacks against them, while we remain unattacked, complicate this friendship. I am to help uncomplicate it."

Well, that was clear enough. Apparently the Commune was as capable of *realpolitik* as the next guy.

"You might have uncomplicated it sooner if you'd thought to tell us Tesla was behind all this," Gordon said. "He was just in England a week past. We could have arrested him and been done with it."

"I would have been very surprised," Gabrielle answered. "For all your enthusiasm, your department is not very successful at making the arrest."

"What are you talking about?" Gordon demanded.

"Two years ago, through private channels, we tell your department we know who killed Sir Henry Bessemer. Do you make the arrest? *Non*. You tell this English gentleman the French are attempting to slander him and he should retain the solicitor. Instead he disappears. Ah! Now we are more careful what we tell you."

"A different matter altogether. Tesla is hardly a gentleman," Gordon said.

"It is hard to know who is, *n'est-cepas*? Tell me, *Capitaine* Gordon, why would Lord Chillingham, the man who amassed his second fortune by purchasing the patents to the Bessemer process from the heirs of the murdered inventor, have cause to allow the murderer to disappear? Hmm? Can you think of a reason?"

"I won't dignify that with an answer," he said and turned away.

Gabrielle shrugged and sipped her tea.

"I have a question that's been bothering me, Mademoiselle," I said. "Maybe you can help. This Old Man of the Mountain apparently has an extensive network of agents and sympathizers and has been assassinating people all over Europe. Why? What does he want?"

"What difference does it make what he wants?" Gordon demanded. "He's a madman."

Gabrielle frowned at that, but I answered before she could. "It matters for two reasons. First, knowing what he's after may help us anticipate his next moves. Second, I talked to one of his guys. You did, too, Gordon. That fellow Grover was someone who believed in something. Understand the beliefs, or goals, which Tesla shares with his followers and we have an insight into his operation." Gabrielle nodded in agreement.

"*Oui*, this is so. He adheres to the revolutionary syndicalist movement, although his methods are so violent he is no longer embraced by the former leaders of that movement."

"Former leaders?" I asked.

"Since the *Association Internationale des Travailleurs* disbanded in 1871, following the success of the Commune in France, there has been no one centrally organized international movement. Some syndicalists centered their efforts in France and the surrounding countries. I know many of those organizers, of course. But those who reject the state as the inevitable enemy of workers followed Mikhail Bakunin."

"Yeah, I know something about Bakunin," I said. "Not exactly a happy guy, as I recall."

She looked puzzled, as if wondering what his happiness had to do with anything.

"I never met him," she said, "but he does not smile in his photographs. Since his death twelve years ago, there can hardly be named a single dominant leader of the movement. *Le Vieil Homme de Montagne* emerges as perhaps the most influential of those who see violence as a necessary tactic to achieve their ends. He perhaps has the ties to the German labor movement through Wilhelm Liebknecht. Liebknecht denies this, of course."

She paused to sip her tea and frowned in thought. I had the impression she was assessing the likelihood of Liebknecht's denial being truthful, and that she had made a similar assessment many times and had never been completely satisfied with the result. Absorbed as she was by her thoughts, I sensed she had, for the moment, become oblivious to the world around her, unaware we were even there, and it made me feel like a voyeur looking at her, as if I spied on her through a bedroom window. She looked up at me, and I felt my ears flush, but how much from embarrassment and how much from arousal I couldn't say.

"He also has contacts to the more radical elements of the British trade unionist movement," she continued, "through Johann Eccarius, who also broke with the Commune."

"Eccarius?" Gordon put in. "You're sure of that?"

"*Oui*, but I must tell you we have no proof that *Monsieur* Eccarius is an active part of his network of agents. I am sorry. I know how enamored you are of arrests."

I saw a sparkle of humor in her eyes then, and Gordon sat back with a scowl.

"Yeah, okay," I said. "But what *are* their ends?"

"Oh. An end to state and private ownership of the means of production. Its replacement with *syndicats*, unions of workers who produce goods to meet needs, not to enrich owners. Trade negotiation directly between *syndicats* rather than between states." She shrugged.

"So," I said, "a seeker after utopia."

"*Oui*, I believe so. His methods are objectionable but his ends well-intentioned, *n'est-cepas*?"

"Non, ce n'est pas ainsi," I answered, and her eyebrows rose slightly in surprise. *"L'idée là sont des forces naturelles qui animent le monde—"* I began but glanced at Thomson and Gordon and saw their faces blank with incomprehension.

"The idea there are natural forces," I began again in English, "which drive the world toward peace and harmony and plenty, and the only things standing in the way of that perfect world are wrongheaded obstructionists—that thinking always ends in blood, and not much else."

"You do not believe the world can be improved?" Gabrielle asked.

"Sure I do. I just don't think it can be perfected. I think the world gets better by affirmative works. It doesn't get better on its own by just killing bad people, but that's what utopianists always come down to. Like most extreme religious movements end up in crusades or jihads or witch burnings. Just kill enough heretics or infidels and God's plan will succeed."

Gabrielle shook her head. "*Le Vieil Homme de Montagne* is not a man religious."

"No, but all those guys have blind faith in something—an unshakable belief in whatever magic mechanism they think drives the world, whether it's God's will, dialectical materialism, racial superiority, or the free market. This Tesla guy's no different. What's his plan? Murder obstructionists. If he just kills enough Tyndalls and Rossbanks, he figures the syndicalist worker's paradise will burst into glorious bloom on its own. It's bullshit."

"I have to agree with the lad," Thomson said, "if not his choice of language. It doesn't seem like a very constructive program by itself."

"*Non*, perhaps not," Gabrielle said. "But it raises the interesting questions. It was your James Madison who said government is formulated to protect the minority of the opulent from the majority, *n'est-cepas?* The question is whether the state, if denied that ability to protect the wealthy few from the many, then has a remaining useful function."

"It's hardly as simple as that, lass," Thomson protested.

"I should say not!" Gordon echoed in rare agreement with the Scotsman. And they were off and running.

I'd said my piece, and I had no dog in this fight, so I mostly listened. Thomson and Gordon argued with passion and enthusiasm; Gabrielle spoke in a simple tone which never seemed to vary in intensity. Her grasp of detail was incredible. The logic and consistency of her arguments were unassailable, provided you accepted the premises upon which they were based. But most importantly, she was tireless. She simply wore Thomson and Gordon down, without appearing to realize that's what she was doing. When an hour into the argument *Intrepid*'s captain sent word requesting Thomson's presence on the bridge, I think it came as a relief to all of us except Gabrielle. Gordon and I bid her farewell at the same time and accompanied Thomson, although Gordon left us as soon as we were away from her.

"Ah, hello, sir," young Ensign Conroy greeted Thomson as we entered the wheelhouse, and then he nodded to me as well. "Captain's compliments and he's occupied at the moment, but we're getting close to the destination and he thought you might like to see the approach."

Conroy handed Thomson a pair of binoculars, but space was at a premium along the broad window at the front of the wheelhouse. I pointed to the portside hatchway, and Thomson nodded. We made our way out onto the open railed platform they called the bridge wing.

"Quite a formidable young lady," Thomson said once we were under open sky. "Badly misinformed, of course, but that's hardly her fault. I think it would take weeks to untangle all of her misconceptions, and who has the time for that now?"

"Or the energy," I added, and he nodded. Even if he could muster the necessary stamina, I wondered who would end up tangled at the end of those weeks, and who untangled, but I kept that to myself.

"Craft ahead," the lookout above the wheelhouse called out. "Bearing green zero-one-five, climbing from twenty degrees down-angle. Range four thousand and closing."

Ensign Conroy and another officer I didn't know came out onto the bridge wing to have a better look. Thomson offered me the loaned binoculars, and I took them gratefully. It took a few seconds to find it. It looked like a zeppelin to me—black gas bag with some sort of structure slung underneath. As it was climbing and pointed almost directly at us, it was hard to see much else about it. The lookout had a good pair of eyes; the black gasbag was almost invisible against the dark backdrop of the Alps behind it.

"One of the old L Zed Fives," Ensign Conroy said.

"Bavaria flies one or two of them, as I recall," the other officer answered. "Probably an escort. Afraid we won't be able to find Kempten on our own, I imagine. Better call the captain, Mr. Conroy. He may want to exchange honors."

"Action stations, sir?" Conroy asked. The other officer hesitated and then shook his head.

"Captain's prerogative."

Conroy disappeared into the wheelhouse.

The zeppelin was already noticeably closer. Four thousand yards was only a little over two miles. We were cruising at about twenty knots, and if he was coming on at the same speed, we were closing the distance at almost a mile a minute. Captain Harding emerged from the wheelhouse. He must have been in the chart room right behind it to get here this quickly.

"I have the bridge, Mr. Longchamps," he said.

"Aye, aye, sir. Our course is one six five magnetic, altitude four thirty, speed nineteen knots. L Zed Five-class zeppelin approaching, climbing to meet us. Range about two thousand and closing. Shall we go to action stations, sir?"

"Not enough time to get everyone assembled at the rate he's coming. Why show our German hosts a crowded, confused deck? No, we'll dip the colors as a salute. Have the signaler stand by."

"Aye, aye, sir," Longchamps went back into the wheelhouse. Harding followed him and left Thomson and me alone for the moment. The zeppelin was down to perhaps half a mile now. It would pass us to starboard, and Thomson and I stood on the portside flying bridge, so I could see a little of its profile. The gas bag was more pointed than the big German zeppelins of the 1930s, and the crew compartment hung a few meters below the bag instead of being tucked right up against it. I studied it through the binoculars, never having seen a real one before. Its tail planes were visible then, but were the same featureless black as the gas bag.

"Germans don't mark their zeps?" I asked.

"Yes," Thomson answered. "Usually a large Maltese cross on the side of the balloon and a smaller one on the tail."

I felt my heart accelerate, felt the first fingers of dopey excitement claw at my brain, and then I saw the gun mount swiveling toward us, a vaguely familiar gun mount which had no business being here in this time.

I dropped the binoculars and grabbed Thomson by the lapels, pushed his back against the outside steel wall of the wheelhouse, and then kicked his feet out from under him. He crashed to the deck with a startled grunt. I ducked down beside him.

"What in blazes—" he started, but then was drown out by the sound of metal impacting metal, exploding glass, and screaming men. Some of the glass from the wheelhouse windows blew out on us, along with tiny beads of molten steel, one of which smoldered on the sleeve of my coat and burned my arm underneath before I could shake it off.

The zeppelin was already past the wheelhouse. I heard its gun fire again—*POW, POW, POW*—but the rounds hit farther aft.

"Stay down," I ordered and Thomson nodded wordlessly, face as white as the clouds.

I ran through the smoky chaos of the wheelhouse, seeing nothing clearly but an oval-shaped panel of blue sky—the hatch to the starboard bridge wing. In clean air I came up hard against the brass railing and looked at the enormous black giver of death slipping past. A small streak of fire shot out from the zeppelin's gondola and hit somewhere behind the superstructure, causing an explosion which shook the deck under my feet. Then the gun started again: *POW, POW, POW.* One of the aft propellers flew to pieces, the rudder jumped and twisted at the wrong angle, the other prop shuddered and came to a halt amid the screech of tortured metal. Then the zeppelin was past us. I watched for a moment, but it showed no sign of turning back on us.

Beneath me I could feel *Intrepid* begin to list slightly to starboard as her speed fell away. I turned back into the wheelhouse. Broken glass covered everything, and all of the bridge crew was down except for Ensign Conroy, who knelt beside the unconscious Captain Harding and pressed his hand over the captain's bloody forehead. The other officer, Longchamps, had lost the back half of his head.

"Captain, wake up!" Conroy shouted over and over.

My head spun, for a moment nothing, made sense. Then I remembered the red lever by the engine telegraph from our earlier encounter with the French, and I pulled it. Five quick bells, a pause, five more quick bells: action stations—as if anyone onboard didn't already know we were in a world of trouble. This would at least bring more people up here, people who knew what they were doing. I held on to the helm for balance and realized the list was getting worse. The petty officer they called the trimsman had nearly lost his right arm above the elbow, and the mangled flesh and bone lay beside him on the deck at an awkward angle. I crunched through broken glass to get to him, pulled him away from the hedge of trim levers, and applied pressure on his inside upper arm to stop the arterial bleeding. Christ, there was a lot of blood!

"Captain, wake up!" Conroy pleaded.

"Conroy, you're in command!" I shouted at him. He didn't seem to hear me, so I picked up a handful of broken glass and threw it at his back. That got his attention.

"What?"

"You're in command. The ship's listing and the trimsman's down. *Fucking do something!*"

He looked around helplessly at the blood-spattered ruin of the wheelhouse, the shattered controls and broken bodies, and then back down.

"Captain, wake up!"

Feet pounded on the steel stairs to the port flying bridge. A naval rating appeared in the hatchway and froze for a moment, taking in the scene.

"Bloody 'ell!" he said. An officer pushed past him and made a quick survey of the damage.

"Better get someone on these trim controls," I told him, "or we're going to tip right over." I didn't know what would happen then, but I couldn't imagine it would be good.

FOURTEEN

October 4, 1888,
Aboard Her Majesty's Aerial Ship* Intrepid*,
Landed Near Kempten, Bavaria

We hadn't tipped over. We were grounded in a meadow while damage-control parties swarmed over the ship. I sat with my back to the wall and watched the activity in the wheelhouse. They had at least swept up the broken glass but several broad smears of blood, red turning to brown, told the story of our brief, disastrous encounter. I didn't help the naval ratings clear away the debris. My knees felt too weak to support me, although I knew from experience that if they had to, they would. Captain Harding, head swathed in a bloody bandage, sat in a chair pulled into the wheelhouse from the chart room, while an officer reported on the damage.

"Both boilers punctured, but Mr. Clyde says he has number one patched with steam up and can have pressure in number two inside of an hour. Starboard airscrew lost, and the port airscrew shaft is bent. Mr. Clyde recommends remounting the port screw on the starboard shaft and says he can give you twelve knots once the work is done. Rudder is jammed amidships, but he doesn't expect a problem freeing it. He can jury-rig the screw in three hours and perhaps make temporary repairs on the boilers, but he would rather spend the night doing the job right."

"Casualties?" Harding asked.

"Lieutenant Longchamp and two ratings dead, yourself and six ratings injured. Dr. Bay says Leading Trimsman O'Donnell will lose the arm, sir."

"What about Mademoiselle Courbiere?" I asked. The officer looked to me.

"Uninjured, sir. The attack distressed her, but she seems quite calm now, all things considered. I was afraid she might become hysterical."

"Never mind that," Harding snapped. "What about our armament?"

"Starboard sponson frozen in place with the gun locked at maximum depression. Z turret totally destroyed. We'll need major dry-dock work to replace it. All secondary armament serviceable, sir."

"They spiked your aft turret," I said.

"I am quite aware of that, Mr. Fargo," Harding said, turning his sour gaze on me. "The question is how they did it, and why."

"No, when I said *spiked*, I meant it. That was a Spike antitank missile they fired at you, built either by Raphael or EuroSpike. What the hell it was doing here is a different matter."

"And that damned gun?" he asked. "It fired faster than a Hotchkiss one-pounder revolver but cut through our armor as if it were mere sheet metal."

"I'm pretty sure it was a Rhinemetal thirty-millimeter *Maschinenkanone*, probably firing sabot rounds."

Harding looked from me to Thomson, who leaned against the wall of the wheelhouse and mopped the perspiration from his flushed face. "Thomson, do you have any idea what this fellow is talking about?"

"Yes, I do. Unfortunately, I'm afraid I cannot explain further at the moment. All I can say is you should listen carefully to whatever he can tell you about the capabilities of these weapons."

Gordon entered the wheelhouse, looking around at the damage. I wondered where he'd been through all of this and spotted the blood dried on his hands.

"You hurt, Gordon?" I asked.

He looked at me wordlessly, as if unsure what I meant, and then raised his hands slowly and examined therm. That slow-motion movement was a pretty good sign of someone coming out of shock.

"No. I'm all right. Someone else's."

My own right hand was bandaged. I'd cut it scooping up glass to throw at Conroy, but I hadn't felt the cut at the time. It hadn't even started bleeding until after things settled down. That was typical, too.

"Why didn't they finish us off when they had the chance?" Thomson asked.

"Turning radius," Harding answered. "They couldn't fire directly astern because of their own airscrews and would have to swing wide to turn back on us, which would give either our broadside mounts or the port sponson a clear shot. Too dangerous with that great hydrogen bag as a target. They couldn't know we weren't at action stations. What I want to know is why the damned Germans are shooting at us."

"It's not the Germans," I said. "At least I don't think so. There were no markings on the zeppelin. This smells of an ambush, maybe by the fellow we're looking for."

"Well, we'll make repairs here overnight and then try to make Munich in the morning. I hope to God you're right about the Germans, Fargo. We're damned near helpless with one screw, a leaky boiler, and half our main guns out of battery."

"There's still the matter of our mission," I said. "We have to examine the incident site."

"Out of the question," Harding said, shaking his head vigorously. "My first responsibility is my vessel."

I looked to Thomson, but he just shrugged helplessly. Gordon had a thousand-yard stare that said his mind was still half an hour back in time.

"If we can get to the incident site on our own, will you wait for us?" I asked.

Harding frowned. "Can't imagine how you'll manage that, but if there's no sign of hostility from the Germans, I'll wait the night and the day tomorrow."

"Smoke on the horizon," the lookout above the wheelhouse called, "nor' by nor'-west, three smudges."

"Those German landships we passed yesterday," Harding said. "If you're wrong, Fargo, they'll shoot us to scrap metal here on the ground."

"Yeah, but if I'm right, they're our ride."

"What do you make of it, lad?" Thomson asked.

I walked around the vehicle, assessing the damage and trying to envision what that fiery moment of transition from my time back to this one had been like. No fun, that's for sure; five fresh graves in the meadow forty yards away bore mute testimony to that.

In some ways it reminded me of the Somerton site we'd looked at earlier, although the impact area was much smaller here. It had that same look of part of one world exchanged with another, and the topography didn't quite line up. WHECOL hadn't been at Somerton, so the shift in time had brought a slight shift in location as well. Here it looked as though the vehicle and a chunk of the surrounding ground had appeared above the surface of the meadow and just fallen onto it. A lot of the surrounding grass was burnt but I wasn't sure if that was from the event itself or a secondary fire afterwards. One side of the vehicle was blackened, and the rear fuel cell had been compromised.

Compromised. Boy, that was a polite word for what had happened. The back two or three feet of the vehicle just weren't there any more, leaving the interior open to the morning sunlight. The edges weren't cleanly cut, as I'd expected them to be, but looked as if they had been melted by a broad-flamed cutting torch. Hard threads of steel hung like shining silver spittle from the yawning improvised mouth, and severed caterpillar tracks lay in twisted heaps around the broken vehicle like spilled entrails.

The circular hole in the top, letting more sunlight in, showed no evidence of violence. The entire remote turret assembly had been carefully removed. That much I'd suspected, as I'd seen it yesterday on the black zeppelin. I wondered how they powered it. My curiosity piqued, I walked around front, lifted the engine access hatch, and looked into an empty engine compartment. Whoever they were, these guys hadn't missed a trick.

"It's a *Schützenpanzer* Puma, the standard infantry fighting vehicle of the *Bundeswehr*—the German army in my time," I explained to Thomson, Gordon, Gabrielle, and Inspector Wolfenbach of the Bavarian *Stadtpolizei,* who stood with them. Gabrielle crouched, an open pad on her knees as she sketched the vehicle and made notes in the margins. Inspector Wolfenbach had already been told, in confidence, of my origins. He clearly hadn't believed any of it but now seemed to be having second thoughts. Thirty-five tons of squat, angular armored vehicle, obviously not from this time and place, possessed a quiet but persuasive eloquence.

Five graves. A Puma could carry nine men —a crew of three and six infantry dismounts. Squads were usually understrength in the field, and there was no telling if all the passengers had even made it through the transition to this time, given that hole ripped in the back end. Somebody had survived, though. No matter how smart the guys in the black zeppelin were, it would take weeks to figure out how to remove that remote turret without damaging it, remove the engine, and install them in an airship so they would actually work—not to mention figure out *how* they worked. Somebody from my time had to have helped them, which was not to say the assistance was rendered voluntarily.

Gordon drifted over and touched the beads of melted steel along the open rear, then peered into the alien interior of the vehicle. He still wore that same blank expression he'd had since the zeppelin attack, which made it tough to figure what he was thinking. After a moment, he looked at me, and his expression was altered. He believed this thing was from a different time, and now he also believed, not just in his head but down in his gut, that I was from a different time as well. Fear had replaced contempt.

I climbed up onto the deck and looked into the now-open turret ring. When I glanced over, I saw Gabrielle studying me with curiosity. She didn't look away at first, but then went back at her work and continued sketching.

"There are brackets for Spike missile reloads, thirty-millimeter ammunition boxes, and seven-six-two belted—what you'd call thirty caliber. All the brackets are empty. I'd guess they have four missiles—three now, since they took out a turret on *Intrepid* with one of them—plus 400 rounds of thirty millimeter, and about 2,000 machine-gun rounds, give or take. That can make a lot of trouble for one or two of your warships, but it's not exactly a conquer-the-world ordnance load."

Thomson scratched his beard and squinted at the broken vehicle. "There's something bothering me. You mentioned the laboratory you worked at was not in Somerton, but rather the countryside, and this vehicle does not seem to have come out at ground level. But your facility *was* in Wessex, and this vehicle was at least in Germany, and quite possibly southern Germany, so in both cases the transition point was close to its origin. You mentioned the date of the incident in your time was early August, but it took place a month later here. Do you suppose the difference in where the Earth was in its orbit around the sun could account for that shift?"

That had been bothering me as well. "I wish it could, but I don't see how. The difference in orbital position is much more than this little shift in location, but it's insignificant compared to the distance the sun has moved in relation to the rest of the galaxy in over a century. By my time we'd been able to measure that speed. The sun's moving through the galaxy at about 40,000 miles an hour, and pulling the Earth and the other planets along with it. That means that in the century between my time and yours, the sun and earth have moved"—I paused and did some quick calculations in my head—"about three and a half *billion* miles. Being a couple dozen kilometers off in terms of where I came out doesn't seem like that big a deal when you look at it in those terms."

What I left unsaid was that if I'd been a couple dozen kilometers—or even meters—off in *altitude*, I wouldn't have survived the experience. These guys had come out a few meters high. What if they—or I—had come out a few meters low? For a moment I felt sick to my stomach.

"Well, how can you account for this difference, then?" Thomson said.

I looked at him. "You're the scientist. You tell me."

Three and a half billion miles. As I thought about it, I realized this was an aspect of time travel I'd never heard addressed in any of the science fiction I'd read as a youngster. For that matter, the physicists at WHECOL hadn't questioned it, either. Why not? They were just swept up in the excitement of the possibility of time travel, I supposed. And for all I knew, maybe some of them *had* wondered about it—I never spoke with any of them directly, only with Reggie. But I think the first question I'd ask if I had a machine bringing things back from the past is why it wasn't just bringing back big scoops of vacuum, because that's about all there would have been hundreds or even thousands of years earlier in the spot we occupied when the time machine was running. How would the machine search out where Earth was back then and bring samples back from it? Something didn't add up, but the answer wasn't in the burnt-out Puma.

"I think we're done here," I said. I'd sure as hell seen all I cared to.

Intrepid had finished its jury-rigged repairs and was already airborne and coming to find us when we were an hour from the crash site. I was happy to switch from the German landship to *Intrepid*. The landships were big on the outside but amazingly cramped on the inside, not to mention hot, steamy, and filthy with coal dust and lubricating grease and oil. Dante would have taken one look around and nodded.

But aside from the comparative comfort of *Intrepid* as a means of transportation, we didn't have a lot to celebrate. We were too late getting to the incident site, and the pride of the Royal Navy had had its ass handed to it by a balloon. The three-hour flight from Munich was looking like a six or seven-hour return flight on one propeller. Gabrielle was no longer confined to the crew's mess, as the room periodically filled with steam from a leaking boiler line—that and the fact that Harding had a lot more on his mind than the danger posed by one unarmed French woman. She joined Thomson and me at the bow railing, but none of us had much to say.

FIFTEEN

October 5, 1888, Munich, Bavaria

Intrepid limped back to Munich well after dark. We met the next morning in the chart room on *Intrepid*'s bridge. Gabrielle joined us and I expected an argument from Captain Harding about a "Frog" coming into his inner sanctum, but I was mistaken. His still-bloody head bandage was reminder enough that, for the moment at least, the French were not the enemy.

The chart room wasn't all that big, and the six of us crowded around the map table: Gabrielle, myself, Gordon, Thomson, Harding, and Inspector Wolfenbach of the Bavarian *Stadtpolizei.* Inspector Wolfenbach's considerable girth contributed to the close quarters; I pegged him at between two-fifty and three hundred pounds. Gabrielle stood to my left, pressed against my arm by necessity, and I enjoyed the sensation.

Thanks to her I knew almost as much about Tesla's location and setup as did French intelligence, which was quite a lot, although much of it was pretty boring, mundane stuff. Gabrielle had recited all of it the previous evening, warming to the subject as she went, becoming more interested as the information became more arcane and obscure. She went on long after Thomson, Gordon, and I started listening out of a sense of duty rather than genuine interest, and then after we began just pretending to pay attention, and she never seemed to notice. In a sense it was a replay of her long lecture about anarcho-syndicalism in the mess hall of *Intrepid* earlier. Coming from anyone else it would have been annoying, but from her it was strangely endearing. We are all suspicious of perfection, and rightly so. Perfection is an illusion; this flaw made her real.

Or maybe that was why Gabrielle Courbiere could be a successful spy; guys got stupid around her, knew they were being stupid, and didn't care. Part of it was because of her looks, no doubt about it. But part of it was her disarming directness and absence of guile. She might lie about facts—provided it was a carefully constructed lie, rich in nuance and detail, and painstakingly internally consistent—but she did not seem capable of deceiving as to her feelings.

"Can we still count on your cooperation, Inspector Wolfenbach?" Thomson asked.

The corpulent policeman bobbed his head, making his jowls quiver. "*Natürlich.*"

Thomson unrolled *Intrepid*'s chart of Serbia and pointed to the mountains along its southwest frontier with Turkish Bosnia and Montenegro. That had surprised me the first time I saw it—Turkey still holding a bunch of the Balkans. I was pretty sure in my time-line Austria had them by now, but wasn't certain.

"*Mademoiselle* Courbiere tells us that Tesla's base is here in Serbia, specifically in the valley of the Uvac River, between Zlatar Mountain and Mutenice Mountains, near the village of Kokin Brod. Two years ago the Serbs built an earthen dam near the village, used explosives to bring down some of the rock cliffs. Since then the valley to the southeast has filled with water. *Mademoiselle* Courbiere also tells me you have been gathering information on this installation, Inspector?"

Wolfenbach nodded and then pointed to the valley, using a finger like a small bratwurst. "*Ja.* Berlin does not, but down here we still remember our friends in Vienna and help them out now and then. If a hound in Serbia has fleas, soon there will be scratching in Budapest, *nicht wahr?* So this is the lair of *Der Alte Gebirgsmann*. Bad country. There are many rumors about horrible things in the hills, we think started to discourage the curious. Also maybe three, four earthquakes, but not large. We know about the dam, but why build it? This we do not know." Wolfenbach shrugged, which threatened to knock a lamp off the wall behind him.

"When he was working for Edison, Tesla did a lot of work with large electrical turbines," I said. "I wonder if he's playing around with hydroelectric power generation."

I looked around but realized the word didn't connect with anyone. "Have there been any unusual shipments of equipment into there?"

"Nine heavy naval guns," Wolfenbach answered, "and glass."

"Glass? As in window panes?"

"*Ja,* window panes. Large sheets of window glass, hundreds of them, maybe thousands. They have been buying as far north as Dresden."

"Armor plate as well?" Harding asked, but Wolfenbach shook his head.

I looked at Thomson, figuring glass might mean something to him, but he simply chewed on the stem of his new pipe, lost in thought.

Gordon tapped the map to bring us back in focus.

"The question remains how we are to reach this base deep inside Serbia."

"That I can arrange, *Herr Hauptmann,*" Wolfenbach said,

Thomson's head came up and he took the pipe from his mouth.

"Please elaborate, Inspector."

"*Die Hochflieger Ost,* the express zeppelin from Berlin to Turkey, stops here in Munich, then Vienna, and finally Sofia before arriving in Istanbul. It makes no scheduled stops in Serbia. However, *Deutsche Luftschiffahrts* AG, the concern which owns the *Hochflieger Ost,* is willing to do occasional . . . *favors* for the imperial authorities, *und* now it seems for us as well. I believe *Fraulein* Courbiere has a particularly persuasive friend."

Yeah, I'd met him two nights before. Wolfenbach looked at Gabrielle with a smile and raised eyebrow, but if he was trying to make a veiled salacious hint, it was lost on her. Veiled hints didn't seem to penetrate her consciousness; if you wanted her to know something, I suspected you needed to just tell her.

"*Zo,*" he said, "your party travels as civilians on *Die Hochflieger Ost* with passage to Istanbul, but when it passes over southern Serbia, it will land in the countryside, secretly disembark your party, *und* then continue on with its voyage. The other passengers will be told a story of some sort. We leave that up to the zeppelin line."

"I'm unclear as to exactly what our plan is once we get there," I said. "But more importantly, how do we get out when we're done?"

"Walk west," Thomson said. We all looked at him, and he tapped the chart with his pipe stem. "It is only a few miles to the Bosnian frontier. The Foreign Office has said we can expect cooperation from the Turks in this. I imagine that extends at the very least to allowing us to flee across their frontier."

"And if they follow us with that damned black zeppelin?" Gordon demanded.

"Leave that to *Intrepid*," Captain Harding said, "providing Johnny Turk lets us use his air space. If we sight that black zeppelin again, we'll see what a salvo of Hale rockets does to its hydrogen cells. Why he's still using a dirigible is a puzzle, though."

"Why?" I asked.

Harding looked around the chart table and colored slightly, as if he had said too much.

"I . . . well, this fellow's an inventor, ain't he? I just—"

"*Capitaine* Harding is perhaps concerned with the stolen Royal Navy liftwood," Gabrielle said.

We all looked at Harding, whose face turned a deeper red.

"How do you know about that?" he snapped.

"I am a spy," she answered, and gave a wonderfully Gallic shrug.

"He stole a shipment of liftwood?" Gordon asked. "And we weren't told of it?"

"We don't know who stole it," Harding answered. "We just know that a White Star aether flyer under Royal Navy charter was seized by its crew during a return flight from Syrtis Major. The passengers and ship's officers were put down on the Azores, and there's been no sign of it since."

"Yes, I remember," Gordon said. "That business with RMF *Prolific* last year. I read of it."

"What was kept from the papers," Harding continued, "was her cargo: the finished lifting vanes for another cruiser of this class, along with refitting vanes for two of our older gunboats."

"He has it," Gabrielle said.

No one seemed inclined to argue the point with her.

"This changes things," Thomson said. He leaned back against the bulkhead and studied the lamp hanging from the ceiling of the chart room, chewing thoughtfully on his pipe. After a few minutes of increasingly awkward silence, his face soured and he shook his head.

"Are you stumped, or have you figured it out?" I asked.

"I believe I understand the business, although it gives me little enough satisfaction. Remember, Tesla has not imported any heavy machinery, at least that we know of. Therefore everything he needs, aside from the items we know he brought in, must have been on RMF *Prolific*, the pirated White Star aether flyer.

"The first critical component, of course, is the vessel's aether propeller. It is useless in the Earth's dense atmosphere as a means of propulsion, but at its simplest it is nothing but a very large, although specialized, electromagnetic field generator, exactly the device Tesla has spent much of his life working on and perfecting. I think it clear he has discovered uses for it beyond simple propulsion in the vacuum of space. He has found a way to concentrate its field, and heighten its power, to the extent that it can tear open a hole between our time and others, such as yours, Jack. As I recall you told us, your Wessex apparatus required enormous electricity."

"Enough to power a good-sized town when they really had it cranking."

"Tesla cannot generate that much power all at once," Thomson continued, "nor is there a central power grid such as in your world from which he can simply draw it. I believe he must generate it gradually and store it, then discharge it quickly through his field generator—the modified aether propeller—to open his portal to other times.

"So, the next question is how can he store that much power? Well, this is where I believe it gets truly remarkable, and I'll say this much for Tesla—the villain thinks large.

"Are any of you familiar with a scientific device called a Leyden jar? No? It is a device for storing electrical charges and then discharging them on demand. It consists of a conductive medium on either side of a nonconductive barrier, a dielectric, in which the actual charge is stored. Its most primitive version is a handheld beaker of water, where the water inside and the hand outside serve as conductors and the glass is the dielectric."

"The window glass!" I said.

"Very good, laddie. Yes, the window glass, enough glass to make hundreds, even thousands of cells. And where does he keep this latticework of glass?"

He looked around the circle of faces. Gabrielle was the one who answered.

"The lake, obviously. The lake he has made. It is his giant Leyden jar."

"The largest Leyden jar ever conceived," Thomson said. "I cannot begin to fathom how much energy it could store. He could accumulate energy slowly, I suppose, were he a patient man. He could run a waterwheel or two, as Jack suggested, or use the steam engine from RMF *Prolific*.

"But the numerous stories of small earthquakes, which I take to be the thunderous reports of his time-rending machine, these point to more frequent uses."

"As I understand what you've told us," Gordon said, "this Leyden jar thing does not generate power. It merely stores it. So where is he getting all this power?"

"Ah, the missing component from RMF *Prolific*, and I do not mean its steam power plant. I mean its cargo of liftwood, along with the vessel's own lifting vanes. Here is a man who has more liftwood than any private citizen, and most governments, on Earth, and yet he still makes use of hydrogen-filled airships. Why?

"He does so because he has better uses for his liftwood. The damned fool has built himself a Forever Engine, and God help us all."

SIXTEEN

October 5, 1888, Munich, Bavaria

I had no idea what a Forever Engine was, but something in those words, or perhaps in the way Thomson said them, sent a surge of adrenaline through me.

"If word of this leaks out. . ." Gordon said, and he leaned back against the wall as if exhausted, his words trailing off for a moment. Then he shook his head, his expression grim. "The colonies on Mars will go up in flames. It's just the sort of excuse the local troublemakers have been looking for. Once that starts, heaven knows where it will all end."

Then he stood forward again, and his eyes turned to Gabrielle.

"*Mademoiselle* Courbiere, you must give us your word that you will not share this information with your government."

"You are wrong, *Capitaine* Gordon. No part of our agreement obligates me to withhold information from my own government."

"This goes beyond our agreement. This is a matter of the lives of thousands of innocent people on Mars."

"Will you keep the information from your own government, *Capitaine? Non?* Why can your government be trusted with this information and mine not?"

Gordon was getting his steam up, so I broke in.

"Would you two just take a break for a minute? All of you seem to know what this Forever Engine thing is. I haven't got a clue, so first somebody fill me in, and then you guys can get back to refighting the Napoleonic Wars."

"*Ja,* I am wondering the same thing," Wolfenbach said.

Gordon glared at Gabrielle for a moment longer, then nodded. Gabrielle shrugged.

"Yes, of course, laddie, you've no way of knowing, nor is it widely known in general," Thomson said. "It's not a secret, of course, just rather arcane. Forever Engine is the translation of an old Martian term—*Makach Khadeek* in Son-Gaaryani, although there are similar versions in all the Martian tongues. Martians agree on very little, Jack, but they are unanimous in their belief that the *Makach Kadeek*, the Forever Engine, is a device of unspeakable blasphemy."

"You mean this is a religious thing?" I asked.

"Not precisely. Or rather, many religious prohibitions in all cultures have a survivalist foundation. In the case of the *Makach Kadeek*, the prohibition is no doubt based on the distorted remnants of earlier scientific understanding, from before Martian civilization went into decline.

"I should start by explaining the device itself. Depending on the orientation of its grain, which appears to follow an internal energetic field in the wood we do not yet understand—depending on the orientation of that grain from tangent, a length of liftwood provides either greater or lesser repulsion from a gravitational mass. This much you already know.

"Now imagine a waterwheel, but with liftwood planks in place of the paddles."

"Like blades," I said, "with one edge facing in and one out."

"Good lad. Now suppose you add something to your wheel. Suppose you add a clever but mathematically very simple system of gears to the attachment points of the liftwood panels, gears which control the orientation of those panels, and tie that orientation to the position of the panels on the wheel. This orients them so that all of the panels on one side generate a repulsive force but those on the other side are neutral. The repulsive force 'lifts' one side of the wheel but not the other. This makes the wheel turn. As the panels come around, the gear mechanism keeps them turned in such a way that they always are neutral on one side of the wheel and repulsive on the other."

"Okay, I get it," I said. "The wheel goes round and round forever. A *Forever* Engine. Good name."

No, wait . . .

"Tesla has made a perpetual motion machine? That's crazy. There's no such thing, can't be, even in a place as screwy as this. I took high school physics. The universe is the universe. There's only so much stuff in it, whatever that stuff is and however it interacts. You still have conservation of matter and energy."

"And momentum," Thomson added. "Do not forget momentum, Jack. You are perfectly correct. A perpetual motion machine is impossible, in the sense it is normally understood, for the very reason you set forth: conservation of matter, energy, and momentum. But a Forever Engine is not a true perpetual motion machine for two reasons.

"First, liftwood simply does not remain active forever. It deteriorates over time, not only in a physical sense, like ordinary wood, but also in terms of its repulsive properties. So a Forever Engine will eventually run down simply from exhaustion of the field characteristics of its lifters.

"But more importantly, the Forever Engine does not create energy from nothing. I now believe, based on what you told me in London, that liftwood redistributes momentum in a system. Normally the gross momentum in the system would remain constant overall. A flier takes off, but later it lands. Even while aloft, the center of mass of the planet and the flyer moves infinitesimally, but their combined momentum within the solar system remains unchanged. You see?"

"I think so."

"Good. But this device actually allows its maker to convert momentum to work energy. In this case, Tesla is charging his giant Leyden jar with electricity generated from that momentum. He gains his energy at the *price* of momentum."

"What momentum?" I asked.

"The Earth's orbital momentum. We believe Mars was originally farther from the sun than its current orbit. The use of Forever Engines as power-generating devices slowed its orbit and caused it to move closer to the sun, began its warming and the subsequent decline of its civilization. That much, I believe, is now clear. And the Martians must have eventually understood it as well."

There was a moment of silence around the chart table as everyone thought that over. Well, everyone but me. How restless the natives were on Mars wasn't my problem.

"That still leaves us with the question of what we plan to do once we get there," I said. Thomson looked up at me and then over to Captain Gordon. Gordon looked around the circle of faces a moment before realizing the call was his.

"Well—I should think that much was clear. Learn what we can about his operation."

Wolfenbach shifted his weight and nearly knocked an inkwell from a side table behind him. Thomson scratched his beard and then shook his head.

"Daunting as I find the prospect, I am afraid our charge is rather more than simply gathering facts. General Buller expects us to deal with the problem, and it becomes clear Tesla has potentially enormous power at his disposal. Whether these incidents which brought us Professor Fargo were entirely Tesla's doing or not, he clearly has some scheme in train. I cannot think it anything but reckless to let him play out that scheme uninterrupted. No, I fear our mission must now be to penetrate his lair and either capture or kill the villain."

Well, that was *their* plan. Mine was going to have to have some embellishments.

Eat, drink, and be merry, or so Ecclesiastes recommends. That night it seemed like pretty good advice, at least the heavy drinking part.

Gabrielle left us to rejoin "Renfrew," and within minutes Gordon left as well, his sullen glare keeping the revelers at arms' length, which that evening spoke volumes about the broadcast power of his personality. Every time Thomson or I turned around, someone offered, *"ein Prosit der Gemütlichkeit!"*—a toast to good fellowship—and they meant it. Hard not to drink to that.

So we ate *Thüringer* brats and *Steckerlfisch*—really delicious little fish grilled on a stick—washed down with too many steins of *Märzenbier.* The *Märzenbier* packed a punch, more like malt liquor, and, before we saw it coming, Thomson and I were both arm in arm, one stumble away from knee-crawling drunk.

In a more lucid moment, I noticed the normally cheerful Thomson increasingly drifting into melancholy. We sat on a low stone wall slightly out of the main traffic pattern and nursed our beer for a while.

"What's eating you, Professor?"

"Tyndall haunts me. We were friends, you know, before all this

Darwin business. As God's my witness, I wish I'd never heard Darwin's name!"

I remembered something from back in London, maybe from Buller's office, something about disproving Darwin's theory of natural selection. The details were fuzzy.

"Gotta stick by your guns," I said, but just to make him feel better.

"Magnetism is an interest of mine, you know that. But temperature is my true passion. Heating, cooling, that's the history of the cosmos, laddie. Everything else is . . . side effects. No one knows heating and cooling as I do. Not half a dozen men can even understand the equations I've derived to model the cooling of the Earth."

"Well, there you go," I said, but he shook his head.

"You don't understand. Temperature—it's all I've got. It's my legacy, and . . . I made an error."

"An error?"

"Aye, an error in computation. The Earth is older than my calculations, old enough . . . perhaps . . . I don't know. But no one's noticed the mistake yet, even though it's been published for over a decade. Who would think to double-check Billie Thomson's sums on something that important, on something about *temperature*? No one but me."

He stared down at his beer stein. No wonder he felt haunted by Tyndall's ghost.

"Well, your secret's safe with me, pal," I said, and patted his back.

He turned and looked at me, eyes empty and hopeless.

SEVENTEEN

October 6, 1888, Munich, Bavaria

I rose early, my head throbbing from too much beer the night before and too much bizarre science. I left the hotel in my improvised running clothes and began jogging under a pale pinkie-gray sky that promised another glorious autumn day. Only a few clouds drifted overhead, and the heavy dew would vanish like magic as soon as the sun showed itself.

I had the streets almost to myself. Down the block a solitary milk wagon made its way, four young boys running back and forth from the open sides to front steps, delivering tin jugs of milk and boxes of butter, panting to keep up as the wagon made steady progress down the street. Another block away I saw a carnival wagon, maybe an early departure from the fair. Other than that, everyone was sleeping it off.

I ran it off instead. I had things to do, a body that wasn't ready to do them, and not enough time, so I ran even though I would rather have rolled over and drifted back into my erotic dream of Gabrielle Courbiere. I might have done so anyway if I hadn't had to pee.

Besides, the dream had become disturbing. She had undressed, and under the black riding habit she was a robot—a shapely robot, like out of Fritz Lang's *Metropolis*, but a robot nonetheless—and it hadn't bothered dream-me. In fact, dream-me was part robot, too. What the hell did that mean?

So I ran. I ran to purge my body of toxins, to harden it for the coming trials, and to scourge it for my sins. I ran to forget unbidden dreams, and I ran to think, to make sense of the inexplicable—trips to Mars on gossamer wings!

Our hotel was a couple blocks south of the *Fliegerplatz*. Despite the cool morning I'd worked up a good sweat by the time I rounded the corner onto Landsberger *Strasse* and the *Fliegerplatz* came into view. I jogged east now, toward the red pre-dawn, with the *Fliegerplatz* to my left. Not much stirred except for a smallish dirigible ahead of me, descending for a landing from the east. I watched it glide almost silently across the Landsberger *Strasse*, nearly brushing the uplifted branches of the chestnuts and oaks and I felt the adrenaline surge as I saw its unmarked black sides. I watched helplessly as it passed directly over the bulk of *Intrepid*, dark and silent on its tie-down pad, and as it passed over I saw a shower of small objects cascade from the dirigible onto the British cruiser. The explosions were small, but there were many of them, crackling like fireworks, all mixed up with the shouts of alarm from the sailors on early watch and the chiming of action stations, all of the sounds soft and distant, not at all like genuine danger.

The dirigible did not land; its engines increased in volume as it climbed and turned to port, toward me, and it began making smoke—thick, oily black smoke, escaping in almost solid coils from the back of its enclosed cabin. I knew instantly it wasn't turning toward me; it was turning toward the hotel.

I sprinted back south across the broad boulevard and into an alleyway. The hotel was three blocks south and four west. My lungs burned for air by the time I reached the end of the alley, but I didn't let up. As I raced across the street, I glanced left. The dirigible cleared the roofs, coming diagonally toward me, no more than a hundred meters away. They'd see me, but from up there I'd just look like some local yokel running in panic.

That wasn't far wrong. I upped the speed, put everything I had into it, legs pounding like pistons, my heart feeling as if it were about to explode, and with no idea what I'd do when I got there. *Warn them!* my brain screamed.

The dirigible was going to get there before me. A warning was going to be too late, unless the dirigible had to mess around for a while trying to land. *Think!*

The hotel was on another broad east-west boulevard, Agnes-Bernauer *Strasse*. They'd have plenty of room to land the dirigible there, but they'd also see me coming from a long way if I went there and turned right.

At the next corner, a block short of Agnes-Bernauer, I turned right. My breath came in ragged gasps, the shadow of the dirigible passed over me, I felt a tingle in my scalp and up my spine, and then suddenly I had my second wind. Adrenaline is a marvelous thing. Behind me I heard the report of a large naval gun. Somebody on *Intrepid* had found a better way to sound the alarm than ringing a bell.

By the time I'd run the four short blocks west and turned into the alleyway, the dirigible had disappeared below the roof line ahead of me and its engines softened to idle. Smoke smelling of fuel oil settled into the streets and alleyways around me. Through the drifting smoke I saw the zeppelin now, or at least a very short segment of it between the buildings at the end of the alley, hovering twenty or more feet above the pavement. A rusty one-meter length of inch-and-a-half iron pipe lay against a trash can, and I picked it up as I jogged down the alley.

I paused at the end to catch my breath and get my heart rate under control. As I did so, I felt the familiar darkness tease at the edges of my vision. I did not fight it this time. I surrendered to it.

I looked cautiously around the corner, across and slightly down the street toward the hotel. Half a dozen ropes hung down from the dirigible, and several men on the ground held on to them, holding the airship in place against a soft breeze from the west, my right. None of them looked armed, and their attention was directed upward. The engine noise was louder out in the street. The carnival wagon I'd seen earlier was parked in front of the hotel, and as I watched, four men hustled Thomson, still in his nightshirt, down the front steps.

I took four or five long, fast strides out into the street and swung the pipe with both hands. The first man holding the rope never saw or heard me coming, and when the pipe cracked the back of his skull he went down like two hundred pounds of dead weight. The man beside him holding the same line started to turn toward me, his face distorted in horror, and the pipe crushed his left elbow, then his ribs, then his hip in three quick blows, and he was down.

The pipe felt good in my hands, balanced and lethal, as I ran toward the second group of linemen.

One of them saw the scuffle and alerted his partner. They let the rope go, and the first one drew a sheath knife from his belt. He held it up, as if to guard against me. I swung the pipe, and he made to duck it, stepping sideways. He ran into the other lineman, stumbled, and the pipe hit, driving the two of them to the pavement in a shower of the first one's blood and teeth.

The buoyancy of the dirigible changed and tugged the remaining linemen up, pulling their feet off the ground for a moment before they came back down. They literally had their hands full, so I ignored them and ran toward the men holding Thomson. The linemen were in dark uniforms, but these four were dressed in bright colors. Of course—*the circus wagon*—a pretty good cover for guys moving around early in the morning.

I heard a gunshot from above and behind me, felt a momentary burning sensation in my left shoulder, but the pain went as quickly as it had come. I was running fast, and the dirigible was bobbing. I'd have to be damned unlucky to get hit by another aimed shot before I got to the kidnappers.

Thomson's face lit up when he saw me. One man held the old Scotsman's arms behind his back, and the other three stepped forward to meet me, knives drawn. Fortunately none of them were packing pistols or this might have been a short fight. I shifted my grip on the pipe, held it like a short quarterstaff.

The first man lunged for me. I broke his wrist with a downward chop of the left end of the pipe and then took him down with a sharp right cross to the head. The other two went wide to either side of me. The quarterstaff grip was a mistake, wouldn't let me keep these two at a distance, and now I needed to fight for time. Police, the army, *somebody* had to be on their way to find out what the ruckus was all about.

I let the pipe slide back into a kendo grip. I launched an overhead swing at one attacker, followed him and swung again as he gave ground. Then I spun and swung from the shoulder at the other attacker, who I sensed, who I *knew*, was closing in on me from behind. He raised his arm to block the blow, and it made a sound like a stick of celery snapping when the pipe hit it. The man, face distorted in pain and broken left arm dangling limp at his side, started to back up, but not quickly enough. I swung again and he went down forever.

I turned back to the remaining thug, but he backed quickly down the sidewalk away from me. I looked to Thomson, but more men now crowded out of the hotel, some in the dark dirigible uniforms, some dressed like carnies—too many of them, and a couple had revolvers.

"*Kein Schiessen!*" I yelled at them. *"Ich bin Fargo. Der Alte Mann wunscht mich lebendig."*

Don't shoot. I'm Fargo. The Old Man wants me alive.

They hesitated; the barrels of the pistols dropped.

I raised the pipe above my head and charged.

EIGHTEEN

October 6, 1888, Munich, Bavaria

"Well, you've got guts, Yank, I'll give you that," O'Mara, the Royal Marine corporal from *Intrepid,* said, shaking his head and looking around. A half dozen of the men from his section along with two Bavarian policemen examined the bodies in the street while several more Marines checked out the hotel behind us room by room. A crowd of over a hundred curious locals clustered around, looking at the visible evidence of violence with the same mix of horror and fascination as motorists driving past a bad wreck.

"Thanks. You want to hold this for me?"

I was trying to bandage my left arm and it was hard to manage it with one trembling hand, especially since both of my arms felt as if they were filled with sand—really hot sand. Every muscle in my body seemed on fire.

He tied the bandage for me as Jenkins, a naval lieutenant from *Intrepid*, came out of the hotel and looked around.

"You did this by yourself? Unarmed?"

"I had a pipe."

"Remarkable," he said, shaking his head. "The Marines shot four of them when they opened fire, but you killed three men yourself. Injured more than that, I daresay, but they got them away."

"They got away with Thomson, too," I said. "That's what matters. Son of a bitch."

I'd gotten tangled up with the mob from the hotel, and the dirigible had dropped a sling and hoisted Thomson up. It dropped a whole bunch of lines with slings at the end. The thugs had overcome me by the time the Marines showed up, were dragging me toward the slings, but they got sloppy in their haste. They had sheathed their knives to use both hands, and I got hold of a nice heavy-bladed one, pulled it out of its sheath, and cut up two of the thugs pretty badly before they dropped me. With a dozen Marines pounding up the street and firing rifle shots, there wasn't enough time to deal with me again, so they grabbed the slings and called it a day. The dirigible had let loose a cascade of ballast water and shot up into the sky, gone just like that.

The water had washed most of the blood off the street.

Now what the hell was I going to do? Thomson was the closest thing I had to a friend here, my guide, the honcho of the expedition. Gordon was probably dead, or Tesla's men would have hauled him out as well.

"Better let our surgeon have a look at that later," Jenkins said, nodding to my arm. "Right now he's busy with casualties from the diversionary attack. Some sort of metal globes that unfolded into mechanical spiders after they landed. Devilish machines, and quite deadly."

"Yeah, I saw some in London. Not that hard to avoid once you get over the surprise, but pretty scary the first time."

He looked at me and frowned, clearly unsure what to make of me, a history professor who ran the decks of his ship every morning and who had done . . . this.

"You may have a broken bone or two as well. You do look frightful, I must say."

"I'm still a little groggy so I think I'll just sit here on the grass for a while, if that's okay."

I probably had a cracked rib or two and probably a mild concussion. Once I went down, they were pissed enough that, orders or no, they might have kicked and beaten me to death if the Marines hadn't shown up. My vision was blurry, and I was sure my nose was broken, but I still had all my teeth. That was good; the thought of having to visit whatever passed for a dentist here was pretty high up on my creepy nightmare list.

Gordon came out of the hotel with the last couple Marines. I experienced a flash of an unfamiliar emotion—pleasure at seeing him. He saw me and walked over, clearly still excited from his narrow escape.

"You're alive! Good Lord, what happened to you?"

"There was a fight. They captured Thomson and got him away. Where were you?"

"Thomson? Gone? I . . . I woke up and had to visit the water closet. I saw them on my way back, and when they tried to overpower me I broke away and made it to my room."

"Barricaded in right proper, 'e was," one of the Marines volunteered.

"You barricaded yourself in?" I asked.

"Yes, of course," he answered and looked around at the others. O'Mara stood and walked toward his men in the street, suddenly interested in what they were up to, and Jenkins and the other Marine followed him.

"I'm just one man," Gordon said. "What the devil did you expect me to do against that mob?"

"Your revolver was in your room. Shoot the first six of them and then beat the rest of them to death with your empty pistol. Or die trying."

He opened his mouth to reply, but no words came, perhaps because there was no anger or accusation in my voice. I simply said what I honestly expected of him. It's what everyone had expected of him, and, as he stood there, I think he knew it was what he ought to have expected of himself.

He looked away and frowned.

"Go to blazes, Fargo. I don't answer to you."

"No, you answer to Lord Chillingham. If we go back empty-handed, General Buller might be willing to give you a revolver and some privacy, but Chillingham won't. Have you met him? I have."

He looked back at me, anger and resentment mixed up with desperation and the hint of panic.

"Of course I've met him. He's my department head. It doesn't matter what you think," he said in a low voice. "Hate me if you like. You're nothing here."

I didn't hate him. I wasn't all that crazy about myself right then.

Not because I'd failed. Success and failure are often beyond our control. But I had killed three men, probably crippled as many more, and after all these years, it had been so fucking *easy!* Every day here took me further from the life I had built for myself, took me further from my daughter, Sarah, until even if I returned she might not recognize me.

Sarah found an old picture of me once, a picture I'd forgotten. For a while she kept it in a frame on the desk in her room. I never spoke to her about it, but after a while she put it in a drawer. She noticed I stopped coming into her room when it was out. She was always very sensitive that way.

The picture was taken in Afghanistan, at Bagram Air Base outside Kabul. There's an MH-60L Black Hawk helicopter from the 160th Aviation in the background on the tarmac, with me and the other eleven guys in my chalk in the foreground, six kneeling and six standing. I'm standing second from the left. We're not combat-loaded; we're just in desert camo pants and tee-shirts. I remember it was a hot day, but we don't look uncomfortable. We look as if all our lives up until that day had prepared us for that place, that moment, and nothing else. That's not true, but that's how we look.

I'm grinning, squinting in the sun, mouth wide and showing bared teeth, white against the brown of my tanned face. I look like a cheerful Doberman, well-adjusted and happy and dangerous. I look like Reggie Llewellyn, but I'm not. I'm not like Reggie Llewellyn.

Gordon stood there for a while, his anger running out of fire, and then he looked out into the street at the line of bodies.

"The Marines said you . . . who *are* you, Fargo?"

That was a pretty good question.

"I'm exactly what I told you. I'm a history professor from the University of Chicago. I specialize in the ancient world. When I was younger, I was a soldier, like you."

"Not like me," he said.

"Okay, not exactly like you. I was a warrant officer, not a commissioned officer. I was a translator, Middle-Eastern languages—Arabic, Pashto, Turkmen, and Daric Farsi. I'm not sure how useful that's going to be."

"We usually hire a local Johnny to do the translating."

"Yeah, how'd that work out for you in Afghanistan?"

His face clouded with anger again, and I could have kicked myself. He hadn't been to Afghanistan, he was ashamed of it, and I'd just rubbed his nose in it. If he froze up, either with anger or shame, this was the end of the road. Thomson was gone. Without Gordon there was no expedition, and then how would I save my world? How would I save Sarah from oblivion?

"You speak German as well," he said after a moment.

"Spanish and French, too. I've got an ear for languages."

He gestured out toward the bodies.

"And that? You didn't learn that as a translator, I'll warrant."

"I got carried away."

"Bloody hell, I should say so! Like some sort of whirling dervish, to hear those Marines tell it."

"Yeah, I know what it looks like, but I'm no super-warrior from the future. I'm a guy pushing middle age who did three tours in Afghanistan, went to school on army money, and made a pretty good life for myself. My passion is history, not homicide, and all I really want is to go back home."

He looked at me and he wasn't buying it, but it was the truth, sort of the truth—a simplified, sanitized version of the truth, but that was good enough for me right then.

"How did I learn to swing a pipe like that? It had nothing to do with the army. As an historian, I got interested in ancient fighting techniques, and I studied kendo. You've heard of it?"

He shook his head. He'd probably never heard of karate or kung fu, either.

"It's Japanese fencing with long two-handed swords, although we use a *shinai*—a bamboo stick—and practice in padded armor. I just went on autopilot and started cracking people's skulls."

"Autopilot," he repeated. I started to explain, but he waved me to silence.

"Very well, I suppose you may be useful for something. I'll at least need a German translator I can rely on. Right now I have to sort through Thomson's papers, see if there's any hint of a detailed plan there. You'd better come along in case any of them are in German."

I got painfully to my feet and started to follow him back into the hotel.

How much faith did I have in Gordon to pull this off? Absolutely none. Hopefully he could get me close enough that I could accomplish . . . what? What did I expect to find at the end of this road? A doorway back to my own time? That for starters, but it wasn't enough. Tesla might be the only guy who could figure this out, but how inclined to help was he going to be? I'd have to come up with some leverage, a bargaining position, some way to make him willing to help me or a way to force his hand.

That might mean preventing this expedition from killing or capturing him, which could be interesting.

And Thomson—somehow I had to get him out of this in one piece. I owed him too much to just walk away, although . . . if I was going to have to scrub this whole world anyway to save my own—this was getting very complicated.

"I suppose," Gordon said almost to himself, "the first thing we need is some tea."

Two hours later, Gordon and I had Thomson's papers and maps spread all over the table in his room, trying to figure out what resources we had and whether he'd actually come up with any sort of plan.

"What I don't understand is how they knew where we were staying. For that matter, how did they know we were even in Munich?" Gordon asked.

"Lousy security in London is my bet." I could have mentioned that Thomson had let slip to Tesla that Munich was our destination, but figured the old Scotsman had enough troubles right now.

Gordon tossed aside the folder of news clippings he had been looking through and shook his head.

"I'm more inclined to think that French tart had something to do with it."

"The charming *Mademoiselle* Courbiere? It's possible, I suppose, but not likely. This was a very elaborate operation, with people in place on the ground and the zeppelin in position to extract them. I don't think it was thrown together in a day. They knew we were coming in advance and had at least a couple days to get ready."

"And how did they know where we were staying?"

"That's the easy part: a guy on the ground watching to see where we went from the *Fliegerplatz*."

Gordon thought it through for a while, frowning the whole time, but he ended up nodding reluctantly.

"Very well, the information probably came from London, not *Mademoiselle* Courbiere."

"I am grateful for your confidence, *Capitaine* Gordon," Gabrielle said from the wardroom's doorway, and Gordon jumped in surprise. The events of the morning had pushed last night's dream out of my mind, but seeing her standing there brought it all flooding back.

"How long have you been here?" he demanded

"I arrived just this moment. The concierge showed me the way. You are injured, *Monsieur* Fargo. How serious it is?"

"I'll be okay. Tesla has Professor Thomson."

"*Oui*. This I hear. The expedition, it is done?"

"Is that all you care about?" Gordon asked, anger in his voice.

"*Non*," she answered. "But about that, it is my duty to care. Yours as well, *oui*?" She spoke without resentment, as if answering a question about the weather.

"The expedition is not done," I said. "Captain Gordon is now in command."

Her eyebrows rose slightly in reaction, but then she nodded.

"Of course. Our agreement, it is still good?"

"I'll have to think about that," Gordon answered.

Gabrielle shrugged and started to leave.

"Wait," I said hastily. She stopped, and both of them turned to look at me.

"It's your call, Gordon, but you can see what we have here to work with. Unless the Bavarians can loan us a battalion of flying monkeys with death rays, we're going to need all the help we can get."

Despite the tension of the moment, Gordon smiled.

"*Flying monkeys with death rays?* I don't think that very likely, so under the circumstances—yes, *Mademoiselle* Courbiere, I will be pleased to honor the agreement made between you and Dr. Thomson. We will be most grateful for any assistance you can provide in finding and apprehending Tesla."

He even made a little bow.

NINETEEN

October 7, 1888, Munich, Bavaria

I'd taken a real beating in front of the hotel, and I didn't understand how much until the next morning. We'd moved back over to *Intrepid* for security, and I shared a stateroom with Gordon. Fortunately he took the upper bunk. When I woke, I couldn't sit up in bed. I had to roll over onto my stomach, flop my legs off the bed onto the deck, push myself upright on my knees, and then stand up using the headboard for support. I felt as if I wore weights on my arms and legs, every joint was full of acid, and a couple key muscles just weren't present for duty. Unfortunately, calling in sick wasn't an option. My head was clear, so at least there was probably no brain damage.

My morning run was out, and I'd have liked another hour of sleep, but Harding had planned a service for the crew members of *Intrepid* who had been killed the previous day and in the first fight with the zeppelin. I wanted to attend. Gordon and I walked over together in silence, each with our own thoughts, under steel-gray skies that smelled of rain.

Gordon had come up with a plan yesterday which had the virtue of simplicity and directness but took those qualities to a dangerous extreme, in my opinion. Maybe he was trying to prove he wasn't the coward so many people thought he was. Fine, but he could do that on his own time. This put the whole mission at risk. More to the point for me, if Tesla was the key to getting me back to my own world, I didn't think shooting our way into his stronghold with a thousand Turkish infantry was the approach most likely to gain his cooperation. What *would* work with a megalomaniac who sent drugged-up fanatics and wind-up spiders across Europe to murder people who pissed him off was another question.

My problems weren't Gordon's, of course, nor were they Lord Chillingham's or the British crown's. As far as they were concerned, I was baggage and bait—annoying baggage and bait in Gordon's view. Any suggestions I made to him were likely to send him in the opposite direction, but we would meet with the Bavarians again after the funeral service. Hopefully somebody at the meeting would do my dirty work for me.

I'd been to two British military funerals in Afghanistan. This one was the largest, at least in terms of casualties: eighteen of them. That was a big hole knocked in a crew of only two hundred.

The bodies were sewn into white sacks made of sail canvas. They must have carried the canvas just for that purpose—*Intrepid* didn't mount sails. There weren't enough Union Jacks to cover all the bodies, so some were covered with white naval ensigns and some by simple bedsheets. All the covers—flags and sheets alike—were wrapped around the body bags and tucked under them to keep them from blowing off in the damp breeze. The bags were lined up in two rows of eight and then two others out front. That would be Lieutenant Longchamps and Ensign Conroy, the two officer casualties, leading the formation.

A company of Bavarian soldiers stood to one side of the arrayed bodies, the crew of *Intrepid* to the other, and an assortment of civilian workers from the *Fliegerplatz* made a ragged crescent between them, forming the bottom of a box protecting the silent dead. A line of Bavarian horse-drawn artillery caissons waited behind them to take the bodies to the military cemetery. Three Bavarian drummers, their drums muffled, provided the only music. An enclosed carriage arrived, and two passengers joined the officers of *Intrepid*: Gabrielle Courbiere and a tall, stout man dressed in black, complete with a black silk scarf over his face.

Harding stood before the company and began with the opening prayer.

"Loving God, you alone are the source of life. May your life-giving Spirit flow through us, and fill us with compassion, one for another. In our sorrow give us the calm of your peace. Kindle our hope, and let our grief give way to joy; through Jesus Christ our Lord. Amen."

The incongruity, the palpable unreality of the moment, washed over me like a cold wave. The South had won the Civil War, the Royal Navy had flying ironclads, there were colonies on Mars, but the Book of Common Prayer hadn't changed. What were the odds? But there was nothing unreal about the eighteen silent white sausages lying on the dark green grass of the landing ground.

We again met in *Intrepid*'s chart room, a more somber group this time, the cause made obvious by Thomson's absence. His place was taken by a young officer in the light blue uniform of the Bavarian Army, complete with dueling scar on his cheek and spiked helmet held under his arm.

I shifted my weight from one foot to the other. Too many damned meetings. It was time to get on with it, to just saddle up and go after these guys. That's not how it worked here. That's not how it worked anywhere except the movies. If it wasn't a meeting with the Bavarian police and army, it was tea with the Afghan village elders to see what they thought we should do next, not because we gave a shit what they thought, but because it made them feel better, for a while, to think we might.

"Captain Harding, what is *Intrepid*'s status?" Gordon asked.

"Short-handed but ready for action. Those blasted clockwork spiders killed one of my officers—young Conroy—and fourteen crewmen. I have six more still incapacitated, but there's no additional damage to her machinery.

"My position has been rendered somewhat complicated by other developments, however. As I am sure you all understand, the safety of the Royal Family is our paramount consideration. It should be obvious we have taken on board a special passenger. This afternoon we will lift off with a heading toward the British Isles."

"You will be returning to England?" Gordon asked.

"I did not say that," Harding answered. "What is important is that we be seen to leave with a heading toward England."

"Elvis has left the building," I said.

Everyone looked at me blankly.

"Renfrew has already left Munich," I explained. "This is a diversion. Who was that dressed up like him at the funeral?"

"Very good, Mr. Fargo," Harding said. "It was one of our black gang. He was the only one in the crew large enough to be convincing. A closed car was added to the morning train to Frankfurt."

"He was on that?" I asked.

"Perhaps," Harding said. "I don't know, to be honest. What I do know is that I also received coded orders this morning via cable through our consulate here, instructing me, once our diversionary demonstration is complete, to support your mission, which of course we will. The entire crew is anxious to strike back at those villains—cowardly bastards, leaving their dirty business to machines."

"What are your rules of engagement?" I asked.

"I beg your pardon?"

"What limits are placed on your actions?"

"Ah, yes. I am not to hazard my vessel beyond what I believe necessary to support the mission, a pretty way of saying if things go wrong it's my head on the chopping block. Well, so be it. More importantly I am under no circumstances to provoke hostilities with a foreign power. In this case that means I cannot enter Serbia, Rumania, or Bulgaria. I can send a small Marine landing party with you, but not in uniform. We do have permission to enter Austro-Hungarian and Turkish territory, however, and have promises of cooperation from those governments."

I had mixed feelings about that. Clearing things with the Austrians and Turks was probably necessary, but a lot of people knew a lot of stuff about this "secret" mission.

"This changes things, I suppose," Gordon said, "although I am not sure exactly how. Can we still count on your cooperation, Inspector Wolfenbach?"

The corpulent policeman bobbed his head, making his jowls quiver.

"Berlin says help, so *ja*, I assign three of my policemen to help. But after the attack yesterday I receive new instructions—from the *Prinz-regent* himself. Now we are joined by *Leutnant* von Schtecker and twenty volunteers from the *Bayerisch Garde Schützenkorps*, all *gut soldaten*, excellent shots, and all with some English."

The Bavarian army officer clicked his heels and did a little bow in Gabrielle's direction.

"We travel in civilian clothes, of course," the young lieutenant explained. "We say it is a hunting trip to Macedonia. Our rifles will be in the baggage until we need them."

"This attack stirred things up?" I asked.

"They ruin *Oktoberfest*," the lieutenant answered, the outrage plain in his voice. "Since the first festival was held we have only interrupted it twice, both times for war. Now a third time? Very well, war it shall be."

Something to remember if I ever wanted to conquer the world: don't get between the Bavarians and a good party.

Gordon unrolled *Intrepid*'s chart of Serbia and pointed to the mountains along its southwest frontier with Turkish Bosnia and Montenegro.

"We are happy to have you, Leftenant. The plan was to have Inspector Wolfenbach direct the *Hochflieger Ost* to make an unscheduled landing somewhere south of Belgrade and drop us off. Now the attack here has caused the zeppelin line to postpone the departure of the *Hochflieger* from Berlin for several days. Perhaps that is to our advantage."

"With Thomson in his hands, how can a delay be good?" Harding asked.

"If Tesla knows all the rest, he may know of the arrangements with the zeppelin line as well," Gordon said. "If he already expects the attack to come from the *Hochflieger*, its delay gives us the ability to attack by a different route, by surprise. We'll have to move quickly, though. The potential for surprise will last only until the next actual passage of the *Hochflieger*.

"Inspector Wolfenbach, if you would post armed guards on the hotel where we were staying, it will help convince any prying eyes that Mr. Fargo and I are still there, waiting for the arrival of the *Hochflieger*."

"*Ja, sehr gut*," Wolfenbach answered.

"Captain Harding, I'd like *Intrepid* to take the entire party to the Austrian military base at Ujvidék, south of Budapest on the Serbian frontier. From there we will take off after dusk and make a high-speed run to the southwest, follow the Turkish side of the frontier all the way down to"—he leaned over the map to read the name—"Višegràd. That's approximately one hundred miles, so we should be able to make it there in four hours from Ujvidék. Does that sound correct?"

Harding leaned over and studied the map, did a quick measurement using map calipers.

"Now that we've got the portside drive shaft straightened and two airscrews mounted, we can make twenty knots again. If we stay well above the mountains, yes, we can make it in four hours. Landing would be tricky except we should be able to descend into the valley of the Drina River here. Let me think. We can make Ujvidék from here in a little under a day. If we leave this afternoon and run through the night, we arrive tomorrow afternoon. That means making the approach run tomorrow night. It's a new moon, so the only light we'll have coming down will be starlight. If this overcast continues we'll have to use floodlights for landing, but that shouldn't be a problem. Yes, four hours there and perhaps half an hour to find your village and land you."

"Good. You drop us off along with Leftenant von Schtecker's men and as many Marines as you can spare. You make full speed back to Ujvidék. I'd like you back on your tie-down pad by dawn," Gordon finished.

Harding straightened up and nodded again.

"Yes, with no one the wiser as to where we've been. Confusion to the enemy. Good show. And you?"

"The armed party will remain hidden," Gordon said, "and we'll need supplies and field gear—tents, rations for a week, that sort of thing. Leftenant von Schtecker, can you arrange for that?"

"*Jawohl, Herr Hauptmann*," the Bavarian officer answered.

"Good. While you establish our camp in the hills, Fargo and I will contact the Turkish authorities. Mr. Fargo will serve as my translator."

"You speak Turkish?" Harding asked.

"Turkmen," I answered. "Close enough."

It wasn't all that close in my own time because in the early twentieth century the Turks had reformed their language, gotten rid of all the Farsi and Arabic borrow words which Turkmen still had. The two languages were actually closer in this world, at least in theory. I figured I could get by.

"After we determine what assistance the Turks will render," Gordon continued, "we will conduct a reconnaissance of the border, determine the best route of advance, and make our way east to Kokin Brod. Given the information Captain Harding has supplied, and the instructions Dr. Thomson was given, I expect at least a battalion of Turkish infantry, and likely a full brigade. Of course, we can't count on Turks for anything lively, but our Marines and Leftenant von Schtecker's men should serve for that.

"From what *Mademoiselle* Courbiere tells us, there are no regular Serbian troops at Kokin Brod—if the Serbs can be said to have regulars at all. Tesla's followers are fanatics, their courage fortified by narcotics, but it is the sort of courage best applied to raids and surprise descents. I find it highly unlikely they will stand for more than a volley or two against well-armed infantry.

"Are there any questions?"

I waited, looked around the table, hoping someone would speak up. Gordon might listen to Harding or either of the Bavarians, but he still wasn't likely to pay any attention to what I had to say. Unfortunately, the three other military types stood there nodding like bobble-heads.

"Just a thought," I said. "Why don't we try sneaking in, keeping the element of surprise?"

"Sneak in with five hundred or a thousand men?" Lieutenant von Schtecker asked. "How?"

"No. I'm thinking a small group to go in, probably the Marines and your riflemen, *Herr Leutnant*. The Turks would follow up and cover the withdrawal. I guess what I'm saying is, why shoot our way in and out, when maybe we can sneak in?"

Von Schtecker looked like he was thinking it over, when Gordon stepped in.

"Mr. Fargo is a professor of history in America. He has an academic's approach to problems—too complicated by half. Simple is better; hit them hard and fast."

"Hard I understand," I said. "It's the fast I'm foggy about. How are you—"

"That's enough, Fargo. We'll work out the details when we can see the lay of the land. But in outline I think we are in agreement, yes?"

All the bobble-heads nodded. It wouldn't do for a serving officer to take sides with some icky academic guy.

"Actually, this use of stealth, it seems sensible," Gabrielle said.

"While I appreciate the intelligence you have shared with us, *Mademoiselle*, I insist that you allow the military men to deal with military matters," Gordon answered. "Now, one more thing. It will be a difficult trek, across very mountainous terrain. I hope you will not take offense, Inspector, but I believe Bavaria's contribution to the expedition will be more than satisfied by the information you can give us and Leftenant von Schtecker's riflemen. I see no need for you to personally accompany us."

"*Natürlich*," Wolfenbach answered. "You are not Hannibal, after all."

Wolfenbach wasn't quite as big as an elephant, but close enough. They all laughed except for Gabrielle, who seemed confused by the reference.

TWENTY

October 7, 1888,
***Aboard Her Majesty's Aerial Ship* Intrepid,**
Aloft over Bavaria and Austria

The rest of the morning and early afternoon we saw to fitting everyone into the confines of *Intrepid*. The dent in her crew made it a little easier, but there was still a lot of disruption. Officers doubled up to accommodate Gordon, von Schtecker, and myself, and Gabrielle got Lieutenant Jenkins' cabin all to herself. The Bavarians got their own section of the crew common quarters, but there were only fourteen berths for twenty men, and, like the rest of the crew, they'd have to hot-bunk it.

We reprovisioned as well, and the Bavarians brought tents and wooden boxes of spare rifle ammunition aboard.

"What you ought to have along is one of those new Maxim guns," Lieutenant Jenkins said as we watched the deck hands carry the supplies below deck. "We're due to get Maxims next refit, but that's not until this winter. We could let you have one of our 8-barrel Nordenfelts, but they're too heavy to haul up and down mountains."

I had some experience humping things through mountains, and I wasn't looking forward to that part of the trip. We'd have to carry probably eight days of food with us, ammunition, at least some climbing gear, and either blankets or greatcoats. It was going to get cold up there and probably wet, if the thickening clouds and rising wind were any indication. We could go part of the way by river, but at some point we were going to have to carry stuff over some crappy-looking mountain roads.

No, we wouldn't be taking along an 8-barrel Nordenfelt, whatever that was.

We lifted off about mid-afternoon and headed north. Once we were out of sight of curious eyes in Munich, we made a wide turn to starboard and ended up heading southeast toward Austria and the Balkans. Visibility closed down to a mile or two and the white wooden deck planks started darkening with a light rain. Massive grumbling thunderheads, flickering deep inside with lightning, pursued us from the west, but we seemed to be keeping our lead for the moment.

The sun disappeared behind the storm front, and we lost whatever remaining light was left within an hour. About six o'clock I saw the lights of a large city off our starboard beam—Salzburg. A signal light blinked cheerfully from the ground, and a signalman clacked back an answer from the Aldis lamp above the bridge. From here on we would be in Austrian air space.

Dinner in the officer's mess that evening turned out to be far more interesting than I had expected. Conroy and Thomson were missing, but Gabrielle and von Schtecker had taken their place, so the number at table ended up the same—ten, since two of the ship's officers were on rotating duty at all times.

Gordon was quiet and withdrawn throughout the meal, glancing at the decanter of red wine on the table once in a while but staying with hot tea. Von Schtecker was also quiet, perhaps because his English was good enough for a professional meeting but not really up to witty repartee. Or possibly he simply didn't care much for British officers, or sailors of any nationality, or people sent by Berlin who had brought a truckload of trouble with them.

Gabrielle, not surprisingly, quickly became the center of attention. For *Intrepid*'s young officers, her presence was a form of sublime torture. On the one hand, she was a strikingly good-looking woman of open and friendly disposition. On the other hand, she was French, a Communard, and an agent of *Le Garde Rouge* to boot. How were they, as officers, to react to that? For guidance they looked to their captain, who seemed in a friendly enough mood.

"Tell me, *Mademoiselle*, how long before you make General Secretary Renault emperor?" he asked as the cook ladled out the steaming potato soup. The officers laughed politely at the captain's joke.

"Me?" she asked. "It is not for me to make the emperors."

"Your people, I meant. It's rather a tradition, isn't it? First Consul Bonaparte became Emperor Napoleon I. President Louis-Napoleon became Emperor Napoleon III. You seem to have skipped Napoleon II, but the pattern seems clear enough."

Although it was phrased as good-natured banter, I didn't like what Harding was doing. He was showing off, trying to embarrass Gabrielle for the amusement of his officers. That's not how I was raised to treat dinner guests.

Gabrielle frowned for a moment in thought, as if actually taking the question seriously. Perhaps she was.

"Well, those were mistakes, you see. I believe most French people understand that. Do the English not?"

I saw a couple faces cloud over then, but one officer covered his smile with his napkin, and another nodded in agreement, pleased at how adroitly Gabrielle had turned the question around on his captain. I wasn't so sure.

Harding looked around, his smile even broader than before.

"Well, I dare say we do, *Mademoiselle*. I dare say we do. It is most agreeable to hear that sentiment shared on your side of the Channel. Now if only you had a proper royal family, things might start looking up over there."

"Ah, but we do, *Capitaine*. In fact, we have three: the Bonapartés, the Orléans, and the Bourbons. The politicians pay no attention to any of them, but that is like your own country, *oui?*"

Harding's smile disappeared, and he put down his spoon before answering.

"I wouldn't say that, Ma'am."

"Really? My friend Baron Renfrew says it all the time," she answered, and then she sipped her soup. "Oh, this is quite good!"

She looked up at the momentarily frozen faces around the table. "What is wrong? Is the soup not good?"

"I think it's great," I answered.

"Yes, it's capital, I'd say," an earnest young midshipman to my right added, followed by a half-dozen other hurried expressions of agreement, to which Gabrielle smiled happily.

Through the fish and then the main course of roast beef, Harding launched repeated argumentative storming parties against Fortress

France, all of them disguised as amusing jokes, all of them taken as neither jokes nor insults by Gabrielle, and all of them ending in Harding's red-faced retreat in the face of a defense as impervious to the attack as it was apparently oblivious to it. Watching this was the most fun I'd had since showing up here.

By the dessert, a plum pudding, Harding had lapsed into defeated silence, but the conversation went on without him. His officers' fascination with and admiration for Gabrielle had only grown with her repeated brilliant escapes from Harding's cunningly-constructed traps.

Was I the only person here who got it? Was I the only one who saw all she was doing was taking the questions literally and then answering them? Apparently so. Maybe this was how most beautiful women got a reputation for brilliant conversation: just about anything coming out of their mouths sounded pretty good. It wasn't that Gabrielle Courbiere was dumb; she was well-read and obviously intelligent. She just seemed oblivious to the most basic social cues.

Over glasses of port the younger officers drew her into a conversation about the ethics of spying, which she naturally answered with the argument that patriotism required service to one's country in whatever capacity a person had.

"But *Mademoiselle*, to what lengths can one take that?" the young gunnery lieutenant, whose name I'd forgotten, asked.

"How do you mean?"

"*Mademoiselle* Courbiere," he said, and then he paused to let the drama build, as if he were the prosecutor and she the defendant in the dock, "would you cut a throat for France?"

"It depends upon the throat," she answered, and then she looked around the table as if the answer were obvious.

And it was, but that did not stop *Intrepid*'s officers from regarding her with a mix of fear and fascination, as if she were a beautiful yet deadly creature from another world. More than either beautiful or deadly, though, they saw her as exotic, enigmatic.

Who could believe she was simply an open book? None of these guys, that was for sure.

When we finished, half the men offered her their arm to escort her safely to her cabin, as if it were ten miles up the Rio Orinoco instead of twenty steps down the hall. I couldn't blame them. The memory of my erotic dream of her two nights before had returned, and my imagination had tacked on a few new embellishments.

She smiled politely to the officers but turned to me.

"Mr. Fargo has promised to tell me his life story and tonight may be our last opportunity for some time. Will you join me in my cabin?"

Sure.

If I'd imagined her sitting languidly, elbow on table and chin resting on her hand, eyes locked on mine in rapt attention as I told the remarkable tale of how I came to this time—and maybe I had imagined that just a little bit—I was completely wrong. Gabrielle's cabin was as small as the one I shared with two other officers, and the ventilation was not as good, so it felt warm and stuffy as soon as we got there. She gave me the only chair and sat in her bunk cross-legged, another advantage of a riding habit instead of a conventional dress. She took a journal and a pencil from the table by her bed, opened it to a blank page, rested it on the desk made by her crossed knees, and nodded for me to begin.

The deal had been to tell her everything about how I came here, and a deal's a deal. I started with what I knew about the research project in Wessex, then my background as a historian, then the world I came from in more and more detail, but steering clear of the subject of aeronautics and the space program. She asked probing questions, particularly about my kendo training and before that my military experience. She took pages of notes in a small, careful handwriting which looked almost machinelike in its regularity.

The room grew warmer as I talked, and I began to perspire. I noticed that she did as well, her skin glistening in the gaslight. After about an hour, she puffed out a breath and stood up from the bunk. She unbuttoned the jacket of her riding habit and took it off, then unfastened her skirt and slipped it down and off, leaving her in blouse and riding breeches. She unbuttoned the collar and cuffs of her blouse and rolled the sleeves up almost to her elbows. Then she sat back on the bunk and picked up her journal.

"Better," she announced.

"Do you mind if I take off my jacket?"

I felt foolish asking, but it seemed the thing to do here.

"No, why would I?" she asked, looking up from her notes. I had already learned none of her questions were rhetorical; when she asked a question she expected an answer.

"Well, some ladies might consider it a sexual advance."

"You do not make the sexual advance?"

I almost said no, but then I thought better of it.

"I do not mean the removal my coat as a sexual advance. I may make a sexual advance later, if I feel it would be appropriate."

She thought for a moment.

"What would determine whether or not it was appropriate?"

"I would only consider it appropriate if I felt you would welcome it."

"I see. You have the eyes which are kind, sad, and hard, all at the same time. But when you laugh, your eyes laugh first. Yes, I think I would welcome such an advance, but first I would like to know more about a thing—what did you call it?—the Tesla effect."

I told her everything I knew about the Tesla Effect, which took all of about fifteen seconds.

TWENTY-ONE

October 8, 1888,
***Aboard Her Majesty's Aerial Ship* Intrepid,**
Aloft over Austria

The next morning I woke in the darkness and felt the rhythmic vibration of *Intrepid*'s engines through the bunk, felt the warmth and slower rhythm of Gabrielle's engine beside me. Her back rested against my chest in the narrow bunk, her bare shoulder rising and falling as she snored softly. For an instant, it was the best morning I'd had since coming here, perhaps the best morning in years. Then a wave of panic swept over me. *What the hell was I doing?*

I pulled away and sat up on the edge of her bunk, sat there shivering, appalled at what I'd done.

When Sarah was just six or seven, my wife and I had taken her to a seafood restaurant. We had to wait before being seated, and Sarah spent the time studying the tank of lobsters which stood beside the hostess station like an aquarium in the doctor's office. After a while, she began naming the lobsters, and I knew: no lobster tonight, maybe never again.

I had called Gabrielle *Gabi* last night, over and over in our mutual passion, our entwined dance of life as we hurtled toward a rendezvous which would enable me, if all went well, to snuff out this time and everyone in it to save my own.

Gabi—naming the lobsters.

Behind me she stirred, then stretched a little, and yawned.

"Ah," she said. "You are awake."

"Yeah." I got up and started to dress. For a moment she rested on her stomach, chin propped on folded arms, face obscured by a soft tangle of golden curls. Then, nude and unselfconscious, she sat up on the bed, crossed her legs, and pushed her hair away from her face. I had never imagined a Victorian woman remotely like her.

"Gabi—*mon surnom*. You would say nickname? Do you have the nickname for your daughter?"

"The Terminator."

Like an incantation, her name summoned her, and, for a moment, if only in my mind, Sarah was there, about twelve or thirteen years old. I guess we always think of our kids as younger than they really are, just as we think of ourselves that way. Sarah looked at me with her knowing smirk, one eyebrow raised when she looked at Gabrielle, torn between approval of "Daddy's hottie" and vague distaste at the idea of "old people sex."

Then she was gone, and my cheeks were wet and my lungs empty of air.

Gabrielle studied me, frowning slightly in concentration.

"You fear for your daughter, she will be impoverished if you do not return?"

I caught my breath and wiped my eyes.

"I fear she no longer exists. But if she does, I had good life insurance. Plus she'll get my IRA and the condo on Lake Shore Drive."

Gabrielle had that look that said she had no idea what I'd just said.

"Trust me, financially she'll be fine."

"What of her mother and siblings?"

"There's only her—her mother died when she was eight."

"Ah, so you are her only family. You fear she will be alone."

"No, she's still got two grandparents alive, plus a bunch of uncles, aunts, and cousins, mostly on my late wife's side of the family. We've stayed close to them."

She looked more confused than before. I was, too. I'd spoken about Sarah as if I would never see her again, as if she would go on but without me. I would save her, somehow. But would I be able to face her afterwards, knowing what I had had to do to accomplish that?

The duty officer had rigged a set of pistol targets to a long outrigger off the port side near the stern, where the Marines normally took rifle drill. I'd already stashed my new revolver, fresh from *Intrepid*'s arms locker, there along with my towel and a box of cartridges. Gordon showed up with his own revolver about when I finished my run. Gordon being up and moving shortly after dawn, and not visibly hung over, was a good sign.

"I see they gave you one of the new Webleys," Gordon said, looking it over. "Do you need help with this? I imagine it's different than the weapons you are used to."

"Thanks. Let me see if I can figure it out first."

With a six-inch barrel, the Webley had a nice heft to it, about two and a half pounds. It smelled of gun oil, and, if it had ever been fired, it had been carefully cleaned afterwards. It was the break-open kind, the frame hinged forward and below the cylinder. I found the release catch and opened it, checked the cylinder to make sure it was empty, then clicked it shut. I cocked it and dry fired it, then dry fired it a couple more times from the hammer-down position. The action was stiff, but the trigger pull was even, if a bit long.

I dug a handful of cartridges out of the box of fifty, slipped all but six of them in my trouser pocket, and loaded. They were nice big cartridges, about the size of a .45.

Gordon had his revolver out as well now. It was different looking, slightly smaller and more complicated in design, with what looked like a hinged lever below the barrel in front of the cylinder.

"It's an Enfield," he explained. "Slightly larger bore, a four-seven-six as opposed to your four-fifty-five, but with a shorter cartridge. I think it makes it more controllable when firing."

I didn't say anything, as part of my new policy to avoid irritating Gordon any more than necessary, but I couldn't help remembering how the "more controllable" low-powered bullet had bounced right off the hashshashin's body armor in London.

"You a pretty good pistol shot?" I asked him.

Instead of answering, he raised the Enfield, took careful aim, and fired at the target on the outrigger. His pistol made a healthy bang and left my ears ringing.

"Jesus, do you guys do anything to protect your ears when you're shooting? It's a wonder you aren't all deaf as posts."

Gordon looked at me as if good hearing was for sissies.

The target was about twenty yards out, so I could see the hole, one ring out from the center. This wasn't competition shooting, so in the black was good enough as far as I was concerned, especially since the target frame was shaking a bit from the wind and engine vibration. The shooting was fine, but his stance was terrible, sideways with his right shoulder forward, right arm straight out, left arm at his side. It was the classic dueling pose, probably good for standing inside a red-coated square and picking off Fuzzy-Wuzzies, but worthless in the sort of combat we were likely to see.

I dug some cotton out of my kit, chewed on it to get it wet, and packed it in my ears, then took my stance—left shoulder forward, both arms slightly bent, left hand supporting and steadying the pistol hand. I raised the pistol but ignored the sights and just focused my eyes on the target. I fired three shots in as quick a succession as I could manage, given the stiff action, and then took a step to the left. The recoil had been strong but controllable. That's the beauty of a heavy pistol like the Webley or the Colt .45 automatic: it can handle a powerful round and not jump all over the place. It felt good to shoot.

Without lowering the Webley, I scanned the target for signs of light.

"Not very good shooting, I'm afraid," Gordon said. "Only one shot even on the paper."

I fired three more rounds, took another step to the left, and then immediately broke open the revolver. A release wheel popped all six empty casings out.

"Better," Gordon said. "At least you're on the paper and one round is in the black. There probably wasn't much call for a translator to actually fire his weapon."

"You wouldn't think so," I answered.

I dug six more rounds out of my pocket, but without a speed loader it took way too long to get all of them in. As soon as I did, I clicked the Webley shut and raised it back into my tactical stance, fired three rounds, and took two steps to the right.

"You might try firing just one round until you've got the hang of it," Gordon said, but then frowned when he looked at the target. "That's actually a rather good grouping. Still low and to the right."

Three more rounds, step to the right, revolver open, spent brass tinkling on the deck.

"Still low and right, not quite as tight as last time, but respectable. Keep at it. You may end up able to hit something after all."

"Thanks. Say, do me a favor, would you? At least keep an open mind about the plan?"

He turned and walked away without answering me. He'd fired a total of one round. For what? Was it even worth cleaning his pistol for one round? Well, that was his business, not mine. I had thirty-eight rounds out of the box still to fire.

Twenty-four rounds later, as I broke open the revolver and ejected the spent brass, Gabi spoke from behind me.

"You have many strange habits while you shoot," she said.

I turned to her and pulled the cotton out of my left ear. She sat on an equipment locker, had on riding breeches and a lacy blouse with big sleeves, open at the throat as if she'd dressed hurriedly. Her loose hair floated around her face in the wind

"Hey, I thought you were going to sleep in."

I clicked the revolver closed. I had started experimenting with holding pairs of rounds between my fingers, like a speed strip, and I was getting faster at reloading.

"Who can sleep with all this bang-bang-bang? Why do you step to the side after you shoot, as if you are dancing?"

"People under stress lose their peripheral vision. They see the world as if through a tunnel. If you step to the side, you step out of their tunnel, and it confuses them. They have to take a moment and look for you."

"Surely not! This is a joke, *oui?*"

"Not a joke, *cheri*. Have you ever fainted?"

She nodded.

"Before you faint, first you lose your peripheral vision, then your central vision loses fine resolution and color. Remember? It is because certain parts of your brain become starved for oxygen. People under stress have similar experiences."

She frowned and thought about that for a moment. Finally she nodded.

"*Bien*. But the target, it does not shoot back. Why make the mincing step now?"

I hadn't thought of it as *mincing*, and I didn't much care for the image that brought to mind.

"If someone does shoot at me, I will be under stress as well. I may forget to step sideways up here." I tapped my head with my fingertips.

"I have to remember it down here," and I tapped my leg, "so I do it over and over again. It's like whistling. You have to think about how to do it at first, but after you whistle enough you don't think about how to make your lips form a certain shape to make a certain sound. You only think the sound, and your lips remember how to do the rest."

"Really? I cannot whistle," she said. "Can you teach me?"

That was something I was learning about Gabi: if you weren't careful, you could get whiplash from the sudden changes of direction in the conversation.

"Sure. I taught Sarah."

"The Terminator," Gabi said, and then looked out past the target outrigger at the clouds floating near the rusty-gold horizon. "If possible you will leave us to return to her, your daughter." She made it a statement, not a question. "Our time has not been kind to you so far. But if it were, you would still leave, yes?"

"Of course."

She turned and looked me in the eyes.

"It is not because she needs you. This you have told me already. It must be because you need her. But why?"

And that was Gabi, too. Maybe everyone who knew my real story wondered that, but none asked it. It was personal, and of course they all knew the answer, or at least knew how *they* would answer the question, which to them was the same thing because they believed that everyone was pretty much the same inside as they were. But Gabi had no such illusions.

"Don't you feel that way about someone in your family?" I asked.

"There is no family. I was my mother's only child. She was not married, so she lived in the convent for a while, and then she left and now she is dead. I was raised by the nuns. I never met my father." She shrugged as if to say this was no tragedy, it was simply what was.

"So tell me why," she repeated. "Please."

I almost didn't answer, but there was an aching need in her question—not a need for me, but rather a need to understand the world around her. It was the first evidence of emotional vulnerability I had seen in her, and it opened my eyes. I understood her. For a moment, just a moment, I saw the world through her head, and none of the people in it made any sense. They argued, laughed, loved, raged, wept, and all for reasons which defied her understanding, all seemingly at random.

A wave of melancholy swept over me as I realized the extent to which she was alone in the world, and probably always would be, standing on the outside of a house watching the party inside through a window, smiling at the jokes she couldn't quite make out, wondering at the cascades of inexplicable emotions, separated from all of it by a single pane of glass which she had no means of breaking.

She at least deserved an honest answer, even if she wouldn't understand that, either.

"It's the only relationship in my life I haven't fucked up."

She looked at the clouds and thought about that for a while.

"It must be good to have such a relationship," she said at last.

I sat down on the locker next to her and put my arm around her, and she rested her head on my shoulder.

TWENTY-TWO

October 8/9, 1888,
***Aboard Her Majesty's Aerial Ship* Intrepid,**
Aloft over Turkish Bosnia

Intrepid shuddered and side-slipped as she pushed through the darkness, rain lashing her deck and superstructure. The weather front which pursued us the previous day overtook us not long after we began our night run into Bosnia. It could hardly have missed us once we'd started heading southwest instead of southeast.

Two trimsmen wrestled with the forest of levers at the back of *Intrepid*'s wheelhouse, fighting the turbulence which rocked the flyer, each change in deck angle altering the power and balance of the liftwood louvers deep in the hull. I had thought this massive steel flyer would be immune to the effects of weather, at least compared to a hydrogen-filled dirigible. I was wrong.

"Try to hold her steady, Wickers, there's a good fellow," Captain Harding ordered.

"Aye, aye, sir," the senior trimsman answered, strain apparent in his voice.

"Wouldn't do to come this far just to fly into a mountain," the captain added.

For a moment the bridge was as bright as noon, the sky to starboard filed with a dozen branching, broken lances of raw electricity, and I jumped despite myself. The sizzling crack and rolling roar of thunder came immediately afterwards.

"Damn me!" Gordon said beside me.

Captain Harding smiled, but it was a calculated, tightly controlled smile.

"Compass house reports two degree drift to starboard," Lieutenant Jenkins reported from the bank of speaking tubes connecting the bridge to the rest of the ship.

"Helm, come two degrees to port and steady back on one seven zero," Harding ordered.

"Two degrees to port. Waiting to steady on one seven zero," the helmsman answered.

"With a sluggish bridge compass and all this gusting wind, our analytic engine isn't much good to us," Harding told Gordon and me. "Just the night for some good old-fashioned navigation, wouldn't you say so, Mr. Jenkins?"

"As you say, sir," the lieutenant answered absentmindedly, his attention on the speaking tubes and the bridge compass.

Beside me Gordon tried to look nonchalant, but I could smell the fear on him through his own rain gear. He clasped his hands behind his back, I figured to keep from fidgeting, but the desire to do something—pace, drum his fingers, tap his foot—was so powerful I could almost feel it, as if he were an overwound clock ready to fly apart.

"How close would you say we were to our course, Mr. Jenkins?" Captain Harding asked. Jenkins licked his lips and thought for a moment before answering.

"I'd say we're a good twenty cables downwind of our course."

"Twenty cables? Really? Well, that *would* put us into a mountainside if we try to come down. I don't think we've surrendered that much ground, though. Let's drop down and see if we can find this river."

"Sir, we're still well short of Višegràd. No need to—"

"Take us down, Mr. Jenkins. Light the bow searchlight. May as well see what we're flying into."

"Aye, aye, sir. Trimsman, two percent negative buoyancy. Bosun, bow light on, twenty degree down angle."

A petty officer closed the collar of his oilskin slicker and ducked out into the rain, then slid down the companionway to the main deck.

"How long is a cable? Do you know?" I asked Gordon, more to make conversation than because I really wanted to know.

He looked at me, eyes moving quickly from side to side like a cornered animal. Confusion, irritation, panic, all played across his face in less than a second, and then he took a breath and was under control.

"Two hundred yards."

Twenty cables times two hundred yards—Jenkins was saying we were more than two miles off our projected course. That was more than enough to put us out of the river valley and over the mountains.

"How does the glass read, Mr. Jenkins?" the captain asked.

"Five hundred fifty fathoms and dropping, sir. Now five forty."

"The tallest mountain peaks around here are twenty-seven hundred feet. Close enough to five hundred fathoms. We'll know soon enough which of us is the better navigator, eh, Jenkins?"

"As you say, sir."

"Of course with this storm the glass is running low anyway, so we're a few fathoms above the read. Nothing to worry about for a few more minutes, anyway. Who's for a nip?"

He took a flask out of his coat pocket and held it out toward Gordon and myself.

"I'm not too proud," Gordon said and took the flask.

"I've noticed that about you," Captain Harding said.

Gordon paused for a moment, the flask in his hand, and as he did the bridge exploded in light around us and another latticework of lightning filled the window behind Harding, backlighting him. This time I didn't jump.

Gordon handed him back the flask.

"Changed my mind."

"Particular about your whiskey, are you?" Harding asked.

"Just who I drink it with."

Harding laughed, then offered the flask to me. I took it and sipped—Irish, like Reggie Llewellyn always carried. I thought about Reggie, what he'd make of all this, but the truth was I never really knew what was going on inside his head. Still, he'd been a friend, whatever that had meant to him, and it had meant something. I remembered his regiment's motto and lifted the flask as a toast.

"Who dares, wins."

I drank again.

"If so, we're on the road to glory tonight," Harding answered as he took back the flask. "Bad as this weather is, I wouldn't count on much support from us once we drop you off. Barring mishap we'll make the run back to Ujvidék by morning, but I think it better we sit out any more of this weather. No point in tempting fate too often."

In other words, once he landed us we were on our own and good riddance. Ever since the dinner that first night out of Munich, Harding's attitude had soured. There had been traces of his contempt for Gordon earlier, but now it had deepened and broadened, including Gabrielle and myself as well. Mostly I'd tried to just stay out of his way.

"Corporal O'Mara has been singing your praises to anyone willing to listen, Fargo," Harding went on. "I've decided to send his section along with you, if there are no objections."

"Ask Captain Gordon. He's in command."

"Of course he is. Captain Gordon, will that be acceptable to you, sir?" he asked with mocking courtesy.

"Yes," Gordon answered.

O'Mara had been "singing my praises," but he didn't have much good to say about Gordon, so that could be a problem for him, and I was sure Harding knew that when he made the call.

Harding was navy, Gordon army. Harding's naval rank of captain was the equivalent of an army colonel, so he outranked Gordon by three pay grades, but Gordon was in charge of the expedition. Maybe that wasn't sitting well. Corporal O'Mara was in Harding's crew, but now the Marine couldn't stop talking about the American with the pipe. On this ship I had the feeling there was room for only one hero, and Gabrielle's humiliation of him at dinner that first night had been the last straw.

So Harding would take care of his ship and get some payback for what happened to his men and maybe rid himself of a "disloyal" Marine, but as far as our mission went, we could pound sand for all he cared—inter-service rivalry and personal jealousy trumping everything else. I'd come back over a hundred years and to a different world or reality or whatever the hell it was just to find the same old bullshit.

"Four eighty by the glass," Jenkins announced, and Harding shook himself as if waking from an unpleasant dream.

"I had better see to my vessel," Harding said. "You gentlemen may be more comfortable belowdecks. If I were you I'd make sure those Bavarians and Mr. Fargo's French trollop are ready to disembark. I believe we are running a bit ahead of schedule."

Gordon shot me an angry look, as if I were to blame for Harding's attitude and manners, but I didn't much care what Gordon thought.

There were only two people in this particular world I gave a damn about—Gabrielle and Thomson—and Harding was about to write them both off because it was more convenient to do that than to do his job. Never mind what I might have to do to them later to save my own world, this moment was real, they were still alive, and this spiteful little shit wasn't just going to turn his back on them.

"I guess it makes you feel big to insult a woman who isn't here to defend herself," I said. "Especially since if she were here, she'd make you look like a monkey—again."

"I won't—" he started, but I cut him off.

"Fuck you, Harding. Fuck you up the ass. That's how it's usually done in the Royal Navy, isn't it? What are the three enduring traditions of the service again? Oh, yeah, I remember: rum, sodomy, and the lash. Which one's your favorite?"

There was a moment of stunned silence on the bridge. Harding stood with his mouth open, face turning red, and then I heard a nervous snicker from one of the trimsmen behind me.

"You're in a bad spot, Harding," I said. "If we come back, you and I might have to have a real serious conversation you won't like. If we don't come back, then no matter how good an excuse you come up with, Lord Chillingham is going to flay the skin from your bones. I guess you're going to have to decide which one of us you're more afraid of."

There I was, using Chillingham as a boogey man again. He was becoming so useful in the role I was starting to feel gratitude toward him for being such an over-the-top son of a bitch. I left the bridge while Gordon wasted his time sputtering an apology to Harding.

I found Gabrielle in her cabin. She sat on her bunk, dressed in a green-grey riding habit, with her gear packed and piled neatly at her feet. I noticed her hands clasped tightly in her lap and her face paler than usual.

"What's wrong, Gabi?"

"I am frightened. The weather . . . it is not good for the flyer, is it? For the trim? If the ship tilts too far to one side, the lifting panels cannot compensate, because they will line up with each other and then they lose all their lift and we fall."

I couldn't exactly reassure her on that point. Flying by jet was safer than driving a car, but they didn't have either of those here. I didn't know much about the safety record of liftwood flyers. I felt a shudder of anxiety myself, but it was submerged in the wave of surprise I felt at Gabrielle's fear. She showed so few emotions it was easy to fall into thinking she was immune to them, but fear was a basic animal instinct.

She cried out as the porthole flashed white, flooding the room with light. She clamped her hands over her ears with the crack of thunder immediately following it, her face wrinkled up and tears streaming from her eyes.

One long step took me across the little cabin. I sat down next to her and put my arms around her, and she clung to me as if to a life preserver at sea.

"I do not like the lightning," she explained in a small voice, trying to choke back the panic. "Or the thunder. It hurts my ears."

"Yeah, it sucks."

"It sucks?"

"That means it's bad."

She nodded her agreement against my chest.

"Did my pistol shooting hurt your ears yesterday?" I asked, just to make conversation and divert her mind.

"*Oui*. All my life the loud noises bother me, more so than others. So I could not sleep while you shoot. But it was good watching you. You are funny the way you shoot."

"I'm here all week."

She lifted her head and looked at me, confusion momentarily replacing the fear.

"Sometimes the things you say—I understand the words but not the sentences."

"Yeah, I get that a lot, mostly from my students. Listen, I kind of kicked a hornet's nest up on the bridge a little while ago. Gordon's going to be pissed—angry—at me and he may try to take it out on you, maybe try to leave you behind."

"We have the agreement. He is not an honorable man?"

"He's a frightened man. To be honest, I don't know what sort of guy he is under all the fear."

"You need to find this thing out, Jack," she said, concern for me momentarily trumping her own fear. "So much for you now depends on him. For me as well, but I still have information he needs which I have not shared."

"Good girl. I figured, but it's good to be sure. He needs me as a translator with the Turks and maybe as bait. Our plan doesn't use me for that, but it's always there as a back-up."

She was right about Gordon. What did I really know about him? He was angry a lot, probably as a cover for his fear. He drank for the same reason, but he'd stopped, and that showed something. What sort of man was he underneath?

Lighting flashed outside the porthole, and Gabrielle jumped again.

"Tell me something about this Tesla guy I don't already know," I said, just to get her talking and take her mind off the storm. "Tell me about his folks, his family."

"He . . . his father was an orthodox priest, well-educated and *très charismatique*. It is said he had many affairs of the heart outside of his marriage."

"No vows of celibacy in the orthodox church, huh?"

"*Non*. Priests marry and raise families, the same as the Protestants. His wife, Tesla's mother, was the daughter of a priest herself, but she was uneducated, unable to read. She memorized many of the Serbian epic poems and recited them to Nikola as he grew."

"Are they still alive?"

"*Non*, both dead. His father died eight years ago. His mother died six years ago, when he lived in France. He was grief-stricken at her loss, so much he suffered the physical collapse. Strange. He broke the ties with his family ten years ago, and yet he was so upset at the deaths of his parents. This is odd, don't you think?"

"People are strange, Gabi, no getting around it. Is there a woman in his life?"

"He had three sisters, all married, but they died in an outbreak of typhus not long after his mother died."

She started telling me where they had lived, what their husbands had done for a living, how many kids they had had, but I shook my head.

"Oh, a woman. You mean the romance? *Non*, he is—what is the word you used?—celibate. He says the celibacy keeps his head clear."

"A lot of nutcases think that."

"Nut case?" she asked and then nodded. "Ah, you mean the crazy person. But is he crazy because he has the different ideas?"

"No, Gabi. He's crazy because he sends clockwork mechanical spiders and assassins high on hashish to kill people who disagree with him. I've met him. Odd guy."

"I have only seen photographs of him. Do you think he misses his sisters?"

I blinked at the conversational sharp right turn, but before I could answer there was a loud pounding on the door.

"Fargo, are you in there?" Gordon shouted from the corridor.

"There's trouble," I told Gabrielle and then raised my voice to answer him. "Yeah, I'm in here. Come on in."

"Is *Mademoiselle* Courbiere with you?" he shouted.

"*Oui*, I am here," she answered.

"May I come in?" he shouted.

I couldn't help but smile. There he was, steaming mad out in the corridor, and still impeccably polite, asking permission from the lady to enter her quarters, and asking it at the top of his lungs.

"*Oui*, you may enter."

"Are you decent?" he shouted.

My grin got bigger as Gabrielle frowned in confusion.

"I believe so, but sometimes I do not think everyone agrees," she called back.

"He means are we dressed," I explained.

"Ah! We have on the clothes," she called out.

There was a moment of silence, and then Gordon opened the door and stepped in, red-faced with anger or embarrassment or both. He made a little bow to Gabrielle before turning on me.

"Thank you, *Mademoiselle*. You are most kind. Fargo, what the bloody hell were you thinking, insulting Harding like that on the bridge? Don't you know we need his help to carry this off?"

"Relax, Gordon. Have a seat."

"I will not relax, and I prefer to stand when dressing someone down."

Gabrielle turned to me, confused again.

"This 'dressing down,' it has again to do with the decency? And why did you insult Captain Harding?"

"Yes, we'd both like to know that," Gordon said.

"So sit down and I'll tell you."

He stood fuming for a few more seconds, but when I showed no sign of budging he looked around the tiny cabin, pulled the single straight-backed chair out from the writing desk, and sat facing us. I turned to Gabrielle first.

"Harding insulted you. I didn't like it, but that's not the reason I insulted him."

I turned to Gordon.

"I insulted him because we need his support and cooperation, and we were not going to get it any other way."

"Just how, in that twisted, convoluted brain of yours, did you imagine this would increase his chances of helping us?"

"He insulted me?" Gabrielle said, curious rather than angered. "What did he say?"

"He called you a trollop. You aren't a trollop."

"*Non*, certainly not. A trollop is a woman promiscuous, or who exchanges sexual favors for money, neither of which am I. You were right to disagree with him. And how did you insult him?"

I told her.

She started laughing, harder than I'd ever seen her laugh. She covered her mouth with her hands and leaned back against the wall behind the bunk, laughing so hard tears came to her eyes. Lightning flashed outside the cabin and thunder shook *Intrepid*, and for a moment she froze, eyes wider, and then she started laughing again, even harder than before, laughing at the lightning too, or her fear of it. I laughed as well, and after a moment Gordon's anger melted away and he joined us.

"Oh God!" he said as our laughter began to subside. "*Rum, sodomy, and the lash?* I don't believe I'll ever forget that."

"I can't claim it. A young British Army officer, alive right now, so I won't tell you his name, will go on to become First Lord of the Admiralty and eventually Prime Minister, at least in my world. He'll say it. He had a way with words."

"I dare say. But really, Fargo, what were you thinking?"

"Yes, Jack," Gabrielle said. "Harding is not a very interesting man, but his good feelings are important to us, *oui*?"

"*Non, cheri.* His good feelings are meaningless. What is important is his cooperation. Gordon, I as much as threatened to kill him if I got back from this, and I did it in such a way that everyone on the ship is going to hear about it."

"Precisely, old man. That's rather the point."

"Yeah. So what happens if we *don't* come back? People will say Harding sabotaged the mission to keep me from making good on my threat. They will whisper that, whether it's true or not, and Chillingham will hear the whispers. That's what I meant when I asked him who he was more afraid of, me or Chillingham. Trust me, Harding's not afraid of me."

Gordon rubbed his chin and scowled.

"Still too damned much of a gamble. More flies with honey than vinegar, that sort of thing. You need to look before you leap, Fargo, or better yet leave all this sort of thing to me. You're just the translator. It would be best if you remembered that."

"This Lord Chillingham, he is a very bad man," Gabrielle said, reasserting her right to change the subject.

"You've met him?" I asked.

"No, but Renfrew has told me enough."

"Interesting," I said. "So we're all in agreement on that point, including the royal family."

"Not so much the queen, from what I understand," Gordon said. "Not that she likes him—too aristocratic for her tastes, I would imagine. But she's not willing to move against him."

"He's too aristocratic for *my* tastes," I said, "but a queen's? That's a little hard to get my head around."

Gordon leaned forward, and for the first time I saw a hint of fire in him, other than just anger.

"You have to understand, Fargo, the old aristocracy, people like Chillingham who own probably four-fifths of the land in England, look down on the royal family. Really they do. They see them as a pack of *nouveaux-riches* German bog-runners, Johnny-come-latelys the lot of them. To Chillingham's way of thinking, when his family won its coat of arms, the queen's family was still cutting peat on Luneburg Heath, and they have no business telling *proper* Englishmen how to run their country. But for all that, the queen won't stand up to him."

"What can she do, anyway?" I asked.

"The one real power the monarchy retains: create lords. She could flood the House of Lords with her own people, but she won't. God knows how the old aristocracy would react, and she's not willing to chance it."

"Her son will," Gabrielle said.

Gordon nodded but seemed to grow angrier as he did so.

"Yes, the Prince of Wales will, once he's king and assuming he lives that long. Fargo, he's the one man in Europe with the guts and brains to stand up to Chillingham and perhaps come out on top, *and you've decided to roger his mistress!* What in God's name were you thinking?"

"I am not Renfrew's mistress!" Gabrielle exclaimed. "We are friends, sometimes we are allies, but not lovers. He is currently enamored of the Countess Warwick, *n'est pas*? And who is this *Roger*?"

Hearing those words from Gabrielle made me feel light in the chest, but that made no sense. Our relationship was based on mutual physical attraction without promise, or even prospect, of a deeper emotional commitment from either of us. Friends with benefits, we'd say in my time. Gabrielle couldn't understand falling in love, let alone do it, and as for me, I didn't want to even think about that, or where this entire quest was inevitably headed. So her words shouldn't have mattered.

But they did.

When I told her people were strange, I meant it, present company included.

TWENTY-THREE

October 8/9, 1888,
Aboard Her Majesty's Aerial Ship Intrepid,
Aloft over Turkish Bosnia

Harding might have been an asshole, but he was a righteous navigator. He dropped us right down through the storm into the valley of the Drina River. The river's surface, visible in the glare of the bow searchlight, danced in angry whitecaps. Wind gusts made *Intrepid* shudder and sideslip, and sheets of rain slammed into the glass windows of the bridge.

As bad as it was down here, it was certainly worse aloft, which is why Harding brought *Intrepid* down as soon as he did. Another reason was the lightning, crackling and exploding all along the banks to either side, as ferocious a display as I'd ever seen in my life. *Intrepid* was struck three times, but as soon as Harding had seen the water, he had dropped the ship's ground cable and raised its lightning masts. All three strikes had grounded into the river below us.

Gordon and I declared an uneasy truce and returned to the wheelhouse as we approached our landing area. It looked like hell out there.

"How are you going to return in all this?" Gordon asked. "You can't go up into those thunderheads, surely."

"We'll follow the river back north," Harding answered. "It flows into the Sava near the Austrian frontier. With luck we will have a break in the weather and can make the run to Ujvidék from there. It's only fifty miles. If the weather doesn't break, we'll have to follow the Sava west to Zagreb."

That would mean not being back at Ujvidék by morning, possibly alerting Tesla's informants to the threat, but there was no point in belaboring the obvious.

"We're going to have to change the plan anyway," I said. "We were going to camp in a meadow down there while Gordon and I contact the Turks in Višegràd. That won't work in this weather."

"What's wrong, Fargo. Don't fancy getting your dainty feet wet?" Harding asked.

"The plan made sense because there are no villages down there in the meadows. They're all up in the foothills, so not much chance of anyone stumbling across us at night."

"And?" he demanded.

"And there's a reason there are no villages on the meadows. It's the same reason they call those meadows 'flood plains.' With this rain, by morning there's going to be a couple feet of water over all that ground and anything not tied down is going to be twenty miles downriver. And no, I don't fancy getting *that* wet."

Harding scanned the riverbank for a while and scowled, trying to come up, I imagined, with a good reason not to agree with me. But facts were facts.

"Very well. If we are going to drop you closer, we may as well take you to the bloody city gates. Mr. Jenkins, take us down to wave-top level, if you please."

"Wave-top level, aye, aye, sir." Jenkins replied. "Trimsman, one per cent negative buoyancy."

"In this weather any sensible person will be indoors, and the lunatics may think we're a riverboat," Harding added and glared at me, daring me to disagree. I returned his look until he turned away.

"Captain Gordon, I'll let the others know about the change in plans," I said.

"Very well. I will join you when we arrive."

I left the bridge into the driving rain, slid down the ladder to the superstructure level and then down the adjoining ladder to the main deck. One of the naval ratings had shown me how, feet on the outside of the handrail using friction to slow me, and I was getting pretty good at it. I opened the hatch into the superstructure just abeam of the midship port gun mount and ducked out of the rain.

The group was assembled in the crew's mess, with the tables

pushed against the walls to make room. I looked them over and shook my head. They were probably all in civilian clothes, but nobody seemed to think about their overcoats. All twenty Bavarians wore identical field gray greatcoats while the twelve Marines wore identical blue-gray coats. Von Schtecker was chatting with Gabrielle, but he bowed to her and crossed the room to meet me.

"We are ready," he announced. "We should be nearing the landing ground, *ja*?"

"Yeah. Slight change of plans: *Intrepid* is taking us right into Višegràd."

"*Sehr gut.* Bad weather for marching, even though the men are well-equipped."

"Yeah, pretty snappy greatcoats."

"*Ja.* All insignia removed, as you said. You see?"

"That'll fool everyone, no doubt."

He looked at me and smiled condescendingly.

"I see, *Herr Professor.* You believe our party of thirty-four men, all of military age and bearing, who speak only English and German and who carry the latest military rifles, would fool everyone if only we had thought to wear different colored coats. I think not, and I must tell you, speaking as a *military* man, that there are advantages to the peasants knowing we are capable of taking care of ourselves. Bandits infest these hills, but they attack only the weak."

He was right. The lack of insignia wasn't so much intended to fool people as to give the two governments what in my time we called "plausible deniability."

I left von Schtecker and joined Gabrielle. Her gear was again at her feet, but I took a closer look this time. A rucksack that looked about three-quarters full. A long blanket roll wrapped in a rubberized canvas ground cloth, with the two ends of the roll tied together. She'd wear that over one shoulder and across her body. She had a canvas haversack for over the other shoulder, a good-sized canteen also on a long shoulder strap, a brown leather gun case, and a leather bandolier with big, thick ammunition pouches on it. Her headgear was a grayish-white cloth-covered cork sun helmet, stained and worn. None of her gear looked new except for the leather gun case.

"You've done this before," I said. "What are you packin'?"

"Many things. Spare stockings and underwear, one clean blouse, some concentrated—"

"No, I meant what's in the gun case?"

"Ah. It is the shotgun. I find that more useful than the rifle in most cases. I used to carry the twenty-gauge with two barrels, but this is a new gun from your country, designed by *Monsieur* John Browning. Have you heard of him in your time?"

"Now and then. May I?"

She nodded, and I unzipped the case and carefully slipped the shotgun out.

"Oh, baby!"

She had a Winchester Model 1887 twelve-gauge lever action, and it was like new. What was I thinking? It *was* new. They'd only been making them for about a year.

"You like?" she asked.

"Shit, yeah. Only thing is, I'm beginning to feel undergunned with just a Webley. The magazine holds five and one in the action?"

"I do not carry it with a round in the chamber. I do not think that safe, but yes, five cartridges in the magazine. The twenty-gauge was adequate for most purposes, but ammunition was sometimes difficult to find. Also the number five buckshot is too light, I think, if the target is a man. The double-zero shot of the twelve gauge is better."

That was certainly true, if a little cold-blooded. Hard to beat double-ought buck for taking down a person.

"You ever shoot a man?"

"*Non,* but nearly so. I have had to threaten to do this thing."

"Think you could put the trigger if you had to?"

"*Oui,*" she answered simply, and I believed her.

"So what made you point a shotgun at someone?"

"Bandits threatened to steal the supplies of our expedition. There were eight of them, *très féroce.*"

"Eight of them, and you with only two rounds. That why you decided to go with a lever action?"

"Perhaps, although against the bandits there were two of us, and Jeanne had both the revolver and carbine, so really we were quite adequately armed."

"Your friend Jeanne sounds like . . ." I started but then I stopped, remembering a famous engraving of a woman with a revolver and carbine facing eight Persian bandits. A surge of excitement went through me.

"*I have fourteen balls at your disposal; go find six more friends,*" I said.

Gabrielle laughed and shook her head.

"Jeanne never said that, but they put it on the picture anyway. They did not put me in the picture, I suppose because I was simply a helpless woman."

"But Jeanne Dieulafoy was—*is* a woman as well. My God, Gabi, you were on the Dieulafoy expedition to Susiana?"

I sat down on the chair next to her, partly because I felt a bit light-headed.

"Yes, it was my first real adventure. And yes, Jeanne is a woman, but no one would consider her helpless or defenseless. You have heard of the expedition?"

"*Heard* of it? I'm an ancient historian. My specialty, other than Roman coinage, is Achaemenid Persia. Jeanne Dieulafoy's photographs of the inscriptions and architecture at Susa are still one of our key resources. Hell, half the books on the Persian Army have her photograph of the Frieze of the Immortals on the cover. Most of those buildings and artifacts were gone by my time, either destroyed or badly degraded by the elements, so all we have is her photographs. Anyone serious about Achaemenid Persia owns a portfolio of her work."

"It would please her very much to hear that. You should meet her when . . ." She stopped, and the excitement left her face. "Oh, you cannot. After this, you will be gone."

We unloaded at the waterfront in lashing rain and then trudged the two hundred yards through scattered warehouses and sheds to the city gates, which were closed and secured. It took another fifteen minutes of shouting and finally a couple shots from my Webley to rouse someone, then another ten minutes before they got someone who spoke Turkish. The garrison was nominally Turkish, but this was Bosnia. Bosnian, along with all the other Slavic languages, was not part of my repertoire.

We got an angry Turkish officer next, shouting at us through the postern window to go away and come back in the morning. It was well after midnight, and he'd probably been sound asleep.

"Tell this scoundrel to open the gate at once, unless he wants my fist in his nose," Gordon ordered.

"Captain Gordon of the British Army sends his respects to the garrison commander," I translated. "The commandant has been told of our coming and will be anxious to see us. We are on an important mission for the Sublime Porte."

The Sublime Porte, the grand gate at Topkapi Palace in Istanbul where the sultan's vizier traditionally greeted representatives of foreign governments, had come to mean the Turkish foreign ministry. The Turkish officer hesitated.

"Look for yourself," I added. "Do we look like a band of wandering gypsies? These are soldiers on a secret mission. We are going to fight the Serbs, with Allah's blessing and your commander's help."

I took a chance mentioning the Serbs, but it sealed the deal. The officer stuck his head out a bit and looked the company over, then nodded and withdrew. We heard a barked order and in a few seconds heard the heavy beam withdrawn from the gate. Then it opened onto a courtyard.

My first view of Višegràd was not very impressive, but it's hard for any town to wow you in the middle of a thunderstorm. The courtyard was no more than thirty yards square, lined with a couple small one-story brick buildings. Lightning flashed, and I saw the suggestion of taller buildings beyond them.

"We need accommodations for our party for the night, somewhere out of the weather," I told the officer.

"My commander will decide that."

"What is your name, *Effendi*?" I asked.

"Lieutenant Kadir Malak."

"Lieutenant Malak, I ask you to think for a moment. Your commandant is asleep. He will wish to rouse himself and prepare a reception for us, but will be embarrassed to make us wait while he does so. May I suggest you send a runner to him now, and that you see to our billeting, giving him time to prepare for us without embarrassment?"

Malak nodded thoughtfully, even as I was speaking, then sent one of the small group of soldiers milling around running into the heart of the town.

"I know of a stable near here where you may stay. You have silver to pay the proprietor?"

An hour later, Gordon and I entered the office of the commandant, a middle-aged officer, slender in the face and limbs but large in the belly. He rose and smiled in greeting as Lieutenant Malak escorted us in. I saw a clutter of telegrams on his desk and suspected he had been catching up on his orders as to how to handle us. There was also a pen and ink, writing paper, sealing wax, and two folded and sealed letters, the wax seals on them probably still warm.

"Gentlemen, peace be upon you," he said in Turkish.

"And upon you," I answered in Turkmen. "May I present Captain Gordon of Her Most Britannic Majesty's Service."

"Staff Major Cevik, at your disposal. Please be seated. I have ordered refreshments. Please."

I translated the introduction, and we all sat in straight-backed chairs, Gordon and I in front of his desk, Malak against the wall.

"Forgive me," I said, "if my Turkish is poor. I speak Turkmen."

"Ah, yes, it sounded unusual. Your accent, it is up-country, we would say, but understandable."

"Your rank—*Erkan-ı Harb Binbaşısı*—it caused me a moment's pause. Do I address you as pasha or bey?"

A major was normally addressed as *Effendi*, the lowest of the three forms of respectful address, but I wasn't sure for a "staff major." Throwing in the possibility of *pasha* was pure flattery. I can kiss ass when the situation calls for it.

Cevik chuckled.

"Bey. Only very exalted men—generals and governors, are pashas."

One servant brought in a silver ice bucket with a bottle of champagne and another brought a tray with three glasses. I had expected coffee, not alcohol. The servant popped the cork and began pouring. Cevik Bey must have seen my look and laughed again.

"You are surprised to see me serve champagne? I am a good Moslem, I assure you. I follow all the teachings of the prophet. But also I love champagne. So I thought long about it. I prayed for guidance, and this is the thought Allah sent to me: champagne did not exist in Mohammed's time, so he cannot have said it was a sin to drink it. You agree?"

In answer I raised my glass in a toast.

"To our joint endeavor," I said, first in Turkmen then English.

Then we got down to business. Gordon laid out our plan: hire boats and travel twenty-five miles up the Lim River to the border village of Uvats. The Lim flowed into the Drina about seven miles upstream from Višegràd. Depending on the speed of the boats, and how fast the rivers were flowing after all this rain, we could make the trip in a long day or a long morning. From Uvats we would have to travel overland. The large Serbian town of Priboj straddled the Lim River just across the border, and Gabrielle had told us Serbian batteries commanded the river, so we'd have to go overland from there. Kokin Brod was only a dozen miles southeast of Priboj, but it was through mountainous countryside.

Cevik Bey frowned through the description, but more in thought than irritation, I thought.

"So, you will not go from here by land? A pity. I know a man who has mules for sale. Very good price."

There was enough regret in Cevik's expression that I suspected he would have gotten a piece of the "very good price."

"Ask him if we can get enough boats to move all his troops upriver," Gordon ordered.

"No, not on such short notice," he answered after I translated the question. "I doubt we can find enough to move over fifty men by tomorrow, and that may cost you a pretty penny. You have silver?"

The fact that Cevik Bey had, in an offhanded and conversational tone, let me know the Turks would not be underwriting the expedition was not lost on me. As to money, Gordon had over five hundred pounds' worth of British, Turkish, German, and Serbian currency in his "war chest," but there was no point in advertising the fact.

"We have silver, Cevik Bey, although our pockets are not bottomless."

"Ah, whose are?" he asked with a shrug.

"Ask him if he will support the mission as he was ordered to," Gordon said.

I did, but with a bit more diplomacy.

"Yes, of course we will help. These Serbs, they make nothing but trouble. They deserve to be punished, and will be. But my orders are we cannot cross in force without provocation. You understand?"

I translated for Gordon and then translated his reply back, but without the insult and profanity.

"The threat posed by the Old Man of the Mountain is as great to Turkey as it is to Britain," I said. "Surely the Sublime Porte intends more vigorous Turkish action."

"Ah, but the Sublime Porte also knows that the world judges the vigor of Turkish actions differently than it does those of others," Cevik Bey answered. "Less than two years ago the Bulgarians raided across the Danube on a regular basis, intent on provoking war. The world paid little attention to the vigor of their actions. But when Turkey responded with force, the world noticed. Great Britain itself noticed, and joined the world in condemning the *vigor* of Turkey's response. 'Outrage' was the word the British prime minister used, I believe, and the British newspapers used stronger words, ugly words.

"So now Britain remembers its friend Turkey. This makes us happy. It makes *me* happy, Mr. Fargo. I have always admired the British."

To prove the point he flashed Gordon an enormous smile. Not knowing the gist of the exchange, Gordon returned the smile, if with less enthusiasm.

"However, our other neighbors are not so friendly as Britain," Cevik Bey continued. "When you are gone, we will still live next to them. So it must be clear to the world that Serbia is the more . . . *vigorous* participant in this incident, and that Turkey acts only in response to their crimes."

"How do you plan to arrange that?" I asked.

Cevik Bey took another sip of champagne and considered his answer.

"I have a battalion of Bosnian riflemen and two mountain guns. I will march them overland to Uvats and wait there. We will cross the border when and if it is necessary to prevent harm to you, our friends."

"How will you know when we are in difficulty?"

"Signal rockets," he answered, and waved his hand as if in imitation of a rocket spiraling up into the sky. "We will send a dozen with you. Send them up if you need help."

"And how will we stay alive while we're waiting for you to march a battalion and drag two guns up those mountain valleys?"

"Ah, I send soldiers with you as well, just not so many as to be a provocation, you see? I sent a platoon of good riflemen ahead to Uvats under a sergeant I trust very much. Also, he speaks English. He was American once, but converted to Islam. He is . . . scouting into

Serbia, actually. But I sent no Turkish officer, so no provocation. You see?"

Not entirely, but it sounded as if the patrol he had out, if it was lost, was expendable. We probably were as well, in his mind. I translated for Gordon to give myself time to think it over.

"It's important you not react with surprise or anger to this," I said to Gordon as a preface. His frown grew deeper, eyes darker.

"Just tell me what the bloody Wog said."

Out of the corner of my eye I saw Cevik stiffen. He may not have spoken English, but he knew the word "wog."

"Look at me, not him when I tell you this. He understands the word you just used. Are you trying to blow this mission up?" I asked calmly, as if discussing the weather. "Are you trying to get the Turks so pissed off they'll send us away and you won't have to go through with it? Because that's how it looks to me, and it's probably how it will look to General Buller as well."

He didn't say anything in reply, but his face began getting red—whether with anger or shame I couldn't say. Probably both—they usually keep company.

"Cevik Bey will back us up with a battalion once we're in trouble," I said. "But for now we get just a rifle platoon he sent to scout ahead into Serbia."

Gordon sat quietly for a moment, lips compressed in a hard thin line.

"One *platoon*?" he said finally.

"Here's a better question: all the local officers along the border were alerted and told to cooperate. How did he know we'd come here and send someone ahead?"

His anger disappeared, replaced by confusion and then curiosity.

"A spy?" he asked.

"Maybe, but I don't think so. Too complicated, too many spies. Maybe he was just being proactive, but I bet he already had his guys out there and is using our appearance as an excuse. We're his fig leaf for maybe going over the line in poking the Serbs."

He thought about it for a moment and then nodded.

"Very well. Tell him we appreciate his help and foresight."

Not bad. I passed the sentiment along, and Cevik Bey smiled again.

"Will you cable ahead to Uvats and have your men waiting?" I asked.

"Unfortunately, the telegraph to the frontier is out of service. It happens fairly often. I have written a dispatch to the commander of the *Jandarma* in Uvats and another to Sergeant Durson, when you find him." He held up the two sealed letters. "Sergeant Durson reads, by the way. Quite admirable for a sergeant. He may not be in Uvats but he was to keep the Uvats *Jandarma* informed of his activity. Finding him should not be a problem."

I translated for Gordon, who took the news without visible reaction aside from a small nod. He was getting better at this.

"You understand," I said to Cevik Bey, "that even with this platoon of riflemen, who I am sure are among your very best, our party may suffer casualties before you can come to our assistance?"

His face became serious, with a trace of sadness in his eyes. "Ah, let us hope not. If so, it would cause me great distress."

"Because of how much you admire the British," I offered.

He smiled, bowed his head slightly, and spread his hands. "We understand each other perfectly. But let us pray it does not come to that. Ibrahim Durson is an excellent sergeant. His men are always under control, and he follows orders exactly. He also never makes annoying suggestions. It is bad for a sergeant to have ideas of his own. Does Captain Gordon not agree with this?"

"He says he likes it when sergeants know their place and keep their opinions to themselves," I translated for Gordon.

"I don't know about sergeants, but I certainly agree with respect to translators."

TWENTY-FOUR

October 9, 1888, On the Lim River, Bosnia

The rhythmic *chuh-chuh-chuh-chuh* of the steam launch's motor, the slap of waves against the bow, and the low German and English conversations of the men packed into the boat seemed small things in the emptiness of the river.

Bosnia had a somber, brooding beauty—granite cliff faces and massive outcroppings from a distance looking like moss-covered boulders, scattered among scrub forest and meadows. The rain had passed on to the east, but a solid roof of dark clouds kept the sun from lighting the glens and woods, made them all home to imagined lurking menace.

Earlier we had seen groups of people on the banks, then a solid flood—families, some with carts, bundles on their backs, livestock, others with nothing but their lives. We passed boats as well, mostly fishing craft. The boats, the people on shore—all headed downriver, northwest. They said nothing to us, nor did they have to. I had seen refugees before.

I wanted to stop, question them, but Gordon insisted we had lost enough time already, were making slow enough progress.

"The river is running so fast this relic of a boat is hardly making headway against it. We need to make Uvats by dusk. We'll find out what's happened once we get there."

I wasn't so sure. The flood of refuges dwindled then dried up, and for the last hour we had seen no one.

I scanned all around us. Gray sky overhead, gray river broken by white chop ahead, and behind, seemingly forever, empty banks to either side—no wonder the men grew jumpy, talked only in lowered voices, checked and rechecked their rifles and ammunition. Gabrielle seemed restless, unsettled.

"What do you think, Gabi?" I asked.

"About what? Oh, the lack of people on the banks? Either the danger has passed or it has consumed Uvats, *oui*?"

Leave it to her to see to the heart of the matter.

"You don't feel like uncasing that Winchester?"

"*Non*. If thirty armed soldiers cannot deal with the situation, I think one more gun will make little difference."

She was right, but I checked my Webley all the same. Danger in the abstract was one thing, but as we grew closer to whatever was happening up ahead, the butterflies in my stomach woke up and started flying around. Gabrielle staring at me didn't help.

"What?" I asked.

"Your wife, how did she die?"

My stomach clenched again, and for a moment I was afraid I was going to throw up. I felt a cold sweat on my face and knew I must have gone pale. I looked away, out over the river, but not for the view, just to avoid her eyes.

No one else here had asked me that. Not polite, you know, to inquire after a chap's personal life. The answers might be embarrassing to everyone, and we wouldn't want that, would we? But Gabrielle's rather limited grasp of social convention was always trumped by her curiosity. Normally I liked that about her. I liked it a lot.

"She . . . um . . . killed herself."

"This is so? My mother killed herself as well. Sometimes I wonder if she did so because of me."

I looked at her. I'm not sure what I expected to see in her eyes. Maybe a hidden pain forced to the surface, a key to unlocking her trapped emotions. Instead I saw a thoughtful frown. Her mother's suicide was another emotional puzzle for which she had no solution.

"Your mother made her own decision," I said. "You can't blame yourself for that."

"Then why do you?"

The launch's Bosnian skipper spoke enough pigeon Turkish to let me know what he was thinking when he felt like it. Now he raised his head to catch my eye, and I was happy for the distraction.

"Uvats. After hill," he said.

I looked upriver, saw a bend to the right about two miles ahead with a large hill on the bank.

"That hill?" I asked pointing.

He nodded. I took a closer look. Faint smoke rose from behind the crest.

"How long?"

His face wrinkled up in thought. Then he let go the wheel and held up both hands, fingers spread, closed his fists, opened them a second time, closed them, opened them again.

"Thirty minutes?"

Nod.

I passed the word to Gordon, who called von Schtecker back to join us. Both officers seemed jumpy to me, both working hard at not showing it. Like me.

"Pilot says half an hour to Uvats," Gordon started. "No telling what sort of a reception we'll have there, so we need to be ready for all eventualities. Now, here's my plan. Once we land I'll take the Marines and find the local gendarmerie. Fargo, you will accompany me. Leftenant von Schtecker, you guard the boats and supplies with your chaps. Be prepared to support our withdrawal if things get hot."

"*Ja, sehr gut,*" von Schtecker answered.

"Mademoiselle Courbiere should stay with the boats, I believe. You know how touchy these Mohammedans are about women," Gordon added.

I knew how touchy some Englishmen were.

"You mind missing all the fun?" I asked Gabrielle.

She wrinkled her nose in disdain.

"I have no desire to walk through a burning town."

Gordon and von Schtecker both gave a small start.

"Burning town?" Gordon demanded. "What's all this, then?"

"Didn't notice the smoke?" I asked and pointed at the smudge above the hill. Gordon and von Schtecker both turned and studied it, frowns creasing their faces. Gabrielle looked at them and shook her head.

Uvats was a sprawling, motionless, nearly colorless town of gray stone and stucco buildings with brown tile and gray slate roofs, spilling down a low ridge to the harbor. The waterfront was abandoned aside from a couple small boats swamped in the shallows and scores of large blue-black crows, fat and unalarmed by our arrival. They studied us not so much with hunger as speculation.

The fire didn't look as bad up close; the heavy rains last night must have drowned most of the blaze. Several buildings in the town still smoldered, and the fires might grow and spread, but for now all they produced were dirty coils of smoke that formed a veil of mourning over the dead town. At least it looked dead.

As soon as the launch bumped against the dock, the Marines scrambled over the gunwale and spread out into a skirmish line followed by the Bavarians.

The air was tinged with the smell of wood smoke, but something else as well, a sour, oily smell that tickled my gag reflex. It made my heart rate climb and sweat break out on my forehead. As soon as I was on the dock, I unfastened the leather cover on my holster, pulled out the Webley, and kept it pointed at the sky, finger out of the trigger guard but ready to go.

"Bloody hell this place stinks of garbage," Gordon cursed, and von Schtecker nodded his agreement.

I looked at the Marines, the Bavarians, and saw some noses wrinkled in disgust, but nothing more. That told me something about them: they'd never been to war, at least not a long, nasty one.

"That's not garbage," I said. "It's decomp."

Gordon turned to look at me.

"Decomp?"

"Decomposing human bodies, lots of them."

Gordon's look of mild curiosity changed to disbelief and then horror, quickly concealed behind a mask of nervous indifference. A murmur ran through the Marines and Bavarians, a ripple of movement as men became alert and scanned the buildings near the waterfront. I heard a zipping sound behind me, turned, and saw Gabrielle kneeling on the dock, uncasing her Winchester shotgun.

"If something happened here long enough ago for the bodies to start to rot," Gordon asked, "why hadn't the Turks heard of it?"

"Weather's been warm and damp, so I'd say this could have happened within the last three days. Why no news of it back in Visegard? Telegraph was out. You heard Cevik Bey. Happens all the time, so no one thought anything of it."

"Good Lord, what happened here?" Gordon asked.

Something bad, that was sure. As if to emphasize the point, a wolf appeared from an alley and stood sizing us up. A rifle cracked from the crowd of men on the dock, a slug knocked a chip from the corner of a building a few feet from the animal, and the wolf streaked back down the alleyway.

Gordon looked around uncertainly. One of the Marines opened the bolt on his rifle, and a spent brass cartridge case clinked musically on the dock.

"You call that shooting, Private Kane?" Corporal O'Mara demanded.

You call that fire discipline?

But it wasn't my army so I kept my mouth shut.

Gordon looked at the steam launch, clearly wanting to reboard and head downriver. But then what? He looked into the silent town and wiped his mouth with the back of his hand.

"Well, let's see if anyone is still here other than the wolves. Leftenant von Schtecker, same plan as before. You stay here with your men and guard the launch and our provisions. Make certain this cowardly bugger of a boatman doesn't run off and leave us hanging. If you hear heavy gunfire, and you are not yourself engaged, send one section to support us, but you are to stay here with your other section and guard this boat."

"*Jawohl, Herr* . . . Yes, Captain."

I glanced back at Gabrielle and gave her a reassuring smile as we set off into the town. She nodded, face serious, and went back to pushing shells into the magazine of her Winchester.

"Any idea where we're going?" I asked Gordon. We'd originally planned on asking directions once we got to town.

"It isn't that large a town. The public buildings will be on the square."

That made sense. We started up the cobblestone street. It wound up the hillside at a slope I felt in the calves of my legs after a dozen paces.

Up close the town looked pretty bad. The street was littered with clothing, broken crockery, soggy paper, the detritus of looting and panicked flight. The rains which put out the fires had left a muddy gray sludge everywhere, ash washed from the sky. Most of the doors stood open, some off the hinges. A lot of roofs had collapsed, the support timbers burned out from under them. What the hell happened here?

Once we were out of the waterfront and onto what looked like the main street of the town, the Marines went from skirmish order into a ragged group, walking up the middle of the street. Shipboard combat was their main duty, and I figured they were trained for use as a landing party as well, but they clearly didn't know much about street fighting.

I moved over to the right side of the street and looked in an open door. A rug shop, with some woven baskets as well. Living quarters were probably upstairs. No sign of recent habitation.

"Anything?" Gordon asked as I turned away.

I shook my head.

"Corporal O'Mara, have the men check out the buildings to either side of the street," he ordered.

"You heard the army captain," O'Mara barked. "Jones, Riley, left side of the street. Williams, Kane, right side. Hop to it."

We hadn't gone more than a block before Kane, the private who'd fired at the wolf, drew back from an open door and vomited.

"Something here, Corp," the Marine with him called out.

I walked over and looked in. Three bodies, and the wolves had gotten to two of them. All were bloated, the skin stretched and shiny. The decomp smell was strong, but there was something else, almost as strong.

"Diarrhea," I said to Gordon as he came up beside me and looked in, white-faced and covering his mouth and nose with his hand. "Looks like these people shit themselves to death. I'd guess cholera or something pretty close."

He took a step back and nodded.

"Small wonder they tried to burn the infected bodies," he said, voice shaking. "Corporal O'Mara, send a runner back to the dock. Tell the Bavarians there is cholera in the town and they are under no circumstances to drink any water until it has been boiled."

"You heard the army captain, Kane. Get going."

Gordon was using his head, which was a good sign. And he knew cholera was water-borne and boiling was an effective prophylaxis. I wasn't sure when folks figured that out, but obviously before 1888, at least in this world.

Gordon walked faster to draw ahead of the Marines and gestured for me to follow. When we were a dozen paces ahead he spoke to me in a low voice without turning to look at me.

"Cholera is endemic to the region. I cannot think people would abandon a town in panic because of it."

"No, me neither. Something else must be going on."

We walked in silence for a few more seconds. Then Gordon cleared his throat.

"I . . . ah . . . cannot say this to anyone else here. I am quite frightened by all of this, to the point that I fear my judgment may be impaired. But I am responsible for the success of the expedition. I cannot appear uncertain in front of the others. You understand?"

"Yep. Been there myself."

"Really? As a translator?" he asked, doubt in his voice.

I glanced at him. It must have taken a lot to open up like this, especially to me.

"The truth is, I wasn't always *just* a translator."

"I see."

I wondered if he did. We walked on in silence for half a block.

"My point is, I'm a bit at sea, trying to sort out what to do next. Everything seems . . . quite different than we anticipated."

"No plan survives contact with the enemy."

He grunted, almost a laugh.

"You've read Moltke, I see. I met him, you know. Not at all what I expected. Of course, he was quite old at the time. I'm rambling a bit, aren't I?"

"Yeah. You want my advice? First things first—find the Turkish soldiers. We can use the extra firepower and someone who speaks the local languages. But if we can't find them, we still have Gabrielle, a map, and the element of surprise."

The street opened into a plaza ahead of us, with a church on the left side and what looked like a municipal building opposite it. Gordon motioned to O'Mara, and a barked command sent two of the Marines trotting toward each building. Gordon took out a cheroot and tried to light it, but his hands trembled too much to get the match lit. I lit a match myself and held it for him while he puffed the cigar to life.

"Thank you," he said quietly.

"Nothing here, Corp," a Marine called from the door of the municipal building.

"No one alive in the church," another called from the other side of the plaza. "Ten or twelve bodies in there."

I heard the pop of a rifle in the distance, from the direction of the waterfront, then another, then a crackling exchange of rifle fire punctuated by the distinct boom of a twelve-gauge shotgun.

TWENTY-FIVE

October 9, 1888, Uvats, Bosnia

I ran.

The downhill slope lengthened my strides, and the buildings flashed by, scarcely noticed blurs of gray and black. I fell on the ash-slippery cobblestones once but scrambled up again, never lost my forward motion, hardly missed a stride.

The gunfire grew louder, and suddenly the waterfront loomed ahead of me. I stopped at the corner of a building, used it for cover, and took a look.

Bodies by the dock, four of them, none in a gray-green riding habit. A jumble of movement at the nearby seawall to the right, occasional heads bobbing up, a couple rifles resting on the edge of the wall and firing across the open ground at targets to my left. I watched and listened for a few seconds—no sign of Gabrielle, and no sound of shotgun fire.

I risked a look farther around the corner to my left—a low boathouse and two sheds. A rifle fired from the door of the boathouse, then another from behind a jumble of crates and nets beside one of the sheds.

I pulled back and heard the pounding of boots on cobblestones behind me, turned and saw O'Mara leading, with Gordon and the rest of the Marines straggling behind. O'Mara stopped at the wall beside me, panting, and I realized I was panting, too.

"What's the plan, sir?" he asked.

O'Mara looked to me, not Gordon, for leadership. I filed that away to think about later, but I knew it was a problem.

The others drew up beside us, and Gordon pushed his way to the front. I knelt down facing them and drew a sketch in the damp ash.

"We're *here*. Hostiles are firing from cover in a cluster of small buildings *here*. Our people have taken casualties and are pinned down by fire behind the sea wall *here*. Our people are returning fire and have the enemy's attention. The enemy is unaware of our presence. We . . ."

I stopped and looked up at Gordon.

"I recommend we use the Bavarians as our base of fire to keep the enemy pinned down, use these buildings to maneuver under cover to the enemy's flank and rear, and attack using surprise to overwhelm them."

Gordon knelt down as well, studied my diagram in the ash for a moment as if it contained some hidden wisdom which might have eluded him, and then nodded.

"Corporal O'Mara, we will use these alleyways to get behind the villains. Mr. Fargo and I will go ahead and find suitable attack positions. Wait for two minutes and then follow us."

I followed Gordon down the alleyway. He stopped at the end, looked around the corner, and then trotted across five yards of open ground to the back of a burned-out house. We made our way past two more buildings before we caught sight of the back of the boathouse. I checked back and saw O'Mara and the Marines hurrying toward us.

"You have done this sort of thing before, haven't you?" Gordon asked. "Any last advice before the others get here?"

Gordon asking me for advice? That was a switch.

"If you just open fire and bang away at them from back here, it'll give them time to adjust psychologically to being flanked. Make a quick charge and take them out before they know what hit them. Assign specific men to specific buildings. And a prisoner or two would be nice. I'd like to know what the hell's going on here."

Gordon nodded and wiped his forehead with the back of his hand. O'Mara and the Marines clustered around us, looking from Gordon to me. Gordon looked at the back of the boathouse, licked his lips, then nodded.

"They're in those buildings. O'Mara, take three men and secure the shed on the right. I will take you four here," and he pointed to the Marines closest to him, "and clear the boathouse. Mr. Fargo, you take the last three and capture the shed on the far side. Take prisoners if possible. We'll make it in one dash, no firing or shouting until we enter the buildings. Is that clear?"

"Don't forget there may be men between the buildings," I said. "I saw one behind a barricade." Gordon nodded, but I wasn't sure he understood. He looked from face to face and then nodded again.

"Let's go."

He turned and started running, leaving the rest of us to scramble to catch up.

I ran across the open ground, passed Gordon as he pushed open the door to the boathouse with his shoulder, heard a shot, then another. I saw a man turn from the barricade beside the boathouse and fired two shots from the Webley at him, saw him go down. I came to the back of the shed, and there was no door or window. I wasn't sure what to do.

I ran around the far side—a window. I broke out the glass, fired two shots into the dark, stepped to the side. A Marine following me put his rifle through the broken window. A shot exploded from inside and he pitched back, blood spraying.

I stepped back in front of the window, saw movement through it, fired twice, heard a cry of pain, stepped aside, broke open the revolver and dug for cartridges in my pocket. The other two Marines knelt by the wounded man.

"You, secure the front!" I shouted.

The closest Marine looked up, eyes wide, face white.

"'Ee's 'urt!" he shouted back.

"Secure the front!"

"'Ee's *'urt!*"

Fuck!

Okay. Tactical breathing. Get centered again.

I finished loading with trembling hands and snapped the Webley closed. I edged to the corner of the shed and looked around the front, listened.

Shouting, men in rage, O'Mara cursing, someone crying out in pain, a pistol shot close by, then another, but nothing from the interior of my shed.

I took two quick steps to the door, looked at the handle but couldn't make anything of it. Was it a latch? A door knob? The shape wasn't familiar, so it didn't register. I took a step back, kicked the door in, and went through with the Webley up and at eye level.

Movement in the dark corner. I turned, almost fired, but he sat in the corner waving a hand in the air, saying something, no weapon visible. His rifle lay at his feet. I crossed the three steps to him and kicked the rifle toward the door, backed away, scanned the shed for signs of anyone else.

Cordage, nets, wooden buoys, the smell of rotting fish and old kelp, but no one else.

"Clear!" I shouted, and turned back to the fellow on the floor.

He wore a shabby uniform jacket and trousers, hard to tell the color in the gloom of the shed but dark, maybe blue. He held his right arm with his left hand. Blood stained his uniform sleeve black but was bright red on the fingers of his hand. He blubbered something I couldn't understand.

"Speak Turkish?" I asked him in Turkmen.

"No. Yes. Little," he answered.

"Stay. Don't move."

He nodded vigorously, then shook his head just as vigorously. Pain creased his face and he started rocking back and forth, moaning.

My ears rang with the echoes of gunfire, but outside I heard only harsh orders in English and men talking rapidly to each other—the post-combat chatters. I stuck my head out the door and looked around. Gordon emerged from the boathouse at the same time, looking dazed. He saw me, but for a moment the image didn't seem to register. He closed his eyes, shook himself, and then walked over to me.

"I . . . is it over?" he asked.

"Looks like it. I have a prisoner here, but he's wounded and he doesn't speak much Turkish. Did you take any prisoners?"

"What? Prisoners?"

He thought about it for a moment, face creased in a frown.

"I don't think so. One of them may still be alive, but he's in a bad way. Maybe he'll survive. No, he's very bad. I don't know." His eyes flicked back and forth, up and down.

He looked at the revolver in his hand as if he'd never seen it before.

O'Mara and another Marine emerged into the open area, dragging another of the men in dirty blue. He saw us and started toward us.

"Here's O'Mara," I said in a low voice, just for Gordon. "Take a deep breath and get your head together."

Gordon looked at me, still dazed, but his eyes cleared and he nodded.

I left Gordon and O'Mara to round up whatever prisoners there were and see to our wounded. I started to walk toward the breakwater, saw our people there stand up and begin climbing up onto the dock, and I broke into a run, heart pounding.

Gabrielle was there, a Bavarian helping her up onto the dock, and I saw blood on her face and coat. She looked at me, face pale and eyes wide, still in shock herself. I stopped in front of her, looked for a wound but didn't see one, touched her shoulder.

"Are you hurt?"

She thought about the question and shook her head, looked around, stared at the bodies on the dock.

"The lieutenant . . . he stood before me when the shots came."

I followed her gaze and saw von Schtecker's unmoving body on the ground. Gabrielle swayed, and I helped her sit before she fainted. I put my arm around her shoulder, and she wept quietly.

We had one Bavarian dead beside von Schtecker and four wounded. One of those probably wouldn't make it. The only Marine injured was the private shot through the throat. He might not make it either, but you never knew. We had killed five "hostiles," captured two of them wounded, and one got away in the confusion—the one between the buildings I had winged as I ran by. I was glad he'd gotten away. Pointless, stupid fight.

We had massacred what was left of the local Turkish *Jandarma*.

The realization that this was nothing but a blue-on-blue fight hit the men like hard. A lot of them reacted with anger—anger at the *Jandarma* for attacking without a challenge or attempt to communicate, anger at Gordon and me for leading them into this mess, anger at themselves for what they had done and what they had felt while doing it. Some reacted with grief for fallen friends, some with depression. Any exhilaration they might have felt at a fight won vanished.

The surviving *Jandarma* corporal spoke and read Turkish. When I showed him the letter from Cevik Bey, he cried.

Once he pulled himself together, he told us what happened in the town. The disease was cholera, but a very virulent form, one that struck people down and killed them within hours of the symptoms first appearing. That spooked the townspeople, and so had the wolves coming down from the hills, more aggressive than anyone had ever seen them, attacking in packs in broad daylight in the town's streets and only retreating in the face of gunfire. Farmers from the hills fled to town, telling wild stories of livestock slaughtered by *azhdaja*. I didn't know the word's meaning but it sounded mythic and I translated it as troll for Gordon.

Panic grew as the death toll mounted and finally everyone fled downriver except for a dozen *Jandarma* who had stayed at their post with their captain. That had taken some guts. The captain died that morning of cholera, four others deserted, and we had done for the rest.

What of the platoon of riflemen sent by Cevik Bey?

They were somewhere across the border, patrolling the north bank of the river, trying to find if the Serbs were somehow behind this plague. I had a feeling one Serb in particular was, but I didn't know how.

"I am uncertain whether to wait here for the return of the Turkish patrol or head out after them," Gordon said after drawing me aside.

"Yeah, tough call, but I'd say head on. There's no guarantee they'll even come back here, assuming they survive. Every day we spend waiting is that much less chance we'll take Tesla by surprise."

"Yes, there is that."

"Also, you've got some morale problems. If we sit around for a couple days, with nothing for the men to do but stew about what happened, things aren't going to get any better. If we keep the men marching hard, they'll have other things to worry about."

He looked away, down the river, and squinted as if trying to see something clearly, but what he was searching for wasn't out there.

"I've rather made a hash of things, haven't I?"

"Nope. You had some bad luck, that's all. Shit happens. What you do next could screw things up, but so far I don't know what you could have done differently. How do you feel? How did the fight go for you?"

"Well . . . I don't know exactly. I mean, it was exhilarating in a terrifying sort of way. I fired a lot of bullets but I don't believe I hit anyone, even as close as we were. I'm rather glad, actually, now that we know . . . well. The thought that it was all unnecessary . . ." He shook his head. "I don't suppose you ever ran into anything like this before."

I laughed without humor.

"Oh, I see. Then what is the best way to avoid this sort of thing happening again?"

"Career change was working pretty well for me until today."

The Greek word *anabasis* means the march up-country. Twice the Greeks used it to mean a heroic march through enemy-controlled territory: the march of the Ten Thousand under Xenophon and the March of the Macedonian army of conquest under Alexander.

We buried our dead. We loaded our wounded and the two surviving Bosnians in the steam launch, along with one healthy Bavarian armed with his own rifle and my report to Cevik Bey on the incident. Once it came time to explain what happened, I didn't want the two *Jandarma* to have the only voice.

We had no pack animals, so we left our tents in the steam launch. As it chugged downriver to safety, we distributed our provisions, ammunition, and Cevik Bey's eight signal rockets among our backpacks and haversacks, determined our march order, and began our own *anabasis*.

TWENTY-SIX

October 9, 1888, The Lim River valley, Serbia

It was late in the day to begin a march, but we needed to keep the men moving and too busy or too tired to think. We ate on our feet—hardtack, although the Marines called it ship biscuit. It filled my belly but made me thirsty.

We marched southeast until sunset and then kept going, slowly and carefully. Sunset came early this time of year, about five in the afternoon, and with the weather it was full dark less than an hour later.

The Serbian border town of Priboj and its gun batteries lay across the river on the southwest bank, and Gordon and I decided our best move was to use the darkness as cover and make our way past it that night. There was a new moon, and enough overcast we didn't even have starlight to see by, so our progress slowed to a crawl. We had to move carefully; the last thing we needed was someone with a broken leg.

I expected to be able to pick Priboj out on the far bank by lights on the waterfront, but there was nothing. The town might have been scoured from the planet, its inhabitants struck down or carried off, for all we could tell. The only evidence of life we heard was the crackle of rifle fire drifting across the water, distant and impotent-sounding, about an hour after dark. We paused to watch the distant fireflies of light, and make sure they weren't firing at us, but it had the sound of a close-in fight to me, people firing as fast as they could rather than taking careful aim.

"Is that the Turkish patrol?" Gordon asked softly as we listened.

"Might be. They're on the wrong side of the river, but who knows?"

We decided to take a five-minute rest break, and I sat down next to Gabrielle.

"How you holding up?"

"I am fine. My load is small compared to the others. Some of the Marines, they fly too much. They are not so used to the walking."

She was right. I'd heard some panting from one of the Marines myself. If they were out of shape, somebody wasn't doing their job back on *Intrepid*. There was plenty of deck space for exercise. With all those companionways up and down, the climbing alone should have kept their legs and lungs strong. It was too late to do anything about it now, aside from keeping an eye on it.

"I was frightened for you back at Uvats."

"Really?" she asked.

"Yes. When I saw the blood . . ."

"Oh. You thought it was mine? *Non*. It was terrifying and so surprising. We had no warning, simply gunfire and men falling. I did not know what to do at first. Then the lieutenant stepped in front of me, as if to shield me. Otherwise I would be dead instead of him. When I heard the shot, felt his blood on me, I must have jumped behind the seawall, but I do not remember."

"You got a round or two off from your Winchester, as I recall."

"Yes. That I remember."

I patted her hand but could not see her expression in the darkness.

The distant firing died away, and the silence was somehow more ominous after that.

"I wonder who won," she said.

A bird screeched, and we both started. Hearing a hawk in the distance was one thing, but this one was close, maybe a hundred yards, and it sounded—bigger. The way a tiger sounds bigger than a house cat when it purrs and the purr comes out as a rumbling noise in the back of its throat that could rattle the china in a cupboard across the room.

"Fricken Teufel," a Bavarian soldier near us muttered.

Another screech answered him, farther away and from behind us in the direction of Uvats. I stood up and listened. More screeches behind us, and then a murmur of frightened conversation ran the length of the small column. Much of it was in German, and I caught, *"To hell with the British,"* and *"Let's get out of here!"*

"Gabi, better break out that shotgun, but stay down. Don't run."

What was the name of the Bavarian sergeant? Müller? No, Melzer.

"*Feldwebel* Melzer," I called out. "Where are you?"

He called to me from near the back of the column, and I made my way past nervous soldiers rising to their feet and checking their weapons. I hadn't said much to Melzer since the fight in Uvats, and neither had Gordon. With von Schtecker dead, he was in charge of the Bavarians, and I don't think either one of us had a good sense of who he was. As I walked in the darkness I tried to reconstruct a mental image of him: average height, stocky, broad jowly face with deep-set eyes, crooked nose, and a pronounced under bite that gave him a defiant, pugnacious look. But he'd never made much noise, and he wasn't barking his men to silence now. I never know what to make of quiet sergeants.

"Your men are nervous."

"*Ja.* Who is not?" He looked around even though there was nothing to see in the darkness.

"Fargo! Damn it, where are you?"

That was Gordon, panic creeping into his voice.

"Back here with *Feldwebel* Melzer."

The babble of conversation up and down the line grew louder, and Melzer just stood there with his thumb up his ass.

"Ruhig in dem Rängen!" I barked in my best drill-instructor voice—*quiet in the ranks.* Whether from instinctive obedience or just surprise, they immediately shut up.

"Fargo, is that you? Speak up, dammit. I can't see a bloody thing."

"Right here," I answered, and Gordon joined us, breathing heavily. Walking the length of our short column hadn't winded him. My money was on fear.

"I don't know what's out there, but we need to get away from them," he blurted out.

"*Ja,*" Melzer agreed, his head bobbing in agreement.

"No!" I said. "Form a firing line with a squad—"

But nobody was listening.

"Make for the foothills to the left!" Gordon shouted. "We'll take cover there, find some trees!"

Take cover? From animals? Now men began running off to the left, the sounds of jingling and clanking equipment almost drowning out their footfalls, but not the renewed screeching of birds, more birds, a large gaggle on the hunt, except they were on the ground, not in the air. I ran back to where I left Gabrielle, and she was still there, sitting in the grass, waiting for me.

"Come on, Gabi, time to haul ass!" I helped her to her feet.

"You said not to run if the others did." Fear made her voice shake, and I could feel it tighten my own chest as well.

"Yeah, I just didn't count on the whole outfit going."

We ran. I ran to her left and a little behind her, between her and the sound of the animals. When she looked back to see if I was there, I yelled at her to run as hard as she could. I kept up with her.

We passed someone down in the grass, trying to get up, but didn't break stride to help. Part of me was relieved we weren't the last stragglers anymore and grateful I wasn't in charge, because then I'd have to stop and help. Another part of me was ashamed of those feelings, but it was a small part and not a very survival-helpful one at the moment.

I tripped, almost fell sprawling, but kept my feet and regained my stride. From its sound and weight I knew I'd tripped on a dropped rifle, and the sudden surge of anger almost overwhelmed me. *Idiot!* Some jackass dropped his rifle and had almost killed me, not to mention himself and his friends when the animals caught up and he was unarmed.

We'd overtaken at least some of the fugitives, but the sound of something coming through the grass was close now. No one was going to stop on their own, and this couldn't end well. The ground cover was higher, thicker here. Branches and tree limbs crunched under my feet, and I saw the darker shape of a tree trunk.

"Come on you lot!" I heard O'Mara shout close by. "Keep together." At least someone was still thinking about their men.

Time to make a move.

"Marines, rally on me! O'Mara, pick a spot for a stand."

"Right. 'Ere's as good a place as any to face 'em. Form up, you bastards!"

I knew the emotions struggling in the men. Their legs wanted to keep running, but their heads wanted someone to tell them what to do. It might be too late, though. The animals, whatever they were, were close, streaking through the brush and tall grass.

I grabbed Gabrielle by the arm to slow her, and we found a small knot of men, hard to tell how many in the darkness.

"Form a firing line facing the animals," I shouted, my voice hoarse. "Do it now! Close up and keep it tight."

And then the first one of them hit us, rocketing though the air in a leap. I only saw it for an instant, but it was the size of a wolf or bigger. It hit a Marine in the chest and bowled him over into the brush, the two of them rolling in a pinwheel of arms, legs, and feathers—big feathers.

"FIRE!" I screamed and got a ragged volley of four or fire rounds. I added two quick rounds from the Webley, firing low and spreading the shots, although the noise and muzzle flash were more important than the potential damage.

"Again! Keep it up."

I heard the bird screeching behind me, the down Marine crying out, fighting for his life. The ragged volley had wiped out whatever night vision I had. Everything was sound and smell now. Sweat and fear, crushed grass and black powder. The crack of more rifle rounds from our firing line, screeches of animals, cries of men going down under them, but not here, farther from the river toward the hills. A wet-sounding thud and the animal on the ground squawked once in pain and fell silent.

"That's done for him," O'Mara said, his voice ragged. "On yer feet, Williams."

"Gabrielle, where are you?"

"I am here," she answered.

An animal streaked past me from a different direction. Gabrielle screamed as she and the bird went down together. I jumped on top, got my left hand into the feathers on its neck, and tried to pull it off, but the son of a bitch was strong! Screeching, ripping cloth, cries of pain. I raised the pistol and cracked the bird on its back—aimed for the head, but it was moving too much. The blow didn't make much impression through the feathers, but I got its attention. It spun and sank its teeth into my forearm, or at least the sleeve of my coat, shook its head, and I felt its strength all the way up in my shoulder.

Its jaws, its head—too big for a bird. *A bird with teeth?* a remote part of my mind asked.

I didn't know who might be in my line of fire but had to take the chance. I pushed the Webley's barrel against its chest and pulled the trigger. Its body muffled the sound. It jerked, let go of my arm, took a step away, and fell over with a whimper.

"Gabi, are you okay?"

"I . . . I don't know. I . . ."

I felt for her, found her, did a quick check on her face, throat, and hands, and didn't find anything slippery with blood. She trembled uncontrollably.

"Hold it together, sweetheart. Okay?"

"*Oui*."

"You carry matches, for your cheroots, right? Dig some out. I need them," I said.

"O'Mara!" I shouted.

"One moment, sir. Cooperson, is that you on the end? You and Williams, half left, two paces forward, and fire to the south. Space your shots. You others keep up your fire but slow and steady, in sequence right to left."

Then he knelt next to me.

"Is the lady all right, sir?"

"I think so, for now, but whatever these animals are, they'll circle around eventually. We need a fire."

"What the blazes are those things, sir?"

"Fire," I repeated.

"Right. A fire," he said, and it was clear it hadn't occurred to him. "Aye, a fire would be a fine thing, sir, and there's wood lying about here, but it's damp from all the rain. It will take some time to get it going."

"I bet we can speed things up if one of the men has a signal rocket."

"I've got one here, sir." He slipped his pack off and set it beside me. "I'll see to some wood."

I holstered the Webley and felt O'Mara's pack with my hands. I found the signal rocket lashed to the top, got it free, and took my first close look at it, although by feel. A sheet-metal cylinder with a crimped cone at one end and a bracket for a launching stick at the other. The stick itself was tied to the rocket. I pulled out my sheath knife, cut the lashings that held the rod to the rocket, and started working at the soldered seam by the bottom.

"Here's some wood, and I'll get more." O'Mara dumped an armload of damp brush and branches beside us and hurried away.

I had the bottom open by now and shook out some of the powder of the propelling charge into the brush.

"Got those matches?"

"Here," Gabrielle answered and handed me a half-dozen and a box with a striker strip on the side. Her hand was steadier now. My own shook enough that I broke the first match, but I took two long, slow breaths to steady myself. The second match lit, and the charge powder sizzled and flared to life, igniting the brush. That got a ragged cheer from the Marines around us.

I worked the top of the rocket tube open, shook out a handful of the powder from the bursting charge, and threw it into the fire, got a nice flash from it and a wave of heat.

I turned to get more fuel, and right there, not more than ten feet away, I saw the eyes of a large hunting bird glowing with the reflected light of the fire behind me, disembodied and seemingly floating in the air. I pulled my Webley out, careful not to make any sudden move, took aim, and fired twice. I sensed more than saw the animal fly back from the impact.

A Marine was down in the grass near me. I could tell at first from the direction of his voice; then I could make him out in the growing firelight. He was praying in a thick Irish brogue.

"Hail Mary, full o' grace, the Lard is with thee. Blessed art d'ou among wimin, and blessed is the fruit o' thy womb Jesus. Holy Mary, Mudder o' Gawd, pray fer us sinners now and at the hour of our death."

But it wasn't the hour of our death. Close, but no cigar.

TWENTY-SEVEN

October 9, 1888, The Lim River valley, Serbia

We kept the fire going, built it up, and had no more trouble from the animals.

Others straggled in over the course of the next hour, more than I thought would have survived. We'd been the Tail-End Charlies, so most of the animals had concentrated on us at first. When we kicked their asses, the flock, or pack, or whatever, lost a lot of its enthusiasm for the hunt. Many of our survivors had thrown away their rifles and packs. Gordon was among those who came in, but he didn't have anything to say at first. At least he still had his pack.

Gabrielle and I had matching bites on our left arms, and she had a slash in her left thigh. She had been wearing her long overcoat over her riding habit, so the teeth hardly broke the skin, but the long knifelike spur on the bird's foot had sliced through her overcoat, skirt, riding breeches, and into her thigh. If not for all those layers, the wound might have killed or crippled her.

I made her take off the coat and black jacket, rolled up the blood-stained sleeve of her blouse, cleaned the wound with rubbing alcohol, and then wrapped it with a clean linen bandage, both from her own haversack. I did the same with her thigh, first cutting away that leg of her breeches up to the hip. The slash looked deep, but it wasn't bleeding all that badly so I just bandaged it good and tight. I pulled off my coat, and she bandaged my arm. I made sure we cleaned all the wounds thoroughly; the last thing we needed out here was an infection.

"You got any antibiotic cream or powder in that first-aid kit?"

"I do not know what that is," she answered.

"No, I was afraid of that."

We had two animal carcasses close by the fire, and we looked them over. They were like the biggest wild turkeys, or maybe fighting cocks, you could imagine, probably seventy or eighty pounds each, but with much thicker, more muscular legs and broader feet. They didn't have beaks so much as long, bony snouts lined with small, sharp teeth. Their heads were too big for birds, though, and featured a flaring transverse crest across the back of their skulls which reminded me of the hood of a triceratops, but in feathers.

Their forearms bore a pretty complete set of long feathers, but nowhere near enough for flight. The substantial and muscular forearms ended in grasping talons. Their main weapons were the long, knifelike spurs on their hind legs, the ones which almost got Gabrielle and sliced up one of the Marines badly. The giveaway, though, was the tail, long and thin and about a meter long, as long as the rest of the bird's body.

Neither the Brits nor the Bavarians had ever seen anything remotely like them. I had. Sarah had gone through a dinosaur phase, and that meant *I'd* gone through a dinosaur phase. I'd taken her to the Field Museum for the opening of a new exhibit on the late Cretaceous period a few years back. It included the first reconstructions of *Velociraptor mongoliensis* after the fossil finds that established it was feathered. The ones in adventure films were featherless and always larger, about man-sized, I guess for dramatic effect, which was over twice as big as the real animals. These carcasses weren't that big, but they were bigger than the *V. mongoliensis* Sarah and I had seen, and the heads looked different, shorter and wider. Maybe they were a related species, like *dromaeosaurus,* or maybe something I'd never seen—something nobody from my *time* had ever seen. Who cared? They were night predators, hunted in packs, and were plenty big enough for me.

The fire burned smoky from the damp wood, and the wind kept changing, blowing the smoke in our faces no matter where we sat. Gabrielle and I got our coats back on and sat together, shoulder to shoulder, near enough to the fire to catch its warmth but far enough the smoke wasn't too bad. At least when the wind gusted around we had time to close our eyes and hold our breath.

We hadn't had a real meal since morning, and once the raptors—I couldn't help thinking of them that way—seemed done for the night, some of the men started eating. None of us considered roasting one of the dead animals, interestingly enough.

I took a tin of bully beef from my haversack and Gabrielle and I shared it, pulling strings of the greasy corned beef from the can with our fingers and spreading them on hardtack. It gave me an entirely new appreciation for MREs.

Don't it always seem to go, you don't know what you got till it's gone?

Somebody got a kettle going, and O'Mara came around with two tin cups of tea for us and knelt in the grass beside me. The tea was sweet with sugar and evaporated milk, almost overpowering the flavor of the tea itself, but it hit the spot all the same.

"One of my lot's still missin'," O'Mara said. "Don't know about the Fritzes. Don't think their sergeant has done a count."

"Okay. Thanks for keeping me up to date, but you need to make a report to Captain Gordon."

O'Mara looked over toward Gordon, standing by himself at the edge of the light circle, and spat.

"Corporal, things are going to get worse here. I'm betting they're going to get lots worse. Undercutting Gordon might give you some personal satisfaction, but it won't keep your men alive."

"The men'll follow you, sir."

"Well, thank you for saying that, but the Bavarians won't, and we need them. All that keeps them here are their orders to work with Gordon."

O'Mara thought that over, chewed on it like a piece of gristle he was reluctant to swallow, but eventually he nodded.

"As you say, sir. You want me to talk to the Fritz sergeant?"

"No, I will. He outranks you. He probably won't take an ass-chewing from you all that well."

That got a smile from him. He rose and walked across the firelit circle to Gordon, came to attention, saluted, and gave a report I could see but not hear. I looked around the circle until I located Melzer.

"I'll be back," I told Gabi.

I walked over to him. He and a knot of his men smoked their clay pipes and cast sour, resentful looks across the fire at Gordon.

"Can we talk?" I said as soon as I faced him.

"Talk here," he answered, his jaw thrust out farther than normal.

"How many men did you lose?"

"Too *verdammt* many, thanks to your officer."

The three other Bavarians with him nodded and murmured their agreement.

"How many?"

He hesitated, then looked at his companions.

"*Heinrich ging unten,*" one of them said.

"*Gerhard auch,*" said another.

"*Nein, ist Gerhard hier,*" Melzer answered. "*Wo ist Burkhardt?*"

"Corporal O'Mara has already taken roll and reported to Captain Gordon," I said. "He is a good noncommissioned officer who remembers his duty."

"Duty to him?" Melzer said, gesturing across the fire to Gordon.

"Duty to his men. Captain Gordon said to run to the trees and take cover. O'Mara did that, kept his men together, and in the trees found the brush and wood for this fire. He followed Captain Gordon's orders and his men lived, except one who lost his head and kept running.

"Where did you rally your men, *Feldwebel*? Where did you stop them from running? The *Bayerisch Garde Schützen*, routed by a flock of poultry!"

The three men with Melzer shifted uncomfortably and exchanged looks, but Melzer remained motionless, his eyes avoiding mine.

"Do your head count. Find out how many of your men are alive, how many still have their rifles, how many are injured and how severely. Make your report to Captain Gordon. Do it now."

I turned and walked away, but after a few steps Melzer's hand on my arm stopped me. He nodded toward the darkness, and I followed him a couple steps so we were out of earshot of the others.

"You speak to me this way in front of my men?" he hissed.

"I gave you the chance to talk in private and you wouldn't, so go fuck yourself. Next time keep your nerve, do your job, keep your men alive. Or I'll find someone who can."

I rejoined Gabrielle, watched Melzer do his head count and make his report, but it wasn't long before Gordon drifted over to us. I was tired of talking, but this was one conversation that couldn't wait.

We stepped away from the fire. He didn't say anything at first. I guess he wasn't really sure where to start.

"I panicked," he finally said,

"Yeah, no shit. Don't do that again."

"That's easy for you to say."

"It's easy to say and hard to do. So what? Someone promise you 'easy' when you put on a uniform?"

I leaned in close and spoke quietly to make sure no one at the fire would hear my words.

"Get those NCOs under control and remind them who's in charge. You've got to get out ahead of them mentally and stay there, tell them what to do next before they think of it.

"You screwed up today. I dragged enough brush over your trail they'll wait and see what you do next, but this is it, Gordon. One more screwup and you will never get them back and this expedition is down to me trying to make it through the mountains on my own."

"I've never been in the field before," he said. "I feel . . . I can't explain it, exactly, but—"

"Look," I interrupted, "back in my own time, when I was still in uniform, sometimes I'd get assigned young soldiers, first time away from home, first time they weren't the center of attention, the center of the universe. They'd try explaining how they felt about it all, and as their squad leader I would counsel them. Know what I'd say? *'Just do your job, kid.'*

"Maybe you had a bad childhood—overprotective mother, overbearing father, whatever. I don't care. I don't care about your mother or your father or how you felt when your pet frog died when you were five years old. They aren't here. You are.

"So just suck it up and do your job."

When I got back to the fire, Gabrielle was curled up and sleeping on the ground, her head cushioned on her rolled ground cover and blanket. I unrolled my own ground cover and spread it behind her, then picked her up gently in my arms and slid her onto it, laid down behind her, and spread my blanket over us. Half of the group was snoring by then, the rest looking as if they were wind-up toys running down even as I watched. Fear and exertion take it out of you, burn up every ounce of go-juice you've got before you even realize it, and leave you dull-witted and heavy-limbed.

Just before sleep closed my own eyes like the curtain after the final act of a play, I heard Gordon come back into the light. He rousted O'Mara and Melzer and had them post sentries.

Good.

I slept a dreamless sleep. I almost always did. I can hardly recall the last time I had a dream I remembered, other than that dream I had of Gabrielle the night in Munich. People who experience combat are supposed to have all sorts of tortured, violent dreams. I knew a few guys who did and a lot more who just didn't talk about it, so I have no way of knowing. When I first got home from Afghanistan, I had some pretty nasty dreams, but not about what actually happened. They were sexual dreams, very vivid, and very violent. Just having had them made me ashamed, made me wonder what sort of creep I really was. Those dreams went away after a while.

A few years later I used to have a dream where I was in bed and Joanne was beside me, asleep, still alive. Joanne was my late wife, Sarah's mother. Nothing happened in the dream. I'd just be in bed and Joanne was beside me. When I woke up, she wasn't there. I'd touch the bed where she had been, just to make sure she hadn't gotten up to go to the bathroom or start breakfast, thinking maybe all the rest of it was the dream. But the bed was always cold. I only had that dream a few times, at least that I remember.

After a while I stopped dreaming altogether, or at least stopped remembering my dreams.

Some people think dreams are a window to your future. If so, I didn't have a future. Either that or the window was closed pretty damned tight. Personally, I don't think dreams mean anything, which is probably why I don't remember them.

Gabrielle and I woke in the predawn twilight. The fire was lower, but the sentries had fed it during the night, kept it alive. I don't know which of us woke first, but both knew by the change in breathing of the other that we were awake. Gabrielle rolled over and faced me, eyes only inches from mine. Her face was streaked with dirt and wood smoke, her hair loose and tangled, and she frowned slightly in concentration, searching my eyes for something, I don't know what. I'm not sure she knew.

"Are you thinking about your daughter?" she asked after a while.

"No. I was thinking about a different little girl."

"Tell me about her."

"She was an orphan. She was physically awkward when she was young, not very good at sports or games, and the other girls always chose her last for teams. She felt like an outsider—unloved and unneeded. She wanted friends but did not make them easily, didn't ever really understand the ease the other girls felt with each other. It was as if everyone else had been told a secret withheld from her. Or perhaps she hadn't been paying attention at the right time, when everyone else learned it.

"Her best friend was a doll, or maybe a stuffed animal, I'm not sure which."

"A doll," she said quietly.

"She found it much easier to bond with the doll than with other children. She could imagine the doll loving and understanding her, while the other children did not.

"The other girls resented the order and discipline of the convent, but she liked it. She liked its predictable, unchanging routine. She thought the nuns would value her more for that."

"They did not," she whispered.

"No. Maybe that's why she left. Leaving the orderly routine of the convent must have been unimaginably hard, the hardest thing she ever did, but she did it. She had determination and courage. She grew into a beautiful, intelligent young woman, and as she did, her physical awkwardness disappeared. But she never felt as if she belonged. Even in the company of others, she was always alone."

Tears welled up in her eyes, but I saw no other sign of emotion in her face. She wiped her eyes and sniffed.

"I have never told you this. I have never told anyone this. How do you know these things about me?"

"You think the world is divided into you and then everyone else, but it isn't. There are lots of people who have gone through exactly what you have. It's a mental condition. No, that makes it sound like a sickness, and it isn't. There's nothing wrong with you, Gabi, not one goddamned thing. You're as close to perfect as God makes us. It's just a slightly different way the brain is organized in some highly intelligent people.

"Napoleon had the condition. So did a lot of great people in history, and some pretty amazing people in my own time. There was a guy named Albert Einstein, he went on—will go on—to become the greatest scientific mind of the twentieth century. He had it. It's called Asperger's syndrome."

"Asperger's syndrome?" she asked. "What does it mean? Why has no one told me this before?"

"Nobody figured it out until the 1940s, and even then a lot of people weren't convinced until decades later. But it's real. I mentored three doctoral students with the condition, all of them unique individuals. They shared some traits, though, and their childhoods were remarkably similar. The physical awkwardness in youth, the social awkwardness throughout life, the difficulty empathizing, sometimes hypersensitivity to noise, fascination with order and routine, sometimes liking to collect things or study things in minute detail—"

"When I research a subject," she broke in, interest growing in her voice, "I find out every detail I can. I fill notebooks, carefully organize them. I have a system I use to label them."

"Sounds right to me."

"Napoleon had this condition? You are certain?"

"Well, judging from what we know about his life and behavior, it's a pretty good bet."

"He was very lonely as a boy, was he not?"

I brushed a lock of hair from her forehead and touched her cheek. "Yes, he was."

"It is real, this thing?"

Is it real? My thoughts went back to a cocktail party, one of those joint things designed to bring all the humanities faculty together. Schwartz from the psych department had me backed into a corner, berating me about how there was no such thing as Asperger's. Patel, also from psych, wandered over, his drink crowned with a small paper umbrella. The caterers did not provide those but Patel always brought his own.

"Is Schwartz on about Asperger's again?" he asked. "One more drink and he will start in on how there is no such thing as post traumatic stress disorder."

Schwartz turned on him. "It's a fucking symptom cluster!" he shouted, jabbing with his index finger for emphasis, sloshing scotch from his glass. "It's not a fucking disease!"

"Ho-*ho!*" Patel said, rocking back on his heels, pleased at the reaction he had provoked. "Ho-*ho!*"

I wasn't a psychologist; I was an historian. What did I know about what was and wasn't real? I knew that if only one person did something a thousand years ago, it never happened, but if ten million people did it, it was a historic trend. What was and wasn't real depended on what we noticed, and then what we decided to call it.

Symptom cluster? What did Schwartz know? Hell, *life* was a symptom cluster.

"It's as real as anything else I know," I told Gabi.

She was quiet for a while, absorbing it all.

"There is a cure for this?" she asked finally, a tiny sliver of hope showing like a line of light under the tightly closed door of her inner sanctuary.

"Gabi, it's not a disease."

Her eyes wandered past my shoulder, her mind somewhere out in the glowing purple of the morning sky on the eastern horizon. Maybe even farther than that.

"I see."

TWENTY-EIGHT

October 10, 1888, The Lim River valley, Serbia

We'd camped in the shade of a wood which stretched up the slopes of the foothills to the north and east. The ground opened up behind us down to the river, and I had a good view of Priboj, across the river and about a mile to the southwest. Its stucco houses with tile and shingle roofs sprawled along the riverbanks and up a ridge gray with granite outcroppings. Smoke rose from the town, thick smoke from burning buildings here and there, but I saw no other movement. There might be a few people moving around down there, but there sure weren't a couple thousand.

Refuse dotted the meadow along the river on the far bank—a cart, bundles of possessions, pieces of clothing fluttering in the light breeze, and silent lumps I took to be bodies. The number of bodies suggested a panic rather than a mass slaughter. No one stopped to bury those people, but we buried our own dead that morning.

Two of the missing Bavarians were still alive, having climbed into a tree and spent the night there. Three of the Bavarians and one Marine were dead, and their bodies weren't in good shape. I didn't know the Bavarians, but the Marine was the youngster named Kane, the one who took a shot at the wolves back in Uvats, and who lost his lunch when he saw the bodies in the building.

We'd started out with thirty-six people, and less than a day after stepping ashore at Uvats we were down to twenty-five. This was turning into a massacre.

And we hadn't gotten to the bad guys yet.

Fear and depression showed clearly in the faces of the men. In my opinion, the Bavarians were finished. They'd taken most of the casualties and, between the dead buried here and the wounded sent back with the steamer, they were down to about half strength. They all had to be thinking about their chances of surviving day two of this death march.

It might have been different if Melzer were more of a leader, but he wasn't and I didn't expect him to suddenly "find himself" in the crucible of combat. I didn't think there was much there to find.

Gabrielle and I ate a breakfast of tinned bacon, ship biscuit, jam, and sweet tea. The Marines cooked and shared with us, so in true British style the bacon was hardly warm. I knew it was sort of cooked before it went into the can, but it was still gross. It was nice of them to share, though, so I smiled and choked it down. Gabrielle didn't seem to mind.

"The weather turns cold," she observed. "We will use up fat to climb the mountains."

From a fuel point of view, I didn't have an argument. Other than that she didn't have much to say over breakfast. She sat quietly with her thoughts, which wasn't surprising. I'd given her a lot to process.

Work details recovered the abandoned weapons and packs, and we leveled the supplies between those of us still standing. Corporal O'Mara walked across the trampled camp area with a rifle in each hand, stopped by us, and held them up for me to see.

"Which one suits you, sir?"

"I'll take the Mauser."

"Don't want poor Kane's Lee-Metford?"

"Your section shot off a lot of rounds last night. Split Kane's ammunition up between your men. I'm betting there's plenty of Mauser ammo to go around."

He looked at the Mauser and smiled ruefully.

"Well, you're right about that, sir, although I wouldn't say it too loud. The Fritzes are a bit touchy this morning."

I took the Mauser, opened the bolt to eject the chambered round, and caught it in the air. It sure wasn't the classic 8mm Mauser cartridge I was used to. It was bigger than I expected, fatter, and a good three inches long, most of which was brass. If it were loaded with modern propellant, this thing would shoot through stone walls, and probably break my shoulder, but I remembered the cloud of smoke over the

Bavarian firing positions at the seawall and the smell of the fight last night—black powder. There was a slight neck-down in the cartridge, so slight I wondered why they bothered, and a round-headed lead slug that had to be 11 or 12mm.

The long cartridge case was rimmed, center-fire, and stamped with "MÜNCHEN" on the base along with a couple numbers that didn't mean anything to me, maybe lot numbers.

There was no box magazine at all.

"So, how does this thing work?"

"The bullet comes out 'ere, sir," O'Mara said cheerfully, touching the muzzle with his finger. "Beyond that you'll have to ask a Bavarian."

O'Mara returned to his men, and not long after that Gordon joined us. I had the feeling he had waited until we were alone. He asked Gabrielle's permission before sitting on the grass beside me.

"I am concerned about the Bavarians," he said.

"Good. You ought to be. I think those animals are all that kept them from slipping away in the darkness last night. How are you going to keep them moving?"

"They are Germans, after all, a martial race bred to obedience. You don't think they will simply follow my orders?"

I considered tackling the notion that people were bred pretty much like dogs, but what was the point?

"No, I don't think so. Not for long, anyway."

"What do you propose?"

I pointed across the river.

"Priboj looks deserted. I wouldn't be surprised if the other towns and villages around here were as well. Whatever's going on, it's not limited to the Bosnian side of the border. Even if someone sees us, the authorities probably have their hands full. Originally we planned to move mostly at night and avoid the towns. I think we can stop worrying about running into the Serbian Army; they've got bigger fish to fry. You got your map?"

Gordon pulled the map from his map case and spread it on the ground. It was about fifteen miles from Priboj to Kokin Brod, most of it over a mountain road.

"We planned on moving at night and off the road to avoid detection. I don't think we have to worry about that," I said.

"Near as I can tell we're less than a mile from this first town,

Pribojska Spa, just past this woods. I say we push through the woods to there and pick up the road. We're also almost out of water, so we need to find some. If spa means the same thing in Serbia as it does everywhere else, it may have natural spring water and we won't have to boil it, but either way we find some there. Another mile to this village—what is it? Banja?—then up the road five or six miles to that last village before Kokin Brod."

"Kratovo," Gordon said, craning his neck to read the map.

"Whatever. That puts us almost halfway to Kokin Brod, and it's mostly downhill from there. We spend the night there and finish the march the next day, or hold up there a day and scope things out. The thing is, it gives us an objective for the day that ends up with us under roofs and behind walls. That's got to sound better to the Bavarians than this."

"They might think marching back to Uvats is better still," Gordon said.

"Well, if that comes up, you could point out that you've got the only translator, so good luck explaining what happened to the *Jandarma* when the Turkish Army shows up."

Gordon smiled for the first time.

"Yes, there is that. Very well, we will march to Kratovo today, and then we will decide how to proceed after that."

The Bavarians weren't happy, but then who was? The important thing was they marched, and they kept their muttered complaints in German. Less than an hour through the woods brought us to the outskirts of Pribojska Spa. The town clung to the sides of a small valley and the mass of the mountains rose abruptly behind it, like a backdrop, covered with forests the color of dusty jade. The grain of the mountains ran from northwest to southeast, and our road to the east would take us along the foothills for a mile or two and then up and across.

A bubbling spring near the road let us replenish our water without having to enter the town. There were still people in Pribojska Spa. I caught occasional movement in a window, a door moving slightly to give someone a view, but the locals kept their distance. We weren't in uniform, but we didn't look like we came from around here. We looked armed and dangerous. The town was large enough to at least have police, but they were either gone or hiding as well. In a way, this was good for morale. It was spooky, but the feeling someone was afraid of *us* made the men feel more confident.

The road meandered, following the increasingly rocky and uneven foothills. Another hour of marching took us to Banja, a narrow string of whitewashed stucco houses, barns, and outbuildings sprinkled along either side of the road. We were greeted by a musket shot at two hundred yards—obviously a warning rather than an attempt to do genuine injury.

"What do you think?" Gordon asked.

The men had spread out into a skirmish line, easily finding cover in the broken ground, and so far they had followed the order not to return fire. The Bavarians stirred restlessly, though, eager for a fight. No, they were eager for an *easy* fight, a cheap shot at redemption for having run the previous night. A ramshackle mountain village defended by some guy with a rusty musket probably sounded like the ticket.

"I think we skirt the village to the north. If whoever's in the village tries something, we'll see it coming, have the high ground."

"The Bavarians seem anxious to prove themselves. I wonder if it might not help things if we give them their heads."

I avoided looking at him. He wouldn't have liked what he'd have seen in my eyes.

"Worst case, there are a dozen armed men in there who tear the Bavarians apart once they get in close, kill or cripple half of them and break the spirit of the rest. Best case? A bunch of murdered villagers, probably a few rapes. Or maybe that's the worst case and a bunch of dead Bavarians is better. Except they're your men. It gets complicated."

Gordon took off his cork helmet, scratched his scalp, and squinted up at the rocky ridge north of the village.

"You think you're so bloody superior," he said after a moment.

"Next time I tell you a story, I'll make sure there are butterflies and kittens in it."

He glared at me but said nothing.

We climbed the slope and made our way past Banja. The Bavarians grumbled until we got to a promontory with a good view down at the place. I called O'Mara and Melzer over and we squatted there on the granite, picking out the barricades by some of the walled gardens, the groups of two or three armed men moving from house to house, keeping us under observation. It wouldn't have been the easy fight it looked like from outside. That gave the Bavarians something to think about.

Half an hour later, we scrambled back down the ridge and returned to the road. The path was straighter after Banja, but after a mile it began climbing steadily and conversation died away. Gordon kept up a good pace, so he had a good set of legs and lungs, but the Marines were showing signs of wear.

"Tell me . . . a story . . . about . . . your daughter," Gabrielle said beside me between puffs for air.

I though for a moment and then told her, my story broken into the same respiratory data packets as her request.

"Little girls look up to their older male brothers and cousins, sometimes hero-worship them a little. When Sarah was about eight, we were at a family picnic. Her cousin Rudy—he was about twelve then—came over and said, 'Hey, Sarah, go over and pinch Joey on the butt. It'll really embarrass him.' Joey was a friend of Rudy's, not family."

"What did Sarah do?"

"She looked up at him and said, 'Forget it, Rudy. I'm not the clown in your circus.'"

Gabrielle smiled.

Telling that story always made me smile, too, filled me with a warm feeling, a glow, but here it just left me cold and tight in the chest.

We walked in silence.

"I have no family memories," she said after a while. "Thank you for sharing yours. Family is so important to people, I see this all the time. It gives great comfort, does it not?"

Not always.

With the setting sun at our backs we trudged up the steep grade. Gordon called regular rest stops, but I saw some of the Marines having a hard time getting back up again after the breaks. Gabrielle wasn't carrying as heavy a load as most of the rest of us, but with her shotgun and ammunition, it was pretty close. She was tiring, but so was I, so were all of us. It was a hard march. She didn't show signs of weakening, though. Nothing wrong with her legs.

There's a reason physical conditioning is so important. Soldiers have to do things like march for hours up a mountainside with a full pack and still do their job. Their job includes staying mentally alert, keeping their eyes open, thinking about what is around them and what it means, and that's really hard if you've burned through all your energy reserves and are staggering along, using all your concentration to just put one foot in front of the other.

So that's how we walked into the ambush.

It was pretty slick, as ambushes go. They caught us where the road leveled for a stretch. The right side dropped down and away at a shallow angle, a rocky field without much cover. A sheer embankment rose to the left, about two meters tall, with boulders and scattered scrub above that—excellent cover and hard to get at, on top of that steep cut.

A voice called out in a Slavic language from ahead of us, from a cluster of rocks near the road. As soon as it did, a dozen rifles appeared to our left from the brush and rocks above the embankment, and when we looked there a dozen more appeared to our front, around the rocks—a perfect L-shaped ambush.

"He says to throw down our arms," Gabrielle said beside me, her voice shaking with fear.

He yelled again, more insistently. I looked around, but they had us cold. No cover to our right, no real way to rush the ambush site to our left because of the embankment, no way to do so to our front except in single file, raked by fire from our flank.

"Gordon," I yelled. "he says to drop our weapons. We better do it."

"What language?" I asked Gabrielle.

"Serbian."

Son of a bitch.

TWENTY-NINE

October 10, 1888, The Lim River valley, Serbia

I slipped the strap of the Mauser from my shoulder and eased it to the ground. Other rifles clattered down around me. The men in the brush and rocks above the road stood up, covering us with their own weapons. They wore uniforms that looked like most of the others we'd seen—threadbare dirty blue faded almost to a grubby gray. They wore faded red caps on the backs of their heads, round to the extent they had any shape at all, like stocking caps but made of felt. The caps weren't at all like the stiff cylindrical fezzes the Shriners wore, but they were fezzes all the same.

"We're going to be okay," I told Gabrielle. "I think we just found the missing Turks."

"I think they have found us."

Well, yes. Now, what was the Turkish-American sergeant's name? Durson.

"*Chavush* Durson," I called out. *Chavush* was Turkish for sergeant.

The men with rifles reacted, exchanged glances.

"*Chavush* Durson?" I repeated.

One of them lowered his rifle and pointed toward the rocks at the head of the column. I walked that way, my hands open and well up over my head.

"Better come along, Captain," I said to Gordon when I came even with him. "You've still got that dispatch for Sergeant Durson from Cevik Bey, right?"

We walked together toward the rocks and a cluster of soldiers.

"Sergeant Durson?" I asked in English when we got to within a half-dozen yards of them.

A very tall, very lean black man stepped forward. He wore three large dark green chevrons, points up and almost reaching his shoulder seam, on each sleeve of his blue jacket. I figured him to be about thirty, but it was hard to tell for sure, His face was lined, skin weathered, from a life spent outdoors. Long face with thoughtful eyes, close-cropped wiry hair, big strong hands resting calmly on his cartridge belt—those were my first impressions of Ibrahim Durson, the transplanted American.

"Who axe me?" Deep, steady voice.

"We have a dispatch from Cevik Bey for you."

Gordon took the sealed dispatch from his map case and handed it over. Durson drew a pair of wire-framed reading glasses from his tunic and put them on, frowned as he read the writing on the outside and examined the wax seal closely, then broke the seal, unfolded the dispatch, and read. He read slowly, his face an unreadable mask.

When he was done he took off his reading glasses and looked us over, then the men behind us.

"*So, Uh gwine maach wit duh buckruh. Dunno w'ymekso.*"

He spoke more to himself than to us, and he shook his head. I wasn't sure if it was from disgust or resignation. He turned to me.

"*Binbashi,*" and Durson raised the dispatch slightly by way of explanation, "*'e tell'e say Uh haffuh do 'um, but 'e sweet mout' me, too.*" He said that with bitterness in his voice. "*Duh tabak got t'irty-fo' soduh, strang, two gud cawpruls. Tabak long fuh grease dem mout'. Oonuh bring rashi'n?*" The question came out as an angry challenge, and his voice rose after that. "*Done soduh crackuhday to daak, spy billige in dayclean, steal biddle. Wore down. Hongry. Done 'nuf!*"

"What?" Gordon asked, looking from Durson to me.

I hadn't caught all of it, but enough to fake it for the moment. *Binbashi* and *tabak* were Turkish, the words for *major* and *platoon*. The rest . . .

"The sergeant has thirty-four men, but they're tired and out of food."

"Well, he can't bloody have any of ours."

"They're your men now, Captain. They won't be able to march very far or fight very hard on empty bellies."

Durson didn't react, but, from the way his eyes looked from Gordon to me when we spoke, I had the feeling he could pick up about as much of my words in English as I could of his.

"Did you live in the Carolinas, Sergeant?" I asked in Turkmen. "You can answer me in Turkish. I need the practice."

"I was born in South Carolina."

"My name is Jack Fargo. and this is Captain Gordon, the commander of the mission."

He looked to each of us wordlessly, anger still in his eyes.

"I am from Illinois," I added.

If that made an impression one way or the other, he hid it well. A wall stood between us, as thick and tall as any I'd ever run into. I'd traded insults with part-time Taliban hotshots in Kandahar's market and felt closer to them than to this man. Part of it was being on opposite sides of the officer-NCO divide, which for me was weird, at least finding myself on the officer end of the relationship, but that wasn't all of it. Part of it was race, but that wasn't all of it, either.

"Let me ask you, why did you challenge us in Serbian?"

"We thought you were Serbs. We expected no one else up here."

Well, that made sense. Good thing they were in the mood to take prisoners.

"We have some silver with us," I said, "enough to buy food for your men. Is there a town nearby?"

"Kratovo, a mile farther up the road, but your silver will purchase only death there."

"The cholera?"

"The *hajduci*."

That was a word I was unfamiliar with in either language. I shook my head and spread my hands.

"They were fighters against us when this was Turkish land, ten years ago. Now they fight for themselves. The Serb soldiers control the valleys, the *hajduci* the high country."

It wasn't the first time in history freedom fighters turned into bandits once the war was over.

"Is there a safe place nearby where we can rest?"

"We have a camp up the mountain, less than a mile from here, *Effendi*."

"Assemble your men, *Chavush* Durson. We will follow you."

I translated the conversation and Gordon shouted for the Marines and Bavarians to pick up their arms and come forward. Durson shouted his own orders and moved off a few steps to get his men assembled.

"What the devil was that gibberish?" Gordon demanded in a low voice.

"He doesn't speak English; he speaks Gullah. I don't imagine Cevik Bey knew the difference. Gullah is a slave patois, West African grammar with a lot of English borrow words, borrowed from British slavers interestingly enough. Most slaves along the southeastern U.S. coast spoke it back—well, still speak it now, I guess."

"You speak it?"

"I've read about it but I don't speak it. I can figure out about half of what he says. Good thing I speak Turkish. Sort-of. His Turkish is very good, by the way."

"Bloody hell."

"You aren't curious how a Gullah-speaking American ex-slave came to be a Turkish sergeant in a Bosnian rifle battalion?" I asked.

"Blasted Turks hire every drunk or ruined European who claims to have been a soldier, make half of them generals. Why not a nigger sergeant? All I want to know is how to get to Kokin Brod."

Occasionally I found myself getting used to this time, forgetting how different it really was from my own, different in ways not visible to the eye. Then a single word, shocking as a cattle prod, could remind me.

"You need to share our food with these men. You understand that, right?"

"Yes, I suppose so," he answered reluctantly. "Don't imagine they'll eat much. I doubt the Turks feed their men all that well. The officers probably steal half their food and sell it."

I wasn't so sure. Their uniforms were old and ragged, but the men looked healthy. They weren't carrying a lot of fat but had pretty good muscle mass. They didn't look to me as if anyone was stealing their rations.

I watched Durson assemble his platoon. The ten men from the boulder barricade had already formed a column of two, and the dozen or so from the embankment trotted forward and fell in behind them. Durson gave an order, his voice clear and loud without having to bark or shout. The leading two riflemen unslung their rifles and trotted forward up the road fifteen or twenty yards to where a faint trail snaked up the hillside. They scrambled up, and, when they were far enough ahead, Durson waved his arm and set off after them.

Gordon started at the head of our own column, and I let it pass until I could fall in beside Gabrielle. I filled her in on what was happening.

"He has the interesting face, this Turkish sergeant," she observed.

"What do you find interesting about it?"

"It betrays nothing of the man."

Our people were already tired from a day of marching on a mountain road. Climbing a trail so steep we sometimes had to use our hands to pull us forward really wore them down. It wore me down pretty good, too, but I made an effort not to let it show.

Gabrielle finally started wilting. She'd hung in so far and shown no signs of exhaustion. Now I saw lines in her face, squinting eyes, pursed lips, and a limp increasingly favoring her injured leg—all signs that she was running on willpower and not much more. I still never heard a complaint from her, though. I helped her along, particularly through the steep stretches.

"Can't be much farther now," I told her.

She gave me a tired smile but didn't say anything.

Our column straggled badly, in part because of fatigue and in part because of the pace the Bosnians set. They must have had steel springs for leg muscles. The slope grew increasingly rocky as we climbed, with ever smaller patches of grass and scrub, but ahead I saw a belt of woods, the trees smaller, more stunted than the ones we had camped in the previous night. When the scouts got there, two more Bosnian riflemen emerged from the shadows and talked to them, turned to watch us as we finished the last hundred yards.

Of course. Durson had over thirty men in his platoon, but only twenty-some at the ambush: two squads with him in the field and the third pulling security at his base camp. The guy knew his business.

I turned and looked back. It looked as if we had bled stragglers, Marines and Bavarians in ones and twos down the hillside halfway to the sharp white line of the road.

We had six or eight miles ahead of us to Kokin Brod, all of it up and down like this, probably most of it on mountain trails instead of a proper road. Our own people weren't going to get to Kokin Brod with enough energy left to put in a spirited assault. I wondered if Gordon understood how desperately we needed Durson's Bosnian mountaineers.

The Bosnians had camped in a clearing in the woods with a mountain spring nearby—cover, fuel for the fire, and a good source of fresh water, with open approaches from above and below which were easy to watch. The tidy and well-organized campsite provided more evidence of Durson's competence.

The sun disappeared behind the western mountains. While our men came in, Durson and his men washed in the stream and said *Maghrib*, the sunset prayer. The prayer continued for perhaps ten minutes, the thirty-odd men bowing and rising in unison, softly chanting.

"It is beautiful in its way," Gabrielle said. "But they do not pray in Bosnian. You know the language?"

"Arabic," I answered, and then when they began the second *Raka'at* I translated for her.

"God is Great. In the name of God, the most Beneficent, the most Merciful. Praise be to God. Lord of the Worlds, the most Beneficent, the most Merciful, Master of the Day of Judgment, to you we worship and to you we turn in need. Show us the straight path, the path of those you have favored; not the path of those who earn your anger or who go astray."

"Strange that they pray in Arabic," she said.

"Catholics still pray in Latin, don't they?"

"That is strange as well."

By the time the last of our men straggled in and got settled, the Bosnians finished their prayers and we started cooking. By pooling our rations we managed to put together a couple pots of pretty good-smelling food. The Bosnians had dug some turnips and still had onions with them. Those and a dozen tins of British bully beef made a decent stew.

The Germans contributed *Erbswurst*, which I'd never heard of before. The *wurst* part made it sound like sausage, and that's what it looked like at first glance, but *Erb* is German for pea. When they unrolled the wax paper–wrapped "sausage" I saw six thick, hard, yellowish tablets, not very appetizing-looking. They dumped a couple sausages' worth of tablets in a kettle of boiling water and in a few minutes had a steaming hot pea soup. I tried it: really good, thick and salty with a hint of bacon flavor.

"*Sehr gut*," I told the Bavarian cook, "but the Bosnians can't have any."

His smile disappeared, and he looked as if I'd insulted his soup.

"Bacon," I explained. "They cannot eat pork."

Understanding came to his face, and then he looked at the Bosnians with pity. I agreed. A world without fatty pork goodness just wouldn't have been quite as bright or warm a place. I looked across the fire at Durson and wondered how a man from South Carolina, land of bacon and ham and pulled pork, had managed to adjust.

Beef stew, pea soup, and hard biscuit. After a long day's march to work up an appetite, they hit the spot. But there was something else, a rich, wonderful aroma I hadn't smelled since coming to this world, hadn't realized how much I missed until that moment.

"Coffee?"

The Bosnians smiled and nodded, one of them pouring me a cup of the dark, rich brew. After thanking them I rejoined Gabrielle. Usually I have a little half and half in my coffee, but this evening I took it black, luxuriating in its rich, unadulterated flavor—bitter but earthy with that distinctive roasted back-taste and, in this one, a hint of caramel and something that reminded me a little of potatoes.

I shared it with Gabrielle. She held the cup between her hands and breathed in its steam, then closed her eyes and drank. As we passed the cup back and forth I felt the muscles in my back and legs finally start to loosen up. It's strange how a stimulant can relax you under the right circumstances.

I took her empty tin plate and looked at her, saw dark shadows under sleepy eyes.

"Lie down and get some rest. If I need a Bosnian translator, I'll find Sergeant Durson."

She smiled and nodded, patted my arm softly, and curled up on the open blanket I'd spread on her ground cloth. I covered her with my own blanket, and in moments the lines in her face disappeared and she began snoring softly.

I looked across the fire and saw Durson watching me, waiting. I rose and found Gordon eating by himself. At least he'd waited until his men were fed.

"Time we brought Sergeant Durson up to speed," I said.

"Up to speed?"

"Tell him what our plan is."

I knelt next to him.

"So, what's our plan?"

He sipped his mug of tea and thought for a moment before answering.

"First, we'll find out if the Turks know anything about Kokin Brod. If not, we will march to a closer campsite tomorrow. Hopefully we can find a place as secure as this one. Damned lucky of the Turks to stumble on it without a proper officer along."

"Well, now they've got you, so their worries are over," I said.

Gordon looked at me suspiciously before continuing.

"We'll see how well defended the area is. We will be moving mostly downhill, on the back side of this ridge. My thought is to leave a small party in this camp, our walking wounded and those too weak to continue. They will send up our signal rockets from here when we are ready to break in and seize Tesla."

"And Thomson," I added.

"Naturally. I doubt the rockets will be seen from down in the Lim River Valley if we fire them from the east side of the ridge, but from up here they'll be visible for miles. Hopefully that will bring our Turkish friend Cevik Bey with the rest of his Bosnian cutthroats. We'll march as hard and fast as we can and meet up with him."

Aside from still not knowing squat about how well defended Tesla was, or how we were going to get in undetected, locate and grab Tesla and Thomson, fight our way back out, and stay ahead of armed pursuers with a prisoner and a fat old Scotsman, up seven or eight miles of mountain trails back to this camp—aside from all that, it was as good a plan as any.

We rose and walked around the fire to where Durson waited for us.

"You know we are here on a mission," I said in Turkmen.

"For two weeks my men and I have had our own mission. We scout these hills, staying ahead of the Serbian Army in the valleys and the *hajduci* in the highlands. The men are tired and hungry, and fear wears them down as well. I keep them going with the promise that tomorrow we march home. Tomorrow.

"We thank you for sharing your food. I will do what I can to advise you, tell you what I know about the land and the enemy, even delay our departure for one day. But my men have done enough."

"Cevik Bey ordered you to help us," I said.

"The extent of the help he left to me."

Shit.

"What seems to be the problem?" Gordon asked.

"Cevik Bey left Durson's cooperation to his discretion."

Gordon's face darkened with anger of his own.

"And now he's balking? Why I ought to—"

"What? What *exactly* ought you to do? Thrash him within an inch of his life? Go ahead, pal, take your best shot. I imagine he's got some experience of thrashings from arrogant white assholes like you. Not recently, and I bet he's waited a long time to even the score. But don't let that stop you. I'll hold your coat."

My words took Gordon by surprise. For several long seconds we all just stood there, three angry men, glaring at each other.

Gordon's anger faded first. He looked away, out into the woods, before speaking.

"We need his help, Fargo. Perhaps if you explained what we are here for, it might make a difference."

I didn't have high hopes, but it was worth a shot.

"We have come to recover a man and bring him back," I told Durson in Turkmen. "Can you at least tell us about the Serbs in and around Kokin Brod and the new lake?"

His eyebrows went up a bit at that.

"We scouted that area three days ago. I have drawings of the new gun mounts and the machinery buildings by the lake. But why does that concern you? The man you want is two miles up this mountain, in the village of Brezna."

"He is? You are certain?" I asked.

"It was from a distance, but I saw him with my own eyes."

He looked from one of us to the other, and his anger gave way to uncertainty.

"You are looking for the old, stout Englishman with the big beard, are you not? From the crashed zeppelin?"

THIRTY

October 11, 1888, near Brezna, Serbia

We made our plans that night and got a good sleep. Gordon, Durson and I spent most of the next morning hiking the mile up the mountainside. Durson knew a good observation post on a spur from the main spine of the ridge, but if we were going to avoid detection, we couldn't chance any more than three of us. Gordon and I expressed our concerns about the raptors, although I had to explain what I meant by the word.

"The *azhdaja*," Durson said. "They are nocturnal hunters, but even then we have little to fear from them. Our second day in the area they attacked. We killed three of them and they have not come near us since. They learn, so they are intelligent, as animals go."

"*Azhdaja*. A *jandarma* back in Uvats used that word, but I'm not familiar with it. The local people know this species?"

"No one ever saw them before a few months ago. *Azhdaja* is a local word, the same in Bosnian and Serbian. In Turkish we would say *iluyankas*."

"Dragons?"

He gave me a hard look.

"No, they are not real dragons, *Effendi*. They do not fly, they do not breathe fire, and they are not very large. The local people simply had no other word for them."

They also had feathers instead of scales, but their mouths were lizardlike, and their crests reminded me of the crests of some oriental dragons and hooded lizards. Their coloration—green and black and flashes of yellow—blended in surprisingly well with the mountainous country, but it also reminded me of how some dragons were colored in art. I supposed dragon made as much sense as anything.

Durson had no more idea where they came from than we did, but my money was still on Tesla. If Tesla really could open doorways to different times, no telling what sort of fell beasties he could bring back.

On the way up the ridge we passed the twisted frame and deflated gas sack of the black zeppelin I'd last seen climbing away from the hotel on Agnes-Bernauer *Strasse*. There was no sign of the gun turret which had shot up *Intrepid*. The gas bag bore a name painted in white Cyrillic letters, which Sergeant Durson deciphered for me—*Djordje Petrovic.* I hadn't noticed it before.

"Petrovic was a famous Serbian warrior a century ago, against the Turks, of course," Durson explained. "Bosnian women still frighten their children with stories of how he ate Turkish babies.

"I do not believe that, myself," he added.

Dense, sweet-smelling purple lilac shrubs sheltered our observation post, which wasn't much more than a half mile from Brezna but was separated from it by a deep ravine, all but impassable, so there was no reason for the *hajduci* to guard this spot. The town lay northeast of us, slightly higher on the main ridge. Beyond it the ground fell away into a deep valley which led down to Kokin Brod, seven twisting miles away.

The town sat near the summit of a long, steep-sided ridge of mostly bare granite. Gardens and vineyards surrounded the town, but the closest orchard stood a quarter mile farther up the northwest thrust of the ridge. A half mile of open ground stretched between the village and closest growth of thick woods to the south, the approach all uphill.

The stone houses of the village huddled together as if taking shelter from the winds which must have come howling in from the west in winter. Stone walls linked the buildings and made the place look like an Afghan hill fort, a comparison which did not put my mind at ease.

I handed the binoculars to Gordon and turned around to face Durson.

"How many men in the village?" I asked in Turkmen.

"About two hundred people live there, so perhaps fifty or sixty grown men aside from the whitebeards. I think a dozen actual fighters. Others would help but without the same skill or enthusiasm."

"Doesn't matter. A dozen good men can hold that place against a small army, unless the army has artillery or air support."

Durson looked at me and nodded his agreement, and his expression grew harder when he did so.

"That would not stop the English from ordering an attack," he added in Turkish, "with my riflemen in front, of course."

There was a depth of feeling there which surprised me. What did a former slave know about the British? Durson saw my expression and shrugged.

"When Britain and Turkey were allies against the Russians, forty years ago, few Turkish soldiers survived the experience of being under English command. The old ones still speak of it."

"Did I mention I'm from Illinois?" I said, trying to distance myself from the Anglophobia.

"Since coming to Turkey twelve years ago," Durson said, "three American gentlemen have sought me out, each one attempting to collect the bounty for returning me to my former owner. One of them was from Illinois."

Swell. So much for bonding.

"Ah, more visitors," he said and pointed over my shoulder toward Brezna.

I turned to look. A black zeppelin, the twin of the wreck we had passed earlier, rose above the skyline in the valley beyond Brezna, and as soon as it cleared the ridge I heard the distant drone of its engines. Gordon heard as well and raised his glasses.

"Damn. Well, that ties it," he said. "We're too late. Tesla will snatch him up and that's that."

Sergeant Durson said nothing.

"What do you think, Sergeant?" I asked.

"I do not know what to think, *Effendi*. I am interested to see what will happen. Farther down the mountain, on this slope but below the wreck of the airship, my men and I found twelve large iron fire boxes with grates on the sides. They were rusty from having been there for months, but had recently been used."

I didn't see what that had to do with Tesla's zeppelin coming to pick up Thomson. Tesla's stronghold was in the opposite direction, on the other side of the ridgeline. They couldn't have been used to signal him.

So what *had* they been used for? If the *hajduci* were going to signal with them, why not put them up on the ridge, where they could be seen from farther away? And why did they need a dozen of them? The Brits didn't need a dozen Aldis lamps to send signals.

I looked at Durson, but his eyes were on the zeppelin approaching Brezna.

"Were the fire boxes all together or spread out?"

"They were spread out, *Effendi*, irregularly spaced over perhaps fifty *kulaçi*—one hundred meters."

Huh.

I settled down to watch as well.

The zeppelin slowed and made a broad circle over the town, came toward us but made a slow turn to its right and doubled back, coming almost to a halt above the open ground on the ridge south of the town.

"Can you see any movement in the town?" I asked Gordon.

"No. The windows are all shuttered. There is nothing moving anywhere except some laundry drying on a line."

The zeppelin hovered there for a few minutes, edging forward against the wind then dropping back.

"There's someone at a window. I think he's shouting at the zeppelin," Gordon said. "Now he's waving. I think he is waving for it to leave. Yes, he wants it to leave. More shouting. He's gone. No, he . . . oh . . . I say!"

Durson and I didn't have binoculars, but we didn't need them to hear the crackle of small arms fire from the village. The zeppelin remained in place for as long as a minute. The first volley of rifle shots died away, and then started up again, less evenly as the riflemen loaded, aimed, and fired at their own pace.

The zeppelin's engines grew louder, higher in pitch, as if someone had reached the controls, or regained their senses. The airship accelerated and turned away from the town, made a wide circle to the south, passing close by our clump of brush and rocks. It drew off, made several sloppy figure eights, as if considering its next move, and then closed on the town.

I knew the sound of the Gatling gun on the airship as soon as it started, that steady pop-pop-pop-pop-pop—I'd heard enough of them in films. The zeppelin passed on the far side of the town from our vantage point and then began circling it, like a C-130 gunship hosing down the target with a minigun. The popping stopped.

"Changing magazines," Gordon announced. "Either that or it's jammed."

The *hajduci* must have figured the same thing. A ragged volley of rifle shots crackled from the ground.

The fight went on for a few minutes longer. Then the zeppelin beat a retreat back down the valley to the east. The airship had a Gatling gun, but the gas bag was made of canvas, the gondola of something light and flimsy. The *hajduci* had stone walls and overhead cover. I imagined some maintenance people would spend a fair part of the day slapping patches on that big black gas bag once they got back to Kokin Brod. No telling how many casualties the crew took.

"Interesting," I said. "Not everyone in Serbia seems to get along."

"I believe the Brezna *hajduci* support the king in Belgrade," Durson answered. "Their neighbors incline more toward the Kradodevici. I have never heard of them shooting at each other, though."

I translated that for Gordon, who looked thoroughly confused by it all.

"Well, if these chaps in Brezna are shooting at Tesla's lot, maybe we can get them to help us out," he suggested, and I translated that for Durson.

"Perhaps they will help you. They will not be happy to see me or my men. The royalists are more moderate in their views than are the Kradodevici. The royalists simply believe all Turks should be killed, while the Kradodevici believe unspeakable things should then be done to our corpses."

I found it interesting that Durson thought of himself as a Turk, but then what else would he consider himself?

"I wonder if this is about money instead of politics," I said to Durson, and he nodded in agreement.

"When I was a child in Carolina," he said, "my mother told me of the wreckers, people on the islands along the coast. The wreckers lived by taking the cargoes from broken ships. When storms did not provide enough wrecks, the people lured ships onto the rocks with false lights, or so it was said."

"I've heard that story myself," I said.

"Yes, many people have, and many people believe the stories of the false lights. But later I became a sailor. I learned the stories of the false lights were legends, fairy tales. They could not be true, and any sailor will tell you as much. At night, ships near the coast do not steer *toward* lights; they steer clear of them."

"Or over them, if the ship is a zeppelin," I said.

"Yes," he answered, and for the first time he smiled. "But perhaps not very high over them."

"And on a moonless night, the light shining through the grates of a dozen iron fire boxes spread out along the side of a ridge would look like the lights of a village on top of the ridge."

"Yes, *Effendi*."

"Especially if everyone in the village was told to keep their windows shuttered or their lamps extinguished on that night."

"It is possible, *Effendi*."

"Gordon," I said in English, "we may be able to do business with these guys. How much cash is left in your war chest?"

Getting back to the camp was a lot easier on the lungs than climbing the mountain had been, but was strangely harder on the legs. You would think going down hill would be easier, and in a lot of respects it was, but it used a whole difference set of leg muscles, and a set you don't use that much. Halfway down, Gordon and I had to call a break. My legs did not feel tired; they simply would no longer support me. While we waited for the strength to return to them, I outlined my plan.

We would return to Brezna that night, or rather to the wood below it. Durson, one Marine, and I would approach the town alone. I would need Durson to translate into Serbian for me. We would have to find some civilian clothing which came close to fitting, but a Marine overcoat would be the main element of his disguise, allowing us to pass him off as my servant.

We would have one of Gordon's leather-wrapped rolls of fifty gold sovereigns, and we would buy Thomson's release. If necessary, we would send the Marine as a runner back to the main party and retrieve the second roll of sovereigns. If the Brezna *hajduci* wanted more than that, everyone was out of luck.

If all went well, we'd have Thomson back. If something bad happened to us, Gordon would still have Gabrielle as a Serbo-Croatian/Bosnian translator. They could make a try for Tesla or attempt to get away.

I told Gordon and Durson followed along—the English was simple enough that he picked up most of it. I'd intended to tell him in Turkman once Gordon agreed, but he was ahead of me and shaking his head.

"Since we are not attacking the village, I agree to help. But there is a problem. All the people in these hills know me by sight, or at least by reputation. I am called *Noć Ubojica*. It means Night Killer."

I translated for Gordon but kept my eyes on Durson, looking for a clue as to what this name meant about the person behind it, but Gabrielle was right. His face gave away little.

"I have killed very few people," he volunteered, "and never at night. I believe my color has to do with the name they give me, that and fear. People are very superstitious. In any case, such a name has its uses."

Yes, it does.

"They know your face?" I asked.

"They know my race and physical build. I do not know if anyone in Brezna knows my face, but it is possible. I have questioned and released many people during patrols into these hills in the last two years. Always I tell them I would kill them, but I cannot because, unfortunately, that day is a holy day on which I may not shed infidel blood." He shook his head and smiled. "So many holy days."

That said something about the guy right there.

"Okay, I'll have to take one of your men. They speak Turkish, right?"

"They speak enough to take orders from Turkish officers, but they would have a hard time understanding you, *Effendi*. What you speak—it is *like* Turkish, I suppose."

We walked the rest of the way to the camp in silence, each with our own thoughts. Once there, Gordon looked at me and looked away, reluctant to say what was on his mind.

"I'll ask her," I said.

He nodded.

"So that's how it is," I finished. "We only have two people who can translate Serbo-Croatian to a language I understand: Durson and you. They know Durson, so he's out. I'll tell you straight up, Gabi, this is really dangerous, and it's not your responsibility. You don't need to do it."

"*Non?* What will you do if I say no?"

"I'll go in alone. There are a fair number of German speakers around here; maybe I'll get lucky. Or maybe some of the older folks speak enough Turkish. Or I'll use sign language. One way or another, I'll work something out."

She sat on the stump of a tree, hands resting on her knees, elbows locked. She looked worn out. A night's sleep and a day resting here while the three of us climbed the ridge and came back had done a lot to restore her reserves, but she still looked weak and bedraggled. She'd washed in the stream and tied her wet, tangled hair back in a ponytail behind her neck, but her riding habit was still dirty and torn from the attack two days earlier.

"Can you even make it up the ridge?" I asked.

She sat up straight, and her eyebrows came together in an angry frown.

"I am tired, but still I can walk your sad little Marines to their knees. See if I cannot."

"Okay, I believe you."

I sat down on the ground next to her and leaned my shoulder against her tree stump.

"I don't want to argue. I'm too tired after that climb today. You could walk my sad little ass into the ground right now."

She put her hand on my shoulder. It felt good.

"I will go with you," she said quietly.

"Yeah, but I'd rather you didn't."

"I know. And I know why."

I looked at her, but she wore that impenetrable look she almost always did.

"I'm not sure *I* know why, so how the hell can you? Besides—it's lots of things."

"*Non.* It is simple. You will soon have to make the decision, yes? And when that time comes, you do not want to be in my debt."

I didn't answer.

"You must discharge your debt in advance, then," she said after a while.

"How?"

"Tell me the truth about you. Tell me what you have told no one else. Share your dark secret."

The Bosnians and Germans and Marines had begun cooking. I smelled boiling pea soup, corned beef, onions, and coffee all mixed with the smoke of the wood fire, the smell of Gabrielle's damp hair drying, the resin scent of the carpet of pine needles beneath us. I closed my eyes and from the forest I heard a woodpecker, distant and empty, as if an echo from the past, as if it were long dead and Gabrielle and I were the only two living things left in the world. My throat tightened, the same tightness I'd felt when Reggie mentioned my dead wife, so far from here, so long ago, a hundred and thirty years in the future.

"I don't know what you're talking about," I said. "I've told you the truth."

"*Non.* You show me the one man, but there is the other, the one you keep locked away. But when he comes out, men die. This I know. Which one is the real man?"

"I am only one man."

"Ah, that much I believe. But who is he? What is his essence? However, you will not tell me today. So I go with you tomorrow, and you *will* be in my debt, and you will have to find a way to answer my question before you leave."

THIRTY-ONE

October 11, 1888, near Brezna, Serbia

We ate and rested that afternoon and began the long, careful climb to the ridge after dark. We brought about half the Marines and Bavarians along, those who weren't injured and seemed to be holding up better physically. The others we left behind to recover their strength. We would need them for the push on Kokin Brod later.

We also brought a half-dozen of the Bosnians, men Durson picked himself. We needed them as scouts, so we dressed them in Bavarian and Marine greatcoats and had them stash their fezzes in their pockets. If they kept their mouths shut they should blend in with the rest, and if all went well no one would see them anyway.

Durson led the way. It was difficult in daylight and all the more dangerous at night, even though the trail never required actual open-face vertical climbing. We took it slowly.

Gabrielle was not much inclined to talk during the climb. I wasn't sure if she was "in a huff" over our earlier conversation. I didn't think so, because so far I had never seen her show resentment or anger. She was about the most even-tempered person I'd ever met so a fit of pique was unlikely, but you just never knew with people.

I waited until a rest break and then made my way forward to find Durson.

"May I sit with you, Sergeant?"

"Of course, *Effendi*."

I sat with my back against a tree trunk, facing the sergeant. We were no more than three feet apart, but I could hardly make out his silhouette in the darkness.

"How long have you and your men been out here, on this side of the border?"

"Thirteen days so far. I plan to start back to Uvats tomorrow."

"I know. We need your help, but I can't fault you for putting your men first."

We sat silently for a little while.

"You mind me asking how you came to be here? It is a long way from South Carolina."

"I was born to slavery, a field hand until the age of thirteen. Then my master sold me to a wealthy merchant, a man who made his fortune as a young blockade runner in the war. Now his ships travel all over the world. I was ship's boy at first, then a seaman."

I wondered how painful a memory that was, but nothing in his voice betrayed suffering. He spoke as if telling someone else's story rather than his own.

"I didn't know they used slaves as seamen," I said.

"It is difficult to escape from a ship, harder still when you cannot read or write, and speak no foreign language."

"Cevik Bey said you read and write."

"Now I do, Turkish and Arabic, but not then," he said.

"I see. So, hard to escape, but apparently not impossible."

For the first time he chuckled, a low rumbling sound.

"No, *Effendi*, not impossible. Twelve years ago I swam ashore in Varna harbor. There was a cholera epidemic in the town at the time, so no one from the ship pursued me. In any case, it would have done them no good. The Turkish authorities do not return escaped slaves."

"Did the Turks enslave you?"

"By then slavery was illegal in the empire. Of course, it was still widely practiced, but God guided my footsteps. I worked carrying and burning the bodies, of which there were many because of the sickness. I did not grow ill myself. An imam, Ilhami Baraket, noticed me, took me in. He is a scholar of the Hanifa school, the most gentle man I ever knew. I lived with him for over a year. He taught me to speak Turkish, to read the Koran, to write, and to question. When I was ready, he helped me join the faith of the prophet."

"That's when you took the name Ibrahim?"

"I was born Abraham. It is the same."

"Ah. So, how did you like the circumcision?"

He made a face.

“That was my least favorite part of the ceremony.”

“I’ll bet. Had your master, the sea captain, been hard on you?”

“He was no harder on me than on any other man in the crew. But they could quit, if they chose to. Some did. Eventually, I did as well.”

“So you made yourself free and then joined the army to take orders from officers?”

“To defend the country and the faith which gave me freedom is an honor. And everyone takes orders from someone. Cevik Bey often gives me missions such as this, where I am away from the officers. That is better.”

Well, I couldn’t argue with that.

“Why don’t they make you an officer? You can read and write, which I guess is unusual for an NCO here. Captain Gordon says they make officers of men of foreign birth, and race doesn’t seem to be a huge problem in the empire.”

“Our officers . . . are not terrible men, but the best of them are ambitious, and so take credit for the achievements of their subordinates. It is not easy for a common soldier to gain the eye of Istanbul.”

Too bad. From what I’d seen so far, Durson had what it took.

After the break, we resumed our trek. We climbed the steep mountain footpath for almost three hours before reaching the crest of the ridge. From there the trail joined a dirt road which followed the spine of the mountain. It wasn’t a super highway, but it was broader and much more even than the footpath. The ridge gained height toward Brezna to the northwest, but much more gradually than the mountain trail.

I moved with Gabrielle and noticed she increasingly favored her left leg, where she had been wounded. When we stopped for a break where the trail met the road, I made her fold back her skirt and let me examine the wound. I had three of the Marines stand around us with greatcoats spread wide to mask the light of the wooden match I used to look at it.

“It is fine,” she said.

“It is not fine. I should have stitched the cut closed when I wrapped it. It’s broken open and is bleeding again. At least it doesn’t look infected.”

"It is fine," she repeated. "Wrap it tightly and, if you wish, you may stitch it once we reach the village."

So I wrapped it up with the last of the clean bandage linen from my kit bag.

After no more than half an hour marching up the road, Durson passed the word to stop. After a moment one of the Bosnian riflemen came silently back along the column and found me.

"*Chavush* Durson say Fargo *Effendi* come forward," he whispered in Turkish. "Very quiet please."

I patted Gabrielle's arm and followed the rifleman forward to the head of the column. Gordon, Durson, and two more Bosnian riflemen crouched in a circle at the side of the road behind some granite boulders. I joined them.

"You should have been up here with me," Gordon whispered. "Find out what the holdup is."

"The scouts have found a guard post," Durson offered without me asking. "Two men, one asleep, the other watching the road."

"They got close enough to see the sleeping guard?"

"They heard his snores, *Effendi*. We will silence them."

One of the Bosnians silently drew a long thin-bladed knife which for a moment gleamed in the faint starlight, but Durson put his hand on his arm and shook his head.

"Can you take them without killing them?" I asked. "It would make negotiating with the *hajduci* a lot easier if we brought these guys in still alive."

"I think so as well," Durson said.

I translated for Gordon while Durson gave his orders to his two scouts. They stripped off their greatcoats, equipment, and jackets and then set off, silently and unarmed, in the broken scrub beside the road.

We waited in deafening silence for half an hour. Then one of the riflemen came trotting down the road and whistled softly. We rose, Durson picked up the rifle and gear of one of the scouts, and I picked up that of the other.

"Your men move well at night," I said.

"For two years we have patrolled these hills, sometimes on this side of the border, sometimes on the other side. Most of these men have been with me that entire time."

Fifteen minutes walking took us to the edge of the wood southeast of Brezna, the one we had seen the previous morning. Before us there was nothing but a thousand yards of open ground.

I hefted the leather roll of gold sovereigns Gordon had given me. The roll was about an inch in diameter and four inches long, but it weighed almost as much as my Webley. A hundred gold sovereigns is nothing to sneeze at. If I held it in my fist like a roll of quarters, and I hit someone really hard, I'd break their jaw and, unless I hit them just right, most of my fingers.

I opened one end of the roll, shook out five of the gleaming gold coins, and handed the rest of the roll back to Gordon.

"This has got to be more cash than everyone in that village put together has ever seen in their lives. If we walk in with the whole ransom, there's no reason to let us go, so I'll take these five as a down payment. I'll take one Marine with me to guard our two prisoners going in, and I'll send him back for the rest of the money once we work out the exchange."

I stuffed the gold coins in the pocket of my overcoat, unholstered the Webley, and handed it to Gordon along with the Mauser rifle.

"Take care of these. I'm getting kind of attached to the Webley. Better keep Gabrielle's shotgun, too."

"You'll want the Marine armed, surely. There are the prisoners, after all."

"The prisoners are tied up. Your guy and I can take care of them. If there's trouble, one rifle won't get us out of it, but it could make things worse."

"I go," I heard.

Gordon and I turned to the beefy, square-faced Sergeant Melzer, the Bavarian NCO. He handed his Mauser to one of his men and then made a fist the size of a small ham and held it up.

"Prisoners will not make trouble."

Melzer. The last guy I expected to pitch in and lend a hand. Huh.

The five of us walked toward the town: prisoners in front, then Melzer holding a rope tied around each of their necks, then me helping Gabrielle along. There was enough starlight to see the creases of pain in her face, even though she insisted her leg was fine.

After ten minutes the outline of the town emerged from the background darkness, its sloped roofs cool black against the slightly warmer black of the night sky. The air was chilled, but sweat ran down my face and it was not simply from the exertion of the walk. Any minute I expected a challenge or a shot, and the closer we got without a challenge, the more likely a panicked outbreak of fire became. Finally, no more than twenty yards from the first buildings in the town, I told Melzer to stop and had Gabrielle instruct the two prisoners to call out and get the town's attention.

It took a few minutes before anyone responded, and then there was a lengthy and heated exchange. Gabrielle gave me a running translation.

"The prisoners say they have been captured by the English. The man in the town thinks they are making the joke."

"It's no joke. *The English are here. Rule Britannia, Britannia Rules The Waves!*" I shouted at the top of my lungs—in English, of course, which they might not understand but were likely to recognize.

"He says to wait." Gabrielle translated the reply which came after several seconds of silence. "He goes to fetch the *voivoda*—the village chief."

She shifted her weight and sucked in air sharply.

"You leg is killing you, isn't it?"

"No, it is merely painful."

And then she slumped against me, gradually at first, but as I tried to support her she went limp in my arms and became dead weight. I got one arm around her back and the other under her legs and picked her up. I felt my arm under her legs grow warm and wet with blood.

"Get 'em moving, Melzer. We're going in."

THIRTY-TWO

October 11, 1888, Brezna, Serbia

After ten minutes of loud and animated discourse in broken German with a couple of the locals, the boss-man of Brezna showed up, still fastening his belt around the long peasant smock he wore over baggy trousers. He was younger than I'd expected, late thirties or early forties, and tall but not particularly muscular. It was hard to read his expression. His eyes were deep set, masked in shadows, a shock of unruly black hair fell across his forehead, and a luxurious flowing black moustache covered most of his mouth.

"You are English?" he demanded in excellent German.

"We're with the English expedition. I'm American, and the woman is French. She has a wound which needs attending."

"Yes, bring her along to my house. Your man, too. He is English?"

"No, Bavarian. We brought two of your guards with us."

He barked an order in Serbian and two villagers leapt forward to cut the two prisoners free. Two more offered to carry Gabrielle, who was starting to stir in my arms, but I shook my head.

"Let us hurry," the chief said and led the way. "You have come about the English scientist, Dr. Thomson?"

"He's Scottish, actually."

The chief laughed.

"Yes, he told me. This is a curious expedition the English mount, to send an American, a German, and a French woman in to rescue their Scottish scientist. But I believe it. The English seem always willing to spill the blood of friends and subject nations, provided it is for a noble cause and makes England richer."

"Everywhere I go," I said, "people love the English."

He laughed again and held open the front door of a two-story stone house. I carried Gabrielle into the brightly lit front room, and the chief hurried past me. The house smelled deeply of garlic and cooked cabbage and stewed tomatoes.

"Bring her this way, into the kitchen. Put her on the stove."

On the stove?

The stove took up half the kitchen and was more like a large brick oven built against a massive stone chimney. There were doors and nooks in the front and on the sides, but the top was bare glazed brick.

"Go on," the chief encouraged me. "In the winter my wife and I sleep here."

I put Gabrielle gently on the warm stove top as a woman came down the stairs at the back of the kitchen, tying her hair up in a kerchief. She was in her thirties, stout of build, average height or a bit shorter, but with strong features, a clear complexion, and dark, piercing eyes. She hurried to Gabrielle's leg and began peeling back the blood-soaked bandage, frowning and shaking her head. She barked an order to her husband, the chief, and he answered with stubborn dignity but then started to leave.

"I return with water. You stay here."

Gabrielle was fully awake now, although still pale, and she propped herself up on one elbow. She and the woman conversed in Serbian a bit, and the woman turned to me and scolded me. I couldn't understand the specifics, but the general tenor was clear enough. Serbian sounded like a pretty good language for scolding people.

"Her name is Mirjana Radojica. Her husband is Jovo Radojica, the *voivoda*. She says you are a fool."

"No argument from me."

Mirjana pointed to the wound and asked a question, and when Gabriele answered I caught the word *azhdaja:* dragons. Mirjana frowned, nodded solemnly, and patted Gabrielle comfortingly on her unwounded leg.

"Ask if she has needle and linen thread so I can stitch up your leg," I said.

Gabrielle translated, which set off another series of dismissive remarks aimed in my direction.

"She says men cannot even sew buttons on shirts. She will stitch my leg, and do it so there is only a small scar when it heals, instead of it looking like the seam in a quilt. Those were her words," Gabrielle explained.

"Got it."

Presently the chief—Jovo Radojica—returned with a bucket of water and moved quickly around the kitchen gathering bowls and pans at Mirjana's direction, pouring water in them, fetching clean rags and jars of ointments. I backed away to get out of the traffic pattern and saw Melzer watching through the door to the front room. I gave him an encouraging smile, and he shrugged in reply. I had to admit that, whatever else happened, it was hard to think of ourselves in much danger. This was all just too . . . domestic.

"The woman fainted," Jovo Radojica said to me from across the room. "We should loosen her clothes."

Without looking up, his wife hit him hard in the upper arm with the back of her hand.

"You don't speak German!" he protested, rubbing his shoulder.

"Know enough," she answered in an accent thicker than his. She unbuttoned Gabrielle's jacket, and she breathed more easily.

"You know what Mirjana means in Serbian?" Jovo asked me. "It means *obstinate*. Her father gave her this name, and he cursed all of us when he did."

Mirjana Radojica shooed us all out into the front room and drew heavy drapes across the door to the kitchen. Jovo sat in the only padded armchair in the room and gestured to other chairs around the fireplace for us. He began packing a long white pipe with tobacco, and Melzer pulled his own pipe out as well.

"So," Jovo began once his pipe was going, lit from coals in the fireplace, "you have come for the Scottish scientist Thomson. The Old Man of the Mountain wants him as well. Why should I risk that one's wrath by giving the Scotsman to you?"

"I don't think you're afraid of the Old Man. If you were, what was that fight with his zeppelin all about this morning?"

"You heard about that? It was nothing. Rumors! These stories grow in the retelling." He puffed on his pipe and frowned into the fireplace. The flames painted his face orange and yellow.

"I did not hear about it: I watched it from a ledge less than a mile from here."

His eyes moved to me and then crinkled in a smile. He shrugged.

"Very well. I get along with some of my neighbors better than others. That is always the way, is it not? I have the crew of his airship, those who survived the crash, twelve men in all. Also his strange gun, although the barrel is bent and will require a master gunsmith to set it right. I thought to ransom the crew, but the Old Man sent word he *might* spare my life if I turned over them and Professor Thomson unharmed, and paid to repair the ship. Can you imagine the arrogance? Then he sent his other ship here to intimidate me. Well . . . things got a little out of hand yesterday. So now I suppose I will have to send his crew back just to settle things down.

"I would dislike giving Professor Thomson to the Old Man, even though it would help make peace. I have grown fond of the Scotsman. He is the only one I can talk to of the wider world. I went to school in Vienna, you know, two years at *Die Akademie der Bildenden Künste*. I wished to paint. Now, mostly I sketch—gun positions, poorly guarded gates, that sort of thing."

"Life's funny that way," I said, and he nodded in agreement.

He turned to face me directly.

"So," he said.

I pulled the five gold sovereigns from my pocket and handed them to him. They seemed to glow in the firelight.

"We will pay more," I said. "This is just to demonstrate we can."

"An impressive demonstration," he said. "Now we haggle back and forth to reach a price. The people in these hills love it, because there is so little else to do. It is a form of entertainment, you see? But I have no love for it, and not enough patience.

"So this is what I do instead. You tell me your price, and I will tell you yes or no. No bargaining. If the answer is no, you leave and the Scotsman stays with me."

"No second chances, huh?"

"No."

He put his pipe in his mouth and turned back to the fire, I guess to let me think it over. I didn't need to.

"One hundred gold sovereigns. The five you have here and ninety-five more."

He continued to study the fire, chewing on his pipe, as if thinking over the offer, but I knew from the way his eyebrows went up at the figure the answer was yes. Maybe he was thinking about whether there was a way to ask for more, but that would have broken the rules of his own game. Finally he turned to me and smiled.

"I will send for the Scotsman."

I sent Melzer with the news for Gordon, but also to tell him we wouldn't be leaving until morning. Thomson had banged his leg up and would need a litter, and Gabrielle would as well, just to be on the safe side. Rigging litters and trying to carry two people down the mountainside in the darkness was just asking for trouble. Besides, Jovo Radojica, *voivoda* of Brezna, was feeling hospitable.

His hospitality did not extend to a dozen or so heavily armed men, however, so the team would have to camp in the woods. It was just as well—I didn't want Radojica giving our Bosnians, or Sergeant Durson, too close an inspection.

I rose when Thomson came to the door, and for a moment neither one of us spoke. His brief time in captivity seemed to have aged him. He walked with a wooden staff and favored one leg, and his face bore several abrasions and bruises, probably from the crash. He'd still been in his nightshirt when Tesla's men grabbed him back in Munich. Now he wore homespun peasant clothing, and if his hair had been longer he could have passed for a gray-bearded village elder. He put his hand on my shoulder, and his face crinkled in relief and grief.

"Ach, look at yah!" he said, his voice thick with emotion, "your eyes black and nose crooked, and I'm that glad to see you. I saw them beating you, Jack, once you went down. I though' you were dead. I did, it's God's truth."

"I'm hard to kill."

We shook hands.

"Come on and sit down, you old fart."

I helped him to a chair by the fireplace, and from the other room I heard Gabrielle.

"Is that Professor Thomson's voice?"

Within moments she joined us, supported under one arm by the formidable Mirjana Radojica, who frowned in clear disapproval of her patient being up and about. It was starting to look like a convention for the walking wounded.

"My word, is that *Mademoiselle* Courbiere?" Thomson asked. "I hardly recognized you."

Gabrielle ran fingers through her straggling hair and smiled weakly.

"I recognized you at once, Professor. But we are so different from when we met at the house in Munich. Was that really only one week ago?"

I took her arm and helped her to a chair as Mirjana dragged a wicker hamper over from beside the wall and then gently raised Gabrielle's injured leg and rested it on the hamper. Through the slit side of her riding habit's skirt I saw a fresh bandage on her thigh.

I pulled a chair next to Gabrielle's and sat, and for the next twenty minutes we caught up. I told the bare bones outline of our adventures, leaving out the rendezvous with Durson's Turks and Cevik Bey's promised intervention once we gave the signal. No matter how Jovo Radojica felt about Tesla, he probably wouldn't be crazy about a Turkish-led battalion of Bosnian riflemen marching through his neighborhood. Thomson told of the flight through the mountains and the crash at night, and Jovo freely admitted to setting the lure for the airship, although he was surprised it had actually worked.

Marjana brought steaming cups of sweet coffee just when a villager knocked on the door. It opened to reveal the returning Sergeant Melzer with Gordon in tow. More introductions followed, along with another reunion between Thomson and Gordon, more reserved than ours had been.

"We need to talk," I said once everyone settled in. I glanced at Jovo, hoping he would give us some privacy. He shrugged.

"What is it you want?" he asked us, looking around the circle of faces. "What is it you expect to accomplish here? I think more than simply rescue my new good friend Professor Thomson.

"I have a problem of my own. He is called the Old Man of the Mountain. He loves Serbia, he says, but he does not love me, and he does not love our king, this I know. He will bring ruin on our nation if he continues with his madness—this I believe.

"I think you intend to do something about him. Tell me if I am wrong."

He looked around at each of us. No one said anything.

"I thought as much. I will not help you in this. Too many of my countrymen are likely to die. Even though my country may need this thing done, I will not bloody my hands with it. But this much I *will* do: my wife and I will go to bed."

He rose, shook Thomson's hand, bowed to the rest of us, and then he and Mirjana went back through the kitchen and up the creaking wooden steps to the second floor.

Thomson looked at each of us.

"Well, then," he said, "I suppose the first order of business is command. Nominally I am supposed to be in charge, but I have some misgivings on that score. Captain Gordon, you have crafted a new plan and brought the expedition here, surmounting what sound like extraordinary obstacles. It would be foolish and irresponsible of me to supersede you at this point, particularly as I am physically unfit to actually accompany our move on Kokin Brod. I know that officially the responsibility is mine, but I surrender command to you on the grounds of medical infirmity. Do you accept?"

Surprise and embarrassment flickered across Gordon's face.

"I do, Dr. Thomson. And I—I very much appreciate your confidence."

"Not at all. Now, tell me what we know about Tesla's plans."

"Well—"

I heard shouts from outside, the sound of running feet. The door burst open and Sergeant Melzer came in, face red with excitement and alarm. Through the open door the sound of angry voices was louder, but I also heard the crackle of distant rifle fire.

"*Herr Hauptmann*, the natives say we have betrayed the truce! There is firing from the direction of our camp!"

THIRTY-THREE

October 11, 1888, Brezna, Serbia

Gordon and I sprang to our feet. I heard two people pounding down the back stairs. Jovo and Mirjana appeared at the doorway in nightclothes, Jovo's face dark with anger.

"By God, if you have betrayed us . . ."

"Do you see a gun anywhere pointed at you?" I demanded. "You have all our leaders under one roof, deep in the heart of your town, with one gun between us, and it's not drawn and pointing at the *voivoda*. If this is a betrayal, it must be the most stupid one in history."

He glanced at each of our faces and saw nothing but surprise and alarm. His frown remained in place, but he nodded. He spoke a word to Mirjana, who turned and hurried back upstairs, and then, still in his nightshirt, he stalked between us and out the door.

"Come along," he said curtly.

I turned to Thomson and Gabrielle.

"You two stay here. I'll be back. I won't leave you."

"Yes, go," Thomson said. Gabrielle simply nodded.

Jovo, Gordon, Melzer, and I ran to the edge of town through a growing crowd of angry and frightened villagers. The sound of firing grew louder and more distinct as we got to the small gate.

The wild-eyed sentry babbled out a sentence in Serbian, and Jovo put his hand on his shoulder to calm him. The *voivoda* replied, the sentry looked around in confusion, then relaxed and nodded. Jovo patted him on the back and turned to us.

"He says the English are attacking us," he explained in German. "I tell him I don't think so, but if they are, the English must be terrible shots since none of the bullets come this way. Tell your captain someone is attacking his camp."

I started to translate, but Gordon nodded impatiently and cut me off.

"Right. The camp is under attack. We have to get back there and sort it out."

"You go. I won't leave Thomson and Gabrielle."

"Don't be a bloody fool! They're safe here, and I need you to translate," he said.

"You'll do okay without me. I'm staying."

He hesitated for a moment, torn between duty and the desire to throttle me. Then he unbuckled his pistol belt and handed it to me.

"You may need this."

"What will you fight with?" I asked, but I took it gratefully.

"A mixed platoon of Royal Marines and Bavarian rifles, I should imagine. I shall be back shortly."

Gordon and Melzer ran off into the darkness toward the distant flashes of small arms fire twinkling through the branches of the woods to the southeast. I wondered what General Buller would think if he could see Gordon now, running into the pitch-black night, toward a fight with unknown enemies, unarmed.

"Is he brave or foolish?" Jovo asked, as if he had read my thoughts.

"He's English," I answered, and Jovo nodded.

The breeze, blowing softly from the northwest, picked up for a moment and carried a soft, faint droning sound which momentarily was louder than the distant crackle of rifles. Jovo heard it as well, and we looked at each other. Bees?

"A zeppelin's engine," Jovo said.

"Get your men armed. The land attack is a diversion!"

I ran toward his house, to Thomson and Gabrielle. Jovo shouted a warning in Serbian behind me. Somewhere a bell rang the alarm. I rounded the street corner before Jovo's house and saw broad black shapes glide over the rooftops ahead of me, making soft whispering sounds. A batlike creature, its wings fully a dozen feet across, settled into the shadows of the courtyard ahead. Its wings drooped to the ground and fluttered awkwardly, and without thinking I had Gordon's revolver out.

Crack, crack, crack.

Three shots and the thing staggered back and then collapsed. I waited a moment for more movement and then trotted toward it.

The thing rested on the ground, an indistinct lump outlined faintly in the pale starlight and the yellow glow of the *voivoda*'s nearby open front door. I prodded the thing with my foot. It groaned. It was not a creature at all, simply a black-clad man in a sort of silk-winged paraglider harness.

He started to move again. I shot him once in the head and ran toward Thomson, Gabrielle, and Mirjana, all crowding in the open door.

"Back inside!" I barked.

They hurried back in, and I followed them and closed the door to a slit.

"Douse that light. Tesla must be either very anxious to have you, Professor, or very angry at Jovo, or both."

I buckled on Gordon's pistol belt, dug four cartridges out of the leather ammo pouch, and replaced the spent rounds. As I clicked the revolver closed, Jovo ran up the street. I held the door open for him.

There was fear in his face. He and Mirjana exchanged hurried words in Serbian, and she disappeared into the kitchen.

"You have seen them?" Jovo asked. "They come like shadows, mostly in the north side of town, I think, while we were south."

The distinctive, metallic rattle of a Gatling gun reached us from outside.

"Ah! Now the damned airship joins the attack," he added.

"It will pin your men down in the south half of the village, suppress their fire, while the air assault consolidates in the north," I said. "Once they are organized, they will push south and clear the village house by house. They'll get here fairly soon."

Jovo looked around the room, fighting against the rising tide of panic. Everything was happening too fast for him. I turned to Thomson.

"I hate to say this, since we just found you, but we've got to leave you behind. Your leg . . ."

"Yes," he answered, and put his hand on my arm as if to hurry me toward the door. "I'd never keep up, and I doubt he means me any harm. You have to go now."

"My leg is injured as well," Gabrielle said. "Perhaps I—"

"You I can carry. We're going down the ridge into the valley. Jovo, we need a back way out, a window—"

Jovo's face cleared, and he nodded decisively.

"Yes, follow me."

He led us into the kitchen, where Mirjana finished tying together the two ends of a rolled wool blanket. She thrust it at me.

"Take," she ordered in German.

"*Danke.*" I slipped it over my head and left arm. "What about you?" I asked Jovo.

"All we can do is give up or die, and dying is stupid, so we'll give up. The Old Man does not butcher Serbs, although he may take his anger out on me. We will see. When the soldiers come, I will say the Scotsman is Mirjana's crazy uncle Sasha from Zagreb, who only speaks German. Perhaps we will have some luck there if the released airship crewmen do not see him."

"And when they ask where Thomson is?"

"The five gold coins will explain his absence, unless Captain Gordon's party is taken as well. Now go!"

Mirjana opened shutters on a window on the back wall.

"It is about three meters down, then twenty meters to the edge of the slope."

I lowered myself out feet first but stopped to shake Jovo's hand.

"Thank you. I don't think I'll be able to repay you."

"Singe the Old Man's whiskers and that's payment enough."

I lowered myself until I hung from my hands and then dropped the two feet to the ground. Out here the rattling chatter of the zeppelin's Gatling gun was louder, along with shouts and screams and the sound of scattered small arms fire in the town. Above me Jovo and Mirjana helped Gabrielle out and lowered her by her hands. I reached up and held her by her waist.

"Got her. Take the weight on your good leg, Gabi."

I eased her to the ground.

"This is foolish. I cannot keep up. You must leave me."

"No chance."

Above me the bright square of the window darkened, filled with Thomson's head and upper body. From behind him I heard loud rapid knocking on the house's front door.

"Laddie, you've got to stop Tesla. He has enough liftwood to have built an engine of enormous power. If the earth's orbital velocity slows even slightly, we move closer to the sun. Temperatures will rise, and it will take very little to produce disastrous results. It—"

"Yeah, melting icecaps, rising oceans, killer storms, mass extinctions—got it. Now close the window, *Uncle Sasha*. I'll take it from here. And watch out for yourself."

"God be with you."

The shutters closed, and the world turned black.

Stop Tesla. Did I even want to do that? I supposed I did, but I also needed Tesla for . . . everything else. Putting those two things together was going to be a really good trick, and I could hardly wait to find out how I was going to pull it all off.

For that matter, Tesla was a smart guy and so far as I knew not suicidal. Wouldn't he have figured out all this end-of-the-world stuff? That was something to ask him, when the time came, but first we just needed to get away. When I faced Tesla, it wouldn't be as a prisoner. Not if I could help it.

We had to get to the edge of the slope, then start down, but my night vision was shot. I put my arm under Gabrielle's shoulders to support her, and we started slowly toward the valley.

"Leave me," Gabrielle said, her voice almost pleading. "I will be all right. You have a better chance by yourself. I do not believe Tesla will harm me."

"Based on what, his record of restraint?"

"He does not harm women."

Huh. Was that true? I thought about it for a couple seconds while we walked.

"He kills people he sees as obstacles, Gabi. In your world most women aren't empowered enough to constitute an obstacle. You are, so no more argument. Pay attention to the trail."

I had enough night vision by then to see faint gray highlights on the ground beneath us against the deeper black of the open sky ahead, where the ground fell away. There was no abrupt drop-off, simply a gradual descent which grew more pronounced at a certain point, and continued to grow steeper with every step until we had to struggle to keep our footing.

We stopped, and despite Gabrielle's protests I picked her up in a fireman's carry, settled her weight so she was balanced, and began backing down the slope using my free left hand as a support against the ground. The hillside was rocky, with woody scrub and vines. It tangled my feet but also gave me good handholds when my feet slipped. I lost my footing several times and slid a foot or two down the slope, I skinned my knees up and felt a couple thorns and splinters in the palm of my left hand.

My gloves were in the pocket of my overcoat, back at Jovo's house. Gabrielle's overcoat and the jacket for her riding habit were back there, too. Being out here in worsening weather without adequate clothing worried me. Hunger and thirst don't kill many people in the wilderness—exposure does. Fortunately Mirjana had had the presence of mind to grab a blanket for us. I liked Mirjana, even though the feeling didn't seem to be mutual. I liked Jovo, too. I hoped Tesla wasn't going to be too hard on them, but sticking around wouldn't have made it any easier.

My feet slipped again in loose shale, and I slid three meters down the slope before I got a good handhold. I stopped for a moment, panting for breath and smarting. The knees were gone from my pants by now, and I could feel my legs bleeding. The fireman's carry is a good way to handle weight if you are upright, but leaning forward like this put a lot more stress on my neck and left arm, and my lower back ached from trying to compensate.

"Okay, we need to change position."

"You should rest a few minutes."

"Can't. Look up there."

She looked up and caught the tail end of a flare rising over the village. Somebody had fired a Very pistol up in the air.

"What does it mean?" she asked, and even as she said it the stutter of the Gatling gun died away.

"Tesla's men have firm control of the upper village. That must have been their signal for the zep to cease fire, so they can move south and clear the other half. We need to get some distance between us and the town. Then we can rest."

I had her put both arms around my shoulders and ride piggy-back as we resumed our descent. That let me use both hands, which was an improvement. After another fifteen minutes all sound of fighting died away, although the drone of the zeppelin's engines remained, growing louder and softer as it circled the town. I wondered if Gordon and the others had fought their way clear. I wondered if Jovo's ruse had kept Thomson safe. Mostly I wondered how much longer I could keep this up.

Another ten minutes gave me my answer. My legs and arms trembled uncontrollably, and when I lost my footing again, I slid on bare rock and scraped my knees so badly it brought tears to my eyes. I couldn't get back up. It was as if my legs no longer received the electrical signals from my brain. I lay there panting for a while, Gabrielle still on my back.

"Are you all right?" she asked.

I slapped the ground beside us with my right hand.

"Camp here."

We rested for a while. Gabrielle started to shiver. With nothing on above her waist but a silk blouse, it was no wonder. I unrolled the blanket to wrap it around her shoulders, and my appreciation for Mirjana grew. She had not simply rolled up a blanket for us. In it she had included a small bag of dried meat, one of dried fruit and nuts, a thin loaf of hard bread, a jar of ointment for Gabrielle's wound, clean linen bandages, and a dozen wood matches tightly wrapped in a small square of rubberized canvas.

"What?" I said, examining our treasure. "No Serbian-English phrase book?"

"I think this was very thoughtful of Mirjana," Gabrielle said in her defense.

"Me, too, Gabi. I was joking."

"Ah," she said, as if she understood.

We ate a little bit, and Gabrielle rubbed some of the ointment on my bloody knees. She wanted to bandage them as well, but I wouldn't let her use all the linen for that. I tore a small square for each leg, just a patch, and pressed them over the ointment. Then I used my pocket knife to cut about a four-inch strip off one end of the blanket, cut that in half, and used each half to wrap around my knees to hold the linen patch in place, and for padding.

I checked her leg as well, but there was no sign of bleeding on the bandages, so the stitches were holding.

"Well, as we sophisticated classical scholars like to say, *tempus* is *fugit*-ing. Let's get some distance between us and the town by dawn."

We rolled our supplies back up, got Gabrielle positioned on my back, and started down again. She dangled her good right leg down and took up some of the weight when the ground allowed it. My night vision was good now, and I'd gotten used to the repetitive motion of the climb. The brush was much thicker here and tore at our limbs and clothes, but gave me better handholds as well, and I could use the resistance of the brush to ease our passage down. We made better time, and my strength lasted longer. We took another ten-minute break after an hour, then started again. We descended for perhaps twenty minutes more before I heard the first shrill hunting cries of the *azhdaja*.

THIRTY-FOUR

October 11, 1888, near Brezna, Serbia

My first instinct screamed at me to keep moving down the ridge, deeper into the valley, but that was flight panic talking. Instead, I stopped. Gabrielle's arms tightened around my shoulders, and I felt her breathing come faster, in shorter pants. She had more reason than I did to panic, having already been laid open once by one of them.

"*Azhdaja*," she gasped. "What should we do?"

I dropped to my hands and knees and eased her off to the right side, on her uninjured leg. Then I took her upper arms in my hands and squeezed, and put as much calm in my voice as I could.

"We're going to take a minute and think."

I looked up the slope. The lights of Brezna glowed in the darkness, marking the top of the ridge. Being able to see it made it seem that much closer, even after all this time, as if we were running in a dream but not getting any farther away. If the valley twisted, if there had been a spur of ground between us and the town, it would have felt more distant. More importantly, if I used Gordon's revolver on the hunting *azhdaja*, nothing would block the muzzle flash from observers up there, or muffle the report.

"These things are nocturnal hunters," I said, talking to myself as much as to Gabrielle. "They probably have better night vision than we do, so being out in the open does us no good. We want to be where the ground is close and there's a lot of undergrowth. That way we can hear them if they get near."

I looked at Gabrielle, but I couldn't make out her expression in the starlit darkness.

"How does that sound?" I asked.

"Yes," she answered, voice trembling but under control. She bit her lower lip in thought and scanned the countryside below us, then raised her arm and pointed.

"Is that a wood down there?"

"Yeah. A little far away if they decide to close on us."

She nodded and looked again. An *azhdaja* shrieked, closer this time and from a different direction, but not in attack distance yet, as far as I could tell. Gabrielle looked toward the sound of the shriek, then looked in the opposite direction.

"There," she said and pointed to a streak of dark shadows, closer than the woods and slightly to our right. I'd already spotted it. I wasn't sure if it was really what we needed or just a freak shadow from a fold in the ground, but we had to try something.

"Okay, mount up, Gabi."

Between the short rest and the adrenaline, I got us over to the dark ground in no time. It was better than I'd hoped for, a very broken arroyo with crumbling shale banks about five feet high right here and lots of tangled thorny brush as tall as our heads, maybe taller. I put Gabrielle down and was about to slide down the bank when I saw her back in the starlight.

"Damn, Gabi! Why didn't you say something?"

I looked closer. I'd been backing us down the ridge for over an hour, through tangled scrub and thorn bushes, with Gabriele on my back and nothing on her back when we started but a silk blouse. There wasn't much of that left now.

"It is all right. We have to hurry."

Heaven deliver me from stoic women. I slipped the blanket roll over my head and then stripped off my jacket.

"Put this on. No talk, just do it."

While she did I lifted the blanket roll back over my head and listened to two *azhdaja* call to each other—one far away and lower down the valley, one pretty close. I wet my finger in my mouth and held it up, felt one side cool in the light breeze. At least the closer one was upwind. It hadn't caught our scent yet.

I slid down the shale embankment as quietly as I could, but the shale was what climbers call *rotten*, crumbling and coming apart under my feet. It sounded like an avalanche to me, but I couldn't tell how much of that was proximity and fear-heightened senses. I helped

Gabrielle down the bank, and then we listened for half a minute, maybe longer. At first there was no sound. Then the closer hunting bird shrieked, a different, more insistent call, and was answered by three or four others from below us and to either side.

"They're hip to us," I said and pulled her toward the brush. The thorns formed a nearly impenetrable tangle, especially in the darkness. I tried pushing into what felt like a weak spot, maybe a gap between two bushes, but after the foliage gave a little, it locked up. I heard *azhdaja* make their hunting shriek again, all of them closer and the one now nearly on us.

"Down," Gabrielle said urgently. "We must crawl under the branches."

I dropped to my knees, and she had already nearly disappeared into the tangle. It was easier down here. The root clusters were easier to see, and there were several inches of clearance before the branches met and formed that impenetrable web. It wasn't hands-and-knees crawling, though; it was right down on your belly stuff, dragging yourself from one root cluster to the next by your hands. After a few yards in, the shale gave way to wet sand and then black mud, still sticky from the heavy rains a few days earlier.

I heard more hunting shrieks, this time seemingly right on top of us, and I felt panic seize at my throat, choke off my breath. A root broke off in my hand. I grabbed at another and felt Gabrielle's muddy boot. She cried out in terror and kicked wildly.

"It's okay! It's just me. Keep going."

Behind me I heard the bushes rustle, and an *azhdaja* squawked in hunger and frustration—at least that's how it sounded to me. The bushes rustled again, and I knew it was coming through.

I reached for another root cluster but felt nothing but mud, groped right and left—we had reached a small clearing. I crawled in next to Gabrielle, who lay prone in the stream bed, panting in fear and exhaustion. Around us I heard at least two, perhaps three of the hunters crashing through the brambles.

I sat up, pulled the blanket roll over my head, and laid it on Gabrielle.

"If one of them gets in, use this as a shield."

I pulled Gordon's revolver from the covered holster, took a breath to calm myself, and waited.

The clearing was actually the center of the streambed. The stream ran sluggish and muddy now, but two or three days ago it had probably been a couple feet deep. Most of the undergrowth had hung on, but the very center of the stream—no more than a meter wide—was clear of brush. The *azhdaja* squawking and struggling in the bushes where we had crawled in made the most noise, but didn't sound like it was making much progress. I figured the main danger was from downstream. That's where most of the screeches had come from, and once the hunting birds got in the middle of the stream, they would have a straight shot at us. I sat facing downstream.

Tactical breathing, in and out. Settle down.

I waited for a clear target, but as I started thinking about it, I wondered why. I didn't really care if I killed any of them. If a shot or two frightened them away, that was fine by me. I decided to take a shot at the bird to my right, the one making all the noise, when I heard scrabbling to my left and higher up.

Gabrielle sat up and clutched the blanket roll.

"What is that?" she whispered.

The answer came in an eruption of flapping and squawking, followed by an explosive crash of brush to my left. One of the *azhdaja* had jumped from the high bank, trying to clear the brush and get to us. Pretty smart, but he'd fallen short.

"Close your eyes!" I shouted to Gabrielle. I turned, closed my own eyes, and fired twice into the noise. A high-pitched screech of pain followed the second shot. Not bad for firing blind, and we'd kept our night vision.

Then a second *azhdaja* leaped from the bank, and this one cleared the brush.

Gabrielle saw him, screamed, and raised the blanket roll, held it up and away from her. The rear talons of the bird ripped into it, and Gabrielle collapsed back under the sudden weight. The bird pitched forward, screeching and flailing, and somersaulted into me—eighty pounds of angry teeth, talons, and feathers.

The impact stunned me, knocked me back into the mud. The bird and I rolled, slashing and striking at each other. A part of my mind told me its legs were the most danger, and when I saw one kicking inches from my face I grabbed it, and then somehow had the other leg—thick, leathery, and muscular—in my other hand. The calm and distant part of my brain reminded me that meant I no longer had my revolver.

The bird twisted in my grip and snapped at me with its teeth, nipped my thigh. I could hold its knifelike leg spurs at bay this way but couldn't do much else.

"More come up the stream!" Gabrielle shouted. "Shoot them!"

"I dropped the pistol!" I shouted back.

She groped the streambed near me, and for a moment Gabrielle, the bird, and I all rolled and struggled together—the bird to kill us, Gabrielle to find my pistol in the shallow water, and me to just break even.

I tried kicking the bird in its face but had to draw my knee up so far to get my foot even with it that I had no strength in the kick. Finally I drew both knees up and got my feet on either side of its head. It wriggled free, but I got its head between my feet again, this time with one foot under its jaw, and pushed down, straightening my legs, pulling its hind legs with my arms as hard as I could. It stretched out, and then I felt a *snap.* The *azhdaja*, its neck broken, continued to struggle, but deliberate attack changed to random twitching and flopping.

Boom! Boom! Boom! Boom! Click, click, click.

Gabrielle had found the revolver. I pushed the still-twitching carcass off of me.

"Give it to me. I'll reload."

She handed it over. I tried to break it open, but it seized up. I tried again and it made scraping, grinding noises but still wouldn't open more than a half inch. I felt at the hinge—it was Gordon's revolver, with that complicated-looking lever arm below the barrel, and the lever was caked with gritty mud.

"*Goddamned worthless Enfield piece of shit!*" I shouted in frustration. "*Where's my Webley?*"

I frantically swished it in the shallow water of the stream and worked it back and forth until it popped open. With trembling hand I pulled cartridges from the leather pouch on my belt, dropped two or three of them, but managed to get the revolver loaded and snapped shut.

I looked up but couldn't see much, Gabrielle's firing having blown out my night vision.

"Can you see them?" I asked.

"*Non*. I hear the one."

Our original friend, the one that had followed us into the brush, still struggled and flailed, but its efforts seemed desperate now. As I listened I heard more of them downstream, but receding rather than advancing. I didn't know whether Gabrielle had hit anything, but if not, the noise and flash had been enough to drive them away. They weren't stupid or suicidal.

I raised the revolver and fired at the *azhdaja* still struggling in the brush, the one that first found us. It made a high-pitched chirping sound, a mix of fear and pain, but it kept struggling. I fired three more times, and it shrieked twice more but still struggled.

"Die, you stupid son of a bitch, DIE!"

I fired twice more and then clicked on an empty cylinder. The bird broke free of the brush, and I heard it scramble up the shale embankment in retreat, then . . . silence.

Gabrielle and I sat side by side, panting, limbs trembling, soaked in muddy water. We looked at each other. I picked a light-colored *azhdaja* feather from her hair and let it drop into the stream.

"Well," I said. "That was easier than I expected."

Then we laughed.

And laughed and laughed.

I had worried earlier that pistol shots might attract attention from Brezna. There was a chance the brush and twisting banks of the streambed had muffled the sound and blocked the flash, but we couldn't take the chance. As soon as we caught our breath, I scooped up the blanket roll, got Gabrielle on my back, and started up the streambed.

"We went down before. Why do we go up now?"

"You tell me," I answered.

She thought about it for a moment.

"If they look from the air, they'll find the dead *azhdaja*. We can do nothing about that. Since we were moving away from Brezna before, they will look for us farther away, not closer, *n'est-cepas?*"

"Bingo."

Then I had to tell her what bingo meant.

We made it about two hundred yards up the stream bank when I heard the engines of the zeppelin heading down the valley toward us from Brezna. We found a place in the brush where the branches were high enough we could wriggle under them. Since the blanket was a dark earth tone, I unrolled it. We crawled under the overhanging brush next to each other, Gabielle's head on my arm, and I pulled the blanket over us to break up our shape from the air. Once we got in position there wasn't much to do but listen to the sound of the zeppelin and wait.

"I was very frightened when the dragons attacked," Gabrielle said, "but the fight, it was quite exhilarating."

"I know what you mean."

"You do, don't you? You have been through this before. The fear—but then the excitement, and I do not know where the one stopped and the other began. Do you know?"

She was chattering, pretty standard stress-release motor mouth, but that was okay.

"I could never tell, either," I said. "They're too mixed up together."

"Yes, those feelings, and others as well, all together."

She turned under the blanket and looked me in the eye.

"Do you know what I wanted to do immediately afterwards?"

I looked back at her and smiled.

"As a matter of fact, I do."

I'd never heard her giggle before, but she giggled then, lying under a blanket in a thorn thicket as Tesla's black zeppelin droned overhead, its searchlight sweeping back and forth across the streambed and the surrounding meadows. The zeppelin passed us by, its attention downstream, and under our blanket I gave in to the moment and did so knowing what would come at the end of the road. As I did, I also knew that whatever came, I would share it with Gabi at the end. If I had to choose one world or the other to save, I would save my daughter but share whatever fate came to this place. That didn't make it right, but it was all I had left to give.

Nature took its course, although not without a few false starts. The ground was hard on the back, had a lot of broken shale and gravel, so, gentleman that I am, we started with Gabrielle on top. That put too much pressure on her injured thigh, threatened to tear the stitches. We tried it with me on top but my knees were so torn up I couldn't manage it. Beat up as we were, we kept at it until our efforts were rewarded, which says a lot for our commitment and perseverance. But they say where there's a will, there's a way, and right then our wills burned so brightly, so intensely, it's a wonder Tesla's balloon boys didn't see them scorching away the darkness.

Later, after our celebration of glorious survival, we rested, all tangled up in each others' arms and clothes and the blanket.

"Do you know what my friend Renfrew said about you?" Gabrielle said sleepily. "He said I would find you interesting. He said, 'Three remarkable men are going on a desperate mission.' He often speaks like that. He described the three of you as, 'The most intelligent and practical-minded scientist of our time, one of the most courageous young officers in our service, and this strange fellow from another time. You will fit right in, Gabi,' he told me. I think he meant because I am odd."

"No. He meant because you are exceptional."

She made a contented sound and gently caressed my chest with her hand.

"I believe he was mistaken about *Capitaine* Gordon," she said after a moment. "That is odd. Renfrew is seldom wrong about these things."

Yeah, why would Renfrew describe Gordon as courageous? Was he just hyping the team to get Gabrielle to agree to help? Maybe. Gordon had never been in combat before. How would Renfrew know anything, one way or another, about his courage? In fact, Gordon had gone out of his way to exchange duty assignments with other officers to avoid overseas service and stay assigned to the intelligence branch in England.

The zeppelin's engine had faded to a distant murmur earlier but in the last few minutes had grown louder and now grew louder still. I leaned out from under our bushes and looked downstream. I could see the location of the airship by its spotlight, which was very close, no more than two hundred yards east. The light was stationary, pointing down into the streambed, and as I watched it settled lower, landing.

"Trouble. They found the *azhdaja* we killed."

"You thought they would," Gabrielle said. "Now they look downstream, *oui?*"

"I think they already did. We need to move while they are still occupied down there."

We rolled up the blanket and started upstream. I put my arm

around Gabrielle and supported part of her weight until we found a break in the brush to our right. I climbed the stream bank and pulled her up behind me, but by then could hear voices, some coming up the stream, some in the meadow to either side, calling to each other to keep station.

We had to move fast. Gabrielle didn't protest when I picked her up in a fireman's carry and started trotting up the gentle slope. There had to be woods up here somewhere.

But the long flight down the valley and the fight with the *azhdaja* had taken more of my reserves than I'd realized. Carrying Gabrielle up the ridge, trying to stay silent, covering as much ground as I could, left my knees trembling and buckling within a minute. We needed to get to cover. The voices grew closer, but I slowed to a staggering walk. My legs just wouldn't move any faster.

"Leave me," she whispered.

No, I thought, without the breath to say it.

I slipped on a loose rock and fell to my knees, pain lancing up my thighs. A voice sounded an alarm behind us. I tried to get up but couldn't at first. I waited for ten or twelve heartbeats, gathered my strength, and rose. I staggered on toward trees I couldn't see but which had to be there. *Had to be.*

A shot rang out behind us, close, but I heard no bullet passage. Just someone sounding an alarm. Not much time left. Had to get to the trees.

Feet running in the grass behind us.

The slope grew suddenly steep. I went down on my knees again and my one free hand. I groped for a handhold, something to pull us up the slope, and felt the root of a tree.

A tree.

We'd made it. I gathered all my remaining strength and pulled us up the slope. I grasped the trunk of the young tree and pulled us farther, pulled us through the sharp scent of pine needles and into the dark shadowed safety of the woods.

That's where Tesla's men found us a few minutes later, exhausted, lying against the trunk of a pine tree.

THIRTY-FIVE

October 12, 1888, Kokin Brod, Serbia

I'd seen plenty of dungeons in movies. The real thing was nothing like either Hollywood or I imagined. Nothing.

The dungeon was small, a single chamber undivided into individual cells. The irregular floor, a slab of unworked bedrock, sloped toward the back wall. The walls themselves were crooked, uneven, some the same natural stone as the floor, some limestone blocks and boulders of uneven size and shape.

Iron rings hung from hooks hammered into the back wall, and they trailed heavy, rusted chains ending in shackles. The wall and floor below it were stained dark brown and black—from rust, I hoped, but I suspected otherwise.

The guards did not speak. They took our shoes, my jacket and shirt, but perhaps in a nod to Victorian modesty left Gabrielle the rags of her blouse. I shouted in surprise and pain when one of them took a small, sharp knife and cut a thin slice of flesh from my left shoulder, put it in a glass tube, and sealed it. Hot blood ran down my arm, dripped from my fingers onto the floor. They attached one shackle to my right wrist and another to my left ankle, then did the same to Gabrielle.

I saw no sign of sleeping pallets, no remnants of food, no provision for human waste, and their absence was a whispered, chilling threat—*you will not need these things.*

Of elaborate and imaginative machines of torture there were none. That surprised me. After the clockwork spiders, I expected some baroque, complicated torture contraptions. Their presence would have been comforting, in a macabre way, evidence of imagination and sophistication, no matter how twisted. But this . . .

There was nothing sophisticated about this dark, cramped, low-ceilinged hole. Everything about it was crude, primitive, and hard. This was not where they broke someone's will, made them reveal, confess, or inform. This was where they chained them to a wall and beat them to death with iron rods.

After they chained us, the guards departed, climbing the steep, winding stone stairway, taking the one lantern with them. They left us shivering in darkness so absolute it made the dungeon the smallest place in the world, and the largest.

"I'm sorry, Gabi," I croaked.

"You should have left me."

"Not an option," I answered.

"You should have left me," she repeated. "They would have stopped looking when they found me, and you would have escaped."

"And then what happens to you?"

She didn't answer for a moment, and then she said, "I would have been all right."

Sure. *Tesla doesn't harm women.* Gabrielle was chained in the same shitty hellhole I was, which I thought brought that proposition into some doubt, but I didn't say so. What was the point? To scare her more than she already was?

For a long time we did not speak. The only sounds were the occasional rattle of our chains when we shifted position, and the slow, steady drip of water in a far corner of the dungeon.

Plop . . . plop . . . plop.

Deep underground, and with the doorway at the top of the stairs closed, there was no ambient light, nothing for my eyes to adjust to, so we both remained blind, isolated. Minutes passed, or an hour, or longer. It was hard to tell.

"Which is the real man?" she said, her voice strangely disembodied in the impenetrable darkness, and loud after so much silence.

"What?"

"You know what I ask. You were the warrior, then suddenly you became the scholar. Why?"

I shivered, perhaps from the cold and damp.

"My wife died. Someone needed to raise our daughter."

"Why did your wife kill herself?"

I took a deep breath. The dungeon smelled of mildew and stone and air no one else had breathed for a long time. It smelled like a tomb—our tomb. Gabrielle was right; I owed her this answer.

"We had a second child, a little boy. Jack Junior. I spent time at home, was there for the baby's delivery. Joanne had trouble with Sarah's delivery, but Jack Junior's went fine. My guys back in Afghanistan needed me, too. I thought she was okay, so I went back to my unit.

"We exchanged some words over that, harsh words. There had been a lot of harsh words. You get used to that after a while, if you aren't careful. Suck it up and do your job."

"There's this thing called post-partum depression. I guess I'd heard of it, but it was something other people suffer from, people you read about. One night, when I was halfway around the world, Joanne sent Sarah to stay with her cousins. Then she took a whole bottle of pills, went to sleep and never woke up."

I paused, and I heard her chains clatter softly as she changed position.

"There is more," she said after a moment.

Yes.

"I remember my commanding officer calling me into his tent, sitting me down, telling me. I remember that instant as if it were ten minutes ago, not ten years. There was this second, just a second, when way down inside of me, in a deep, deep corner of my soul . . . I was relieved. All the arguments, the recriminations, the long silences that measured her growing frustration and disappointment—all that was over, and I was glad. I was glad she was dead.

"Then my commander told me . . . before Joanne killed herself, she'd smothered little Jack."

I remembered that moment again, as if it had just happened, remembered the bright morning sunlight through the partly open tent flap, how it had fallen on my hand but strangely had not warmed it. I remembered the sound of someone working the bolt on a fifty-caliber machine gun, cycling it twice, getting ready for the morning supply run over to Zareh Sharan as if nothing had changed. I felt the crushing certainty that this additional death was the inevitable punishment for my moment of terrible, unforgivable gladness.

We didn't say anything for a long time, just listened to the sound of the water dripping.

"So your daughter is all the family you have left, *oui*?" she said eventually. "Still, it is strange you change your life so completely for your daughter alone. Do not the other people in the army raise children?"

She said it thoughtfully, intrigued by the mental problem this presented but untouched by the enormous tragedy I had just revealed, unaffected by the admission of my terrible sin. Something about her detachment made it easier for me to talk about it as well, as if she saw the event from a different angle, a different dimension, and hearing her voice let me step, just for a moment, into that dimension where the death of my wife and child was just a thing, a thing different from other things, but still just a thing.

"Yes," I said. "People in the army raised children. Some were single parents. It was hard for them."

"I do not think hard things frighten you. Ah!" she said, as if she finally understood a great mystery. "You believe in ghosts."

"No. I don't believe in ghosts. What are you talking about?"

"You believe you killed your wife by your actions, and so you killed yourself, your old self, the self which made these actions, to make it up to her. But unless she is a ghost, she cannot see this thing, cannot accept your act of atonement. So you must believe in ghosts.

"And the old Jack Fargo, the one you killed, he does not remain dead, does he? Another ghost."

Ghosts! What did she know? She had Asperger's. She had a giant hole in her mind where other people had empathy, where other people understood what went on in the heads of the people around them. What did she know about me or about ghosts?

"Family," she said at last, and there was a distant, thoughtful sound to her voice, as if she talked to herself. "Always it comes back to family."

An hour, or two, or five later, the door at the head of the stairs creaked and scraped open. Light flooded down the stairs and illuminated every corner of our tiny world, or at least it seemed so, as dilated as my pupils were. Men clumped down the steps and brought lanterns of blinding brilliance with them, forcing my eyes closed until they adjusted to this new reality.

"So, again I meet the man from the future," a familiar voice with an Eastern European accent said in English.

"So, again I meet the king of the shitheads," I answered.

He didn't say anything right away, but then responded, "Can we dispense with verbal sparring? There is a great deal I would like to discuss with you about your time."

"My time? How about yours? You know, Thomson thinks you're going to destroy the world with your gizmo, which will have some pretty serious ramifications on my own time, don't you think? We're all pretty attached to having a world to live on."

"Of course he thinks that," he answered, and I heard laughter in his voice. "The Earth will fall closer to the sun, temperatures will skyrocket—am I right?"

"Something like that."

"Despite your words, you do not seem overly concerned, Professor Fargo. Tell me, do *you* believe I am going to destroy the Earth by melting its icecaps?"

I opened my eyelids a slit. The light burned, but I could see.

"No, you're too smart for that. You're going to destroy it by altering its magnetic field."

I could see him well enough to know that took him by surprise. He leaned back, and his eyes widened for an instant, then narrowed in suspicion.

"Thomson says this? Thomson thinks he understands magnetic fields, but no one alive understands them as I do."

"Except for me," I said.

"*You?* You teach history. What do you know of electromagnetism?"

"Not much by the standards of my day, but I took high school physics in 1998, so at least I know what makes the Earth's magnetic field work, which is more than either you or Thomson do."

Anger struggled with curiosity for control of his face. Curiosity won.

"Tell me your theory," he said.

"Well, it's been a while, but as I remember, an astrophysical body generates a magnetic field with kinetic energy from planetary rotation acting on an electrically conductive fluid, in our case molten iron in the Earth's core. What you end up with is a gigantic electromagnetic dynamo. And you're slowing it, aren't you?"

He paced slowly back and forth in the confines of the dungeon, frowning in thought and occasionally glancing at me, as if gauging my honesty.

"Did Thomson fill you up with this story?"

"No. I didn't figure it all out myself until today. I had a lot of time to think about stuff down here. But Thomson may put it together himself. He's a pretty smart cookie."

Tesla shrugged at that, dismissing it.

"He was, until my men shot him down, along with that Captain Gordon and the others. Jovo Radojica, the *voivoda*, as well. Ah, I see that surprises you. Yes, all of them, gone, hunted down on the slopes of the mountain and shot like dogs. But what does it matter? Even alive, Thomson posed no real threat to me. Most of the men who might have are already dead."

Thomson dead? Gordon dead? Maybe Durson and the others as well, or at best scattered fugitives, hiding in the rocks and brush of the mountains. I never really thought Tesla would deliberately kill them. That came from being too many years away from the life of violence, from getting used to the idea that a unique personality could somehow protect you from the worst of life's reversals. It came from the notion that if you had an interesting enough story to tell, you would get to finish telling it. But you don't always.

My stomach twisted, and suddenly I vomited. There wasn't much to come up, other than stomach acid, but I brought it up and then gagged again. Gabrielle and I were alone, chained in a dungeon, with no one left to rely on but each other.

I licked my lips and tasted bile. Now what?

What had Jovo said at the end? *Singe the Old Man's beard.* It wasn't much, but it was all I had left.

"Tesla, the problem really smart loners like you always have is they underestimate the power of collective thought. The British are assembling a committee to look into this and they'll put the pieces together."

He scowled.

"A *committee*! Look into what?"

"Look into why Big Ben is running fast. I read about it in the *Times.* They're trying to figure out why they had to slow the pendulum by four tenths of a second a day. I didn't think anything of it when I read it, but now I understand. Big Ben isn't running fast; the Earth's running slow. Your Forever Engine gizmo is not slowing the Earth's orbital speed, is it? You're not repeating the Martian mistake. It's slowing the *rotation* of the earth, bleeding off rotational momentum and turning it into electricity, a great big turbine. But it won't take long for the British observatories to figure out the rotation has slowed slightly, because the night stars are going to rise and set at the wrong times. Put that together with the survey work of the Royal Navy—"

"*What* survey work?" he demanded.

"The magnetic mapping surveys they've been doing for decades. They've measured a slight decrease in the Earth's magnetic field in the past year. They don't know what it means—yet. But they'll put it all together, because you didn't count on the reduction in rotational speed reducing the magnetic field."

He stared at me for a long moment, then shook his head.

"How can I believe you were able to reason this through with such limited information? You are not a scientist. You teach history."

"I'm smarter than I look," I said.

"I must think about this," he said abruptly and turned to go.

"Wait!" Gabrielle called out, the first words she had spoken in hours. "There is something I must show you."

"Ah, the French spy," Tesla said, turning back to us. A guard shifted his lantern to illuminate her, and she squinted in the light. I noticed Gabrielle and I had both become monochromatic, and not simply from the harsh lighting. Now that we were dry, our hair, skin, and clothing had all turned the gray of the streambed.

"I warn you," he said, "I am immune to your charms, even if they were more . . . presentable, but especially now"

"I would never attempt to seduce you. It would be highly inappropriate," she answered.

"An interesting choice of words. What is it you want?"

Gabrielle's blouse hung open almost to her waist, showing her upper undergarment. She reached in and drew out a locket.

"To show you this."

I'd noticed she wore a locket but hadn't thought anything of it. Now I realized it was the only jewelry she ever wore. I suppose I subconsciously put that down to proletarian austerity, the whole *Garde Rouge* thing. Suddenly I wasn't so sure.

Tesla stood motionless for a moment.

"Is this a trick?" he said.

"*Non.* Have one of your men open it if you like. It is simply a locket with an image inside."

"Why would I care about that?"

"That is for you to say," she said.

He hesitated for perhaps half a minute, then reached forward and swept the locket from her hand, opened it with his eyes on her face, searching for a reaction in advance, then held the locket up close to a lantern and looked.

He said nothing at first, did not react at all, until the seconds rolled on and his lack of movement itself became a reaction.

"Where did you get this?" he asked without looking up, his voice strained.

"It was my mother's."

"Why did she have it?"

"It was an image of her lover, the man who was my father but whom I never met."

"They put you up to this. They concocted this story for you. Admit it!"

"*Non.* My mother traveled in the Balkans as a young woman, was seduced by a married man, returned to France carrying me, and died without ever telling me who was my father. All I have of hers is the locket. When I grew older, I came to work for Le *Direction Centrale des Renseignements Généraux,* the DCRG. I did many things, but last year my superiors assigned me to research you. I am the very meticulous researcher. I sought out everything about the subject. When I did, I found an image of your father—*our* father.

"I told no one, but I made certain that when an expedition was sent to find you, to it I would be indispensable."

Tesla lowered the locket and took a step closer to Gabrielle, leaned forward to examine her more closely.

"And France?" he asked. "Do you feel no loyalty to your country?"

"I try," she answered. "I try, but a country is not real. The people, the cities and towns, the rivers, these things are real. But the country itself lives only on maps, and in the imagination of people. It is hard to be loyal to an imaginary thing."

He nodded in understanding.

"A person must be loyal to something," he said, "a principle, an ideal, some great goal."

"*Oui*," she agreed. "And I have searched for such a thing all my life. What is worthy of loyalty? This is what I found: people are loyal to the family. For soldiers, the regiment is the family. Many people imagine their family encompasses an occupation, a political movement, even an entire nation, but their loyalty to it is strong only so long as they believe it is still their family, *n'est-cepas?* Always it comes back to family."

Always it comes back to family.

Of course it did. Gabrielle never stopped asking me questions about Sarah and Joanne, about my family, the things which happened to us, how we felt about each other and why. Had this whole trip really been engineered by Gabrielle just to meet her half-brother, her only surviving family?

She said it would be "highly inappropriate" to seduce Tesla. Boy, talk about understatement! As I sat there and watched them in profile, her looking up, him looking down, any doubt I had as to their common ancestry vanished—both brilliant, both eccentric, both socially . . . odd. Tesla probably had a leg up in the brains department, and Gabrielle was a lot more concerned with finding her heart in all this, but here were two branches from the same tree.

When I had rattled off the famous and brilliant people who were likely Asperger's candidates, I had left out Tesla, even though he was near the top of the list. I'd done so because I thought that revelation might horrify rather than comfort Gabrielle. Now I remembered something else about Asperger's: it was usually transmitted through the male line.

Tesla gave an order in Serbian to the guards. One of them unlocked Gabrielle's fetters, and Tesla helped her to her feet.

"I am not yet sure what to do about you," he said to her. "But we have a great deal to talk about before either of us can make an intelligent decision."

"Yes," she said. "I believe that is so."

She glanced at me, then turned back to Tesla.

"Jack Fargo will not be hurt? He has been very good to me."

"I may have need of him. I will explain all that in due time. For now I have to leave him here. I think I will win him over, but I cannot afford to let him escape before I do so."

"*Oui*," she agreed. "He is very dangerous."

They started to leave, Gabrielle limping and Tesla supporting her weight, but Gabrielle paused at the foot of the stairs and turned to me again. She looked at me intently, frowning in concentration the way she always did when trying to solve a puzzle.

"I *told* you to leave me, Jack. I *told* you I would be all right."

THIRTY-SIX

October 13, 1888, Kokin Brod, Serbia

Woe for the wooing of disaster-fraught women.

At least that's what Euripides figured, and he must have known a thing or two about the subject. Half-naked, bleeding, shivering with cold and smelling of vomit, I sat chained in Tesla's dungeon alone—as alone as I had been the first day in this world. More so. I had nothing that first day. This day I'd had people I'd come to care about and then lost them all, either to death or betrayal. I tried to imagine Gordon, Thomson, and the others dead, tried to and failed. And Gabrielle . . .

Gabrielle's was the most bitter loss. The others had left my side through no choice of their own; Gabrielle had meant to all along. All along. Why?

During World War II, the U.S. built airstrips on a lot of remote and primitive Pacific islands and flew in cargo to sustain air and naval bases built there. The local base troops passed on food and some hardware to the locals, partially to keep their good will and partially out of natural generosity. It didn't amount to much for the U.S. armed forces, but it constituted unimaginable wealth for the islanders. When the war was finished, the U.S. troops left, and the cargo stopped coming.

Religions sprang up on a lot of those islands, religions collectively called cargo cults. Their followers would build imitation air strips, use old scrap metal to build dummy airplanes, and light fires at night like runway landing lights, hoping to lure back the cargo. If they went through all the right motions, they figured, they would get the good stuff and be happy again.

Gabrielle had started her own one-person cargo cult.

She had latched on to family as her cargo, and figured if she found a blood relative and acted as if they were a family, everything else would happen magically. She had a powerful and orderly mind, but in some respects it was unsophisticated. The biological component of family was easy for her to understand, easy to define and confirm, so that's what she had grabbed hold of with the desperation of a drowning woman clutching a life preserver. And she *was* drowning—just not in a way most people could see.

Gabrielle had asked which man I was. Was I the man I had become by chance or the one I had later become by choice? As I thought about it, I wondered if her question had as much to do with her own choice as it did with mine.

It seemed to me that choice reflected the true self, but Gabrielle had suggested my choice was not made for me, or even for Sarah, but rather for Joanne, my dead wife. She thought it was a form of suicide. Is choosing a life path which subordinates your own sense of person to someone else's expectations a form of suicide?

Maybe it is.

Which man was I? It was a question with less meaning for me than I think it had for Gabrielle, but often the questions posed by folks with Asperger's made little sense to others. The three Asperger's doctoral candidates I mentored at UC had remarkably similar childhoods, which is why I could peg Gabrielle's so closely, but they were distinctly different adults. All of them struggled with interpersonal issues. In some cases they had trouble with day-to-day maintenance of relationships; in other cases the whole concept eluded them.

Ann Girrardella alone had not finished her degree, and she had been the least socially adept of the three. She never understood "that romance stuff," as she used to say. She ended up a veterinarian, which was a good match for her. She liked animals, in a thoroughly unsentimental way.

Gabrielle reminded me of Ann in some ways, in her honest bewilderment concerning intimate relations of the heart, although Gabrielle was more determined to crack the mystery, whatever it took.

So here I was, chained in a lightless dungeon, all alone, and at Tesla's mercy. I should have been thinking about options, escape, turning the tables. Instead, all I could think about was Gabrielle's prospects and difficulties, after she had switched sides, betrayed me, left me here to rot.

I felt weightless, unattached to anything, not simply alone in the world but alone in the universe, the cosmos. What right did I have to feel loss at the deaths of Thomson and Gordon when I was hell-bent on destroying their world to save my own? What right did I have to feel betrayed by Gabrielle when the betrayal I contemplated dwarfed hers?

Would I find a way to save my own world, save Sarah and everyone else I had known from extinction? Hard to see how, but if I did, if I managed to extinguish this world and every soul in it to save my own, would I be able to face Sarah with that atrocity on my conscience? "Hi, Honey, Daddy's home. Guess what I did to save your life?"

A world, an existence, has a right to self-defense, a right to preserve itself, and it fell to me to be the instrument of that preservation. Tough luck for me. But would I do what needed doing when the time came? Yes, I would.

Yes, I would.

I just could not imagine surviving the act, could not imagine going about life afterwards. Perhaps it would have been different if I had not named the lobsters, but I didn't think so.

The door at the head of the stairs creaked open, light flooded down into the dungeon, and Tesla and two burly guards joined me. I steeled myself for a beating, but that wasn't what this was about at all.

"This business with the rotational momentum of the earth and its magnetic field," Tesla began without preamble. "I still do not understand how you came to the conclusions you did based on such little information. How is this possible?"

"It's my specialty. It's the reason I'm here, actually. The people who brought me into the Wessex project did so because I can make logical inferences with limited data—I can connect the dots when nobody else can. Also, I have a really good memory—for some things, anyway. That helps."

"It is hard to believe," he said.

"It's my gimmick. Some people do card tricks. Now, *those* are hard to believe."

He stood there quietly for a while, thinking that over.

"What does your good memory tell you will be the result of a reduced magnetic field?"

"The big thing is solar wind and cosmic rays. The magnetic field deflects them. Reduce the field and more will start getting through, which will increase the cancer rate. The solar wind will start stripping some of the atmosphere, too. I don't know what the threshold levels are for serious results. If you stop now, maybe the effects won't even be noticeable."

"A large steam power plant will produce sufficient power," he said, "but building one here two years ago would have been obvious and difficult. The Forever Engines I use were more practical for my immediate needs, and . . . the concept intrigued me. But I will stop soon."

"Sure, you can stop any time you want. Spoken like a true junkie."

"I do not know what that word means. I assume it is unflattering, but that is neither here nor there. What happens in this time will be of little concern to you.

"I have penetrated the curtain between different times repeatedly and reliably. If you are as astute as you claim, you must have realized this already. I offer you a way back to your own time, back to your daughter. Gabrielle tells me this is what you desire above all other things. I tell you I think she has misunderstood your purpose here, has misunderstood exactly what has happened. I realized when you made that slip of the tongue in London and then tried to cover it up. You remember? Concerning alternating versus direct current?"

I knew exactly what he meant, but I didn't feel like throwing in my cards yet. He might be bluffing. "What do you mean?"

"Oh, such transparency! You are not from our future, Professor Fargo, but a different one. But you hide this fact while revealing the rest. Why?"

"You tell me."

He shook his head impatiently. "Still you try to mislead and confuse when all is revealed. You do this to mask your intentions. What are they? You mean to do violence to our world, I think, in order to save your own. Is that not your purpose? Come now and tell me the truth. Nothing is gained by these pointless denials."

Maybe nothing was gained by them, but I'd be damned if I'd admit it to him. We traded stares for a while, and finally he shook his head again.

"You are a fool, Fargo. You think you can extinguish this reality? How? I think there is as much danger of you erasing my world's existence as there is of fairies being real, as there is of you becoming a rose bush by simply wishing it so.

"No, the only real danger you pose lies in your capacity for extreme violence. I owe you a debt for keeping my sister safe on her odyssey here. Also, she seems to feel an attachment to you, which makes her anxious concerning your health in this dungeon. So this afternoon I will have a room ready for you upstairs in the house—one with suitable security. You will find it more comfortable than this. I would like to converse with you about your world. If you accommodate me, I will accommodate you."

"What do you mean?"

"I will send you back to your time."

This was where I'd figured I'd be arguing with Tesla, trying to find a way to persuade him to send me back, find something I could do to make it worth his while. Instead, he was offering me almost exactly what I wanted. So why wasn't I jumping at the chance? Well, it wasn't enough, was it? Going home wouldn't save my time.

"Thanks for nothing."

He looked at me and frowned, then paced the length of the narrow confines of the dungeon, across the cell and back.

"Very well. Answer my questions about your world and I will give you access to my research findings on my experimental time soundings. I cannot guarantee the answer you seek—or believe you seek—is there, but it is all I have to offer you. When you believe you have an answer, I will send you wherever in time you desire, provided it is within the physical capacity of my apparatus."

"Somebody from the German Army vehicle from my time survived the transition to this time. That was obvious. Why don't you ask him about my world?"

"So stupid! The soldier survived the journey of over a hundred years and then died when the zeppelin crashed on the mountainside. That gave me another reason to kill Radojica, as if I did not have enough already."

I'd have liked to talk to that fellow myself. Speaking with someone from my own time would have made this all seem less surreal.

Tesla paced back and forth again. Was he just upset over the soldier's death, or was there something more? Why was he offering me everything on a platter? Why was he willing to risk annihilation of his time and world for answering questions about my world? Sure, there would be answers to some questions about lines of scientific progress which might help him out down the road, but was it worth the gamble? I couldn't see that it was. That must mean either he needed to know something very important—vitally important—about my time or that he did not believe there was anything I could do to threaten his world. Maybe he just wouldn't deliver on the promise when the time came.

Still, what did I have to lose? I wasn't getting anywhere in this dungeon. Even if his offer of a return to my time was a lie, access to his research notes might tell me something. After that I'd be on my own, but I'd been on my own all along.

"How are you going to get me back to my time, or any other, without turning me to ash? Going through your hole in time seems like a game of Russian roulette."

Tesla smiled and relaxed. "Oh, that is elementary. I have been experimenting for over a year, and I derived the formulae for adjusting the electrical input based on mass transference and temporal deflection easily. It was only the coincidence of your laboratory people aiming their device here at the same time as mine was active which set off that violent and very distorted effect. They must have used an extravagant amount of power. But normally I have experienced no such ill effects. The birds the locals call *azhdaja*, for example, survived the transition from their time to ours."

He must have brought a whole flock of them back. There were a lot of *azhdaja* wandering around, and no one had seen them until the last couple of months, so there hadn't been time for them to breed and populate, unless they grew really fast.

"I will have a room for you upstairs this afternoon," he said. "In the meantime, consider my offer."

He and the guards climbed the stone stairs and left me in the dark with my thoughts and my throbbing left arm.

All I had to do was say yes. Study his notes, find a clue to what was happening, and if all else failed just go home, hope I got there in time to see Sarah one more time before the effect wave extinguished us. But then I'd never get to see her graduate, see her find someone to spend her life with, build a family, maybe even end up with a few grandkids of my own to spoil.

Or maybe . . .

Could Tesla return me even earlier? Ten years earlier? Early enough to save my wife and son? Why not? The idea came like a flash, left me sweating and dizzy. If I could figure a way to save the whole world, why couldn't I also fix it to save Joanne and little Jack? If I was going to surrender my life, maybe my soul, to save my world, that didn't seem like too much of a reward to demand.

But a remembered voice nagged at me as well: Jovo Radojica's last words spoken to me.

Singe the Old Man's whiskers, and that's payment enough.

Was that a debt I could ignore?

Two guards came for me an hour later. Gabrielle and I had been blindfolded when they brought us here, and this time they covered my head with a canvas sack, I guess to keep me disoriented. They shackled my wrists together in front of me and led me up the stone stairs, down wooden hallways, up a carpeted set of stairs, more hallways, and then a warm, humid room. They pulled the hood off and I found myself in an austere but clean bedroom with a steaming tub of water in the middle of the floor. The guards waited till I stripped off the filthy rags of my clothing then gathered them up and left.

I slipped cautiously into the tub, but the water wasn't all that hot; it steamed more because the air in the bedroom was cool. I scrubbed myself until the water turned gray and I washed with particular care the patch on my left shoulder where they'd taken a chunk of my hide when I arrived. I resisted the temptation to soak; I didn't know when Tesla would show up and didn't want to be at a disadvantage, however slight, when he did. I dried off with coarse towels and found clean clothes folded on the bed—a little large but close enough once I pulled the belt tight. There was also gauze and tape, which I used to dress the wound on my shoulder.

The bedroom had a single door, which was locked, and a single window, covered on the outside by substantial-looking iron bars. For furniture the room boasted a single bed with a covered chamber pot underneath, a desk and straight-backed chair, another straight-backed armchair in the corner, a dresser with china water pitcher and bowl, and a wardrobe with a clean shirt and clean pair of trousers hanging within. The desk drawers were empty while the dresser held two pairs of long underwear and two pairs of woolen socks.

I put on a pair of the socks and settled into the armchair to wait. Within a quarter hour I heard the door unlocked. Tesla entered, a leather portfolio under his arm and two big guards in tow. He moved quickly, but not nervously—a man with a lot of things to do and a purposeful approach to getting them done.

"Have you considered my proposal?" he asked without preamble.

"A bit, but I have some questions. Assuming you can get me back to my own time—"

"I can," Tesla said with confidence.

"Yeah, okay. Assuming you can, how do you know you can hit my time exactly? What if I come out fifty years in the future? Or fifty years in the past? Fifty years is nothing compared to some of the time differences you're playing around with.

"For that matter, what if I come out, say, ten years in my past and meet myself? Does the time-space fabric rupture or something? Or is that possible?"

Tesla's eyebrows went up slightly.

"Interesting questions, which I expected you to ask. There are vibrational properties unique to the objects from each point in time, properties which manifest themselves in a particular type of spectroscopic analysis I have perfected. Using this, I can calibrate my device to access that precise time."

I touched the bandage on my left arm, hidden by my shirt.

"Is that why you carved on my arm with a knife yesterday? To get a sample of me for spectroscopic analysis?"

"Yes, of course. And that is why there was no need to take such a sample from Gabrielle."

"Is that how you brought back all those *azhdaja*?"

He smiled

"Exactly so. I sent several large oxen through with iron filings implanted in their flesh. Then several hours later I recalibrated and exchanged a large number of rocks for a surprising number of these avian predators. I had hoped to capture a single large predator. Usually small animals do not hunt large ones, you know, unless they do so in concert. Unfortunately, this animal engages in collective hunting. Most of them escaped and seem to be thriving in the hills."

"Where they are killing people. Your people. They almost killed Gabrielle twice."

"And you twice saved her life, I understand, for which I am grateful. But as to the larger picture, the food chain will adapt to them."

"Yeah. Like Asian carp in the Mississippi River."

He nodded. Of course, he didn't know that in my time Asian carp had all but ruined the Mississippi ecosystem.

"That Roman coin I brought with me—you were anxious to recover it as well."

"Yes, and my agent managed to pass it to the man who escaped from Dorset House. It arrived here shortly before you did. But its spectroscopic properties were confused."

"Now that I have answered your questions, I hope you will be sensible and cooperate," Tesla said. "Dinner at 7:30 PM," he said over his shoulder as he left, and the guards closed and bolted the door behind them.

I sat there and thought about the coin for a while. What had Tesla called its time signature? *Vibrational properties.* Why would they be confused? Maybe because the melted plastic from my time got mixed up with the silver of the coin from the past.

Yeah. That had to be it.

THIRTY-SEVEN

October 13, 1888, Kokin Brod, Serbia

Two guards came to collect me for dinner—one a beefy fellow in peasant smock, the other in the black uniform of Tesla's zeppelin crews, with his left arm in a cast and sling and his right hand resting on the grip of a revolver thrust into his belt. The peasant gestured down the hall and walked at my side. The *pistolero* followed at a distance.

I turned and looked at him, and his eyes burned with hatred.

"Do we know each other?" I asked in German. He said nothing, and his expression remained frozen.

Oo-kay.

The house looked new and was more modest than I had imagined when I was blindfolded—plain, but spotlessly clean. The hardwood floors were varnished but not stained. The plaster walls lacked decorative wainscoting or crown molding. The coarse brown carpeting on the stairs clearly was intended only to muffle noise.

We descended a broad staircase to the main floor, ended up facing a large front door, but turned right into the dining room. I started composing a mental map of the place, now that I could see.

Tesla and Gabrielle, already seated, waited for me. Tesla sat at the head of the table, Gabrielle to his right. The circles under her eyes bore testimony to our arduous journey here, but she looked rested, even fresh otherwise. She smiled when I entered, and I saw a light in her eyes I hadn't seen before. She had found her family, a goal to which she had devoted herself with single-minded determination for quite some time, and I wasn't entirely blind to what that might mean for her.

It wasn't my place to judge her about other responsibilities and loyalties. Realistically, I had to be near the bottom of that list in any case. Because of all we had gone through together, and all I'd shared about my own life with her, it seemed like longer, but the truth was we had only known each other for nine days. I had no claim on her, and no right to judge her betrayal. Still, I couldn't bring myself to smile back.

"You are well, Jack?" she asked.

"Better, anyway. Amazing what a bath and a nap can do sometimes. A meal won't hurt, either. You okay?"

"Yes," she said, and she smiled at Tesla. "I am quite well. I have already learned a great deal more about my family, things which simple newspaper reports and gossip could not tell me."

Tesla returned her smile and gestured to the seat to his left, across from Gabrielle.

I sat and the peasant guard left, although the black-clad *pistolero* remained, standing discreetly in the corner behind me. I turned and glanced at him.

"I understand that you are a dangerous man, Dr. Fargo," Tesla said. "Dangerous in many ways, perhaps, but also in a personal, physical sense. I do not wish to have to shackle you, but I need to take precautions with my own safety and that of Gabrielle."

"I wouldn't harm Gabrielle."

"But you do not deny that you might harm me. That is understandable, given your circumstances. I hope to persuade you otherwise, but in the meantime I prefer to have a guard present, one who understands the necessity of vigilance. Dragomir is one of the men you attacked in Munich. The local doctor says he will probably lose the use of his left arm. He is unlikely to underestimate the danger you pose, and will certainly not hesitate to shoot you should you attempt violence. Only his loyalty to me keeps him from doing so now."

I looked at the guy again.

"Dragomir. Ich entschuldige mich für das Schädigen Ihres Armes," I said. *I apologize for the injury to your arm.*

His expression didn't change, and I didn't know if he even understood German, but I made the effort anyway.

All violence has victims. I lived in a time—two times now—where sometimes there were no obvious alternatives to violence, but that didn't mean I had to tell myself fairy tales about how everyone I hurt deserved everything they got. That was one lie I'd given up a long time ago.

A servant brought steaming bowls of vegetable soup and a platter of thick-sliced bread which smelled freshly baked. My mouth watered, but I made myself eat slowly, partly because I didn't want to get sick, partly because I didn't want to show weakness to Tesla.

"Have you considered my offer?" Tesla asked as the soup bowls were cleared away. "Surely you understand there is no other way to return to your daughter. That, I understand, is your principal motivation."

I looked at Gabrielle. She wore a confident, happy expression, and Tesla seemed at ease as well. Suddenly I saw my edge, if I could figure out how to leverage it. Both of them had very limited, simplified views of human motivation and behavior. Gabrielle understood me only in terms of my love for my daughter, and had communicated that to Tesla. For the moment, the most important thing was to play to that belief. It gave me the most options down the road. I made up my mind.

"Okay, I'm in."

For the rest of dinner Tesla began his "conversation" with me about my world, which amounted to an interrogation, but that's what I figured. He was uninterested in our space program and had surprisingly little interest in weapons technology, given his ongoing fight here. I would have thought he'd want some more goodies like the gun turret his men had scavenged from the Puma back in Bavaria, but that wasn't the case. Instead he was much more interested in the data infrastructure of my world: the Internet, wireless communication, satellite GPS systems, the data cloud. Those things fired his imagination, would leave him lost in thought for several minutes after a round of answers, and then suddenly full of an entirely new line of questions.

This went on long after dinner was done and the dishes cleared away. His other interest, not surprisingly, was magnetic fields, and he sucked whatever information I had on the subject as a man might suck the marrow from a bone after stripping every shred of meat from it. Magnetism and planetary magnetic fields led to the solar magnetic field, or rather series of changing magnetic fields, and how the current thinking in my time was that changes and collapses in local solar magnetic fields led to solar flares.

The largest known solar flare had happened in 1859, when Tesla was just a little boy. He didn't remember it but had heard stories of the electrocution of telegraph operators and the brilliant night auroras. A flare of that intensity would have fried most of the communications and computer systems in my world.

After an hour or so, Tesla finally pushed back from the table.

"Fascinating conversation, but it grows late and I still have work to do before I retire. I now have a good deal to think over, and for that I am most appreciative, Professor Fargo. Tomorrow perhaps we can discuss what you know of particle accelerators. The guards will see you back to your room."

He rose and bowed to Gabrielle before leaving. Once he was gone I got to my feet as well, but Gabrielle spoke for the first time since the dinner dishes had been cleared away.

"Jack, I know you must think ill of me, and I cannot blame you. I feel no guilt over what I did, but I feel something. Regret, I suppose. I am uncertain I can accurately characterize it."

"It's okay. You don't owe me an explanation."

"No, I do not think so, either. But I wish you to be comfortable and even happy, if that is possible. I found this book in the library." She leaned over and picked up a heavy volume from the floor and placed it on the table. "It is about the subject dear to you, I think. Perhaps it will remind you of your home."

I walked around the table and picked up the book: the first volume of Gibbon's *The History of the Decline and Fall of the Roman Empire*. Despite myself, I smiled.

"Thanks. Nothing helps me sleep like Gibbon."

She smiled in reply, oblivious to the irony in my words, but then grew pensive.

"Why do you think it so wrong to believe in the possibility of a perfect world?" she asked.

I looked down at the book for a moment, tempted to let the question slide, to tell her maybe it wasn't such a bad thing after all. What did it matter to me anyway, one harmless lie more or less? But I'd let enough lies stand for the last ten years.

"Because only that belief can make otherwise-sane and good-hearted people commit unspeakable evil."

We said our polite good-nights, and the guards followed me back up to my room and saw me securely locked in. I undressed, but as soon as I slipped under the cold sheets I thought better of it, rose, and put on a pair of long underwear from the dresser. Then it was just me, Edward Gibbon, and a gas light. The Gibbon volume had been about as thoughtful and tender a gesture from Gabrielle as I figured she was capable of, and reading Gibbon's carefully measured prose probably would bring back pleasant memories of graduate school at the University of Illinois.

I picked up the volume and had a sudden thought, one which should have occurred to me sooner except I'd had a lot on my mind. What had three years, as opposed to three months, of Galba as emperor done to the history of Rome? It didn't make any difference to my mission, but as an historian I was curious. I opened Gibbon to find out.

Huh!

THIRTY-EIGHT

October 14, 1888, Kokin Brod, Serbia

Breakfast next morning was hot porridge and coffee, normally not my favorite flavor combinations, but the coffee was strong and rich, sweetened slightly with whole cream. I needed the coffee; I hadn't slept well much the previous night—way too much to think about. Gabrielle sat quietly through the meal, eyes down, her happiness of the previous day less in evidence. Was it our conversation of the previous evening?

"Are you okay?" I asked.

She looked up and studied me intently for a moment.

"I am very concerned about you," she said.

"Me? I'm going home. You're the one staying here, with the Turkish Army on the way and the British and German armies behind them. Why worry about me?"

"She is concerned you surrendered too quickly yesterday," Tesla said. He sipped his coffee but studied my reaction over the rim of his cup.

I shrugged.

"No need to worry. Best way I can keep Sarah safe is to stick with the program, right? Besides, there's nothing keeping me here."

She looked back down at her porridge. I'd meant it to hurt and it, had, but instead of satisfaction I felt shame. Wasn't I the guy who'd said I had no right to judge her?

"Thanks for the book, Gabi. It made for interesting reading."

She looked up and smiled.

"Book?" Tesla asked.

"Gibbon's *Decline and Fall*, Volume One. She loaned it to me from your library. I wanted to read about Emperor Galba, and I made a very interesting discovery. There never was an Emperor Galba in your history."

"Really?" He smiled an odd, knowing smile. "That is not my field of expertise."

"It did pique my curiosity. When can I have a look at your research notes?"

"I have work in the equipment building this morning, so this would be a good time. They are in German. I trust that will not be a problem."

Once the breakfast dishes were cleared away, we took our leave of Gabrielle, and he and the guards accompanied me back up the stairs. My initial impression of the house as being small was not correct. It did not have the rambling splendor of Chillingham's manor house, but it had as many or more stories. The first floor's kitchen, dining room, study, library, and sitting rooms were topped by bedrooms on the second and third floors, then a large laboratory on the fourth floor. I lingered a moment by the door to the laboratory, looking in at the banks of electrical instruments, and rubbed the bandage on my left shoulder.

"This where you did your spectrographic analysis of my skin?"

"No, that equipment is elsewhere. I have already calculated the settings and required power levels for the aether-field manipulator. I will transfer the settings to the machine when we are ready to proceed."

"Still cranking the power gizmo, huh?"

"Actually, I have enough accumulated power to make the transfer now. I do not want to completely drain my reservoir, however. If the Turks should actually manage to organize an attack, I need a reserve of electrical power."

"I don't think the Turks are coming. Nobody left to send them the all-clear signal. Even if they did, what would you need power for?"

He didn't answer me but gestured for me to follow into the laboratory. He pointed to a chair by a clear desk, and I sat. In a little while he came back carrying a thin folder of papers and a small bound book. I had expected more, and Tesla probably saw that in my face. He again flashed that same odd smile.

"I have decided to save you some time," he said. "Your discovery of the nonexistence of the emperor on the coin tells both of us something, doesn't it? I assumed it was from your timeline, and you assumed it was from mine, but we were both wrong.

"You are free to examine all of my research files, which are along that far wall. The assistant I leave with you, who speaks German, will help you if you so desire. But I believe all the information you need is in these papers here, consisting of two artifacts from time, along with this book from my library. How did you describe your talent? An ability to *connect the dots*? Well here are two dots—or perhaps three, counting this book—which I look forward to seeing how you connect. I will rejoin you for lunch."

And then he left.

I picked up the book first and looked at it. It was in German, with a publisher's imprint of 1765, a memoir of the campaigns of 1758 and 1759 in Saxony during the Seven Years War by the Austrian field marshal Prinz von Pfalz-Zweibrücken. I put it aside for the moment and spread the folder's contents—four pieces of paper—on the desk blotter. Two were clearly the artifacts Tesla had mentioned, and the other two were sheets of accompanying explanatory notes.

Before reading them I took a moment and just looked at them. The notes were in German, written in a careful, extremely regular hand, looking almost machine-generated. It reminded me a little of Gabrielle's writing. I remembered that Tesla's technical education had been in Austria, so scientifically he probably thought in German.

The two artifacts had been printed on letter presses in the curlicue-choked German typeface called *Fraktur*. I'd read a lot of nineteenth-century German journal articles on Achaemenid Persia in this typeface, enough to give me headaches trying to tell the capital F from J—and forget about capitals B, R, and V.

One sheet was a piece of oversized newsprint folded in half, scorched along the bottom but mostly intact. The sheet was an interior page from a newspaper, *Die Frankonische Neu Zeitung*, dated January 7, 1759. The main story dealt with rumors of the defeat of a French army under Marshal Soubise by the forces of the King of Prussia commanded by his brother Prinz Heinrich near a Saxon town called Torgau.

The accompanying notes described the newspaper page, gave details of the settings of the Aether Field Manipulator—which made no sense to me—and listed April 28, 1887, as the experiment's date.

The August page from a calendar from 1759 constituted the other artifact. The first twelve days of the month had been marked off. The back of the page, labeled *"Kalkenhof im Thüringerwald,"* was a lithograph of a manor house in a rustic setting. The explanatory notes were identical except for the date of the experiment, which was in early December of 1887.

That was it.

I read through the experimental notes again but found nothing new. I compared the machine settings. Even though they were gibberish to me, they were identical gibberish, every entry exactly the same.

I read both sides of the newspaper page again, thinking maybe there was something important hidden in the articles, but found nothing. Besides, if there was, what could the calendar page mean? The back was a picture and the front unremarkable except for the days marked off.

I leaned back in the chair and stared at the ceiling, trying to understand what Tesla had seen. After twenty minutes I started thinking it was just an elaborate head game designed to lock my brain up for a day or so, a riddle to which there was no answer.

If anything, it confirmed my concerns. Tesla had used identical settings on his machine, and yet it had brought back items from different times.

And then I sat bolt upright in the chair and felt the adrenaline surge through my body with a rush like cocaine. I got it.

Son of a bitch!

I grabbed the von Pfalz-Zweibrücken memoir and paged through it until I found an account of the winter fighting. That pretty much capped it—there was no battle at Torgau in January, at least not in this timeline.

So I had a coin from 71 C.E. which clearly was not from my timeline, and was not from Tesla's, either. I had two artifacts from 1759 C.E. which were not from Tesla's timeline, and which were from different points in whatever that other timeline was, even though the machine settings were exactly the same—same settings, same timeline, but different times. How could there be three—no, *at least* three—timelines going, two or more temporal-event waves scrubbing one past and replacing it with another? I didn't think there could be. I checked the dates again. *And there it was!*

I broke out in a sweat, and my hands shook, but not from fear:

from excitement. How often do you get to see how the universe really works? All those smart guys at the Wessex lab had been wrong—or at least the ones who came up with the temporal event wave theory. There was no event wave. There was no such thing as time travel, odd as that sounded sitting here in 1888. When Tesla returned me—assuming he kept his half of the bargain—I couldn't pop back out ten years before the Wessex incident and save Joanne and Jack Junior. They were gone, lost to me forever, but Sarah was not.

That knowing smile of Tesla's—he had figured it out as well. He wasn't afraid of me destroying his timeline, because that's not how the universe worked. Now all I had to do was play along with Tesla, tell him whatever he wanted to know, and then go home. I didn't have to destroy this world or any other, did not have to go back home with the blood of billions of people on my hands. I didn't have to eliminate Gabrielle to save Sarah.

I looked out the window which I had scarcely noticed when I came in, and I saw a cloudless blue sky framing the mountains, the slopes painted gold and orange by autumn leaves and sprinkled with pale purple from the wild lilacs which seemed to grow everywhere in riotous abandon. How had I not noticed before how beautiful the mountains were? I might actually miss them when I went home.

Home.

Tesla, lost in thought, said nothing for the first quarter hour over lunch. Finally he emerged from his reverie and looked at me.

"You asked me a question earlier, Dr. Fargo, about the precision with which I could return you to your own time," Tesla said after a moment. "Have you found your answer in my research notes?"

He glanced at Gabrielle and smiled. The smile appeared condescending to me, and Gabrielle looked down at her soup, her own smile gone.

Tesla must already have spoken to her about my question, told her he had left the folder with me, and now he expected me to admit the problem was beyond my ability to solve. This was a demonstration of the limits of my intellect for Gabrielle's benefit, and for a moment it made me angry and defensive.

Interesting—and stupid, like some kid trying to impress his girl. I wasn't some kid. Gabrielle wasn't my girl. Not now.

Since I had figured out the problem, this was an opportunity to embarrass Tesla, but I couldn't see an upside to that. On the other hand, I wasn't sure that pandering to Tesla's desire to humiliate me was going to help my cause, either. The unembellished truth was probably the best path in this case.

"Can it be that the answer escapes you?" Tesla asked. "It seems so obvious to me."

"It took me the better part of an hour to figure it out, but I managed," I answered.

His eyebrows went up slightly, and then I saw a flicker of amusement. He thought I was bluffing.

"Ah. I see. So tell me, how will I manage to deliver you to your correct time?"

"I assume you have repeated the experiment and obtained the same results. These results are illustrative and typical, not unique."

Tesla shifted in his chair, less confident than he had been a moment before. "Obtaining verifiable dating of samples is difficult in most cases, but, if we are speaking of the same thing, then I can say that I have not a single experimental result which contradicts the factual evidence of these artifacts. They are simply the clearest illustration of the phenomenon."

I nodded and took a drink of water. I took a moment to think about how best to explain the artifacts, at least as I understood what they meant.

"The mistake the scientists in my world made was thinking they had a time machine of any sort. Once they did enough experiments, they would have figured out the truth, but since they're all dead and the Wessex facility is probably a big crater in the ground, I'm guessing it will be a while before anyone tries that again, at least in my time—I guess I mean in my *world*.

"The old law of conservation of matter, energy, and momentum is the real clue which should have tipped them off—there's only so much stuff in the universe, and if it simultaneously exists throughout time, then it is not finite, is it? It is infinite.

"I'm not sure I'm expressing that very well, but there are just a lot of issues with the universe completely re-creating itself every instant, or nanosecond, or whatever the universe's quantum of time is. There are even more issues with the universe existing as separate complete products at every instant throughout time, products which can be independently accessed.

"Here's the bottom line: the only reality is *now*. The future is a possibility and the past is just a memory; the past is not a bunch of stuff still down there in the basement you can go back and rummage around in. It's funny, but Omar Khayyam, the twelfth century Persian mathematician and astronomer, in one line of poetry, captured the essence of reality which escaped the understanding of all the scientists in the Wessex project:

"'*The moving finger writes, and having writ, moves on.*'

"Time travel, as the Wessex scientists understood the concept, is impossible because there is no other time to travel *to*."

"And yet here you are," Tesla said with a smile.

"Yeah, here I am. Your experiment—that was the nail in the coffin. You brought back a newspaper page from 1759. I have no idea how many times you had to repeat the experiment until you found something else you could establish a date for, but two hundred and seventeen days after the first experiment, you succeeded; you brought back a calendar page also from exactly two hundred and seventeen days later in that timeline. Two hundred and seventeen days elapsed time in both timelines—that was no coincidence.

"The answer is not time travel—it is multiple parallel universes, which is another theory which was gaining some traction in my time. Maybe some of the scientists at Wessex thought that was the answer, but I wasn't there long enough to find out. Maybe they went with the temporal-event-wave theory because it was the most dangerous explanation and so they couldn't afford to ignore it, just in case. Maybe they had other guys working on the multiple-universe angle. I'll probably never know for sure, but it doesn't matter now, does it?

"I suppose there are many parallel universes—what we called timelines before—but in each of them time advances like a wave, and the only substantial reality in each of them is that universe's 'present,' the location of time's wave front at that instant. The present just happens to be at a different time point in each of them.

"To answer my own original question, I have been in your universe for about a month. When you return me to my universe, you will return me to it a month after I left. You will return me to that time because that is the only time there is."

I looked at Gabrielle, and she looked from me to Tesla, looking both relieved and intrigued.

"So, do you know why the base-time wave front is different in each of these universes?" I asked.

Tesla looked at me for a moment, his expression unchanging.

"I do not."

I felt a slight adrenaline rush. As certain as I was that my conclusion was correct, there was always the possibility I had overlooked something and gotten it wrong. Tesla, by his expression and demeanor, had confirmed it. The three of us knew something no one else, on this world or my world, knew, something fundamental to how the universe was ordered. I found that pretty exciting, no matter what else happened next.

"So here's my next question: How can you be sure you can get me back to my own universe? Have you accessed it before? For that matter, how can you get me to a precise location in that universe?" I thought again about the seeming impossibility of finding the needle that was the exact location on a world when there was a difference of billions of miles between where it was here and where it was in that universe.

He sat there for a moment not speaking. I got the impression he had figured out how this conversation would unfold, and it had gone completely off the rails. Now he took some time deciding out how to regain control.

"No, I have not accessed your plane of existence before. I have been unable to access any plane with a more advanced time than our own, but that is in part an energy issue. My calculations suggest the energy cost to open a portal to a more advanced plane is substantially higher than to the less advanced one. I suspect there are inertial issues involved in this. But I have accumulated enough energy to do so, and now that I have you physically present, I have the means to target your plane directly. As I explained, the vibrational properties of items from your world can be measured and used to calibrate the instrument.

"As to precise places within that plane of existence—I will only say that location may not be as significant in the universe as I once thought. It is at any rate not a tremendous barrier to surmount, provided the vibrational properties of the associated local material in this plane of existence are known. Once this business with the Turks is finished, I shall be happy to demonstrate."

That was great news, right? I was going home, and I wasn't going to have to be a mass murderer, a destroyer of worlds, to do so. So why did I feel like I was waiting for another shoe to drop?

THIRTY-NINE

October 14, 1888, Kokin Brod, Serbia

After lunch, Tesla took me on a walking tour of his compound. Gabrielle remained behind, claiming her leg still bothered her, so it was just Tesla, me, and two big guards. One guard walked between Tesla and me, and the other, with revolver in hand, walked behind us. This *pistolero* had a bandaged head, probably a souvenir of our fun together at *Oktoberfest*. Apparently Tesla had decided to take no chances, even after my agreement to help him.

First he took me back up the stairs. We passed what appeared to be storage rooms and servants quarters on the fifth floor and then, past them, climbed a narrow stairway to the attic and then up a ladder to the roof.

An observation platform, supported by iron girders, topped the peaked slate roof. We climbed a steel spiral staircase to get up there, and even on the way up I could see enough to appreciate the view. A dozen outbuildings and smaller structures huddled around the house, and the two or three dozen homes and shops of the village of Kokin Brod sat securely under its view a quarter mile down the gentle slope, halfway to the lake.

We had a crisp, cool, bright autumn afternoon for our inspection. The sun sparkled off the lake which stretched east of the compound for several miles, filling what had clearly once been a river valley. A well-worn road snaked down to the shore of the lake, ending at a cluster of two large, new buildings, and a third, smaller one nestled close by the shore, all inside a wire fence. One of the larger buildings was taller and very long, with a semicylindrical curved roof: zeppelin hanger, wide enough for three of them side by side. I couldn't tell anything about the other structures, but I remembered Durson saying he had mapped the position of new "machinery buildings" along the lake.

I turned and looked west, up the valley toward the main peaks of the mountains. The day was clear enough that I could have seen all the way to Brezna, and the ridge Gabrielle and I had fled down, except the valley twisted and a tall spur blocked my view.

I looked back at the east and counted nine gun positions grouped in three clusters of three each. One cluster sat on high ground to the north of the lake and another sat on a low hill a quarter mile south of Tesla's compound. Both had excellent fields of fire up the valley in addition to covering a slice of the northern and southern approaches. The third cluster was farther east, on the south side of the lake, and covered that direction. Each trio of guns was laid out in a triangle, so two guns could always fire at any one target and no angle of approach was left uncovered.

"Impressive setup. How'd you pay for all this? Royalties on your inventions that good?"

"I receive very little from my past endeavors. Your Mr. Edison stole most of my discoveries. The Russian crown subsidizes my work now."

"The Romanovs? Seriously? Why on earth would they subsidize a guy who wants to pull down every edifice of inherited wealth and power? Don't they not know how to spell 'anarchist'?"

"I have no love for the czar, nor he for me, but my attacks are directed primarily at Britain and Imperial Germany. The Russian foreign ministry operates under the foolish belief that its enemy's enemy is its friend, or at least its useful tool. The czar's agents have been quite useful, particularly in establishing my network of . . . sympathizers."

He was serious. He thought he was putting one over on the Russian secret police. Just because someone's a scientific genius does not make him politically astute.

I glanced around the observation platform. Heavy riveted iron or steel formed the raised palisade, certainly bulletproof. I saw short vertical metal pipes, a couple inches in diameter, welded to the back of the palisade. A couple metal footlockers were spaced along the base of the palisade. I started to open a lid but turned to Tesla to see if that was okay. He nodded.

Gatling gun, and a dozen or more loaded magazines. The locker protected it from the weather, and it would take about ten seconds to pick it up and drop the post of the pivot mount into the steel pipe.

The southwest corner of the platform was partially enclosed and roofed. Inside I saw what looked like a couple old-style telephone receivers on cradles and narrow observation slits on the walls. The ones on the west side had a good view up the valley.

"Is this your command post?"

"Only in the event of unwelcome intruders. From here I can direct the fire of all of the defensive batteries. I have never had to use it, nor do I look forward to doing so now. I do not enjoy violence, but I am left with little alternative."

Yeah. At the Battle of Fredericksburg, after watching the cream of the Union Army slaughtered in front of St. Mary's Heights, Lee had said to Longstreet it was good war was so terrible, or men would grow to love it too much. Bullshit. Everyone who sent people off to kill said they hated violence, but just didn't have an alternative. I think the truth is they all loved it, but were just embarrassed to admit it. Tesla was no different.

We descended through the house and walked down the gravel-covered road to the lake.

"So I get you want to bring down the old order, break the back of inherited wealth and power, all that stuff. But sending assassins hopped up on drugs to kill elderly scientists—how's that fit in?"

He looked at me, and his eyebrows drew together in an impatient scowl. "There is a war under way in this world, a silent war, so silent most people do not even recognize it. I will not accept the world order the Lord Chillinghams would impose. Were it within their power, the Iron Lords would turn the entire surface of this continent into a smog-choked industrial slum populated with destitute wage slaves, all simply to sustain their own luxury and idleness.

"Science will transform the world. The question is: *Into What?* What would you have the future of the world be, Dr. Fargo? Shall science elevate the lives of people everywhere? Or shall it enslave them? It is really that simple."

It was never that simple, but there was some truth there. I'd met men whose sense of entitlement came close to Chillingham's, but I'd never met one who seemed so capable of turning that lust for power into reality.

"Okay, Chillingham is a bad guy," I said. "But you lost me getting from there to murdering Professor Tyndall and those other men."

"The members of the X Club? They were Chillingham's tools, even though they never met him. They were the most serious threat to my plans in the long run. They could also have been the most effective opposition to Chillingham and the men he represents, the forces of inherited power. But they chose to work with the system he sits at the center of, like a spider in his web. They paid the price of that choice."

"Bad actors," I said.

"Excuse me?"

"People who commit bad acts—that's what some of my former bosses called them. Kill enough bad actors and pretty soon no more bad acts."

"Exactly so," he said.

Jesus!

I thought about the elderly birdlike Tyndall, and a dozen other academics of advanced age, and the idea of them being the nerve center of a secret revolutionary resistance to Chillingham and the British Iron Lords was laughable. It showed how tenuous was Tesla's grasp of political reality. Here was a guy fighting "inherited power" and financing his struggle with money from the Russian czar, probably the last absolute ruler in Europe.

"Why not ally with the French instead of the Russians?" I said.

"I admit to the logic of that, in the ideological sense," he said. "Gabrielle has mentioned the same thing, and we discussed it yesterday at some length—*en Francais,* of course. You believe me naïve, but I know that one or two of my men may be agents of the Russians, reporting my activities to them, but none of them speak French. In this way I exercise care.

"The short answer as to why—support from Russia was forthcoming when it was needed, while France seeks alliance with Austria and Turkey, two of the most absolutist powers in Europe and the principal architects of Serbia's travails. While I have no more loyalty to the fiction of the Serbian state than Gabrielle does to the fiction of the French state, it currently provides me with a secure base of operations. Beyond that, France has no desire to overturn the European order. Perhaps once, but no longer. They have become comfortable with the status quo. In the long run, who I ally with is of less moment than what comes of it."

Our walk brought us to the wire enclosure by the lake. Tesla waved to a black-clothed guard, who pulled the gate open. Tesla paused to chat with him in Serbian for a moment. He called him by name, and the conversation was casual, the boss asking an employee how he was doing.

I looked the defenses over as we went through—certainly not impregnable. A single row of barbed-wire fence formed the perimeter, better for keeping out wandering livestock than determined infantry. A handful of guard posts dotted the grounds ten or twenty yards in from the fence, but they looked to me as if they were for protection from the weather rather than small arms fire.

One thing I did notice: the compound was not teeming with people. Tesla didn't have an army here, or at least not a very large one. We passed two guards at the gate, and I saw two others making the rounds of the perimeter. The doors to the zeppelin hanger stood open, and I saw a half dozen more men there, working from scaffolds to repair the airship's gas bag.

In the real world the job of evil genius didn't automatically come with a couple thousand loyal minions. Tesla had enough men to guard his compound, maintain his equipment, crew two airships—but not necessarily all at the same time. I'd banged up a few of his men, and Jovo had made an even deeper dent. His engineered crash must have killed or injured some of the remaining crew of the first airship—the *Djordje Petrovic*—and Tesla said three crewmen of the second ship were wounded in the fight I saw. I knew at least one man died in the night attack on Brezna, because I killed him myself.

I glanced back at the bandaged *pistolero* accompanying us. Tesla said he used men who had reason to hate me as guards, and that made sense. But there was probably another reason to use walking wounded for this sort of grunt duty—he was short of manpower.

Tesla led the way to the second building, about half the size of the zeppelin hanger, which still made it huge. As we walked, he gestured to a third building by the lakeshore.

"That is our hydrogen-separation building. We divide water into oxygen and hydrogen by means of electrolysis, although it is not operating today."

"Down for maintenance?" I asked.

"No. We simply have no immediate need for more hydrogen. We use it only to fill the lifting cells of the zeppelins and in several small fuel cells carried by the flying ships. Given its combustible nature, it is better to separate it only when needed rather than storing quantities of it here and there."

He was right about that—hydrogen was volatile as hell. Who from my time and place didn't remember the newsreel footage of the *Hindenburg* exploding and burning? *Oh, the humanity!* Small wonder Harding had looked forward to putting a couple incendiary rockets into Tesla's zeppelin the next time he saw it.

"Ever think about using helium instead?" I asked. "It doesn't burn."

"It would be a superior lifting agent, if I could obtain it. The Americans control most of the world's reserves, however, and are not generous with it."

We reached the second building, and Tesla paused, touching the handle of the door, thought for a moment, and turned to me.

"You are extraordinarily fortunate, Dr. Fargo. What I am about to reveal to you, no more than twelve other people have seen."

He pushed open the double doors, and we entered. The first thing I noticed was the humid air. We walked down a corridor ten meters or so long and then out into the open floor of an enormous workshop, high-ceilinged and dark. Tall portable hissing gas lights illuminated a few work areas, scattered islands of yellow light in the ocean of gloom. I expected noise, but the building was nearly silent.

The corridor ran down the broad open center of the building, flanked by rows of workbenches and assembly areas. Beyond them tall wooden shelves lined the walls, filled with dim, irregular shapes.

I looked at the items on the workbenches and assembly areas. Most of them made no sense, but I recognized several partially assembled clockwork spiders, a primitive electric arc welder, a bicycle with training wheels and a metal shield covering the front, a lot of different-sized electrical motors (maybe some sort of electromagnetic field generators?), a Gatling gun mounted on a four-wheeled cart with a small steam engine, what looked like an oversized riveted metal diving suit on three steel girder stilts, a really big gyroscope, a circular sheet metal platform about a meter across with a brass railing around it and mounted on a dozen enormous steel springs.

Ahead of us lights illuminated several large machines, eerie in their silent but continuous motion. As we got closer, I got a good long look at them, and, despite my natural inclinations, I felt a sense of awe.

Three identical machines, each about three meters tall and wide, and twice as long, stood in line, attached to thick raised concrete slabs with bolts as thick as my forearm. Gleaming brass and steel made up most of the machines, but a large wheel, very much like a turbine blade, was the central component of each. The hub and rim of the wheels were metallic, the blades wood, and as the wheel turned I saw the blades change angle within the wheel, just as Thomson had predicted.

Pipes ran overhead and sprinkler heads sprayed a fine mist of water on the wheels. I remembered the liftwood blades of *Intrepid* growing hot when they lifted. The water spray must be to cool the liftwood panels. This explained the humidity in the building. It was noticeably warmer near the machines.

I only saw four workers in the building, clustered around the generators and an even larger machine farther back. All of them wore long white canvas coats, leather gauntlets, and dark-tinted goggles pushed up on their foreheads. A bald, wrinkled fellow, thin and stooped, greeted Tesla and gave him a report in Serbian. I couldn't understand it, but I'd heard enough by then to know the distinctive sound of the language. Tesla smiled and patted his shoulder, then called out to the others, smiled and waved.

The attitude of the workers here was the same as the guard at the gate and others I'd seen here—respectful without being servile. These were not soulless minions; they were dedicated people who shared some sort of common vision. They followed Tesla out of respect, even affection.

"Good news?" I asked.

"The generators still operate at 84 percent of their original capacity, which is somewhat higher than I projected. The liftwood loses potency over time, but I had very little good documentation on how quickly it would decline given this level of continuous use. Come. This next machine should particularly interest you. The Martians called their momentum generator a Forever Engine, but only because they did not understand its function. But this, by opening portals to other planes of existence, possibly infinite in their variety, slices of time reaching back to Creation and possibly forward to the extinction of the universe—this is a true *Forever Engine*."

The machine behind the three generators towered another three or four meters over them, and the building's roof had been modified to accommodate it. As I thought about it, I figured the building had probably been built around it. Even in the quiet gloom of the workshop the machine seemed alive, enormously powerful, a tiger waiting patiently in the jungle shadows. Six enormous wire-wrapped armatures radiated from a central shaft, and three massive arms projected from the surrounding frame, ending in some sort of insulated housings, apparently a focusing device for whatever it was that came out.

"So this is what an aether propeller looks like, huh?"

"That was the core device, although this is heavily modified. The purpose is completely different, but both effects are produced by manipulation of electromagnetic fields."

"These big arms shape the field somehow?"

"They are critical when using the device as a propeller, but some field shaping is also important to its current function," Tesla said. "The fine manipulation is done with . . . well, it is done. That is what matters. My original modification to it envisioned its use as a directed-energy weapon, but the effect produced was quite different, as you know."

"So that's why back in London you found it amusing that the Wessex accelerator was originally intended as a weapon. Small world—*worlds*. So, you got this one all lined up to send me back?"

Tesla looked at me, and his expression changed—a mix of suspicion, amusement, and maybe grudging respect.

"I thought it better to wait until I was prepared to initiate the operation myself. You have persuaded me that your ability to 'connect the dots,' as you say, is formidable. I cannot imagine how you would discern the operation of this machine, but I am prepared to accept that limitations of my imagination are not necessarily the same as those of reality."

The idea of figuring out how this thing worked had occurred to me. I didn't think I could do it on my own, but I bet Thomson and I could have figured it out between us, if he'd lived to get this far. Figuring out the spectrographic vibration thing, or stumbling across the exact settings needed to get me home . . . those were different stories.

"One thing I've been wondering about," I said. "What were you trying to do when I came into this world? Obviously you were cranking your gizmo at the same time as I popped in or there wouldn't have been that echo effect in Bavaria."

Tesla paused and thought for a moment before answering. "As I am returning you to your own world soon, I suppose it does not matter that you know. The modified focus arms are a recent adaptation I have made which allow me to aim the apparatus's effect at a considerable distance from this laboratory, although at an increase in power requirement as well. My intent was to repeat my experiment with the *azhdaja* but instead of bringing them here, transport them to central London along with whatever other predators the process might sweep up. My intent was purely to cause terror and confusion, undermine the faith of the populace in their authoritarian government. Can you imagine the reaction to a score of *azhdaja* running through the halls of Westminster Palace, perhaps even in parliament?"

"You have that sort of accuracy?" I asked. He shrugged.

"I was still experimenting. I expected some drift, some errors in the calculations at first, but expected to be able to refine the process over time. Once I had done this in London, I would repeat it in the other major capitals of Europe. No palace, no fortress, no remote manor house, no matter how well guarded, would be safe. However, instead of prehistoric animals emerging in London, a village in the countryside exploded and you appeared. Imagine my surprise."

"Imagine mine," I said.

"Yes, I suppose so. This is purely speculation, but I believe the two energy discharges, which were coincidentally simultaneous, must have drawn each other together. As the power used by your Wessex facility was far in excess of my device, it displaced my target point all the way west to Somerton, while displacing your energy effect only a few kilometers to the east."

I wandered over to a tall metallic cabinet by the wall, its face made up of over a hundred small drawers, each one labeled. I looked at the labels: detailed latitude and longitude descriptions sometimes followed by a location. I found the one for London, pulled it open and looked inside. Dirt.

"This must be your database of locations, right? Material from this world which you can use to calibrate your projector to link with the corresponding physical material at the other end?"

"Very good, Dr. Fargo."

"And the echo effect you got in Bavaria?" I asked. Tesla shrugged again.

"I am still considering that. I have no firm hypothesis yet, but we have barely begun experimenting in this field. It was an interesting and unexpected result, and fortunate for you. Had some of the energy not been drawn off for that transfer, the effect in Somerton would have been even more catastrophic. I cannot believe you would have survived the event.

"But I am expecting visitors this afternoon. Come, we must return to the main house."

I looked around the lab one last time as we left, trying to see if there was anything I'd missed, something here I could use to take control of the situation if it came to that.

Nothing.

FORTY

October 14, 1888, Kokin Brod, Serbia

We walked back up to the house, but the guests he expected did not materialize. The nearby villages were supposed to send militia volunteers to help defend against the Turks believed to be on their way. Instead, most of them sent their regrets. Between the *azhdaja* and the reports of Turkish marauders in the area, no men could be spared. Tesla's angry reaction told me I was right about one thing—he was long on hardware and short on bodies to man the defenses.

We retired to his library, he to brood in an overstuffed chair, me to trade "make my day" looks with my personal *pistolero*. Before long, Gabrielle joined us. She looked at me for a moment, her expression a mixture of sadness and concern, but not guilt as far as I could tell.

"Nikola," she said, "the people in the kitchen just told me they saw signal rockets burst in the air high above the ridge, one every five minutes for half an hour, the evening before last."

"What of it?" Tesla said, but then glanced at me. "You smile, Dr. Fargo. You know what that means?"

Smiling? Probably grinning like a little kid was more like it. Yeah, I knew what the rockets meant.

"Serbia celebrates the Fourth of July in October?" I ventured.

"*Non*," Gabrielle said. "It is the signal for Cevik Bey to cross the frontier and march to the aid of *Capitaine* Gordon's party."

"That would be the party that was wiped out," I said. "Gee, I guess somebody survived after all. I wonder who?"

Gabrielle looked from Tesla to me, and then she nodded in understanding. Tesla had lied to us.

"Your expression betrays you, Dr. Fargo," Tesla said. "Are you rethinking your position? Let me remind you that if the British and Turks take this facility, you will lose the means of returning to your own world. Is that the result you desire?"

No, it wasn't. So why had I smiled? I guess I was glad somebody I knew might still be alive. He was right, I needed for him to win in order to go home, but I didn't have to rejoice in the fact. *Singe the Old Man's whiskers. . .*

"You really like the number three, don't you?" I said.

Tesla looked startled.

"What do you mean by that?"

"Three gun redoubts, laid out in a rough triangle, each redoubt with three guns. Three machinery buildings. Three Forever Engines. An iron walking machine with three legs. Your quarters are on the third floor, the third door from the stairs. You have four buttons on your jacket and five on your vest but in both cases button only the top three. There's room in the hangar for three zeppelins, even though you only have one here now. With one crashed on the mountainside, I'd say you have another one out there somewhere on another mission. Is it waiting for the *Hochflieger Ost*? Bet you wish you had a radio right about now, huh?"

He stared intently at me, and his right hand moved to his jacket, fiddled with the fourth, unbuttoned, button, but he did not button it.

After an uncomfortably quiet dinner, we all turned in. I think all of us knew that tomorrow would bring some sort of a decision. Despite Tesla being shorthanded, a guard stood watch outside my door, and Tesla locked the bolt behind me himself. After about fifteen minutes or so the guard unbolted the door and opened it to let Gabrielle in.

"It's polite to knock," I said.

"En Francais," she said. I remembered that was how she and Tesla kept the locals from understanding what they were saying. I nodded. "If I come again I will knock," she continued in French, "but I have come to tell you something and must leave quickly. This is difficult for me. My path is confused." She frowned in distress for a moment but continued. "My brother is convinced that with the inquisitiveness of your world and its vast scientific and industrial resources, it is only a

matter of time before they return to this world, particularly once you tell your story there. Then they may be the architects of our future here. He does not believe your people will side with him."

"He's right. So he's not going to send me back after all." I'd been waiting for the other shoe to drop, and here it was.

"Yes, he is. He will do as he promised. However, that is not all he plans to do. He has a plan which I do not understand—it has to do with electromagnetic fields, which he understands better than I. But be believes he can use his device not simply to transmit material between the worlds, but electromagnetic energy itself."

"Maybe. Don't see why not. So what?"

"He listened to everything you told him about solar flares, their potential effects on your world and how they are triggered by changes in the sun's magnetic field. He plans to cause a large solar flare in your universe. He says it will kill no one but will destroy much of your technological base. Is this possible?"

I say down on the bed. *Possible?* I didn't know if he could actually trigger a solar flare from here, but if he could—*damn*. A big enough flare, just one as big as the 1856 flare, would pretty much fry the processors of every private and commercial computer in the world, not to mention scrub their memories, end satellite communication, crash every stock market, and bust every bank in the world. It might not kill anyone directly, but millions would die from its effects eventually. It would end my world as I knew it.

"Yes, it's possible."

"I cannot help you, Jack. You understand? My loyalties are with my brother and this world. But I thought you should know this. Perhaps when you are back with your daughter you can make precautions so the two of you will be safe. He says he must build up and discharge the energy in the lake at least three times to create the necessary effect, which will take over a month, so there will be time for you. Now I must go."

Once she'd left I washed as thoroughly as I could in the water basin, did my toilet, changed into clean clothes, and lay on the bed. I wasn't sure I could sleep, had lots to think about, and if something happened suddenly in the night, I wanted to be ready. I left off my boots as a concession to civilization. One thing was sure: I couldn't let Tesla follow through with his plan. I didn't know if he could really carry it off, but that didn't matter. I couldn't take the chance. No matter what else happened, Tesla couldn't be allowed to follow through on this plan.

I dozed for an hour or two, but woke with my mind teeming with the possibilities of the coming day. I knew Tesla was weak in personnel, but his defenses were set up to be mutually supporting, and with telephone wire strung to all of them, he could probably move his men around to where they were needed most. If Cevik Bey came, he would have about five hundred or more men with him. I would be surprised if Tesla had a tenth that number, but they would be manning Gatling guns and cannons firing explosive shells—formidable force multipliers.

In most heroic action stories the Turks would come howling down the valley and Tesla's men would fire until their guns glowed with heat, cutting down hundreds of the attackers, and it would all come down to the last handful of Turks trying to overwhelm the last handful of defenders. But that's not what it would be like. After two days of hard marching over the mountains, the Turks would be tired. If they were good soldiers, and the Bosnian riflemen were supposed to be some of the best the Turks had, they would put in a determined attack. But no one was here to commit suicide, especially if there was no prospect of success.

Fifty or a hundred unanswered casualties would be enough to break the Bosnian attack. If they had the notion the defenders were suffering as well, if there was a prospect of success, they might keep coming even with those losses, but it would be tough, and there was no hard science involved in this. I'd seen a battalion-strength attack stopped dead in its tracks by four casualties. You just never knew what would happen on Game Day until you suited up and kicked off.

I thought about Gabrielle and where she stood in all this as well. She stood with Tesla. That stand brought her less joy than I think she anticipated, but she clung to the decision with the desperation of someone who has already tried everything else. In her mind, this was her last shot at humanity, whatever she imagined that to be. I wondered if Asperger's was a net asset or liability for a spy. It was hard to tell, since she was the only spy I knew in this world.

No, that wasn't quite true, was it? I knew two spies. Tesla had told me enough to figure out who his man was on the inside in London. If

I had the chance, I'd have to tell Thomson that bit, if Thomson was still alive. Okay, I knew two spies.

No . . . wait. A question had nagged at me for a while, and finally I had the answer to it. I knew *three* spies.

I heard a sound in the hall and sat up in bed. A scratching—the sound of the bolt being carefully opened. The hall was as dark as the interior of my room, but as I heard the door open I saw a shadowy face appear in the opening. A hand knocked lightly on the door, as if to wake me.

"Gabrielle?" I asked.

"Terribly sorry, old man, but I'm afraid it's just me."

"Gordon?"

"Keep your voice down," he whispered. "And give us a hand with this guard, would you? There's a good fellow. The brute must weigh sixteen stone!"

FORTY-ONE

Early hours of October 15, 1888, Kokin Brod, Serbia

I helped Gordon and his companion drag the unconscious guard into the room. The companion took the guard's place on the chair outside, I closed the door, and Gordon and I tied and gagged the guard using strips torn from my bed sheet.

"Who's your helper?" I asked.

"Radojica's cousin Zoran. He and his father, Jovo's uncle, are helping us."

"Jovo's alive?"

Gordon's face darkened.

"No. Tesla's thugs took him out into the town square and shot him. I suppose that's why his relatives are willing to help us."

"They speak English?"

Gordon smiled again.

"Not a word. They speak a bit of German, so the Bavarians have been translating for us. They masqueraded as local militia yesterday, brought some hams and onions right in here while you and Tesla were off somewhere, said it was supplies sent from their village. The cook showed them the way to the pantry on this floor and pretty much ignored them after that. Zoran managed to unlock a window on the main floor before they left, and here we are."

"How did you manage to communicate with him getting up here?" I asked.

"Sign language. We couldn't risk talking in any case."

"What about Thomson and the others? Tesla told me his men killed all of you."

"Two of the Bavarians were wounded in the fight, but both will survive. We fought off the attack on the ridge, and Thomson managed to pass as a local somehow, so he escaped detection in the town."

Tesla had lied about everything—everything except Jovo.

Gordon wore the clothes of a Serb hill man, and his eyes followed mine as I looked him over.

"I look the proper *bashi-bazouk*, don't I?" he said with relish.

"*Hajduci* is the Serbian term. *Bashi-bazouks* are Turkish. Folks around here are sensitive to the difference. So this is a rescue, huh?"

"Quite so. We weren't sure where they were holding you, but the guarded room seemed a good place to start. Do you know where Mademoiselle Courbiere is held? We'll collect her next and be on our way."

Yeah. That was going to be a problem.

"She's on the next floor up. Her room is right next to Tesla's."

Even in the darkness I saw his expression harden.

"The cad!"

Gordon had the wrong idea on that score, but I didn't feel like setting him straight. *Cad* was simple, *brother* complicated—too damned complicated right now.

If we could get to Gabrielle, I didn't see why we couldn't get to Tesla and maybe wrap this whole thing up right then, and I said so, but Gordon shook his head.

"There is a light up there, and voices. It sounds as if there may be several guards, and they are awake. Can't chance it, I'm afraid. Just trying to get you was risky enough, but it seemed worth the gamble. We didn't want Tesla embarrassing us by using you or Mademoiselle Courbiere as hostages."

"You mean that would have stopped you?"

He scratched his head and smiled.

"No, and that's what could have been so embarrassing, you see?"

Despite the situation, I smiled.

"You're enjoying this, aren't you?" I said.

"I confess I am a bit, which is rather surprising."

Someone knocked softly at the door and then opened it a crack.

"Everything is all correct?" a man asked in heavily accented German.

"Yes. You must be Zoran. Are the guards still moving around upstairs?"

"Yes. I count four voices."

I translated for Gordon.

"We will wait twenty minutes. If they do not settle down or move off by then, we will have to go," he said, and I translated it back to Zoran.

The door closed, and we stood there for a moment.

"You do understand the necessity, don't you?" he said. "To leave her here, I mean, if we cannot effect a rescue?"

"I do."

"She is a professional agent, after all. She understood the risks when—"

"I understand."

More than he could imagine. Gordon looked away, clearly uncomfortable. It had to go against the grain for a Victorian officer and gentleman to leave a lady in distress, even a French *Communard*. It sure rubbed me wrong.

He didn't think capturing Tesla would work, either. Tesla was too likely to make noise, wake up the guards. Of course, there was always the possibility of *not* taking him prisoner, but I didn't share that. Murdering someone in their sleep, even someone like Tesla, was not in Gordon's playbook, and it sure wouldn't get me home.

"So what's the big plan?" I said.

"Cevik Bey is attacking at first light, down the valley, with his rifle battalion. We are to make some sort of diversion. Beyond that there isn't much agreement. I was thinking . . . well, perhaps you had some thoughts on how we might proceed."

So that was the real reason for the daring rescue—a consulting gig.

"I've got a couple ideas," I said. "Tesla's bunkered up pretty good here, and bristling with guns. He's not getting the help from the locals he was expecting, though, so he's shorthanded. I think we can work something out, provided Durson is willing to pitch in."

"Oh, I don't think that will be a problem. That Durson chap is quite remarkable—for an American of course," Gordon said and smiled. "He's as good an NCO as I've ever seen. Bloody Turks are mad not to make him an officer, considering the riffraff they regularly hire."

"So put in a good word for him when this is all done."

"You honestly think the Turks will pay any attention to a simple captain?"

"If we pull this off, they'll listen to anything you have to say. If we don't, we won't have to worry about it."

He nodded thoughtfully, and we stood quietly for a little while, waiting for the guards to go away or go to sleep.

"Where's Thomson?" I asked.

"Still in Brezna. He wasn't physically up to the trek down here, so he's lying up there until we're finished. We'll pick him up on our way back. It seems Jovo salvaged a fair number of components of Tesla's crashed zeppelin, and the doctor has enlisted most of the town in assembling a powered hot-air balloon of some sort from the wreckage."

"Think he'll manage it? It would save us having to hitch a ride back with the Royal Navy."

Gordon chuckled softly.

"I doubt it will fly, but at least he's occupied. Quite a remarkable old man. Do you know what he told me after we got back to Brezna? He made a miscalculation in the age of the Earth. My uncle, Professor Tyndall, was correct in his beliefs all along. Thomson will publish his retraction as soon as we return to England. Can you imagine? I wonder if anyone alive could even have discovered his error. But he is willing to risk ridicule to honor a dead man with whom he could hardly exchange a civil word when they were alive. Quite remarkable. Well, he's safe where he is, and we will pick him up after this business is finished."

"Assuming everything goes according to plan," I said, but something nagged at me. "The problem is Tesla has a surprise up his sleeve, something to do with electricity. I just don't know what it is."

"We have a surprise as well," Gordon said. "Harding has returned with *Intrepid* and is bringing it across the border tomorrow to support the attack. I rather suspect he has considered how being surprised twice by the black zeppelin will look back in London and has decided he needs to do something spectacular to salvage his reputation. Well, whatever his motives, he's here. Let Tesla try to use his zeppelin tomorrow, with an armored cruiser aloft—and this time at action stations with guns manned."

"It's something else."

Gordon slapped me on the arm.

"Whatever it is, we'll find a way to deal with it."

Gordon seemed different, more confident. It reminded me of the conclusion I'd come to earlier.

"So, how long have you been a spy?" I said.

He froze for a moment, then he laughed softly, but the laugh sounded forced.

"Well, I've been in military intelligence for ages now, if that's what you mean."

"It's not, and you know it."

He took out his pocket watch and checked it, but there was still plenty of time.

"Well, I'm afraid—"

"Can it, Gordon. You're busted. You've gone to great lengths to exchange out with officers in your regiment to stay in England, in the intelligence office, rather than take the field overseas."

"Yes, as General Buller was so quick to point out as well. But as you recall, he concluded I was a coward, not a spy."

"I know. But Gabrielle told me the Prince of Wales described you as 'one of the bravest officers in our service.'"

Gordon shifted and looked down.

"I can't imagine why," he said.

"I couldn't, either, especially since I got the feeling in Munich you two had never met. Thomson actually introduced you, and neither you nor the prince batted an eye."

"What's your point?" he said, a hard edge now in his voice.

"You gave me a little lecture about British politics, and how the Prince of Wales is the only man in Britain who can stand up to Lord Chillingham. It was pretty clear where your sympathies rested in that matchup."

"What of it?"

"Well, I got to asking myself a question. Why would someone who admired the Prince of Wales, and loathed Chillingham, ruin his reputation to stay assigned to the one branch of the army under Chillingham's direct control? And why would the prince think that was an act of bravery? And then I got it: you're the prince's spy on the inside of Chillingham's organization."

The silence dragged out for almost a minute before Gordon spoke.

"I won't answer that," he said.

I laughed. "It wasn't a question."

He looked at me intently for a moment, then his expression softened, and he smiled.

"Did he really say that about me? One of the bravest officers in the service?"

"Gabrielle said he did, and the term he used was 'in *our* service.' That was another clue. You know how royalty talks; he said *our* when he meant you were in *his* service. For what it's worth, I think what you're doing takes a lot of guts."

He took the revolver out of his sash and hefted it in his hand, getting the feel of it.

"Perhaps, but it's not the same thing." He brandished the revolver. "This dashing about with bullets and knives flying, or those damnable killer birds—well . . ."

"I know, physical courage is different. But honestly, if you have the one, you can learn the other. It's a matter—"

"—of muscle memory. Yes, yes, I remember, teaching your body to respond correctly. To tell you the truth, I was nearly worthless every time the shooting started. But then during the attack on Brezna, I was so preoccupied with the troops under my command, and not making a hash of things, I forgot to be frightened about myself."

"Yeah, that's pretty much the trick," I said.

"Well, you might have told me so," he said, a trace of indignation in his voice.

I chuckled again. "Doesn't do any good to tell someone. That's one you just have learn on your own."

He checked his watch again and then sat down in the chair by the desk. I pulled the armchair over and sat beside him.

"Speaking of spies," I said, "Professor Meredith is Tesla's man in London."

"Meredith? The cabinet science advisor? That round little nothing of a man?"

"Sometimes they're the ones to watch out for. Tesla told me his agent passed the coin to his assassin. I saw Meredith give the coin to the thug that got away, just before he went through the window. It was the only time Meredith broke cover once the attack started."

"I don't remember that."

"You were still . . . out of the room when he did it."

He smiled ruefully and shook his head.

"Meredith—who could believe it? You know, I really was going for help, odd as that sounds. It seemed to make sense to me at the moment."

"Unless people are very well trained, most of them will panic in the face of a sudden and unexpected emergency. Only good training, or a lot of experience, prevents it."

"I've wanted to ask for some time, how do you know all this?"

"Well, experience for one thing. You already figured out I wasn't *just* a translator. But after my wife died, they pulled me out of the field, moved me into training. That's when I learned most of the scientific end of the physiology of stress response. It's pretty fascinating science. I liked training people, too. That's probably why I got into teaching afterwards."

We sat quietly for a few minutes. He looked at his watch again.

"Time to go. Oh, I brought something for you," Gordon said.

We walked softly to the door, and I saw a bulky, rifle-sized package lying against the wall.

"Just in case there is trouble."

He handed me Gabrielle's leather gun case.

I unzipped it and pulled out the Winchester twelve-gauge, carefully worked the lever to check the magazine, made sure it was empty, then loaded five rounds from the ammunition bandolier. I carefully lowered the hammer, clicked on the safety, and slipped the bandolier over my head and shoulder. I nodded to Gordon I was ready.

He opened the door a few inches. Zoran turned to us and shook his head. I could still hear the voices from upstairs. Gordon closed the door and turned to me.

"We can't wait any longer. Sergeant Melzer and Corporal O'Mara will begin squabbling if I'm not there to sort things out."

I thought about Gabrielle at the top of the stairs, alone in bed, and I wondered if she slept. Was she able to switch off at night, like a machine? Or did she lie awake and wonder about all the things she had dreamed of for years, wonder what it meant when dreams come true in ways we never quite expected, and what she would do next, now that she'd come to the end of her rainbow. I took a deep breath.

"Okay. Let's go."

We managed not to set off any alarms on our way out. Clouds

masked the thin crescent moon, and we ran noiselessly across the soft grass to the wooded foothills, then climbed for twenty minutes at a pace that left Gordon and me both panting. The clouds parted for a moment, and moonlight illuminated the valley behind us, turning the big house silver, the surrounding landscape dull iron, the lake oiled steel. I stared, finding it hard to think of it as real, as a place where flesh lived, until Gordon touched my shoulder and nodded after our guide. Again we climbed.

Durson's voice called out from the darkness ahead. I couldn't make out the Serbian, but I caught the teasing tone. Zoran, our guide, turned and made a sour face.

"Your friend the Night Killer says we make too much noise," he said in German.

"Tell him we wanted him to hear us coming so he wouldn't be surprised and wet himself," I said.

Zoran grinned and passed on the message. Durson's laugh came back as a low rumble in the night.

"I'm surprised to see you here," I told Durson when we entered the clearing. I glanced around—no fire, men well dispersed, very little activity except men cleaning their weapons and checking their gear.

"Your Professor Thomson is very persuasive, even through a translator. Also, I've made new friends," he answered, and then repeated the last part in Serbian for Zoran. Zoran held his right bicep with his left hand and gave him the finger. Nice to know some things never change.

"We have a difficult task ahead of us," Durson said, studying me. "Captain Gordon says you are a soldier of experience. That is surprising. I had thought you were a gentleman."

"Man, were you wrong."

He looked at me a moment more and then nodded.

"You have thought about the problem?" he said.

Gordon stood beside me and motioned Sergeant Melzer and Corporal O'Mara to join us.

"I've thought about if for most of yesterday and all the way up the mountain. Cevik Bey will attack at sunrise? We can count on that?"

"His column passed Brezna this afternoon," Durson said. "We left a heliograph team in the village and exchanged messages with him. The attack will come tomorrow."

"And *Intrepid*'s joining in?"

"Yes. We are to help with diversionary attacks, although I am uncertain what effect a diversion will have."

"No effect at all. Cevik Bey doesn't need a diversion. Tesla can bring four field guns to bear on the attack down the valley, and potentially on *Intrepid*. Harding and Cevik Bey need us to silence those guns. Fortunately, Tesla's defenses are set up to stop big attacks from outside, not small ones coming from inside the perimeter. If we're going to do this, though, and do it without getting half our people killed, we'll need the defenders occupied elsewhere, looking elsewhere.

"The main attack will be *our* diversion."

FORTY-TWO

October 15, 1888, Kokin Brod, Serbia

The clouds and moon cooperated, denying any watchful eye the aid of a reflection from gunmetal or a shadow flickering across open ground. Durson's men moved like silent phantoms, a single-file column which quickly vanished into the uneven foliage along the banks of the lake. Gordon's men—Melzer's riflemen and O'Mara's Marines—moved more slowly, but they didn't have as far to go. They disappeared into a shallow drainage ditch a hundred yards east of the southern gun redoubt.

Five minutes passed—no challenges, no alarms. Durson and his men would take another half hour to get into final position, but I couldn't afford to wait any longer. Already the mountain peaks to the west were distinguishable as ink black against a charcoal sky.

I signaled Zoran and we rose from the underbrush in our improvised ghillie suits—gray-brown wool blankets with branches, sprigs of foliage, and long tentacles of hanging moss pushed through slits in the fabric, the whole thing worn as a hooded cloak. There wasn't a lot of ground cover, but October leaves had piled up around the flower beds and low garden walls on the east side of the big house. We got there well before first light and settled in. Between the dead leaves, and a couple pruned branches from a waiting burn pile to break up our shape, we became all but invisible by the time the sky grew pink in the east.

The lights were already on in the big house, and angry voices carried over the still-dark lawn from open windows. They'd figured out I was gone, probably untied the guard and not gotten much of an explanation from him. Tesla would really be pissed now.

Torches appeared at the main doorway, flickering light played across the lawn, and a half-dozen guards searched for some sign of our trail. We hadn't made any effort to hide our tracks when leaving, but they still didn't manage to find anything. Tracking at night is damned near impossible unless you're a pro, and none of these guys were. After about twenty minutes they got tired of looking and went back inside.

I knew it wouldn't be much longer, so I gave my equipment a final check, maybe as much from nerves as foresight. Gordon had given me a Very pistol to signal when we were clear of the building or when Tesla was dead, whichever came first. The design hadn't changed much between the 1880s and my own time. The flare cartridges I was used to were about half the diameter—better propellants and bursting charges—but the design was the same. I stuck it in my belt in back, where it wouldn't get in my way.

Gabrielle's ammunition bandolier had open loops holding twelve-gauge rounds with leather flaps which snapped over each of the ten groups of five rounds. I'd loaded five, and there were three more empty loops—rounds she'd fired at the waterfront in Uvats—so forty-two rounds more. I opened the snaps and took inventory: ten deer slugs, fifteen number-eight birdshot, and twenty-two double-ought buckshot, including five in the magazine. That was a good all-around load, but the fifteen birdshot rounds were less useful for what I wanted. I thought for a moment. If I knew what situation I'd end up facing, I could decide on a mixed load, but I didn't, so for now I stayed with buckshot.

I sat with my back to the stone wall and waited. The big house had settled down after the tardy discovery of my absence. The distant report of a field gun caused renewed activity and shouted orders, but this time the activity had a more practiced sound to it. Men closed and bolted the front door. Rusty hinges squealed in protest, and metal rattled and clanged as servants closed heavy iron shutters over the windows. After ten or fifteen minutes, these sounds faded as well and silence settled over the lower floor of the house. I listened but heard nothing for a while, then caught the faint rattle of rifle fire and a distant field gun firing. The attack had begun.

I motioned to Zoran. We rose and moved across the thirty yards of open ground to the rear of the house. We faced the east side, the side away from the direction of Cevik Bey's attack, and I counted on all hostile eyes being on the valley. I also figured that, once I'd broken out and escaped, the last thing they would expect was a return visit. The firing grew louder, and the distinctive metallic rattle of a Gatling gun joined in from the roof of the house.

We'd already worked out our means of entry. We dropped our ghillie suits on the ground, and I leaned forward against the brick wall of the house. Zoran scrambled up my back, onto my shoulders, and then used the prominent stone facing work for handholds to climb the last meter or so up to the second-floor balcony. He lowered a knotted rope, wound around the stone railing, and I climbed up behind him.

We paused there, waiting to see if our ascent had alerted anyone—nothing. I already had the Winchester out, and now Zoran unslung his own weapon, a short breech-loading carbine.

We moved the iron shutter aside, and I went through the door to the interior, with my shotgun pointing straight ahead and braced against my shoulder, a buckshot round in the chamber. Empty room. We moved quickly to the door, cracked it, looked out, moved out into the empty hallway. I glanced down the main stairs and saw a heavy iron girder dropped into brackets to either side, holding the front door closed. It would take an explosive charge to force it open, and we might need reinforcement, but we'd already worked this out as well. The door was Zoran's job—open it and then hold it until I came out or good guys came in. I pointed down to it, and Zoran nodded and started down. I headed up to the next floor.

The stairs creaked softly, no matter how carefully I climbed them. I felt sweat trickle down my face and neck, and I paused to dry my palms on my shirt.

The third floor was empty as well, but the sound of two men talking in loud voices drifted down the open staircase. I knelt for a moment at the foot of the stairs and leaned against the balustrade, steadying myself, gathering myself, feeling the blackness around the edges of my vision take shape like a living thing emerging from the fog. I did five cycles of tactical breathing and figured I was as settled as I was likely to get.

I started up the stairs, shotgun up and at my shoulder, my left hip sliding along the banister for support and balance. Halfway up I could tell the voices came from my right, so I turned and let my butt rest against the banister. I moved slowly up until I could see the top of one of their heads, and then I dropped into a crouch. If I could see his head, he could have seen mine if he'd looked in the right direction.

One more complete cycle of breathing, and then I sidestepped quickly up the stairs, the shotgun aimed at their voices and then at the upper torso of the closest one as I cleared the banister at the top. They stood in front of a door, their rifles lying against the wall behind them.

The one a little farther from the stairs saw me first. His eyes grew wide. The other one turned and saw me as the first one cried out in surprise.

"Hands up!" I shouted. "*Hande hoch!*"

Maybe they didn't understand German. Maybe they didn't hear anything through their panic. The closer one turned and grabbed for his rifle, and the other one started to as well.

"*No!* Stop where you are. Hands up!"

Nobody listened.

My first shot took the closer guard in the side as he rose and turned with his rifle, slammed him back against the wall. He slid to the floor, leaving a bloody smear on the wall. My second shot hit the second guard right below the chin and slightly to one side. It nearly took his head off.

I took a moment to look at them. Even with all my breathing exercises, my heart rate shot through the roof and my peripheral vision had gone, but I looked hard at them, trying to make myself notice anything that might be useful.

They were dressed as local farmers, not in the black of Tesla's air crews.

I knelt and checked the first guard—he still lived, but red foam bubbled from his mouth with every breath. I kicked the two rifles down the stairway and left him. If he woke up, he could make his peace with his maker. I didn't feel like hurrying him along.

I kicked in each doorway on the floor and did a cursory search, but couldn't waste too much time here. The noise of the Winchester would probably attract attention, even in the middle of a battle. I pushed two more buckshot rounds into the magazine as I took the stairs to the fifth floor two at a time.

Four men moved cautiously through the main hallway toward the stairs. As my head cleared the level of the floor and I saw them, they called out and raised their own weapons. I had the advantage of being in the stairway, effectively down in a hole and under cover while they were wide open in the corridor. One fired, but the rifle shot went high and to the side. I fired and dropped him. I crouched down to lever another round into the chamber and stepped two paces to the side. I stood up; two men fired, but their aim was off, expecting me to come up where I'd been. I fired and dropped the man who had not fired. I worked the lever for another shell while the two still standing fumbled frantically with the bolts of their rifles. I fired again; a third man went down in a spray of blood, and the fourth man dropped his rifle, raised his hands as far over his head as he could, and began babbling in Serbian.

It was very hard not to shoot him, because I was in a rhythm, a groove, and it was easier to just keep going, but I stopped myself.

I climbed the rest of the stairs and motioned with the barrel of the Winchester for him to back away from his rifle. I kicked it and the other one close to it down the stairway. One of the men on the floor groaned and writhed in pain. I let go of the shotgun's front grip to point at the wounded man with my heft hand and motioned the uninjured guard to drag him into the closest bedroom. He scrambled to do it, eyes wide with terror.

I'd have given a lot right then for a pocket full of plastic quick restraints. Instead, once they were in the room, I used the butt of the shotgun to break off the interior door handle and closed the door on them. Now all there was between me and the observation platform above the roof was the unfinished attic.

Rapid steps thudded down the narrow stairs to the attic. I pushed another round into the magazine, but that was all the time I had before the first man scrambled out of the narrow doorway to the stairs. He looked around, not sure what was going on, and I caught him with a quick shot to the hip which spun him around and dropped him. He crawled away into an open room, but he left his rifle behind, so he was out of the fight. Another man stuck his head around the corner of the doorway, and I drove large splinters of wood from the door frame but missed him.

I put two more rounds into the magazine and moved to my left, toward a doorway, when a rifle cracked from behind me and I felt as if someone had hit my right leg with a baseball bat. I went down and rolled onto my left side. Ahead of me someone looked out the doorway. I fired, and the shot went high but drove him back.

I wriggled a little closer to the stairway, raised my head and looked down. The first guard I'd shot down there, now almost covered with his own blood, struggled to work the bolt on one of the rifles I'd just kicked down to him.

Son of a bitch. Talk about no good deed going unpunished.

I crawled away from the stairway. At least that guy wasn't coming up after me.

A hand holding a revolver appeared at the doorway to the attic stairs. It fired once in my general direction, disappeared, appeared and fired again. The shots went high, but sooner or later he might get lucky. I fired and knocked a lot of plaster dust away but wasn't accomplishing much.

I crawled to a doorway, pushed open the door with my shoulder, fired another round at the stairway, and rolled in. I did a quick scan of the room—an empty bedroom with four thin blanket-covered mattresses on the floor. Servants' quarters.

I worked the lever, ejected the spent casing, but saw the empty loading slide in the receiver. I was dry. I fed in three buckshot rounds, then felt higher on the bandolier and pushed two deer slug cartridges in behind them. I chambered a round and waited.

I leaned away from the doorway and checked my leg. It hurt like hell, but the wound was a simple in-and-out, two-thirds of the way down the thigh and behind the femur. No broken bone and no compromised artery. I was a lucky guy.

I coughed, realized the corridor had filled with black powder smoke. My eyes burned and my mouth was dry. I was out of practice with a shotgun, and I hadn't held it tight enough against my shoulder, so my whole upper right arm and shoulder felt on fire.

The revolver appeared at the doorway and fired a round, withdrew, then came back to fire again. It must have been a single-action revolver and the guy had to cock it by hand each shot. Before he could fire again, I aimed at the wall just beside the splintered door jam, about where I figured his center of gravity would be, and fired a deer slug. It punched through the lathe and plaster wall and I heard a scream of pain from the other side. It wasn't a short scream of alarm; it was a cry of genuine agony, and it went on and on, rising and falling, pausing for ragged gasps of air.

Across the hallway the guy locked into the bedroom started banging on the door and calling to his pals. I put a round through the door deliberately high, just to scare him, and the pounding stopped.

This was getting me nowhere. I had to get up to Tesla, and I couldn't see any good way to do it except over the bodies of all these guys. The *pistolero* in the attic stairway still screamed, but the sound grew distant. They must be pulling him up the stairs. I pushed a buckshot round in and then a deer slug and chambered it. I used the shotgun as a prop to get to my feet and then limped down the corridor, the shotgun trained on the opening. Ten feet from the stairs someone looked around the corner, saw me, and ducked back in alarm. I corrected for where I figured he'd pull back to and fired a slug through the wall. I heard him hit the stairs and then he slid down and out the door into the corridor, arms and legs awry like a discarded rag doll.

I stopped at the bottom of the stairs, reversed the shotgun so I held it left-handed, leaned it around the corner and fired it at a forty-five-degree angle upward. Men cried out in pain and fear. I worked the lever and repeated, and again, and again.

I loaded five more rounds of buckshot. There were only three more buckshot rounds left in the bandolier. That was okay; I was just about there. Once I cleared the attic I'd gather up a couple loose revolvers for the fight on the roof.

I chanced a peek around what was left of the door frame, just a quick out and back. Someone up there was waiting for me and fired a pistol shot, but I was too quick for him. I immediately stepped out and fired two quick rounds up the stairway. I saw a flicker of motion as the man up there scrambled back to safety. The stairs seemed covered with twitching, bloody bodies. One of the men coughed, then raised a rifle toward me. I shot him, driving him back against the stairs, and he slid two or three stairs down until he got tangled up with another body.

I counted five guys on the stairs, four of them in black. It seemed like more, but that was it, and two or three of them were still moving, were probably more stunned than really hurt. I had to get past them quickly, before they regained their senses—either that or stand here and execute all of them, and I didn't feel like doing that. I climbed carefully, trying not to step on them, because I didn't want to lose my footing.

I loaded three deer slugs as I climbed. I figured I'd find out where the last guy up there was, get him to move, and try to put rounds through the floor into him. I heard boots scrape against coarse wooden planks ahead of me and slightly to the left. I made a guess and fired at an angle to put the slug through the floor. As soon as I did, the guy stood up and fired his revolver into the stairway. It knocked plaster dust from the wall into my face. I closed my eyes, chambered a second slug, and fired blind, levered another round in and fired again.

I took two steps up as I worked the lever and opened my eyes. He was a black-clad zeppelin crewman, and I'd caught a piece of him, taken a chunk out of his left shoulder. He'd fallen back to the floor, sitting with his back to the ladder up to the roof. He cocked the revolver and fired. I felt the round graze my left side. I raised the Winchester and fired into his center of mass. It killed him, but he didn't know it right away. He cocked the revolver and fired again. Missed. I took another step up and fired, finishing him.

Then the world exploded in white stars and went black.

FORTY-THREE

October 15, 1888, Kokin Brod, Serbia

I could hardly climb the stairs to the roof. The guy I hadn't seen, the guy hiding on the other side of the stairway, had hit me in the back of my head, probably with the butt of his rifle. I was lucky to still be alive. I'd regained consciousness as I'd started vomiting, a sure sign of a concussion. The back of my head felt twice its normal size, and every inch of it hurt. Only his prodding with a revolver, and the wild, terrified, hateful look in his eye, made me climb. It wasn't hard to figure why he looked that way. How many of his friends had I just killed or crippled?

At the top I crawled onto the metal observation platform. Still too dizzy to stand, I sat, waiting for whatever came next. My wounded leg hardly bothered me anymore. Want something to stop hurting? Make something else hurt worse.

I looked around. The observation platform was all but empty. One man tended a Gatling gun on the west breastwork, although he had no targets at the moment and his attention was locked on the aerial scene above the valley. Other than the gunner, only Tesla and Gabrielle occupied the platform as my captor climbed up behind me. Gabrielle held a revolver in both hands and stood between Tesla and me, her expression guarded, protective. She looked at the blood stain on my leg with concern for a moment, but then must have decided it was a minor wound. She looked me squarely in the eye, and I read her expression at once.

Nothing has changed. I stand with my brother—my family.

I looked away, followed the gunner's gaze and saw the most

remarkable battle I'd ever seen. A mile away, *Intrepid* cruised down the valley at no more than a thousand feet of altitude, trailing its wake of coal smoke, battle ensigns snapping in the wind. Much closer, only a few hundred yards away, Tesla's zeppelin finished a turn and began its run back toward the lake. *Intrepid*'s appearance must have caught it by surprise as it worked over the Bosnian rifles from the air. It had no chance against an armored cruiser.

"I am happy you joined us, Dr. Fargo," Tesla said, then looked at the black-uniformed crewman guarding me. He asked a question in Serbian, the crewman answered in a voice heavy with anger, and Tesla's expression darkened, astonishment mixed with rage.

"All of them? You killed *all* of the men I sent for you?"

"Not all. I locked two of them in a bedroom, and a couple of the wounded will live," I said.

"How?" he demanded, his voice rising.

"Give me a gun and I'll fucking show you."

Whatever he would have answered was preempted by the roar of two heavy guns discharging in quick succession. *Intrepid*'s main batteries had fired, and I saw the zeppelin shudder, shock waves rippling through the canvas skin of the gasbag. The rounds must not have hit anything substantial, though; they passed through the bag without exploding.

The ground battery on the opposite side of the lake fired its two guns which bore on *Intrepid*. One round hit, exploded against the cruiser's lower port-side hull. The flyer shuddered and rocked for a few seconds, but pressed on through the smoke of the explosion. Good armor, probably more than a three-inch gun could penetrate unless it found a vital spot.

Tesla barked an order to the gunner, who ran across the platform and slid down the ladder.

"He will free the men you imprisoned," Tesla said, his voice still heavy with anger.

"I killed all those guys and here you are, same as always. There's a lesson in that, Tesla. You can't fix the world by just killing people."

"How do you know unless you try?" he asked.

"*Try?* Jesus Christ! If killing bad people could make a place better, then once Reggie Llewellyn and I and a few thousand of our closest personal friends got done with it, Afghanistan would have been a fucking paradise! I got out of the fixing-the-world-through-firepower business because it doesn't work, and you can look it up."

Tesla's zeppelin passed the house, only about fifty yards north of us and shedding altitude as it went. I heard a sizzling roar from *Intrepid* and saw a dozen or more fire trails shoot away toward the zeppelin. Harding had said something about firing incendiary rockets at the zeppelin the next time he saw it. These streaked out, some of them veering to the sides or up and down, the pattern spreading and losing coherence as the rockets closed on the zeppelin. I braced myself for a hell of an explosion.

Nothing. Harding should have waited until he was closer. Every rocket streaked harmlessly past the zeppelin, or corkscrewed away from it. One rocket slammed into a lower floor of the house, but I didn't even feel a tremor in the observation platform. Tesla ran back to his command bunker, lifted one of the phones, and barked Serbian orders into the mouthpiece.

A bugle call, faint in the distance. I heard small arms fire as well, and across the lake I saw men scramble up the bare hillside toward the gun emplacements. Closer still I heard a cheer. I pulled myself up by the east iron breastwork and saw infantry swarming up and over the earthen parapets of the closer gun position. That would be Gordon down below and Durson across the lake, storming the gun redoubts. Their timing couldn't have been better.

"Give them all the orders you want, Tesla," I yelled to him. "I think your gunners have other things on their mind."

Tesla and Gabrielle both came to the east breastwork and looked down. Even from here I could see the fight was savage and violent, and was going to end quickly. Tesla being shorthanded meant all the men in the gun position manned the two cannon facing west. Gordon and his men had swarmed over the east parapet and were in amongst the gunners almost before they knew they were under attack. I saw black-clad gunners and white-smocked militiamen going down, others raising their hands, and in moments it was over. Someone stood on the parapet and waved a rifle pressed into duty as a flagstaff, with the red, blue, and white Union Jack fluttering from it.

Tesla's crippled zeppelin, still making at least twenty knots, collided with the ground, dragging its control gondola across the rocky slope of the hill. The airship listed to starboard, dragged its two starboard engine mounts along the ground. Spinning propellers broke free and pinwheeled away, slicing another long, ragged gash in the gasbag. To the west, *Intrepid* had closed the distance sufficiently that I could hear its deep rhythmic machinery. Across the valley a Turkish flag went up over the northern gun position—Durson's men danced in triumph on the parapets.

I started wondering how *Intrepid* would know not to come in and blow apart the building, with me and Gabrielle in it. I didn't have a flag handy but . . .

Huh!

The guy who caught me hadn't checked the back of my waistband. The floppy peasant smock Tesla had given me to wear covered the flare pistol, so he hadn't seen it, either. I could still signal *Intrepid* and the others that I had control of the house.

Now all I had to do was get control of the house.

"You're finished, Tesla," I called out. I used the breastwork for support and pushed myself to my feet. "It's time to throw in the towel."

Gabrielle looked from me to Tesla with growing alarm.

"They have the gun positions, Nikola. Is there anyone left but us?" she said.

Tesla's surprise and alarm changed to grim determination.

"They have not won, nor will they. All they have accomplished is death and more death—and for nothing. I will not forget your part in this, Fargo. Gabrielle, stand away from the north parapet. It is in the line of fire."

Line of fire?

He walked quickly back to his command bunker, picked up a phone, and gave an order.

I saw movement in the building compound, light reflected from moving metal. A section of the roof of the domed building, the one holding the Forever Engines, slid back. A platform rose in its place, a platform carrying the aether propeller apparatus and three technicians. Heavy cables snaked away from it into the building interior. The mount pivoted, elevated, aimed at *Intrepid*.

Tesla raised the telephone receiver again and gave an order, a single word. It must have meant *Fire*.

The apparatus cracked when it fired, but not with the detonation of an explosive charge. My scalp tingled, and I saw Gabrielle's long hair stand out from her head in every direction. The air itself seemed to crackle with static electricity as an intense white beam flickered for an instant, touched *Intrepid*, and—changed it.

Intrepid seemed to waver, slip out of focus, and then it returned to crystal clarity but altered. Parts of the superstructure and hull were gone, and for a moment I caught a glimpse of another world, an orange-painted bridge lit by bright sunlight under blue cloudless skies unlike the overcast gray heavens here. Volcanic jets of live steam erupted from *Intrepid*'s interior, and debris from the ship and that other world, all mixed together, hurtled through the air. Among it, incongruously, I saw a green station wagon tumbling end over end until it crumpled into the ground and exploded.

A spiderweb pattern of sparks played across the surface of the flyer, like St. Elmo's Fire. Half of the cruiser's metal fittings glowed cherry red with heat, and the wooden deck planks burst into flame. *Intrepid* continued at its same speed but began listing and falling away to port. In moments it listed farther, nosed down, gained speed, and then slammed into the ground three hundred yards from the house.

The structure of the flyer's hull buckled, collapsed. Shell lockers started to explode, one after another, lifting whole sections of hull or superstructure, twisting it into an unrecognizable pile of blackened, burning wreckage.

We all stood for perhaps a minute, watching the ruin Tesla's weapon had made of the pride of the Aerial Squadron of the Royal Navy. Tesla stepped out of his command bunker to watch as well. The beam had also passed over the north end of the platform and the metal breastwork there and on the east side glowed and had twisted slightly, the plates thicker, puffed out like cookies baked in an oven. For a while the only sound on the roof was the ticking noise of cooling metal.

"That was from your world, Fargo," Tesla said after a moment. "A small sample of what is to come. I was certain the projector would serve as a satisfactory weapon, but it is nevertheless gratifying to see it perform in action, as opposed to a laboratory test."

"Two hundred men dead, and you find that *gratifying*?" I said.

"What of the men you so casually killed fighting your way to this roof?" Tesla asked.

"There was nothing casual about what I did, and you'll never see me gloat about it."

Tesla shrugged and stepped back inside the bunker. He picked up the telephone, then turned back to me.

"The projector will now destroy—or rather displace—the men who captured the two gun positions. Which one shall it eradicate first? Would you care to decide?"

He waited for a moment, as if he thought I might actually answer, and then spoke into the receiver.

No.

Tesla wasn't going to just zap them like a bunch of ants under a magnifying glass, not after all those men had gone through. I couldn't let that happen.

My guard's attention remained on the burning wreck of *Intrepid*. My leg still wasn't working right, my left arm had stiffened at the shoulder, and I was dizzy from the blow on the head. I doubted I could disarm him in a fair fight, but this wasn't going to be fair.

Gabrielle's eyes were on me, but for some reason she did not call out to the guard until it was too late. He turned to face me just as my left shoulder slammed into him and drove him backwards. He backpedaled to regain his balance and suddenly found himself backpedaling in the air. He'd have fallen straight down the opening into the attic except his momentum carried him back and he hit the edge of the opening in the platform, tumbled down flailing the air, bounced off the railing of the spiral staircase, and slammed into the slate roof with the wet crunch of breaking bones.

My left shoulder bled more than before, aggravated by the impact, but for now I just ignored it. I lifted the metal trapdoor with my right hand, let it drop shut over the opening, and bolted it, just in case the gunner came back.

I turned to Gabrielle.

"I'm going to stop him," I said.

"I will not let you harm him," she answered and cocked back the hammer on her revolver.

"You going to kill me?"

She raised the revolver, aimed, and fired. I collapsed to the iron platform, my left foot a fiery white-hot nova of pain.

"*Non*," she answered. "I will not kill you."

I expected the first flash of pain to subside, but it didn't, not right away. The pain came in waves, almost paralyzing me, shutting down my brain. I caught my breath and then concentrated on the pain, willed it down, forced it into a corner of my mind. It still left me gasping, but after a few seconds I could at least think.

I crawled to the east side of the platform, pulled myself up to my knees using the iron breastwork, although the metal had become brittle and powdery, like old plaster, and part of it crumbled under my weight. I looked over the edge. The zeppelin had come to rest right on the shore of the lake. Its gasbag settled and lost shape even as I watched, the hydrogen escaping out and carried over the lake by a faint westerly breeze. Tesla's technicians were turning the projector toward the gun position held by Gordon and his men. That made sense; they were closer to the house, more of an immediate threat. Once they were gone, the gun would "displace" Durson and his men, and then it would work over the woods up the west valley, scouring out Cevik Bey's Bosnian riflemen.

We had all come so far together. It couldn't end this way.

I reached into the back of my pants and pulled out the flare pistol. Gabrielle raised her revolver and cocked it again.

"I will not let you harm him. Please, Jack, do not make me shoot you again."

Behind her Tesla looked out of the bunker with detached interest at the vignette playing itself out here.

I looked at Gabrielle, saw the tears in her eyes, but saw the determination as well. I think part of my mind had known for some time I probably wasn't going to make it home, but right then was when it hit me with absolute certainty. I'd reached the end of the road, and it wasn't the end I'd planned for. I was never going to see Sarah again, never see her grow to womanhood, never bounce those grandkids on my knee, but in a sense that was okay. It was okay because Tesla wasn't going to hurt her or the world she lived in. I was about to make sure of that.

I'd already done everything important for her I could. I'd raised a fine, strong, resourceful woman. Time to let go.

I raised the flare pistol, and Gabrielle cried out in alarm, but I pointed it away from Tesla and she relaxed. I pointed it toward the eastern sky and fired. The pistol made a loud pop, like a firecracker, and the red flare sizzled up and out to the east.

"A pointless gesture," Tesla said, having come out of the command bunker to watch the denouement.

The flare reached the top of its trajectory and started down toward the surface of the lake.

"Tesla," I said, "you're a real wiz when it comes to electromagnetism, but you've got a lot to learn about some other things. Here's a new word for you: *thermobaric*."

The descending flare sparkled when it hit the first of the dispersed hydrogen over the lake, then—

I felt the explosion rather than heard it. I felt it inside my head, in the roots of my teeth, in the pressure levels in my eyeballs. The detonation first pulled at me, trying to suck the air out of my lungs, and then slammed me a couple meters back across the roof, leaving me gasping and stunned.

I'd used the dispersing hydrogen of Tesla's crippled zeppelin to make my own fuel-air explosion, an aerosol-enhanced detonation so powerful the first "Daisy Cutter" bombs had been used to turn triple-canopy jungle in Vietnam into instant landing zones. I'd never been this close to a really big thermobaric explosion before. I was a little surprised to still be alive.

I couldn't hear, my vision was badly blurred, and my lungs felt on fire, but I pushed myself onto my hands and knees, dragged myself back to the breastwork, and then pulled myself up to look over it.

People began to stir in the southern gun redoubt; they were stunned but not dead. That was good—I'd managed to not kill Gordon and his people, so Durson's crew, farther away across the lake, would be okay as well..

All three of the machinery buildings were reduced to burning rubble. Tesla's workshop building had been torn open like a kid's present, its contents scattered and burning, and small pieces of debris slowly fluttered upward—liftwood from the Forever Engines, a king's ransom of the stuff, floating away like ashes on the wind. I wondered how long it would float around up there before it lost its mojo and settled someplace, like tired old helium balloons.

The key to my world's location, the biological roadmap to my home, had been down there, too. That was one less thing to worry about, not that I thought I'd be around to worry about anything much longer.

The most remarkable sight was the lake itself. It churned and boiled as electricity arced across its surface, discharging into the shoreline, lacing through the three ruined buildings. As I watched, my hearing returned and I heard the sizzling, cracking thunder, like a dozen lightning storms all at once. Then I heard Tesla as well.

"*GONE!* Ten years of work, all gone! Do you know what you've done? *DO YOU?*"

He stood by the east breastwork. He ran his trembling hands up into his hair and tore a handful out, held it out as if to show me, opened his hand and let the breeze carry the hair away. His eyes rolled, were wild, incredulous, insane.

For once, I had nothing to say. There was nothing left to say, nothing left to do.

Tesla groped at his waist, pulled open the holster on his belt, drew his pistol, cocked it, pointed it at me—

A shot rang out, but I felt nothing. Tesla spun around, blood spraying from his right shoulder. He looked unbelievingly at Gabrielle and the smoking revolver in her hand. Her face twisted in an agony of grief as tears flowed down her cheeks.

"We will not hurt him anymore," she said, her voice shaking.

Tesla leaned back to gain his balance, but when his hands came to rest on the warped iron breastwork, it buckled and crumbled under his weight. Arms flailing, he pitched backwards over the edge and fell, his shout cut off by the crash of breaking slate as he hit the sloped roof.

Gabrielle cried out in alarm and ran to the breastwork, arrived just as Tesla's ragdoll-limp body slid over the edge of the roof and fell from sight. She gasped, eyes wide with the realization of the enormity of what she had done. She stood motionless for a long while, looking at the spot where Tesla had disappeared. Then she looked down at her still-smoking revolver.

She reversed it in her hand so her thumb was through the trigger guard, cocked it, raised it in both hands so the barrel rested under her chin.

She pulled the trigger with her thumb.

The hammer fell forward . . .

. . . and slammed into the web of skin between my right thumb and forefinger.

She had stood four or five meters from me. I had a concussion, a bullet in my right thigh, a shattered left foot, and I was on my knees. Somehow I had gotten to my feet, crossed those four or five meters, and gotten my hand in the way of the revolver's firing pin. I had no recollection of doing it, and no idea of how I managed, but I did.

When she realized she was still alive, when she realized what I had done, she sank to the platform and collapsed against the iron breastwork. Her face dissolved in tears, her mouth an open downturned wound, like the thespian mask of tragedy, and she sobbed uncontrollably.

"You should have let me die," she said, and she repeated it over and over. I sat on the platform beside her and put my arms around her.

"I couldn't."

"My only chance . . . my only hope . . . gone forever. I destroyed it. *I* destroyed it! There is nothing left for me."

I held her for a while, let her cry. Even as we sat there, I knew she was going to get better. She had made a choice, the right choice, without even knowing why it was right, had made it on instinct. In time she would figure out why—family is not about shared blood; it's about shared life, and what we give up for each other.

"You were looking for a heart, Tinman," I told her. "You had one all along."

Smoke rose from the opening in the roof, and I realized more smoke billowed from the west side of the house. The single incendiary rocket fired by *Intrepid* which hit the house must have driven through the wall and started a blaze. It would spread quickly, particularly up the carpeted wooden stairwell. How we were going to get down through that, especially when I couldn't even walk, was a pretty good question.

A shadow fell over us, and I became aware of an irregular droning which had grown louder in the last few minutes. I looked up, and a much-patched sausage-shaped black balloon passed overhead, no more than ten meters above us. A single engine mounted behind the wicker passenger basket smoked and misfired, but kept running, driving the propeller. A dozen cables ran back to the improvised-looking rudder, now cranked to the side to keep the balloon in a wide turn over the house. These must be the salvaged remains of Tesla's zeppelin which had crashed near Jovo's village.

Thomson looked over the edge of the basket, eyes hidden by aviator goggles but his unmistakable white beard flying in the wind.

"Jack!" he called out over the drone of the engine. "Do you and the young lady require a ride?"

FORTY-FOUR

May 21, 1889, London, England

Seven months later, Gabrielle and I stood in Buckingham Palace, which is really nice, by the way. Liveried servants escorted us, along with a dozen or so others, up a curving marble double staircase, down a long corridor, and into a holding tank—they called it the Cross Gallery. I had mostly healed by then, but I still used a cane to take a little weight off my left foot.

A score of people already there fidgeted in formal attire and made nervous small talk. We watched them but didn't mix. I didn't know anyone there, I wasn't particularly good at small talk, and I wasn't nervous. I'd been through too much for a Royal Investiture to frighten me, or even excite me all that much. Besides, Gabi and I had grown comfortable with our own company.

I kept expecting to feel a sense of loss, the return of that black shroud of depression I'd fought so desperately ten years ago, but so far I remained free of it. I didn't feel that I'd lost Sarah. She still lived, that *world* still lived, and I had not had to destroy this one—and my soul—to save it.

My faraway thoughts must have showed in my eyes. Gabi's hand found its way into mine and brought me back. I smiled.

After a few minutes a familiar face appeared at the door—Sir Edward Bonseller, secretary to the prime minister, now completely recovered from the wound he had received at Dorset House eight months earlier. He scanned the small crowd, saw us, and walked briskly over. He thrust out his hand.

"I did not shake your hand before. I hope you will accept the offer now, Dr. Fargo, along with my congratulations."

"Thanks. May I present *Mademoiselle* Courbiere of the DCRG?"

Bonseller hesitated for a moment, then smiled and kissed her hand.

"I am pleased to meet you, *Mademoiselle*. We have all heard of, and admire, your remarkable contribution to the expedition's success."

No one but Gabi and I knew what really took place in Tesla's stronghold. What we'd told everyone else was a better story, better for all concerned.

"I hope you are enjoying your trip to England," Bonseller continued. "Is this your first visit here?"

"*Non,* although it is the first time I come without the disguise."

Bonseller froze, unsure what to say next, until Gabrielle put her hand on his arm.

"I made the joke," she said.

He smiled uncertainly, and his face colored.

"How are *you* feeling?" I asked. I figured he'd welcome a change of subject.

"Splendid, now that this business with Tesla has been concluded."

The cremated bodies we'd found in the burnt-out ruins of his house were unidentifiable, but I was satisfied it was over. We hadn't cracked his network of assassins and spies yet, but with his passionate energy gone as a motivating force, the organization would probably unravel quickly.

"I don't know if anyone has told you the order of precedence," Bonseller said, "but the queen is meeting with the three new barons now. After that she will confer the six knighthoods. We have one new recipient of the Garter, a Thistle, two Baths, and then the two CMGs, including you."

"Companion of the Order of St. Michael and St. George," I said and shook my head. "Who'd a' thunk it? I'd have settled for just the help getting a U.S. passport—and thanks for that, by the way—but the star will look good here." I tapped the breast of my jacket next to my brand new *Légion d'Honneur*.

"*Oui,*" Gabrielle said and squeezed my arm. "I think the two will make a handsome couple."

Bonseller shook his head with a sigh of resignation. "The invitation did specify the display of all orders, didn't it? The Prince of Wales was quite insistent you receive the CMG. He will be present for your investiture, by the way. He was also insistent Gordon *not* receive the Distinguished Service Cross. All we could manage was the Conspicuous Gallantry Medal and a promotion to brevet major. It's a damned shame, if you ask me, but the prince wouldn't hear of it. Pity Gordon has to suffer for the prince's animosity toward Gordon's superior, Lord Chillingham, but I suppose there's nothing for it. Royalty can be remarkably petty sometimes."

"That seems unlike Renfrew," Gabrielle said with a slight frown, and Bonseller colored again in embarrassment at the hint of intimacy.

I didn't say anything. If the prince went to these lengths to keep Gordon's cover secure, I wasn't about to screw things up. Besides, Gordon had what he really wanted—an answer about himself, and a medal to confirm it.

The sliding panel doors which led to the ballroom opened. Thomson walked into the gallery and beamed as soon as he saw us. He made to kiss Gabrielle's hand, but she embraced him and kissed him on the cheek, and he returned the gesture with sincere pleasure. I offered him my hand.

"May I be the first commoner to greet you as your lordship?" I asked.

He shook my hand and then Bonseller's, who excused himself to round up the other candidates for knighthood.

"First Baron Kelvin," Thomson said with a broad smile. "It has a ring, doesn't it? They named the barony for the River Kelvin in Glasgow. It flows right by the university."

"Yeah, and there's something you should know. You've worried about your legacy, how history would remember you, and I haven't been able to offer much comfort on that subject. I'd never heard of William Thomson, but then I've hardly heard of any scientists from this time."

"It's all right, laddie," he said. "I'm satisfied with what I've accomplished, and that's more important than fame, isn't it?"

"Yes, it is. But I just want you to know that there's a reason I never heard of you. I can think of only three scientists from this era who left such a lasting impression that any kid who ever took a science course learned their names: Thomas Edison, Nikola Tesla, and Lord Kelvin."

He looked away and flushed, then he sniffed and cleared his throat, smoothed his beard.

"Well, that is . . . quite gratifying."

I imagined it was. I hadn't heard from Gordon since I'd returned to England the previous week, except for a brief note and an attached document hand-delivered three days earlier. The note simply read, "You may find this interesting. Best regards, G." The enclosed letter from the Turkish general staff thanked Gordon for his detailed report on the action at Kokin Brod, and in particular for his description of the part played by *Lieutenant-designate* Ibrahim Durson.

Yes, quite gratifying.

HISTORICAL PERSONAGES

The following characters in the novel are based, loosely, on historical personages. All other characters are entirely fictitious. These are listed in their order of appearance in the novel.

JOHN TYNDALL (1820-1893)

Tyndall was a prominent mathematician and physicist known for his work in diamagnetism, thermal radiation, and atmospheric processes. His greatest contribution may have been a series of seventeen books which popularized physics for laymen. In 1888 he had just retired from his position as professor of physics at the Royal Institution of Great Britain, due to advanced age and declining health.

THE X CLUB

Odd as it may sound, the X Club was very real. It consisted of nine gifted scientists who supported the theory of natural selection and the principles of academic liberalism—which they defined as "devotion to science, pure and free, untrammeled by religious dogma." The nine members were Thomas Henry Huxley (the founder/organizer), George Busk, Edward Frankland, Thomas Archer Hirst, Joseph Dalton

Hooker, John Lubbock, William Spottiswode, Herbert Spenser and John Tyndall. The club formed in the 1860s. By the 1880s the nine men had all become prominent in their fields, and quite influential. Despite a degree of jealousy from non-members, all of the members of the historical X Club died of natural causes.

WILLIAM THOMSON, 1ST BARON KELVIN (1824-1907).

Most widely know for his work on temperature (the Kelvin scale is named after him) Thomson was also a renowned mathematician and engineer. He was instrumental in the successful completion of the Atlantic Cable (which also made him very wealthy), and he invented the adjustable compass adopted by the Royal Navy in the 1880s, which was designed to compensate for magnetic variation and the amount of iron used in naval hulls. His greatest contribution to modern science was to lead the movement to segregate physics from the other natural sciences by organizing it around study of the heating and cooling of the universe.

His feud with the X Club membership was based on differences over Darwin's theory of natural selection. Thomson rejected Darwin's theory based on his calculation of the age of the Earth. His calculations were flawed, but the error was not discovered until the first years of the Twentieth Century. There is no reason to believe Thomson discovered his own error during his life.

Thomson was made the 1st Baron Kelvin in our world in 1892. In this world his contribution to the expedition against Tesla accelerated that award by three years.

GENERAL SIR REDVERS BULLER, VC (1839-1908)

Buller rose to prominence in the mid- and late-1800s in the series of colonial wars the British Army fought. He won his Victoria Cross in the Zulu War and by 1888 had been made Quartermaster General of the army and had a seat on the powerful Army Board. In the novel his career is sidetracked by the murder of Colonel Rossbank, and Buller's reassignment to military intelligence. In fact, his historical career progressed without serious interruption until the Second Boer War, at the turn of the century. A series of defeats of troops under his command led the government to retire him, a scapegoat for the public's broad dissatisfaction with the Army's performance in the war.

Buller was tall and heavy-set, naturally strong but tending to fat in his middle years. His speech was abrupt, and he was short-tempered, irritable, and inclined to sound like the stereotypical gobbling British senior officer. The historical Buller was, in fact, one of the inspirations for the fictitious Colonel Blimp. For all that, Buller was very sharp, practical-minded, and not much inclined to sentimentality, at least at this stage of his life.

ALBERT EDWARD, PRINCE OF WALES (AKA BARON RENFREW), LATER KING EDWARD VII (1841-1910)

Crown prince and heir apparent to the British throne, Albert Edward was estranged from his mother, Queen Victoria (who blamed him for his father's death) and largely kept out of government and the affairs of state, at least on a formal level. He cultivated a public reputation as a playboy, and he kept company with some of the most beautiful and notorious women of Europe. He traveled frequently, ostensibly for pleasure, and went under the title "Baron Renfrew" on his unofficial junkets.

In fact, Albert Edward was an intelligent and politically sophisticated man, using his reputation for unconventional behavior to travel where official representatives of Britain would not, and associate with those they could not. He had a remarkably egalitarian view of the world and made speeches on the subject of religious and racial tolerance which reflected a sensibility more in keeping with society a century later than that of his own time. In 1910 his support of progressive causes brought him into conflict with the conservative majority in the House of Lords when they refused to pass "The People's

Budget." At that time Edward VII considered appointing additional Lords to insure passage of the bill, but died that year before carrying through his plan. Some believe his death was brought on, in part, by stress from the looming constitutional crisis.

Albert Edward stayed in Dwight, Illinois, in 1860 while traveling under the name Baron Renfrew. Renfrew Park in Dwight is named in his honor.

NIKOLA TESLA (1856-1943)

Tesla's early years unfolded largely as related in the story, except that his sisters were not victims of typhoid. Tesla was as brilliant and creative as depicted in the novel. While quite eccentric, and increasingly paranoid in later life, he never displayed the capacity for violence with which the novel credits him. Chalk that up to the alternate universe.

Tesla displayed mounting symptoms of obsessive-compulsive disorder as he grew older, including a well-documented preoccupation with the number three. As depicted in the novel, he remained celibate for most of his life, and he also developed a hypersensitivity to light and sound as he aged.

His lifelong preoccupation with projected power may very well have led him to develop an energy weapon. Late in his life, his interests turned to development of exactly this sort of directed-energy beam weapon, which he called a "teleforce" weapon.

The novel's theoretical basis for Tesla's "force-bearing aether" as related to the Higgs Field is an extrapolation from Tesla's writing on a "field of force" and somewhat from his dynamic theory of gravity, at least so far as it is understood at all. This, combined with his occasional interest in "free energy," would have made the Forever Engine a natural for him.

Tesla's choice of a location for his artificial lake is an obvious one. In the 1960s Yugoslavia dammed the Uvac River near Kokin Brod and created Lake Zlatarsko, the third largest lake in modern Serbia, on the same site as that in the novel.